FORGED
BY FLAMES

FORGED BY FLAMES

A Dragon's Breath Novel

Susan Illene

Forged by Flames
Copyright © 2016 by Susan Illene

www.susanillene.com

ISBN-10: 1-5398881-7-7
ISBN-13: 978-1-5398881-7-8

Model image obtained for the creation of this novel's cover was licensed for use from Josh McCullock photography. Cover design by Jeff Brown Graphics.

DEDICATION

To my family for all their support.

1

BAILEY

I clutched the steering wheel and searched for a threat, any threat. The last gasps of autumn were approaching now that November was almost over, which meant dragons on the west side of Norman, Oklahoma had been out in force searching for enough food to get them through the coldest days of winter when they'd be stuck in their dens semi-hibernating. Though there were still plenty of cows and wildlife in the nearby countryside outside of town, some of them had developed a taste for humans.

"Where in the hell are they?" I glanced over at my slaying partner, Conrad, who sat in the passenger seat of the truck. He held a loaded crossbow with the front aimed at the floorboard, ready to lift and shoot out the window if we came across danger. Conrad wasn't flame-proof like me, but he could do some damage from a distance while I went after the dragons up close with my trusty sword. He'd been working out more too and building up his already toned muscles to give him that much more of an edge. The extra strength came in handy if he had to release a rapid succession of bolts or carry me to safety if I got badly injured during the fight.

The dark-skinned nineteen-year-old—wait, that'd be twenty since his birthday was two weeks ago—gave me a grim look. "You've killed so many of them, I'm willin' to bet they're hiding from you."

I ground my jaw. "Only three this week and it's Wednesday. I need to kill more."

Conrad had no idea how much I needed it, considering the dark and deadly side of me was something I tried to keep well-hidden from my friends. Slaying was the only way to bring relief to the irrepressible instincts that drove me to attack dragons wherever I could find them. To a certain extent, I'd learned to control myself, but lately I hadn't found many reasons to bother. The motivation to curb my killing desires had been for the sake of the red shifter dragons—some of whom I'd become allies with since they weren't a threat to humans. I hadn't seen much of them lately, though.

"Maybe we could address the big elephant in the room," he said, arching a brow.

I stopped at an intersection and leaned forward in my seat, taking the opportunity to get a better look around for any fire-breathing beasts. "We're in a truck—not a room."

"You know what I mean, Bailey."

I didn't look at him or say anything. It was a topic I'd been avoiding for a while now.

"Ever since we rescued those kids you've been actin' different. You're all weird and cagey and shit. About the only time I see you smile is right after you kill a dragon." Conrad ran a hand over his short tufts of hair that he'd started growing out recently. "Don't think I didn't notice this all started about the time Aidan stopped comin' around."

I stiffened. He wasn't wrong, though Conrad wasn't aware of the full story. No one knew that after we fought a major battle against the pure dragons at the Norman airport—to rescue a group of children and push the clan out of town—Aidan and I had met again later that night.

Fresh from battle and our blood still pumping, the attraction between us had been higher than ever. Aidan had also been working through his feelings because he lost his father—the pendragon—during the fight. They hadn't been on the best of terms, which only made him feel worse. Alone in Aidan's lair, we'd taken comfort in each other's arms. It had been one of the most amazing experiences of my life, and the scariest.

Considering he was a shape-shifter, a rare breed among dragon-kind compared to the pure beasts that outnumbered them ten-to-one in the world, and I was a slayer born to slaughter all fire-breathing creatures, it probably wasn't the smartest move on our part. Still, it was one of those moments I'd remember forever.

We'd grown close over the months he'd been training me to slay his enemies—the pure dragons—and I'd learned to trust Aidan despite my instincts. In his human form, he could be more civilized than half the people I'd met since D-day (the arrival of the dragons) six months ago. Despite that, a relationship between us couldn't work. I'd been doing my best to accept that the same way I had to accept fighting dragons for the rest of my life. Slayers didn't get sick or age. They always died in battle and usually before they reached thirty. Every day I survived was a gift. I had to do everything I could to get back to my family in Texas before my slayer heritage got me killed. Aidan was the key to doing that, and I needed to stop thinking of him as anything more.

"The new pendragon is keeping him away," I said, pressing on the gas pedal. The truck jerked forward, and we continued our way north on 36th Avenue.

"Yeah, I bet he did after he found out about you." Conrad paused and narrowed his eyes at me. "But do you think the pendragon suspects you and Aidan are getting a little too close?"

I jerked the wheel, almost sending us off the road. It took a moment to get the truck under control again. "What are you talking about?"

"You ain't foolin' me, girl. You've got that whole angry and bitter vibe goin' on. That's the real reason you started spending almost every day out here huntin' dragons—to avoid thinking about what you can't have."

I tensed, realizing Conrad was right. For those first few weeks, after I last saw Aidan, I stayed at his lair most of the time until the need to hunt dragons overwhelmed me. It hurt not being able to see him. Then Aidan's sister, Phoebe, came by and told me her brother had been sent far away to patrol their clan's borders. I'd realized I needed to stop fantasizing that there could ever be anything serious between us. My family needed me, and I'd nearly allowed my emotions for a dragon shifter to make me forget about the people I loved. If not for the giant chasm running parallel to the Oklahoma border with Texas, separating me from my mother and step-father, plus a huge clan of pure dragons who wouldn't be easy to get past, I'd have gone home already.

"I know it can't ever work," I said, shooting Conrad a look. "So I don't want to hear another lecture."

His eyebrow raised in disbelief. "But do you really accept it?"

"It doesn't matter what I accept. What matters is I know what I have to do," my voice came out clipped.

I didn't want to talk about this with him or anyone else. The more I discussed it, the more it bothered me—and not just because of Aidan. There were still days where I woke up surprised the world was filled with dragons, and that I was expected to slay them. Never mind that I might have begun to fall in love with one of the damn beasts. My future was never supposed to be like this. I'd just finished college when the apocalypse began and had meant to return home to my parents' ranch to help them run it. Then my whole life spiraled out of control on that fateful day back in May.

The only thing I could do now was keep slaying the beasts that were ruining the world and work on getting back to my family.

Conrad was quiet for a minute. "Alright. I'll let it go, but only cuz you look miserable enough without me making it worse."

I snorted. "At least you've got someone you can care about openly."

"Yeah, that's true," he said, smiling at the mention of Christine. We'd rescued her and her daughter after a tornado struck Norman shortly after D-day. That was the beginning of her and Conrad's relationship, though they'd gotten even closer after we rescued Christine's daughter, Lacy, from a dragon that had kidnapped her and a few other human children in town.

"It's good you have somebody," I said, truly happy for him.

"Thanks," he replied, then frowned and looked away.

"What is it?"

He shook his head. "Nothin'. Let's just find some dragons for you to kill."

That was strange. Conrad usually didn't keep anything from me, but I wouldn't push him for now. The tone of his voice made it clear he wasn't ready to open up about whatever was bothering him.

"Okay, but I'm here if you need to talk."

He glanced at me. "Yeah, I know."

In the middle of the road ahead, a middle-aged woman with long, brown hair streaked with gray appeared out of nowhere. I slammed on the brakes, jerking us forward in our seats as the tires screeched across the pavement. The truck came to a stop about twenty feet from where she stood.

"I'm going to kill her," I swore, rubbing the side of my neck where the seatbelt had dug into my skin.

Conrad slowly removed his clenched fingers from the dashboard. "Not if I get to her first."

We hadn't seen Verena in weeks. The sorceress revealed herself when and where she chose. Mostly, you had to be useful to her in some way, or she didn't waste her time with you. It didn't escape me that if she was showing up now, she wanted something. I glanced at my pistol where it rested in the center console, but before I could make up my mind on whether to carry through with my dark thoughts, I found myself unbuckling my seatbelt and getting out of the truck. The damn sorceress had taken over my free will again.

Fighting every step, I nevertheless made my way toward her. It irritated me to no end that while I could feel every part of my body, I couldn't control myself. Too bad being a dragon slayer didn't diminish her ability to manipulate me. Sometimes I wondered if sorcerers were the ones who created slayers like me in the first place—to battle the beasts for them. All I knew was that my race had been around for thousands of years, and the ability to fight dragons was passed down through the family lines. We got greater speed, strength, and immunity to fire, but magic still worked just fine on us. It was damned inconvenient.

Verena clasped her hands together in front of her. The slender woman was wearing a purple, flowery skirt and a beige tank top today. It seemed wrong that she could look that normal with so much power behind her hazel eyes. She was born more than a thousand years ago, but according to her, she'd been under a sleep spell when the dragons were sent to another dimension, and she didn't wake up until a little over twenty years ago. By outward appearances, she looked like she was in her early forties. I wouldn't have called her beautiful, more like average with a thin nose that looked like it had been pinched a few too many times, but she kept herself clean and well-groomed—which was better than a lot of other people since the apocalypse.

"What do you want, Verena?" I asked through clenched teeth.

She lifted a brow. "It's time."

The tight hold she had on my body eased a fraction, allowing me to speak without struggling as much. "Time for what?"

"To repay me for the favor you owe," she said, an Irish lilt in her voice.

I tensed. No matter how much I'd anticipated this would come up eventually, there had been no way to prepare for it. Last summer, Conrad had been shot by some human looters, and he'd been dying. I'd had to do something to save him. This was before my friend, Danae, discovered she was a sorceress with an affinity toward healing. The only person I knew back then who might be able to help was Verena, so I'd taken a chance on her. She wasn't a very strong healer, but she had enough skills to keep Conrad alive and eventually get him back on his feet. I'd been willing to agree to a future favor in return without even knowing what it might be because he was my friend, and I'd do anything for him. There'd been no choice at the time.

"So what's it going to be?" I really hoped it didn't involve something horrific.

Verena smiled. "Nothing as dreadful as what you're thinking. You will be going on a journey soon to locate a long-lost artifact—an orb to be precise. Once you have recovered it, you will give it to me. That is all."

"Um, I hate to break it to you, but I don't have any upcoming travel plans, and I don't know anything about a lost orb." Her hold on me was slowly slipping—she couldn't maintain it for long—and I managed to wiggle my fingers.

"You will soon enough," she said, confident.

I wasn't sure how Verena's predictions worked, but she did seem to have a knack for knowing about things that would happen in the near future. That must have been how she could always find me. If she said I'd be going on a journey, then it was probably true. "Why do you want this artifact?"

She gave me a cryptic smile. "I have my reasons, but they aren't any of your concern—yet."

From the corner of my eye, I caught sight of two dragons flying in the distance. They were headed toward a nearby neighborhood. What little hold the sorceress had over me was quickly diminishing with my need to fight the beasts, and I took a step forward. It appeared when it came to dragons; they took precedence over her magic.

Verena followed my gaze and a look of satisfaction came over her. "I see you've got work to do."

I forced my gaze back to her, needing an answer to my question before I could leave. "What is so important about the orb?"

"It is a matter of life and death, and I must have it." She narrowed her gaze. "Do not even consider giving it to anyone else...or you will regret that decision."

"What are you going to do? Kill me?" I took two more steps toward her, glaring.

"Oh no, my dear." She shook her head. "But you do not want to find out what happens when you forsake a promise made."

Maybe not, but a sorceress who liked to take control of my body without my permission and manipulate me couldn't be up to any good if she wanted an orb. Never mind the question of why she couldn't get it herself. "I'm not giving it to you."

Her expression turned ominous. "Think very hard about that because if I don't get it, very bad things will happen to you and those you care for."

My palm grazed the hilt of my dagger, strapped to my leg harness. "If you hurt my friends, I will kill you."

"I am not the one you need to be worried about." Her gaze turned pitying. "Just get me the orb and all will be well."

"You can forget it if you think..."

A breeze swept over us, and she disappeared. Damn it all to hell—I still needed answers! Where was this orb supposed to be located? Why did she want it, and what did she plan to do with it? Most important of all— what would happen if I did somehow get the thing and didn't give it to her?

Up in the sky, I caught sight of the dragons swooping toward a neighborhood down the street. The terrifying sounds of human screams rose up, chilling me to the bone. One of the beasts blew flames at a target I couldn't see, but I knew there had to be people in its fiery path. I had to hurry if I hoped to save the neighborhood in time. Curse Verena for distracting me from my job when people were in danger.

I spun toward Conrad. "Get me my sword and move the truck off the road."

He was already ahead of me, tossing the sheathed blade in my direction. "Here!"

I caught it by the handle and took off running. Conrad knew the drill well enough to know he had to hang back until the battle was over. Then he'd help me clean up the mess that came after.

2

AIDAN

Warm air glided through Aidan's scales and past his wingtips. He enjoyed the comforting feel of it, knowing there wouldn't be many days left like this in the year. They'd just suffered through the first major cold spell last week. Every morning, frost had covered the thick vegetation of southeast Oklahoma, and his breath had fogged the air. Aidan and his patrol partner, Falcon, had barely been able to muster the energy for their border patrols.

Dragons did not handle low temperatures well. Once it became cold enough, they would have to hibernate through most of it. As shape-shifters, Aidan and Falcon could change into human form and withstand the winter weather better, but they wouldn't cover nearly as much ground on foot. Their clan, or *toriq* in the dragon language, relied on the patrols to keep them safe. The primary advantage they had was that the green dragons on the other side—the *Bogaran*—were pure and could not shift or handle the cold as well as them. Aidan and Falcon had only seen one of them in the past week, and that one had flown sluggishly on its side of the border, paying little attention to the red shifters on the west side.

The recent calm had been a welcome respite from the tensions between his toriq—the Taugud—and the dragons in Arkansas. The Bogaran weren't happy with the shifters confiscating a stretch of their territory and pushing them out of Oklahoma. They'd attempted several raids over the border in the past few months since they'd lost it, but they didn't make it far before Aidan, Falcon, or some of the others patrolling the area had stopped them. With any luck, the arrival of winter would cease the Bogaran's attempts altogether. They had more than enough territory for a toriq their size, perhaps five thousand dragons taking up half of Arkansas and part of Louisiana. They did not need the small section they lost. It was the main reason Aidan and his people had been able to take it without much difficulty last summer.

Do you smell that? Falcon asked telepathically. The red dragon flew a short distance ahead with his nose sniffing the air.

Aidan inhaled deeply and caught a faint whiff of Bogaran stench. *There are two of them nearby—about three miles southeast of us.*

The warm weather has brought them back out. Falcon let out a snarl and led the way closer to the border.

They flew over a forest of trees that rose and dipped with the rolling terrain. Most of the vegetation had withered and yellowed with the approaching winter, but there were still pine trees dotting the landscape to break the monotony of color. Aidan hadn't seen many humans since he began his patrol duties in this area. Before his toriq took over, the pure dragons had laid waste to numerous towns. Some of them had been burned completely to the ground with only scorch marks remaining. Very few things could survive dragon fire, and human-made structures were not among them. They still found some houses and neighborhoods left alone, though. The Bogaran must have been saving them for future raids, but the Taugud would never allow that to happen now. The shifters preferred to live in harmony with humans whenever possible and protect them from the pure dragons.

Aidan had attempted to make contact with the clusters of humans he occasionally scented, but even in his human form they were too suspicious and fearful of him to talk. He'd grown tired of pulling bullets from his body—not that they could do much damage—and decided to let them be. Humans needed time to see the shifters meant them no harm, and Aidan could hardly blame them for their anxiety.

His gaze caught on two green dragons coming over the trees in the distance. They had slender necks and shoulders leading to large, round bellies. Their forearms were short without much of a reach, but they had sharp talons protruding from their feet and long tails that could whip around in the blink of an eye. Full grown pure dragons could be almost twice a shifter's size or more. Their weight and strength made them difficult opponents, but not impossible to defeat.

The wind picked up, bringing with it the distinct stench of dragon urine. The Bogaran patrol was marking its territory on the other side of the border. It was a warning to those from any other toriq to stay away. The beast within Aidan growled, demanding he cover the scent with his own. His inner dragon had different priorities and did not care about politics or rules. He existed as a separate entity, almost always trapped within the recesses of Aidan's mind, but he could be even more feral than the pure dragons. It was a constant battle to keep him contained.

As far as Aidan knew, most shifters did not have to live with their beasts constantly trying to claw their way to the surface, but he'd always been more in touch with his inner dragon—even more so in recent months. His relationship with Bailey had somehow brought that side of him out. Beast liked the slayer and wanted Aidan to form a stronger bond with her. Something about the slayer called to him, defying all reason.

One of the Bogaran roared and let out a billow of fire. The flames hung mid-air for a moment before extinguishing. *Why don't you come over and join us?*

Aidan winced at the menacing voice inside his head. The dragon had spoken telepathically in a method any of their kind could hear within a short distance. Falcon growled, signaling he had heard the message as well.

Aidan and his patrol partner flew until they were no more than a handful of wingspans from the border and stopped. They wouldn't cross the invisible line, but they did make it clear to the two Bogaran males that they would get a fight if they came much closer. The green dragons hovered approximately fifty feet away, and despite their taunting, they knew the odds were not in their favor. Their bodies might be larger and stronger than the shifters, but they were also slower and less agile. Would they risk it anyway? Aidan and the beast inside hadn't gotten a good battle for a while. He half-hoped the dragons would give him a reason to let off some steam.

Think we'll get a fight? Aidan asked Falcon, using a private line of communication.

The other shifter, who was a few hundred years older and more experienced, glanced at him. *It is difficult to say. We have already killed several members of their toriq who made that mistake.*

That much was true, but the last deadly battle they'd faced against a Bogaran patrol was nearly four weeks ago. Aidan doubted the peace could hold much longer. These dragons were young adults, judging by their shiny, unmarred scales. They couldn't have been more than fifty or sixty years old. This could very well have been their first important assignment since leaving their mothers' nests, and they'd be looking to prove themselves. It was rather surprising they'd been entrusted with such a task.

I believe they might risk it, Aidan said.

The green dragons inched closer. Falcon let out a warning growl, one that should have struck fear in the youths' hearts. The Bogaran paused for only a moment, however, before continuing forward. Like two children, they were edging closer to forbidden fruit.

Falcon shot a look over his shoulder at Aidan. *I think you may be right.*

Are you too scared to meet us? one of them taunted.

Stay on your side, Aidan warned. As much as he wouldn't have minded a good fight, battling these young ones would be too easy. He would get no joy from hurting or killing them.

The green dragon on the left let out a snort. *And if we don't?*

You will not live to regret the decision, Falcon replied.

The youths let out enraged growls and surged forward. Aidan and Falcon prepared themselves for the moment their opponents reached them, each taking a battle stance with their claws out. They adjusted their altitude to about five-hundred feet off the ground, forcing their attackers to come up to them. That left enough room for maneuvering, but it wasn't so high they couldn't survive a fall.

Just as the four of them were about to clash, a loud roar sounded from behind the Bogaran youths. They spread their wings wide and jerked to a halt right before crossing the border. A moment later, a large green beast came into sight. Its body was so massive that it had to be almost three times Aidan's size. They only grew to that proportion if they primarily dined on human flesh and lived to become ancients—rare dragons who survived well beyond the normal life expectancy. Bailey's first kill had been an ancient, and it was a miracle she'd survived that battle without Aidan's assistance. The slayer's advantage had been that her opponent underestimated her.

Shifitt, Aidan cursed. *That one will not be easy to take down.*

It was coming toward them fast, eying Aidan and Falcon like it wanted them for its next meal. And with a dragon such as that one, it was entirely possible. Had this been a setup to bring them closer? The gleam in the younger Bogarans' eyes made him suspect as much. No wonder they'd been brave, though they were quickly backing away now.

I can handle the big one, Falcon said, *if you take care of the other two. I do not want them attacking us from behind if we only concentrate on the ancient. That is likely what they are planning.*

Aidan eyed his patrol partner. He was the strongest warrior in their toriq, but would that be enough against this raging beast?

Are you certain? Aidan asked.

Falcon kept his gaze on the incoming dragon. *Yes.*

Left with no other choice if he didn't want to insult the warrior, he went after the two younger Bogaran. They'd moved a short distance away, but not far, and they were already gazing at Aidan with the confidence of two fighters who thought they had the advantage.

From behind Aidan, he heard Falcon clash with the older dragon. Their roars and growls filled the air, and it was all he could do not to turn around. Instead, he kept his focus on the younger ones.

Aidan stretched his arms out, using his greater reach to advantage, and slashed at the closest Bogaran's eyes before it could touch him. The dragon yelped and wrenched away, swiping at his bloodied eyes. A talon cut through the edge of Aidan's right wing. He jerked as pain rippled through him, but it would take a lot more damage than that to bring him down. He turned to face his attacker. Because of the pure dragon's shorter forearms, he'd had to come very close to make that slice. Aidan reached out and grabbed the youth's head. Using all his strength, he dragged the Bogaran through the air and rammed him into his friend. Their wings collided and crumpled into each other. The blinded one clawed at the air, unable to keep himself aloft. He fell, heading for the sea of trees below.

The other dragon regained control of his wings and went after Aidan again. His jaws opened wide, spewing a stream of fire. It blinded Aidan but didn't stop him. He reached through the flames and grabbed the youth's upper and lower jaw, knowing exactly where they'd be. With a wrench, he pulled them far apart until a crack broke the air. The dragon let out a strangled scream, his flames dying down. Aidan grabbed one of his wings and spun him toward the trees where his friend had disappeared. He could only hope this served as a lesson to all the Bogaran that the Taugud were not to be taken lightly.

With one last glance to be certain the youths would not be coming back for more, he flew toward Falcon. The warrior was still locked in a deadly battle with the larger dragon. Blood and wounds covered his body. He was holding his own so far, but the weak flapping of his wings and his slowing strikes said he didn't have much left to give.

Aidan altered his flight path. He could not help his friend from the front without getting in the way, but he could attack the green dragon from behind. As the ancient bit into Falcon's arm, Aidan flew straight into the large beast's back. He wrapped his arms around the dragon's neck and with all his strength, he squeezed. It was a lot like trying to break the trunk of an old tree with one's bare hands. This ancient was built sturdy and strong. Aidan failed to even cut off his air supply, and the dragon continued to gnaw on Falcon's arm. This was going to require far more drastic measures.

He hooked his feet into the dragon's belly, while still holding the neck, and spoke telepathically to Falcon. *Fold your wings and force the ancient to take your weight.*

You can't be serious, the warrior snarled.

Aidan could hardly blame him. *I know it will hurt, but you are going to have to trust me.*

After a slew of curses, Falcon complied and folded his wings. As soon as Aidan saw it, he did the same. The ancient had to flap twice as hard now that he held the weight of two shifters. Still, he did not let go of Falcon's arm. Aidan caught the top of the green dragon's right wing and pulled it downward at an awkward angle. They began to plummet. The ancient growled and let go of Falcon, who spread his wings to take flight again.

Move away. I will take it from here, Aidan said.

He couldn't see if the warrior did as he instructed. The ancient was twisting its head around, attempting to snap at Aidan with razor-sharp incisors. Shifters might have the greater reach in their arms, but their necks were short. Not so with the pure dragons. They could turn their heads behind them, though Aidan had always gotten the sense it was awkward for them. His grip loosened when one of the ancient's furious snaps grazed his snout. With his feet, he dug his talons into the dragon's back and legs to rip through the scales and into the softer tissue underneath. The dragon twisted and jerked, causing Aidan to lose hold of the beast's right wing where he'd still been clutching it. He could barely hold on with his remaining arm now. His opponent was stronger than anything he'd ever fought before. They spiraled through the air as the ancient did everything he could to knock Aidan off of him.

Then he felt a jerk, and they were both being pulled downward. The dragon let out an angry roar.

Let go! Donar screamed into his head.

Where had his cousin come from? He was supposed to be down in Texas helping the Faegud with their masonry work as part of the new treaty agreement. Aidan had been so busy fighting the ancient he hadn't kept track of where they were going, but surely the battle hadn't gone that far south. The toriq lived a couple of hundred miles away, by human measurement.

Trusting his cousin, Aidan let go and backed away. He looked down to discover Donar and another shifter tearing at the bottom of the ancient's wings as he attempted to stay in the air. Falcon returned to the fight and bit into the green dragon's neck, crunching it with his powerful jaws. The ancient's struggles weakened, and within a few seconds his body went slack. Donar led a countdown, and they each let go of the dragon at the same time, allowing the body to plummet to the earth in a crumpled heap. Aidan soared to the ground, landing next to the ancient to check its breath. The dragon showed no sign of life. With the gaping wound in its neck, exposing the insides of its throat, Aidan didn't doubt it was dead.

Donar landed next to him, folding his red wings. *Dear Zorya. That was a big beast. I don't think I've ever seen one that large.*

Neither have I, Aidan said. *What are you doing here? I thought you would still be in Texas.*

My time there ended yesterday, so I returned to the fortress. Donar paused to nod at Falcon and the other shifter who landed nearby. *I thought I would be able to relax for a few days, but this evening the pendragon sent me to fetch you.*

Why? Aidan asked.

The pendragon had made it very clear he wanted Aidan to stay far away from the fortress and the human town of Norman, which why he'd been on border duty for the last two months. Nanoq didn't want

23

him anywhere near Bailey and didn't trust that Aidan would stay away from the slayer on his own. It was ridiculous since he had no intention of breaking his promise, but the pendragon was still solidifying his place as the toriq's new leader and would not take any chances. Nanoq was already uncomfortable with the idea of a slayer in his territory, and that Aidan had allied with her in secret. It would take time to earn his trust again.

Then a grim thought occurred to him. *Does this have anything to do with the mating festival?*

He did not say, Donar replied, shaking his head. *Only that you must come at once, and I had to bring your replacement with me.*

I assume that is him. Aidan glanced toward the shifter who had arrived with his cousin. He didn't know him, other than he was one of the toriq's stronger warriors. If Falcon must be left with someone else, especially now that he was wounded, that male would do.

Donar followed his gaze. *It is.*

Then let us go. I would like to be back in time for the midnight meal. Aidan didn't want to think too hard yet on what could have caused the pendragon to call him back. Whatever it was, it had to be important, but he truly hoped it had nothing to do with the mating festival. Now that Aidan had been intimate with Bailey, he wanted no other female. She might be a slayer, but he'd decided once the time was right he would claim her as his own. He was confident she would return his feelings and give their relationship a chance.

3

AIDAN

Aidan and Donar flew for several hours to reach the Taugud fortress. The sun set during their journey, but clear skies and a full moon made their travel easy enough. Occasionally, they caught the scent of wood burning. With the nights turning cooler, some humans were risking using their fireplaces. They had no idea dragons could scent the smoke from miles away—not that shifters would bother them over it.

The fortress came into view ahead. Moonlight reflected off the walls, rendering the dark gray stone almost luminescent. Shifters in human form paced the ramparts and stood in the guard towers rising from each corner. There hadn't been any direct attacks on their home in a long time, but they remained vigilant. It was only a matter of time before the pure dragons tried again. Long ago, the fortress had been designed so that no one could enter in their beast form. Every rooftop and wall had sharp spikes protruding from them. There were also tall obelisks with pointed ends rising from the wider walkways to discourage landing in the open areas.

No dragon could fly into the keep without severely damaging its wings. Shifters had learned thousands of years ago that this was the safest way for them to live, but it didn't mean they were completely safe in their homes. There had been attacks in the past. If enough of the pure dragons came, they could eventually break down the fire-proof walls with brute force. Aidan knew of this happening once after the fortress was built—long before he was born. His toriq suffered many losses in that battle, but they did manage to prevent the invaders from gaining entrance. The one damaged section was subsequently rebuilt and reinforced. The pure dragons had long since learned they would have to engage in a protracted battle and be prepared for many of their brethren to die if they wished to destroy the fortress and its inhabitants. They seemed to have given up on the idea for now, but shifters knew better than to take their safety for granted.

Aidan landed in the clearing in front of the fortress and changed to human form. His camrium uniform closed over him like a second skin. It was soft and supple, comparable to the human version of leather. The difference being they processed their cloth differently, and they made it fireproof. Shifters could blow flames in human or dragon form, and their skin ran so hot it could burn most types of materials, given enough time. They had no choice except to wear special cloth derived from the *black camria* plant and reinforce it with magic. Aidan had manufactured several of Bailey's warrior uniforms with the material so that she could fight her battles without risking the loss of her garments in dragon fire.

Donar grunted. "Are you ready?"

"As I will ever be." As much as Aidan missed living in the fortress, there had been one advantage to his border guard assignment. He could avoid what he was about to face, and it wasn't the pendragon that concerned him at the moment.

They headed for the gate entrance, and the two shifters standing there stiffened. A gleam of distrust filled their yellow eyes when their gazes caught on Aidan. It had been that way ever since the battle with the Shadowan a couple of months ago when his toriq discovered he'd been working with a dragon slayer. Bailey had stepped into the fight when she saw the shifters were becoming overwhelmed by the pure dragons. It didn't matter that Aidan had made an ally who helped his people—they didn't like that she was a slayer. Their two races were natural-born enemies, and it was difficult to change that way of thinking.

Nanoq, the pendragon, didn't send Aidan away only because he was angry about Bailey. He also sent him to the border to give the toriq time to recover from the shocking news. Unfortunately, it didn't appear as though enough time had passed.

Donar gave Aidan a commiserating glance, and they continued on their way. No one knew his cousin had helped Bailey train to fight as well. It was best if Aidan took the full blame for that and kept anyone else involved out of it. Such as his sister, Phoebe, who only discovered the secret a couple of weeks before the others in their toriq.

The walk through the main thoroughfare filled him with discomfort. Shop vendors and artisans each gave Aidan the cold shoulder as he passed by them. Shifters milling about stepped out of the way, unwilling to even brush shoulders with him. His gut clenched. It hurt that they couldn't see past their prejudices to realize he'd allied with the slayer for their benefit, and he would never do anything to put his brethren in danger.

The only people who didn't give him bitter looks were the humans. There were about a hundred of them living in the keep, mostly refugees who'd crossed into the dragon dimension, Kederrawien, before it merged with Earth a little over six months ago. They had no reason to distrust a dragon slayer and likely enjoyed the idea of someone among their race who could fight back.

Aidan and Donar nearly made it to the end of the thoroughfare when Ruari stepped into their path, his bald head gleaming in the moonlight. He was a large male with heavy muscles and a warrior's build, but his physique was just for show and intimidation. If one paid close attention, they could find signs of deceit and treachery swimming in the shifter's yellow gaze. Ruari preferred to avoid physical confrontations by making himself appear too large to fight. His real talent lay in attacking his enemies through more underhanded means—ones Aidan had been the recipient of a few times over the years. Ruari used lies and manipulation to get what he wanted.

"I can see you are getting the greeting from our brethren you deserve, brother," he said.

Aidan gave him a hard look. "At least I've been making myself useful. What have you been doing?"

His brother had always been the jealous type. The moment Aidan began to build any esteem among their people, Ruari always found a way to ruin it. He might not have had a hand in their brethren's current dislike of Aidan—a miracle considering his brother found out about Bailey days before everyone else—but Ruari would be sure to stoke the flames of their toriq's mistrust.

The shifter smiled. "Not to worry—the pendragon sends me out on regular missions. I've caught glimpses of your slayer running about fighting the Thamaran recently. I must admit she's a pretty thing, if a little skinny for my taste."

It was all Aidan could do to hold himself in check and not attack his elder brother. Ruari had a way of getting under his skin, but he'd had two centuries to get used to the barbs and insults. Aidan would not fall into his trap, especially with so many observers there to witness it.

"If she was fighting the Thamaran, how could you have seen it?" he asked, lifting a brow.

Ruari shrugged. "She stays close enough to our border it is not difficult to observe from our side."

"That's brave of you, brother. I didn't think you had the courage to get that close to the pure dragons on your own," Aidan said, unable to help himself.

"You would be surprised what I'm capable of," Ruari growled.

Phoebe, their sister, pushed her way through the crowd. She was a large-boned woman with toned muscles and the ideal build for a female warrior. Her long, black hair was pulled back with a tie on top of her head and left to hang down in the back like a horse's tail. Only a single strand of silver fell across her face. She had light, olive skin, and features that made every available male in their toriq stare when she walked past. The stride she took left no one in doubt of her confidence or lack of concern about what they thought of her.

She took one look at their older brother and narrowed her eyes. "Don't you have guard duty right now?"

Ruari's face turned red. "That's none of your business."

"If you plan to keep standing here harassing our younger brother, I'll make it my business." She put her hands on her hips. "We both know what you're doing, and it needs to stop."

That was Aidan's sister—the peacemaker among siblings. After a moment of hesitation, Ruari stomped off. He didn't like being outnumbered, and he didn't have their eldest brother, Zoran, to back him up anymore. Zoran was currently locked in the dungeons for his complicity in an attempted murder and would stay there until it was time for his banishment. He'd made the mistake of conspiring to kill the man who later became pendragon—the fool. Aidan was rather ashamed he was related to two such evil brothers and figured it probably didn't make things any easier for him with the clan. Only Phoebe continued to cast a bright light for their family. They'd fallen far from their previously lofty position in recent months, and even the esteem his sister garnered could only help them so much.

"He's been miserable and lonely," Phoebe said, watching their elder brother go.

Aidan snorted. "Good."

"I second that," Donar added, finally breaking his silence now that their company had left.

He hated Ruari to such a degree that Aidan worried one day his cousin might kill him. Donar had a temper simmering below the surface he hid well, but if he ever let it loose outside of battle, the results could be devastating. Most people didn't know that about Aidan's cousin, considering he kept to himself and didn't show off his fighting skills, but Ruari had played a part in Donar nearly dying from poison. His cousin wouldn't forget that for a long time, and his anger might eventually take over his better judgment. Aidan would have to do his best to keep an eye on him.

Phoebe clasped their arms. "It's good to see both of you. Things haven't been the same without you two here."

"I missed you too, sister." Aidan returned the gesture.

Donar echoed a similar sentiment. He wasn't as close to Phoebe, but the two of them got along reasonably well.

She stepped back. "I won't hold you any longer. I heard the pendragon wants to see you right away, but come visit me when you have time."

Aidan nodded. "I will."

He and Donar left her behind and finally reached the castle at the center of the keep. It was massive with a great hall in the middle and several wings leading from it. There was a balcony near the top where the pendragon's accommodations were located, as well as walkways for the quarters on the upper floors. Aidan maintained a room on the first level near the rear of the castle and not far from the kitchens. Because he was a member of one of the high families and his father had been the previous ruler of their toriq, he reserved the right to stay there.

He looked forward to making use of his room again, considering it had been a long time since he'd slept in a bed. He and Falcon usually rested in the woods near the border after patrols so that they could wake at a moment's notice if they heard anything suspicious. Dragons might become especially lethargic near dawn until early afternoon, but they could fight the urge to sleep for an hour or two with the right herbs. Spies used that trick quite often. As a result, border guards could never truly be off duty or allow themselves to sleep anywhere comfortable.

With Donar staying by his side, Aidan passed through the great hall where it was filled with busy human servants. Few of them looked up from their work. Most were preparing for the midnight meal that would commence in less than two hours. Aidan followed a series of corridors until they reached the pendragon's office. The large, heavy door was closed, but muffled voices could be heard within. He knocked once, caught Nanoq's terse command to enter, and stepped inside.

Aidan gave a brief bow to the pendragon, then his gaze shot to Kade. What was his uncle doing here? The last he had heard, Nanoq removed the restrictions on Kade not being able to leave the library—something he'd not been able to do in centuries because of his wild predictions about the future and eccentric behavior—but Aidan hadn't expected his seer uncle to be here of all places. His father, the previous pendragon, had wanted nothing to do with his seemingly insane brother. Apparently, their new leader felt much differently.

"Uncle," Aidan said, dipping his chin.

Kade's lips twitched. He might be about nine-hundred years old, but he only appeared to be in his fifties by human standards. Aidan's uncle had long, wavy black hair that reached his shoulders and light olive skin. Only the lines around his eyes and forehead gave away his advancing years. He probably still had a century or so left in him before he'd go on to meet the dragon goddess, Zorya.

"Aidan." The pendragon drew his attention back his way. Nanoq's lips had thinned, and there was a grim look in his eyes. "Your time at the eastern border has ended...for now."

Aidan frowned. "I don't understand."

"Unlike your father—Zorya be with him—I am not as skeptical of your uncle's prophecies. He has recently come into one in particular that is of great concern to me." Nanoq worked his jaw. He was a warrior and a man with strong convictions. If he chose to put faith in Kade's predictions, he did not do so lightly.

Aidan glanced at his uncle. "The page?"

When he was young, Kade went through a period of blackouts where he had visions of the future. He'd carefully written each of them as they came, but in a strange twist, the details were wiped from his memory right after they were copied onto parchment. Even with re-reading them, it was difficult for him or anyone else to retain the information for long, assuming they understood it at all. This added to the impression that Kade must have been crazy. As he grew older, these events stopped and his predictions turned into minor ones he could recall, but few believed.

The tome containing the revelations went missing a century ago. Aidan's uncle had blacked out again, so he had no idea if he'd been the one to hide the prophecies or if someone else had taken them. Kade had been searching for the book ever since. About two months ago, he found a sheet of parchment with one of his revelations copied on it. This was the first sign that the tome might still be around, but they couldn't understand a word of what was written on the page. All Kade had known was that it was important, and it likely had something to do with an artifact and going on a journey. How his uncle even knew that much, Aidan couldn't say.

"I have finally found a way to translate it," Kade said, rubbing his face. "And the message it contains is far worse than I imagined."

Aidan stilled. "How so?"

"For many centuries," Nanoq said, taking control of the conversation, "there have been tales of an orb that could control dragons. One that was lost nearly three thousand years ago. Most thought it was a myth, but the story has continued to persist down the ages. The pure dragons are especially fearful of it because there are those among them who claim to be descendants of the ones who were affected. They say there are sorcerers who can harness the power of the orb and make it work for them."

A shudder ran down Aidan's back. The very idea of being manipulated and controlled by anyone did not sit well with him. Did the sorcerers not have enough dangerous magic already without having to add such a powerful object to their arsenal?

"It is difficult to separate rumor from truth," Kade added, coming to stand next to the pendragon's desk. "But the page I translated has revealed that the orb was hidden long ago in this region. It was broken and separated into three pieces in the hopes it could never be used again for ill purposes. But my prophecy says it will be if we do not find it first."

"Where is it?" Aidan asked.

"I am still determining the precise locations of the fragments, but I am getting close. I am almost certain at least one fragment is in a cave that thieves have used for refuge—wherever that might be. The text is in an ancient Aramaic dialect, which is not easy to decipher or else I might have more details already. I've only got the help of a servant who once specialized in that area of history to help me. In fact, it wasn't until he visited the library a few days ago that I learned in which language it was written. I know not why I wrote it in that particular dialect." Kade shook his head. "But I suspect that was a common language in the world at the time the orb went missing."

Nanoq sat back in his seat, frowning. "Except that it wasn't spoken in this land where the orb was hidden. Your prophecies are more than a little confusing."

"I am well aware." Kade sighed. "But I do not believe a written language existed in this region to use from that same period."

Aidan shifted on his feet. "Why bring me into this?"

The pendragon drew in a breath. "It is not as simple as sending a few shifters out to recover the pieces. Your uncle's translation has revealed specific details of what we will need to obtain the orb. Certain…types of people and difficult tests will be involved to get past the spells protecting the fragments."

"Such as?" Aidan prompted.

"There must be a dragon—though it need not be pure—and a human present." Nanoq hesitated, a grimace forming on his face. "A sorcerer and dragon slayer are required to be there as well."

"A dragon slayer?" Despite the fact Kade had told Aidan months ago that he and Bailey would be going on a journey together, he had not guessed it would be for something like this.

"Yes." The pendragon appeared sick at the thought. "Whoever hid the orb made it so that only a group with all the races working together could ever reach it. They must have known it would be nearly impossible. In addition to that, the text says slayers can be controlled by the artifact as easily as dragons—should it ever be forged into one piece again."

Aidan wouldn't say it out loud, but while the slayer element surprised him, he was actually less pleased about a sorcerer needing to participate. "Isn't it too dangerous to allow a sorcerer to come as well?"

"Yes and no. Though they are the only ones who can harness the orb's power, they cannot forge it back together. Only the fire from a dragon who has the second flames can do that, which your uncle has informed me you have." Nanoq gave Aidan an ironic look—few knew that secret about him, but now the pendragon could be added to the list. "Having said that, the text does mention the process for acquiring the third and final piece will make it whole again. If we choose a sorcerer who has only recently come into their power, they should not be able to control the orb at all."

"There is none in the fortress like that," Donar said, speaking for the first time since they entered the room. He had held back, stationing himself by the door.

"That is true," the pendragon agreed, then turned his gaze to Aidan. "But if my spies are correct, your dragon slayer has a sorceress friend who has been studying the art of healing since coming into her powers. One with such talents would be the least threatening choice, assuming she passes a vetting process and you agree to the selection."

Aidan considered it. While Bailey's friend, Danae, was no weak-willed woman, he did not believe she would use her powers for evil purposes. At least, not at this early stage. Most sorcerers did not turn to the dark arts until they'd been practicing magic for many years. He suspected that overuse of it tainted them somehow. Danae had only been learning to use her powers for a few months and only for healing purposes. She was as close to non-threatening as they might hope to find if they must bring a sorceress along on their quest.

"I agree. She would be a wise choice," Aidan answered the pendragon.

"Then it is time that I finally meet your slayer and her friend." Nanoq folded his hands in his lap. "We will go after first meal tomorrow. For now, you are going to tell me everything you know about them."

4

BAILEY

I lifted the bandage from my bicep, wincing. The gash was deeper than I thought and hadn't quite stopped bleeding yet. The dragon I'd spotted in the west Norman neighborhood yesterday had killed two people and injured several others as it burned and tore its way through their home. It fled as soon as it heard me coming. Conrad and I spent several hours trying to figure out where it had gone with no luck. Feeling guilty that I hadn't saved the people in time, I'd gone back out this morning and finally found its nest. One thing I'd come to learn about fire-breathing beasts—they woke up cranky and didn't particularly care for swords swinging at their necks. It lost in the end, but I'd gotten a few bruises and a sharp talon across my arm for my efforts.

At least the sturdy uniforms Aidan had given me protected my body from most damage. The dragon's claws had caught me in the leg as well, but the black camrium pants had shielded my skin there. It was only my upper arms and most of my shoulders that were bare. I had a jacket, but it was still too warm out and it restricted my movements. When you were fighting dragons four or five times bigger than you, you needed every advantage you could get.

"So have you picked out any names for the baby yet?" I asked Trish, patting the bandage back into place.

She was sitting a few feet away on a chair, rubbing at the slight swell of her belly. Mostly all she wore these days were t-shirts and yoga pants, and she'd pulled her red, curly hair into a bun on top of her head. There was a soft glow emanating from her porcelain skin that only a pregnant woman could produce. She looked beautiful, but she still had almost five months to go until the baby was born. I tried not to worry too much about how difficult it would be when that time came. The father of her child, Justin, was still working on finding a doctor who could help with the delivery. So many people were leaving Oklahoma ever since word got out that there was a place on the East Coast where the remnants of the U.S. government and military had established a safe zone from the dragons. Despite the fact it was almost a thousand miles away, some people were willing to take the risk traveling. No one in our neighborhood was going, though. Everyone here knew the shifters wouldn't bother us, and that we were safe staying put.

This afternoon, we chose to enjoy what was probably one of the last warm days of the year. A rumor was going around that this was going to be a rough winter. We'd had our first post-apocalyptic Thanksgiving a few days ago, and everyone had been discussing it. I was pretty sure the intel originally came from Javier, the sorcerer who ran the downtown Norman district. He had a knack for knowing things like that, and now that he'd made some kind of deal with the local shifter clan, he wasn't hiding his presence anymore. People could come and go from there as they wished, trading things the sorcerer wanted for food or medicine.

Trish gave me an incredulous look. "You're over there bleeding all over my porch, and you're worried about what name I might give the baby?"

I dropped my gaze to the cement, searching for any signs of blood. There was one drop.

Conrad snorted. "Getting banged and bruised up is a daily thing for her." He was sitting next to me on the porch steps. "I'm beginning to think Bailey doesn't feel pain anymore."

I used my good arm to knock him in the shoulder. "This is not a *daily* thing."

"Damn near," he said, shaking his head at me.

Conrad liked going after dragons almost as much as I did, but I suspected seeing me get hurt over and over again took a toll on him. He kept warning me that one day I would die doing this. He was probably right, but I couldn't let myself think about that. My instincts drove me to fight whether I wanted to or not, and every one of the beasts I killed meant human lives were saved. It was something that stayed at the forefront of my mind every moment I wasn't out fighting. In the areas where the pure dragons roamed, people died on a daily basis. I was the only one who could fight back and prevent those deaths. Conrad knew that, which was why he almost always came with me on the hunts to help. He didn't think it should be my burden alone. We couldn't save them all, though I sure wished we could.

"So have you picked any names or not?" I asked Trish again.

She worried her lip. "Well, I was thinking if it's a girl I'd name her after Justin's mom—Grace. She died when he was young, but I know he still misses her."

"That's sweet," Conrad said, a dimple appearing in his cheek. "But what if it's a boy?"

Trish shrugged. "No idea, but Danae thinks it's a girl. She says she has a feeling about it."

"With as good as her magic is getting," I said, leaning my back against the porch railing. "She's probably right."

"It's goin' to be fun having a little one runnin' around here," Conrad mused. For a guy who tried to act tough and snarky all the time, he sure did love kids. The woman he was dating had a five-year-old girl. It was amusing to watch how ridiculous he could act once a child was around, like nothing embarrassed him, or at least he didn't care what anyone thought.

For me, I preferred to keep them at a distance.

"I was six years old when my mother had my youngest brother, Paul," I informed them, gazing off into the distance. "For the first few years, I hated having him around because he took all my mom's attention. In the beginning, all they do is cry or sleep. Then they start getting into everything, and it's impossible to watch them every moment of the day. He'd sneak into the garden and track mud all over the house or bang on the chicken coop and drive the birds crazy. We just couldn't stop him from getting into trouble, but once he got a little older, it wasn't too bad."

Trish frowned at me. "Was that speech supposed to be encouraging?"

Conrad snickered.

"No, it was a warning. I'm just trying to prepare you for what to expect, but at least you'll have the whole neighborhood to help. Your kid is going to be spoiled—even if we don't have electricity or TV anymore." I forced a smile. "It will be okay."

I was trying really hard to be a supportive best friend, but it wasn't always easy. Trish had picked a bad time to have a child, even if she hadn't planned it. We had no way of knowing what kind of troubles might come next. The arrival of dragons felt like it was only the beginning, and everything was still in chaos. I didn't have the same kind of hope for the future that I once did. Maybe fighting and killing dragons every day had dimmed my outlook on life, and what a child would face coming into this world. Maybe a part of me worried I couldn't protect it, and if something happened I'd blame myself.

"Damn, check out Danae. She looks like shit." Conrad nodded toward the woman walking down the street toward us.

Danae had been pushing her healing abilities to the max to keep up with a recent flu outbreak. She couldn't make it go away entirely, but she could help speed up the recovery process. Trish and Conrad both got it last week and had become Danae's first patients. They were better in about thirty-six hours, but they were young. Some of the older people in the neighborhood were getting hit harder, and she was struggling to help them. At least she didn't have to worry about me. Since I'd become a dragon slayer, I didn't get sick anymore.

Danae had her blond hair pulled back in a semibun that didn't look too different from a bird's nest. A light sheen of sweat covered her forehead, and her green tank top had wet spots on her chest and under her arms. She always washed up after she worked on a patient, but it seemed to take a few hours for her to cool down from doing serious healing magic. I wasn't sure which of us had the worst job since the apocalypse happened. We'd both come into abilities we didn't have before and felt the need to use them to help people no matter the cost to ourselves.

She nudged my foot off the bottom step and plopped down, sighing heavily. "I'm exhausted."

"You look like it," I said.

Danae glanced at my wounded arm and frowned. "I'd help if I had anything left to give."

"Don't worry about it. You know it will be almost good as new in a few hours."

"It's too bad we don't have any energy drinks left." Conrad studied Danae. "You look like you could use one."

"One? I could drink four of them in a row right now." She gave him a weak smile.

"How's it going with your patients?" I asked.

She closed her eyes and leaned her head back against the railing. "I don't know if I can save Stu—he's pretty delirious right now—but I think Norma is going to make it okay."

Norma was a sixty-year-old woman with a chicken coop in her backyard who shared her eggs with everyone in the neighborhood. She could be a little grouchy, but she had a big heart. Stu was a widower who looked like he was around ninety, though I didn't know his exact age. He wasn't quite sound of mind anymore, but we all tried to look after him. He liked to sit on his porch and tell us stories about WWII. Sometimes we weren't sure he was aware of all the changes in the world. At least once a week he'd stand in his yard yelling and asking if anyone else's electricity was out. We hadn't had power since the day the dragons arrived over six months ago. Still, it was nice to think someone could keep on pretending things were normal.

"I'm sure you're doing everything you can," I told Danae, giving her a pat on the arm. I didn't want to put pressure on her, but I hoped both her patients pulled through. We'd lost too many people already, and I wasn't ready to lose any more, no matter their age.

"Thanks," she said, opening her green eyes.

The sound of barking came from down the street, and we all sat up a little straighter. Bomber, a former police dog, was standing in the middle of the road and staring at something to the south. He belonged to Jennifer, but she was still inside her house resting from when she came down with the flu last night. She'd probably let him out to get some exercise. He made a good guard dog and always let us know if any strangers were getting close to our area. We had a brick wall around most of it, which discouraged the majority of potential looters, but some still tried to sneak in.

"What is he barking at?" Trish asked, leaning forward in her seat.

I squinted into the sky and caught sight of several distinct shapes in the distance. A group of red dragons flew this way. It took another minute for them to get close enough for me to make out one in particular I recognized. I stood up. "It's Aidan and a few other shifters from his clan."

My heart fluttered in my chest, though I tried to ignore it. I hadn't seen him since the night we slept together. He'd warned me that it might be a long time before we saw each other again, but I hadn't thought it would be two months. No amount of telling myself that we couldn't be together stopped the small thrill that ran through me. Neither did acknowledging the fact he was a dragon, and I was programmed to kill his kind. The closer he flew, the more I wanted to rush off and get some water to wash away the mess I'd made of myself during my latest battle. My face and hands were clean, but I needed to change my clothes and put a fresh bandage on my arm.

Stifling the urge to prepare myself like I was going on a date, I stood still and waited for him and the other shifters to reach the neighborhood. They knew what I was, and there was no point in hiding the evidence. Not to mention the beast I'd killed today was one of their enemies, too. They should be glad I did it.

The red dragons landed in the street about fifty feet from where we stood in front of the porch. All four of them lit up in flames, and about a minute later they reappeared in their human forms. I tried not to focus on any of them in particular, but I couldn't help checking out Aidan once his face emerged. There was a warning in his eyes. Whatever this was about, it wasn't a social call.

One of the men moved in front of the others and led the way. He was large and muscular with short, black hair and medium-olive skin. Something about his distinguished features and the way he carried himself told me he was in charge. Could this be the new pendragon Aidan's sister, Phoebe, had told me about? She'd stopped by a few times when she could get away from the fortress to update me on news of Aidan and help me perfect some of my fighting techniques.

"I am Nanoq," the shifter said, coming to stand a few steps away from where I met him in the yard. His gaze ran up and down my body in a way that said he found me lacking. "I am pendragon to the Taugud clan. Are you the dragon slayer?"

I decided I didn't like him right then and there. "Only on Thursdays. I take the rest of the week off."

"Today is Wednesday." He focused on my bandaged arm. "And it is clear you have been fighting."

He knew the days of the week? The shifters must have adopted even more human customs than what I'd heard about so far. "Oh, right. Guess I can take tomorrow off, then."

Aidan's pained expression pleaded with me to take this more seriously. He was right, but I didn't like the way Nanoq was looking at me—like I was a bug to be squashed—and it had set me off.

The pendragon stared past me. "Which one is the sorceress?"

I tensed. Shifters could sniff magic users out, but since two women sat on the porch some distance away, he probably couldn't tell who was who. I didn't like the idea that he was interested in either one of them. If he got near Trish, though, I'd kill him. As for what he wanted with Danae, that worried me as well.

"That is her," Aidan said, coming forward to point at Danae on the steps.

Why was he pointing her out? There had better be a good explanation for this.

The pendragon gestured at the other two shifters with him. "Take the sorceress. I'll handle the slayer."

"Wait." The moved around me before I could stop them. "What is this about?"

"You must come with us," Nanoq said.

"No." I shook my head. "You need to explain what is going on first. I am well aware that you guys aren't big fans of slayers or sorceresses, so we're not going anywhere until you promise you aren't planning to kill us."

Though I didn't think Aidan would let that happen, I couldn't be one hundred percent certain of how deep his clan loyalty lay, especially after two months since we'd seen each other.

Nanoq's jaw hardened. "Cooperate, and you won't be harmed."

I couldn't help it—I looked at Aidan for confirmation. "Is this true?"

He looked like he was about to answer when the pendragon took hold of my arm. "You will address me and only me."

"Remove that hand before I remove it for you," I said through clenched teeth.

Sparks shot from his eyes. "Try. It will only prove how dangerous you truly are to my people."

Damn—he had me there. This had to be some sort of test.

"What's goin' on here?" Earl shouted, his country accent stronger than usual. That was typically a sign he was angry and ready to shoot someone. Even I didn't get in his way when he got in that mood.

The Vietnam vet walked up the street with a rifle in his hands, aimed at the shifters. Justin and Miles were on either side of him with their own weapons at the ready. Justin—Trish's boyfriend—held Bomber's leash, which explained why the dog hadn't attacked the shifters when they landed. I almost smiled. My human and canine friends didn't have a prayer against Aidan's people, but that wouldn't stop them from trying to protect me.

I jerked out of Nanoq's hold. "Don't worry, Earl. I've got this."

The pendragon looked at me. "Is he the leader of this..." he paused to gesture at the houses around us, "place?"

"Yes, he is." I didn't even live in the neighborhood anymore, only visited. Aidan's lair was my primary residence because I preferred living alone.

"Stay here," Nanoq ordered me. He gestured at Aidan, and they walked together toward Earl, uncaring of the weapon the old man pointed at them. Aidan shot a quick look back at me with an apology in his gaze. I wished I could speak to him without anyone hearing, but the only way we could do that was if his inner beast took over his body and used telepathy.

For several minutes, the men talked in the middle of the street while everyone else in the neighborhood came out to watch—most of them had been hiding up to this point. After Nanoq promised he was not there to harm anyone, and in fact needed our help, Earl reluctantly lowered his rifle. I was torn as to what to do and glanced over at Danae where two shifters held her. She still looked tired, but also a little angry. We'd both had a rough day already and now this? What did the pendragon want with us? If not for the fact I could hear Nanoq continuing to insist he was there with good intentions, and Aidan was backing him up, I might have put a stop to their visit. But we needed peace with the shifters who now ruled our territory, not war.

I caught a rush of movement from out of the corner of my eye.

Stu was racing out of his house with no shirt on— unless you counted a scrawny chest full of gray hair— and his eyes were fever-bright. "The demons are here. The demons are here!"

"I got this," Conrad called out, running across the street to grab the old man.

"No." Stu struggled against being led back inside. "We have to stop them before they take all our candy."

Conrad pulled a Jolly Rancher from his pocket and gave it to Stu. "Don't worry, man. I got us covered."

Excitement lit in Stu's blue eyes. He glanced down the street toward the shifters, who had returned their attention to Earl, then quickly snatched the candy. Conrad had no trouble getting him back into the house after that.

Another five minutes passed before Miles' voice rose up in a vehement tone. "You're not taking them anywhere. I don't care what good reason you claim to have."

Though he and Danae had never acknowledged their attraction to each other, there was obvious chemistry between them. Miles was always protective of her even while scowling in her direction. Sometimes, I wished they'd just stop fighting and get to the kissing part. The problem was that they were each too hard-headed and independent to see what was right in front of their eyes—no matter how many people pointed it out to them.

"I swear by the dragon goddess, Zorya, that as long as your woman does not pose a threat, she will be returned to you unharmed," Nanoq vowed.

"She's not my woman!" Miles said, outraged.

The pendragon glanced at Aidan. "Is he daft in the head?"

I couldn't hold back a snicker and heard one come from Trish as well. Danae just frowned.

"He's in denial," Aidan replied.

"I would be too if I cared for a sorceress," Nanoq muttered.

"They gotta leave by their own free choice," Earl interjected. "It ain't anyone's decision but theirs if they wanna go with you."

Nanoq turned toward me. "Will you come?"

"Does your promise of safety go for me as well?" I asked. At this point, I'd grown curious enough about what the pendragon might want that I was actually considering leaving with him. Since he hadn't tried to kill me right away, there had to be something more to his being here. It would also be my chance to prove I wasn't a threat to his people—if I could control myself. He didn't make it easy.

"In the name of Zorya, you will be safe." He paused. "As long as you cooperate."

I considered it for a moment longer and told myself it wasn't just because I wanted to stay near Aidan. "Fine. I'll go."

The pendragon looked at Danae next. "And you?"

She met my gaze with a question in her eyes. I doubted the pendragon would lie if he was invoking the dragon goddess' name. They took their vows very seriously. The tricky part there was—how did Nanoq define cooperate and what would he be asking of us?

"It's up to you," I said.

She lifted her chin. "Yeah. I'll go, too."

One of the shifters next to her produced a camrium blanket in his hands. He must have pulled it from *shiggara*, a sort of mystical place where they could store a few things and retrieve them at will. That was also where they kept their clothing and weapons when they were in dragon form.

"Wrap this around you," the shifter ordered.

While she did that, Nanoq walked up to me. "I will be the one to fly you, but you must not fight me after I shift or this will not go well."

I wanted Aidan to carry me, but I suspected the pendragon knew that. He probably only let Aidan come to give us a familiar face.

"Just keep your talons to yourself," I warned.

"I could say the same to you." He nodded at the sword and dagger strapped to my leg harness. "You'll need to leave those behind."

"Don't trust me?"

He gave me a feral grin. "Consider this a test. You'll want to pass it if you wish to continue living in my territory."

Damn. I knew it must be something like that.

5

BAILEY

I kept my gaze trained to the horizon, taking calm and steady breaths, and did my best to ignore the large shifter holding me against his chest. He wasn't Aidan. Flying with Nanoq while controlling my instincts was much harder. My fingers twitched with the urgent need to turn in his arms and claw his eyes out. The only thing that helped was Aidan flying ahead of us. Despite his being in dragon form, his presence calmed me.

I will not allow any harm to come to you, Bailey, his beast spoke to me telepathically in a soothing voice. *Relax and keep your eyes on me.*

He'd been giving me reassurances ever since Aidan shifted into dragon form and let him take over. Nanoq had no idea. It was supposed to be highly unusual for a shifter's inner beast to communicate with anyone, much less a dragon slayer. Beast liked me, though. I'd begun to think he might even like me more than

Aidan did, but Phoebe once told me that the animal within them acted almost entirely on instinct and desire. Their thinking was simpler. They didn't care as much about the potential consequences of their behavior or how others might perceive it. Aidan had to be the one to take responsibility for both of them and anything they did.

I wished I could communicate back to Beast to thank him for his help.

The spirals and tops of the fortress guard towers appeared in the distance. We weren't flying high enough to get a full view, but I could see enough to note it was constructed with dark gray stone. And if the spikes protruding all over the rooftops and walls were any indication, the place was built to be intimidating.

I'd avoided going anywhere near the fortress until now. A lot of images had come to mind when Aidan, Phoebe, or Donar mentioned it, but my imagination had clearly been lacking because it was far larger and more imposing than anything my mind had conjured.

Just south of the fortress, I got my first aerial view of the new mountain range that had sprung up out of nowhere on D-day. The jagged peaks rose to several thousand feet high from the base, making the tops of them visible even from Norman. Their blue-gray coloring provided an amazing sight for those of us who were used to only seeing the flat plains of central Oklahoma. The range went on for as far as I could see, though I'd heard they only took up about fifty square miles. Anyone who wished to pass them had to go around since there hadn't been time for roads to be built through them yet. For now, the dragon shifters were the only ones with full access.

Nanoq's grip on me tightened, and he started descending toward an empty pasture.

I tensed, wondering if he planned to have us walk the last couple of miles. We landed with a thud on a muddy field. A flash thunderstorm had struck sometime in the early hours of the morning, dumping several inches of rain. In the heat of the summer, it would have dried already, but this was late November and the temperature hadn't quite reached seventy degrees that afternoon. It didn't help that clouds had been covering the sky for most of the day, only allowing the sun to peek out briefly this morning.

Nanoq let me go, and I moved a couple of steps away from him, glancing toward the spot where the other shifters had landed. The one who held Danae let her go as well. She stood there with a strained expression on her face, and her fingers clutching the black camrium blanket wrapped tightly around her.

"I think I just developed a fear of heights," she said, shuddering.

I gave her a weak smile. "You and me both."

Aidan lumbered toward me in his red dragon form. None of the shifters had changed into their human bodies, and it didn't look like they were planning on it. He stopped in front of me, rising onto his hind legs. There was a time when having a ferocious-looking creature like him come close would have scared the crap out of me, but I'd grown used to it over the past six months. If anything, I had to resist the urge to hug him.

Black cloth appeared in his big, red hands, and he lifted it with a talon.

I stared at it. "What's that for?"

I am sorry, little one, but the pendragon does not trust you yet. Your eyes must be covered and your hands bound before we finish the journey to the fortress. Please do not fight this. The less threatening you appear to him, the easier this will go. He pushed the cloth into my chest since obviously no one else could know he was talking to me, so he had to make some kind of physical gesture.

"Take it," Nanoq said with a growl.

I just barely made out what he said. Until then, I hadn't realized shifters could speak in their dragon forms, but I could see why they usually didn't bother. The words came out mangled and almost incomprehensible.

"Fine." I took the cloth from Aidan.

As I unfolded it, I realized it was a hood to go over my head. I grimaced. This was going to suck so badly, but they wouldn't be bringing us to the fortress—their home—unless they had a very good reason. It couldn't be to kill Danae and me since they could do that anywhere. Something much bigger had to spark their coming to get us and the expression in Aidan's yellow gaze said as much. I had to trust him that going along with this plan would be worth it.

I glanced at Danae, who'd also been given a hood by one of the shifters next to her. "Let's just put the damn things on and make them happy."

"Remind me never to go anywhere with you again." She lifted the hood and glared at Nanoq. "I've got patients to look after. If they die because I wasn't there to take care of them, I'm holding you responsible!"

The pendragon let out a puff of steam.

She gritted her teeth and shoved the hood over her head. I followed her example, putting mine on next. The cloth was woven together thickly enough I couldn't see through it, but it was loose enough that I could still breathe, and some hints of light made their way inside. Aidan took hold of my shoulder and turned me around, grabbing my wrists to pull them together. Despite his long talons, his fingers were surprisingly dexterous and careful as he put the manacles on me.

I began to breathe harder inside the hood, panicking at the thought of allowing myself to be bound while traveling with a group of dragons. His thumb grazed my palm in a soothing motion. I exhaled the air in my lungs slowly, forcing myself to calm down. He wouldn't let anything happen to me—I had to trust him. No way did he spend all that time training me only to let me die now. Never mind the attraction that still burned between us despite my best attempts to ignore it.

The cold shackles weighed heavily on my arms after he let go. They were tight, but not so tight they cut off my circulation. The pad of his thumb grazed me one more time and then he stepped away. I overheard Danae cursing where they must have been binding her. She used to be a soldier, and she'd served over in Afghanistan a few years ago, but she'd never been on the receiving end of this kind of treatment. It had to be tough for her, too, not to fight.

Nanoq took hold of me once more, and we lifted into the air.

A few minutes later, we touched down again. The ground was sturdier and drier here. Considering we were on a slight slope, judging by my footing, the rain water must have drained off after the storm. The pendragon let go of me. I sensed the heat of his flames as he shifted into his human form. Aidan had mentioned the fortress was designed so that no one in dragon form could enter it. Would we be going through the front entrance? That would be embarrassing, even if I couldn't see the people gawking at me as I passed with manacles on my wrists. I supposed it had been a kindness that he didn't have Danae and I trussed up while we were still at Earl's neighborhood. That would have caused a world of trouble.

Nanoq's hands gripped my hips, and he threw me over his shoulder. The air whooshed out of my lungs as my head swung down behind his back. His arm locked around the back of my thighs, making it rather difficult to move or adjust myself. This was ridiculous. He could have led us to wherever we were going, rather than make us feel like sacks of potatoes. Did he seriously think I'd tried to escape at this point? Sure, if I got angry enough, I could break my chains and get free, but I wouldn't have allowed them to be put on me in the first place if I planned that. Or maybe he was more worried because we'd arrived at the fortress and he couldn't risk me getting loose among his people. I hated that I had to prove myself to the shifters, even if logically it made sense.

I inhaled a deep breath and caught Aidan's scent a few feet away. It reassured me and gave me the strength I needed to tolerate my poor treatment. One advantage to being a slayer was that I had heightened senses. Not as good as the dragons, but enough to give me an edge I didn't have before my transition. It was rather ironic that they couldn't scent my kind the way they could a sorcerer, though. I could sniff them out at close range, but the only way they could figure out I was a slayer was after I attacked them with superhuman strength—or I failed to burn in their flames. There was also a birthmark on my wrist as a sign, but my bracers covered that.

The pendragon began walking, and a moment later we started moving downward like we were descending stone stairs by the sound of it. The air turned cooler the farther we went. The tiny rays of light that penetrated my hood before were gone, and I was surrounded by complete darkness. I bounced with every step Nanoq took. It was hard to say how much time passed or how long we walked, but I estimated it to be about ten minutes. The only sound I heard during that time was booted steps on the stone and the occasional drip of water. He was taking us through an underground route where I assumed no one would see us enter the fortress. The hood and shackles made more sense now. This was probably a secret passage of some sort, and the pendragon didn't want us to learn the location.

Nanoq set me down on my feet and pulled the hood over my head. I immediately ran my gaze around, thirsty for information. We were in a small room constructed entirely of dark gray stone. One table with a glowing lamp set on top was at the center of the space, as well as two chairs—nothing else. They'd shut the door before I could see anything beyond that. Aidan stood in the corner, partly in the shadows. I couldn't make out the expression on his face, but I got the sense he was uneasy.

Nanoq pointed at a metal chair. "Sit."

"Where's Danae?"

"She is close. Do not worry about her."

I narrowed my eyes. "She's my friend. I need to know she is okay."

"You will see her soon—if you both cooperate. Now sit," he commanded.

I straightened to my full height, which was almost a foot shorter than the pendragon, and stuck my chin out. "I'll cooperate, but if anything happens to her, I'll hold you responsible."

Nanoq ground his jaw. "You would do well not to question me."

He had no idea how hard it was not to punch him right then. I settled into the chair, making a point to do it slowly. It wasn't easy to pull off since they'd left the chains around my wrists. I didn't know if I should be honored that the pendragon saw me as such a big threat, or offended.

Nanoq came to stand on the opposite side of the table. "How long have you known you were a dragon slayer?"

That question was easy enough to answer. "When Aidan told me a little over six months ago."

"When did you complete the rite of passage?"

"About three and a half months ago."

Before I'd completed the rite, my enhanced abilities were limited and unreliable. It was only after I made my first kill and consumed some of the dragon's heart that I underwent the full transformation to become a slayer. It took several days, but after it was over, I became immortal. My body was stronger, and I healed a lot faster. Aidan said I could still die if my wounds were grave enough, but I would never age. I was locked into looking twenty-two years old for as long as I lived.

"Your first kill was an ancient?" he asked.

"That is what I'm told. All I knew at the time was that he was big, mean, and ugly with horrible breath."

Nanoq's lips twitched. Good to know he had a sense of humor in there somewhere.

He paced in front of the table, quiet for a moment. These were simple questions that he probably knew the answers to already. I could only assume this was a test to see if Aidan's version matched mine, and then he'd move on to something I probably wouldn't like. My last conversation with Verena came to mind. Was her prediction coming true, and if so, what would I do about it?

"How many dragons have you killed?"

I shifted in my seat. "I lost count after twenty, but that was a couple of months ago."

After a while, the kills began to blend together. I didn't take pride in slaying dragons, though relief did come from slaying the ones who hurt humans.

Nanoq leaned down and put his hands on the table, locking his gaze on me. "You have shown considerable restraint by not attacking my people. Why is that?"

I frowned. "What do you mean?"

"Other slayers do not care whether they kill pure dragons or shifters. Why do you?"

"Aidan showed me you're not a threat to humans." I glanced at the man in question, who gave me an encouraging nod. "He was willing to teach me and protect me until I became strong enough to battle on the shifters' side. I've never been given a reason to fight you."

At least, not on purpose. There was that one time with Ruari, Aidan's brother, but I managed to stop before killing him and let him go. I wasn't about to tell the pendragon about that. It wouldn't matter that I'd still been working on my control back then and couldn't help attacking. The pendragon would probably see it as proof I might still target his people.

Nanoq lifted his brows. "He protected you?"

"Yeah." I didn't look at Aidan this time.

"From the pure dragons?"

"I couldn't become a full slayer and his ally if I was dead." I scooted forward in my seat. "He did what he had to do to keep me alive until I was ready. If you re-call, that worked out for your clan when you fought that battle with the Shadowan. A lot more of your people would be dead if I hadn't stepped in to help."

Nanoq stared at me. "That is the only reason you remain alive now."

"How kind of you," I said, bitterness tainting my voice.

"It means more than you can possibly realize. Especially considering a new threat has emerged, and I am considering asking for your help resolving it." His gaze moved to the door. "Yours and your friend's, if you both prove trustworthy enough."

"And how are we supposed to *prove* trustworthy?"

"Cooperate in every way I ask," he said.

"I've been doing that."

He gave me a skeptical look. "We'll see. Now tell me about the other sorcerers you know."

"There are just two more—Javier and Verena. Neither are my friends, and I only deal with them when I have to, and there's no way around it." That was true enough.

"Have either of them asked for special favors from you?"

I tensed. "Javier asks me to bring green dragon scales for him when I can. He uses them for some kind of protection spells."

"We are already aware of that, and we've sanctioned him to continue doing so as long as there are no red scales involved." He gave me a warning look.

I lifted my chin. "There hasn't been, and there won't be in the future. I don't need you to tell me that."

"Are you saying you would never do anything that could potentially harm my people?" he asked.

"Yes." I stared up at him. "As long as you don't harm humans." That was the main reason I wanted to build an alliance with the shifter clan, and why I was willing to put up with Nanoq's crap. One day, I'd be heading back to my family in Texas. I needed to know the people in Norman would be safe after I left.

"What has the other sorcerer asked of you?"

I dropped my gaze. "Nothing really—until yesterday."

The tension in the room thickened as Nanoq and Aidan exchanged glances.

"And what did she ask of you yesterday?" the pendragon asked.

This was going to take some explaining.

"First, you have to understand I owe Verena a favor. My friend, Conrad, got shot by some human looters a while back. He was close to dying. At the time, Danae didn't know she was a sorceress yet, and the hospitals were a mess. Verena was the only person I knew who might have been able to help. She saved his life, but in return, I had to owe her an unspecified favor. She didn't ask for it until yesterday." I wished I could say I regretted the decision, but I hadn't had a choice at the time. Keeping Conrad alive was all I cared about.

"And what does she want?" Nanoq asked in a menacing tone.

"Some lost orb, but she wouldn't tell me what it's for."

The air thickened, and when I met the pendragon's gaze it was thunderous. "Did you tell her you would give it to her?"

I shook my head. "I refused. She said that if I didn't, I would pay a price for breaking my word, but I still didn't agree to it."

"Do you know what breaking your promise to her will mean?" His tone was quiet and deadly.

"I'm guessing whatever she is planning with that orb is not good. No matter what happens, I won't give it to her," I said.

"You can't know that for certain." Nanoq turned to Aidan. "Get Xanath in here now."

"You can't mean to…" Aidan began. There was a look of outrage in his eyes.

"Now!"

He hesitated. For a moment, I thought he'd refuse the order, but then a resolved expression came over his eyes, and he left the room. A cold chill ran through me. Something told me I wasn't going to like this Xanath person.

6

AIDAN

Aidan escorted Xanath down the dark tunnel passage, both of them moving stiffly. The most powerful sorcerer in the fortress wasn't called to the dungeons often and never for anything good. Aidan would have liked to say all of this man's kind were evil, but Xanath had a kind heart, and he didn't like hurting anyone. He only did it when ordered, and if lives were at stake. Otherwise, he preferred reading in his room at the sorcerer's tower at the far rear of the keep.

At two-hundred and thirty years old, the aging man claimed to have seen more than his fair share of death. Sorcerers usually didn't live much longer than humans, but Xanath didn't practice magic often, so he was able to focus most of his powers on prolonging his life. Still, he'd aged in the past few decades. His body had gotten leaner, and he had a stooped back, resulting in him shuffling his feet when he walked. Aidan had to slow his steps considerably to keep pace.

"You say I am to probe the mind of a dragon slayer?" Xanath asked, peering over at him through a fall of gray, curly hair.

"Yes."

The sorcerer's blue eyes turned thoughtful. "I am getting the impression you are not pleased about this."

Aidan needed to choose his words carefully. "The slayer was open and forthcoming during questioning, and she has never posed a threat to the Taugud. I am not comfortable forcing her to endure a mind probe. She willingly came here after we promised no harm would come to her. It is not right for us to return her trust by invading her mind in a way that could potentially destroy it."

"There is much you are not saying." Xanath stopped in the middle of the corridor and put a hand on Aidan's arm. "How close are you to this slayer?"

"I have trained her and fought alongside her in battle," he answered.

Xanath gave him a knowing look. "That is not what I asked."

Aidan had to take a chance because the sorcerer would soon know everything, whether he liked it or not. "Most would say we are closer than what is appropriate. I would ask that you keep those details to yourself, as they bear no relevance to the matter at hand."

"If I am to understand your uncle and his prophecy correctly..." Xanath paused, and his eyes took on a slight glaze. "The closeness of your relationship to the slayer may very well be what allows you to recover the orb."

Kade had said something similar, though never in front of the pendragon. "I would still prefer you not reveal any intimacies you discover in her mind. Whatever has happened between us, it is not anyone else's business."

The sorcerer chuckled. "I have not met this slayer yet, but I can see you care for her very much. You've already risked more than others would for her. The question you must ask yourself is how would your behavior differ if there was no attraction between the two of you?"

Aidan looked away. He didn't have an easy answer for that, though Zorya knew he'd asked it of himself enough times.

"I gathered as much. Something tells me her weakness for you is just as great." Xanath gestured, and they resumed walking.

"How can you be so certain?" Aidan asked.

"Because your inner dragon has accepted the slayer—I can sense his protectiveness of her—and he would not do that if she did not feel just as strongly about you. The beast can discern things you cannot."

Aidan allowed silence to fall between them. The underground tunnel was long, and it took time to reach the section where they brought prisoners for questioning. Sconces holding lit torches were positioned about every twenty feet, barely penetrating the thick darkness. A shifter could see well enough to walk, but the human servants had to carry their own torch or lamp when they traversed down here. Their eyesight wasn't strong enough for them to see much farther than their hands in front of their faces.

When they got close to the door where Bailey was being held, Xanath slowed and murmured to Aidan. "Whatever is in this slayer's mind, I will only tell the pendragon what he needs to know. As long as your relationship with her does not pose a threat to anyone, your secret will remain safe."

"I would ask that you not harm her, either," Aidan said, not bothering to add what he might do if that happened.

Xanath's expression turned grim. "If it were up to me, I would not be here at all. You must help convince her not to fight me. I'm afraid that is the only way this will go well."

"Of course." Aidan dipped his chin.

They reached the chamber and entered. Nanoq had moved to stand by the wall, but he stared at Bailey with only a hint of civility in his expression. He'd lost a few relatives to dragon slayers over the years, causing him to have an even greater bias against them. It didn't matter what Bailey said or did to prove herself. Nanoq must have been planning to have the slayer's mind probed all along. That was the real reason he made his promise of safety contingent on each woman cooperating—because he knew it would come down to this.

How had Aidan not seen it before? He'd been a fool to think Nanoq would simply question Bailey and let her go afterward. The pendragon had no compunction about doing whatever it took to protect his people.

Of the times Aidan had watched the process before, it had not gone smoothly in any of them. Xanath might have reassured him that Bailey would be fine as long as she didn't fight the mind probe, but they couldn't be certain about that. The one thing Aidan did know was that the moment it appeared Bailey was being seriously hurt by it, he would put a stop to the process. Consequences be damned.

"What is it you wish me to search for?" Xanath asked the pendragon.

Nanoq's expression hardened. "Anything relating to the sorceress, Verena. I also want to know the slayer's intentions toward the Taugud. Does she mean us any harm, and would she betray us if it meant she could save herself."

Xanath's brows drew together. "Has she sworn an oath of fealty to you?"

"No, but she has made a pact with Aidan. That is nearly as binding."

The sorcerer glanced at Aidan. "A full pact?"

"All except her half of the blood ceremony."

Bailey made a disgruntled sound. "Look, I'm not trying to hurt any of you. The fact that I allowed you guys to fly me here—in your dragon forms—should have proved that. Not to mention I *let* you guys shackle me, and I've answered every question you've asked. What more do you want from me?"

"You brought her here in your dragon forms?" Xanath asked, giving them a look of incredulity. "And she did not give you any trouble?"

It was well known that slayers had no control over their instincts, and they would attack any dragon they saw that came near them. Some could show restraint if a shifter were in human form, but even that didn't happen often. Xanath had not been fully informed of Bailey's ability to contain herself.

Nanoq grunted. "She did not give us any trouble."

It must have killed him to make that admission.

"Are you certain she is a dragon slayer?" Xanath asked.

"Many of our warriors have seen her survive the flames and kill dragons. She is a slayer," Nanoq reassured the sorcerer.

"How is this possible?"

Bailey smiled at Xanath. "I let Aidan chain me to trees and make me get used to seeing him in his dragon form until I didn't try to break free anymore. Then I practiced my control while out hunting the pure dragons. It took a while, but I got the hang of it."

There was even more to it than that, but he wasn't about to admit he'd held Bailey close during the days it took for her to transition into a full slayer. She'd learned to find his scent comforting and safe, which helped to desensitize her to the scent of his kind. Aidan knew the pendragon wouldn't be pleased to hear about those details, though.

"Why would you care to control yourself?" Xanath asked her.

Bailey glanced between the sorcerer and pendragon. "Aidan saved my life the day the dragons started coming to Earth. It didn't totally make me trust him at first, but he can be pretty persuasive when he wants to be, and he made a good argument that it was easier working with each other than against. Besides, I only saw the green dragons hurting people, not shifters. That helped convince me."

Everyone stared at the tiny woman who sat in the chair with her arms shackled behind her back. She didn't look like she could hurt much of anything. Bailey had gained some muscle through her training, but she was still unusually small for a slayer.

The pendragon's gaze turned thoughtful. "There was no one else to train you?"

"No." She shook her head. "I didn't even know I was a slayer until Aidan told me. One day I was a normal woman with a normal life, and the next I found out I was born to do a job that would get me killed sooner rather than later. It's not like I had much choice in the matter."

"You could have chosen not to complete the rite of passage," Nanoq said, crossing his arms. "The urge to fight dragons would have faded eventually."

She gave him a questioning look. "And watch people I care about die while the town was being torn apart? Could you have done that?"

A range of emotions crossed the pendragon's face, but he said nothing.

Until that moment, Aidan suspected Nanoq had not fully considered what Bailey had faced in recent months, and the difficult choices she'd been forced to make. Before their arrival, the slayer was a young woman with a bright future before her—one that she'd spoken to him about during their training sessions. Then she was thrust into a new world where it was her sole responsibility to take on hoards of dragons that attacked the territory where she lived. If not for Aidan, she would have had no one to help or teach her. Even with his assistance, she'd had to take on a great deal by herself. He couldn't be with her all the time.

Nanoq cleared his throat. "She is unusual for her kind, which is the only reason I'm considering her assistance with the orb."

"And you wish me to probe her mind anyway?" Xanath lifted a brow.

The pendragon hesitated for only a moment. "I do. Until I can be reassured of her motives, I cannot trust her with this task."

Aidan ground his teeth. For a brief moment, he'd thought Nanoq might relent.

Xanath turned his gaze to Bailey. "Do you know what it means to have your mind probed by a sorcerer?"

"You're going to dig around in my head." She gave Aidan a nervous glance. "And find whatever information you want in there."

The sorcerer nodded. "But you must cooperate. If you fight me at all, there could be irreparable damage done to your mind."

She swallowed. "Will it hurt?"

Aidan wished he could wrap his arms around her right then, rather than just stand there doing nothing.

He wanted to protect her from this. It killed him to stand by without intervening, but he had to trust that she was strong enough to handle the probe. To interfere before giving her a chance would risk the mission to recover the orb and endanger their lives in more ways than one. Aidan would only step in if it appeared she could not handle the sorcerer's intrusion.

"It will only hurt if you fight it." The sorcerer gave her a reassuring look. "Otherwise, there will be some discomfort at the beginning when I enter your mind, but it will fade as you grow used to my presence there."

Bailey looked at Aidan, and he did his best to reveal his thoughts in his eyes. It was a decision she had to make for herself. She wavered for a moment, and fear overtook her expression. Aidan realized she needed to see his confidence in her if she was to agree to this. He gave her a curt nod. That was all it took for the panic rising in her to abate and for her to regain her courage.

"Do it." Resolve filled her gaze. "I can handle it."

Xanath came around the table, bringing the chair with him so he could sit while he worked. The beast within Aidan growled. His inner dragon did not like what was about to happen, and now that it was coming to pass, Aidan had to fight to keep control of his body.

The sorcerer put his hands on Bailey's head. "Prepare to open your mind to me."

She shuddered, but then she took several calming breaths. Aidan had worked with her a few times on meditation to assist with her discipline exercises. That would be useful now. With each breath, her body relaxed until even her eyelids fluttered shut. Her face took on an almost serene appearance.

"Good," Xanath said in an approving tone. "You are doing very well."

"What should I think about?" Bailey asked.

"Think about Verena. Let me see her, and the meetings you've had with her."

The sorcerer's fingertips tightened against Bailey's head, and he scrunched his brows as his magic began to swell around her. Aidan tensed. This was the most dangerous time when Bailey had to either accept or reject the invasion. How she handled it would decide whether she'd be hurt or not. He prepared to leap forward if necessary and push Xanath away. The pendragon took a step closer as well, as if he anticipated exactly what Aidan might do. Nanoq was strong and one of the toriq's best warriors, but he would not win this fight. Aidan would let his beast reign free and do whatever it took to protect Bailey if it came down to it.

"That's it. You've let me in, and I see her." The strain on Xanath's face eased. "Good girl."

Bailey didn't appear in any pain. She continued breathing in and out as if nothing harmful was happening to her. Aidan had been almost certain she would have at least resisted in the beginning. She opened her eyes and looked at him. The message there was clear—she knew he would have stepped in if she fought the mind probe. She'd also understood what the consequences would have been if that happened. To protect Aidan, she would endure this. His chest tightened, and he couldn't even name the emotions he felt at her sacrifice.

The minutes dragged by as Xanath worked inside her mind. Bailey flinched once, but a calm word from the sorcerer, telling her that she had nothing to fear settled her back down. Toward the end, a tear trailed down her cheek. Aidan had no idea what memory Xanath had examined, but it must have been a painful one. Her gaze was clear, though, and her mind was still intact.

Finally, the sorcerer let go and pulled away. "I have learned all I need to know."

"Tell me," Nanoq commanded.

"The slayer is no threat to us." He sat back in his chair, worn from using his powers. "The deal she made with Verena was done under duress. Bailey would have returned the favor, though, if the sorceress had asked for something more reasonable. She has no intention of giving the orb to Verena—no matter the cost to her."

Nanoq and Aidan exchanged alarmed glances. They had confirmation now that they were not the only ones seeking the orb. This did not bode well.

"She will not hand it over even if it means her friends could be hurt or killed?" the pendragon asked.

Bailey bowed her head, and a shuddering breath escaped her. Once again, Aidan wished he could take her in his arms and make everything go away. Instead, he kept his expression stoic. Appearing not to care was the best way to protect her for the moment.

"I honestly believe once the slayer knows the orb's purpose, she will not give it to Verena, even at the risk of her friends' lives," Xanath said and turned his gaze to Bailey. "She is a smart woman capable of seeing how high the cost would be if she did so."

The slayer looked up at Nanoq, her gaze hardening. "I'll kill her first if that's what I have to do."

Xanath patted her shoulder. "From what I can see, this sorceress is elusive. It may not be that easy."

"We'll see," Bailey vowed.

The pendragon asked the sorcerer a few more questions before appearing satisfied. "Very well. I am almost convinced she will suit our needs, but we still need to test her friend."

"Is anyone going to tell me why this orb is dangerous?" Bailey asked, giving them all annoyed looks. "I'd love to know what has you so worried you'd drag someone like me—a slayer—into this."

Now that she'd cooperated in every way they'd asked, she was getting testy. Aidan couldn't blame her.

"The orb Verena wishes you to obtain for her can control dragons..." Nanoq said, tone ominous, "...and slayers."

Bailey blanched. "There's something like that out there?"

"I'm afraid so." The pendragon's lips thinned.

"We can't let her have it."

"I am glad you understand that," the pendragon said, nodding at her.

"Where is it?" she asked.

Nanoq didn't answer right away. He stared at her, weighing her worthiness and all that he'd learned about her today. Had she managed to gain enough of his trust?

"It was lost thousands of years ago. We thought it was only a myth until recently, but now we know it was broken into three fragments. Each of those is hidden somewhere in this region, though we are still narrowing down the precise locations for where to start looking. According to our source, it will require a very specific group of people to recover the orb," Nanoq informed her.

Bailey frowned. "What kind of group?"

"There must be a member with dragon blood, a sorcerer, a human, and a slayer." He shifted on his feet. "They must be allied and working together in order to pass the tests protecting each orb fragment."

"If it's that hard, Verena shouldn't be able to get it. Why not just leave the pieces hidden?" Bailey asked.

Aidan had wondered the same thing until his uncle had told him the rest of what he translated from the page.

"According to the prophecy, someone very powerful—we don't know who—will find a way if we don't obtain the orb first. A reign of terror will follow once they have it and many will die." Nanoq's gaze darkened. "That is not a risk we can take."

"So what about Danae?"

"If she proves trustworthy, she will be the sorceress to go with you," Nanoq said.

"Why not him?" Bailey jutted her chin toward Xanath.

The pendragon glanced at the man in question. "He is too old to make such a treacherous journey, and I am unwilling to risk allowing any of the other sorcerers we have at the fortress go, either. We need someone whose magic is used to help, not hurt. Aidan believes your friend could be the right one."

In fact, Aidan was surprised Nanoq was telling the slayer this much. He'd thought the pendragon would keep her in the dark for as long as possible. Something had happened during the interrogation to make him believe she was at least somewhat trustworthy.

"Will Xanath have to probe her mind, too?" Bailey asked.

"Verena has tampered with your mind," the sorcerer stepped into the conversation. "From what I saw, she gave you back all of the memories she'd clouded, but I have no way of knowing what she has done to your friend and neither do you. The only way to be certain is for me to look inside."

Bailey's shoulders slumped. "And if Verena did do something to her?"

"I will attempt to fix the problem. The sorceress is powerful, but her control over the mind is not as great as my own. As long as your friend does not resist, it should not be a problem. But if not, we will have to judge her as a threat—even if it is not her fault," he answered.

"And what would you do then?" Bailey's voice held a thread of anger in it.

Nanoq answered this question, "If her mind has been altered in a way that makes her dangerous, and she cannot be fixed, we will have to confine her. Should we believe that is not enough to guarantee our safety, she will have to be executed."

"You're not killing her," Bailey said, her brown eyes flashing with outrage.

The pendragon gave her a hard look. "There is just as much chance that Verena made her a threat to you and other humans as much as us. Would you want someone around your people who may turn at any moment and hurt them? I believe I saw a pregnant woman among you earlier today."

Bailey rose to her feet. "Danae has spent the last week using her magic to help people sick with the flu. She has fought to protect her friends countless times since this whole dragon invasion started, and she's healed me when I've needed it. She's not a threat!"

"Let us hope so," Nanoq said.

She was quiet a moment, her mind clearly racing. "If you're going to convince her to cooperate, it would help if you let me out of these shackles. I've spent a lot of time around Aidan and trust him, so I was willing to let your sorcerer probe my mind without a fight, but she's going to be harder to convince. Seeing that you've freed me would go a long way to earning her good will."

The pendragon worked his jaw. "Would you swear an oath to me that you will not harm anyone in this fortress and that you will not attempt to leave without my permission?"

"How long do you plan to keep me here?" Bailey asked.

"I cannot answer that for certain at this time, but it should not be for more than a few days."

Bailey glanced at Aidan and then back to Nanoq. "And if someone attacks me, am I allowed to defend myself?"

"No one will attack you," he said, a promise in his eyes. "You and your friend will remain down here, and the guards will have orders not to allow anyone into this area except who I authorize."

"Fine." She exhaled a breath. "I promise not to hurt any of your people or try to escape."

Aidan stepped forward, unable to hold back any longer. "Bailey, do you recall what it means to make that promise?"

"It's a blood oath, isn't it?" She swallowed. "The one I didn't complete before?"

Because he couldn't bear to make her carry through with it after he saw how barbaric she found it. He nodded. "It is."

Her shoulders tightened, and everyone waited for her answer. "I'll still make that promise."

The slayer never ceased to amaze him.

When the pendragon reached for his dagger, Aidan stopped him. "I will do it."

"Are you certain you can?" Nanoq gave him an inquiring look.

Even he saw there was more to their relationship than they admitted, which was worrisome, but not something they could do much about now. This had to be done. It wasn't a matter of whether Aidan could thrust a blade into the woman he cared about or not. He only knew he would rather do it than let the pendragon hurt her—never mind it was the only way to keep his beast in check.

"I am." Aidan pulled his dagger and turned to Bailey. "Do you remember how it is done?"

She nodded slowly. "Yes."

"It will hurt, but you will heal," he said as a reminder.

And by stabbing her, he would be proving his loyalty to his toriq and the pendragon. His true reasons for doing this didn't matter. Aidan knew where to strike to bring about a believable amount of pain, but cause the least amount of damage. It was the best he could do for her. Pain and blood were part of the dragon way of life. By swearing a vow to one of their kind, she'd agreed to step into their world, and she could not take that back. He'd taught her enough to know that.

Bailey stared into Aidan's eyes, her gaze becoming resolute. "Do it."

His respect for her grew. His little dragon slayer had grown into a strong woman during these past months.

Aidan pulled up her camrium top enough to expose a small section of her stomach. It was all he could do not to admire her flat belly and light olive skin as she continued to stare at him, trusting him despite what he was about to do to her. Just two months ago, he'd kissed her in this spot and reveled in the softness of her skin. Aidan hated to mar such perfection. His only consolation was that she would heal without a scar. He waited until she exhaled her breath, then thrust the blade into her. She let out a small cry and bowed over, the chains at her wrists rattling as she pulled at them. He couldn't allow her discomfort to affect him— not now with the others watching.

Aidan pulled the blade from her and set it on the table. "Sit."

He couldn't help her in any way. According to custom, that would be an insult and imply she was weak. This was the reason only the strong were even allowed to give such oaths. He had to watch, hiding his emotions, as she unsteadily fell back into the chair. Blood poured from the wound he'd given her, leaking onto her camrium pants. Aidan couldn't see Bailey's face since she'd ducked her head down, but he could hear her ragged breathing. She was bravely doing everything she could not to make any more sounds of pain.

He pulled a key from his pocket and came around behind her. Wasting no further time, he took the shackles off her wrists. Slowly, she brought her hands around to grip her belly. Some of her hair fell into her face. Aidan wanted to push it away and look into her eyes. Instead, he retrieved his blade and drew a cloth from shiggara to clean it before putting it back in its sheath.

A few minutes later, Bailey removed her hands and checked the wound. Because he'd made it a clean cut, the bleeding had already slowed. Soon it would stop, and her skin would begin to knit itself back together. In another day, only a faint trace of the wound would remain, and a day after that it would be gone entirely. Aidan reminded himself of these things in an attempt to make himself feel better about it.

Bailey lifted her head and gave him a weak smile. "Can I have a cloth?"

He gave her a fresh one. She used it to clean up as much of the blood as she could, then pulled her top down to cover the wound and handed it back.

"We can talk to Danae now?"

Aidan looked at the pendragon.

Nanoq nodded. "Bring her in."

7

BAILEY

I stood slowly, gripping my belly. My aching shoulders begged me to stretch them after having my hands shackled behind my back for hours, but I couldn't bear to do it. My stomach hurt too much. The sharp pain wasn't nearly as bad as the time a dragon knocked me off an office building roof—that had been much worse—but I definitely didn't feel all that great.

Aidan had stabbed me just as hard as I'd stabbed him last summer. From a human woman's standpoint, it hurt that he could even do that to me. From the dragon's view of things, he'd just shown how much he respected me. When had my life become this complicated? I hoped he understood how much pride and fear I'd had to swallow to let his people take me, confine me, invade my mind, and then stab me. Never mind the promises I'd made. This kind of thing didn't happen to normal people, but life on Earth hadn't been normal for a while now. I could either roll with the punches or get slapped down by them.

Taking a fortifying breath, I shuffled my way to the wall. Danae was going to need the chair, and I wanted to present a strong front, even if all I really wanted to do was lie on the floor and curl into a ball. Better yet—sleep until the pain went away. Rest always sped up the healing process, but it wasn't a luxury I could afford at the moment.

Aidan returned with Danae a few minutes later. Once she was in the room and he'd shut the door, he pulled the hood over her head. Had they left it on her this whole time? Her blond hair fell in tangles to just past her shoulders. The look in her eyes said her patience was wearing thin, and she wasn't going to tolerate their crappy treatment for much longer. I understood how she felt.

"Sit," the pendragon ordered, indicating the chair I'd just vacated.

She took the seat and glanced at me where I stood leaning against the wall. Her brows drew together. I probably looked pale, but at least the black camrium cloth hid any blood stains, and I'd wiped the excess off before my bleeding made much of a mess.

"Are you okay, Bailey?" Danae asked, running her gaze up and down my body.

"Just peachy." I forced a smile.

Nanoq glanced at Aidan. "Peachy?"

"Humans say strange things. What relation a fruit has to her current condition, I do not know," he said, then came to stand next to me. He winked at me before focusing his attention on Danae. I'd told him what "peachy" meant months ago when he heard it the first time, but he probably enjoyed keeping his pendragon in the dark about that one. If you couldn't defy your pendragon in a big way, do it in a bunch of small ways.

Now it was time for me to play my part. If I wanted Danae to survive, I had to make sure she didn't fight Xanath or the shifters. I gave her a meaningful look. "I need you to cooperate with these guys."

Her expression turned flat. "After one of them stabbed you in the stomach? I can sense your injury from here, Bailey. Why would I cooperate with them after they hurt you?"

And this was the main reason I'd chosen to stand. If she'd found me huddled on the floor, I wouldn't have stood a chance of convincing her. At least if I acted like my wound wasn't a big deal, she might consider listening.

"Don't worry about me." I waved a hand. "I asked for it."

Danae narrowed her eyes. "Nobody asks to be stabbed in the stomach. That's ridiculous."

"Dragon customs are a little different from humans, and anyway, you know I'll heal in no time," I said, forcing myself to stand a little straighter. *Please, God, let this wound heal soon.* It was all I could do to hide the pain radiating across my abdomen and play it off like it was nothing for Danae's benefit.

"If you think I'm going to let them stab me, you're crazy." She scowled at the shifters.

"That will not be necessary, and I would not ask it of you." The pendragon moved closer to her. "But we will need you to answer some questions."

She gave him a suspicious look. "Like what?"

"Tell us about your relationship to the sorceress, Verena."

Danae's face twisted. "She helped train me when I first discovered I had healing powers, but I stopped going to see her a couple of weeks ago."

"Why?" I asked, already knowing the answer but needing her to tell them.

"There's something...dark about her." She paused, and a shudder ran through her body. "Like if I stayed around Verena much longer, she'd taint me, too."

"That was a wise decision," Xanath said, easing into the chair next to her.

"You're a sorcerer too, aren't you?" She studied him. "I can feel the magic coming from you."

"The fact you need to ask tells me you are still quite new to your abilities."

She lifted her chin. "Maybe, but I've learned a lot."

"That is what the slayer tells us." Nanoq drew her attention back to him. "But we need to assess how much the sorceress has affected you. To do this, you must allow Xanath to probe your mind."

She pulled back in her seat. "Uh, no. I'm not letting anyone mess around in my head."

"Danae, he really needs to do it." I pushed off the wall and came closer to her, ignoring the pull of my wounded stomach. "Verena messed around in my head, and Xanath thinks it's likely she messed with yours too, especially because you spent more time with her."

"I also believe that your instinct to get away from her was your subconscious trying to protect you," the sorcerer added.

Her green eyes sparked. "How do I know you won't mess with my mind, too?"

She had a point, but the whole time Xanath had been peering into my head, he didn't hide his activities. He was very careful to keep me aware of what he saw and did, including sharpening my memories of Verena. It made it a lot easier to trust him and let him keep going. If he'd rooted around in there while obscuring his actions, that would have made me fight against him. When he'd showed me the cloudy scenes with Verena, I'd seen what she'd done. How she'd made me forget the exact location of her home and even visits I'd had with her. The sorceress had invaded my mind and manipulated it, leaving me feeling violated, but Xanath hadn't been that way. He'd been kind and gentle, pushing no more than absolutely necessary. I didn't get the bad taste in my mouth with him that I did with Verena.

I related all of this to Danae, explaining why it would be a good thing to let Xanath inside.

"It's still an invasion of my privacy," Danae argued.

"Don't you want to know what she's done to you?" I asked, giving her a pleading look. She didn't know yet that this would happen whether she liked it or not. Better to let her think it was a choice. "There's a possibility Verena has put subliminal commands in your mind for you to hurt people. Do you really want to find out about that after it's too late?"

Danae gazed at the back wall, her jaw hardening as she considered it. "How do I know this sorcerer won't do the same thing?"

"I would not," Xanath said, appearing offended. "You need only open your mind, and you will see."

She sighed. "Will it get me out of these shackles?"

"Once we are assured you pose no threat to us," the pendragon responded.

"Please, Danae. Cooperation between them and us has to start somewhere." I gave her a pleading look. "We both know they have the power to force us to do whatever they want, but instead they're asking first."

Danae's shoulders slumped. "Fine. Let's get this over with."

The tension in me eased. Danae was a smart woman, and she had to see we only had one way out of this mess.

Xanath pulled the chair closer to her and gave her the same instructions he'd given me. "I need you to relax and open your mind as much as possible."

"Easier said than done," she grumbled.

It took a minute before the tension lining her face eased. Slowly, Danae took deep breaths in and out.

Her eyes closed and her body relaxed a little more as the sorcerer's calming voice rolled over her. Now that I watched from a distance, I saw how his power could mesmerize a person. No wonder I'd managed to let my guard down. It had been a lot easier than expected when he'd worked on me.

Danae jerked hard when he began his infiltration.

Xanath blanched at whatever he found. "The sorceress has put strong barriers around your mind that I cannot penetrate. Only you can find a way to unlock them. Imagine there is a large door in front of you, and you need a key to open it. Envision the key in your hand."

Thick tension filled the room. It was all I could do to stand there while my friend struggled against whatever was going on in her mind.

"Okay, I've got it," she said.

I expelled a breath. If things went bad, would I need to step in? Could I?

"Good," Xanath said soothingly. "Now put that key in the lock."

Danae's brows wrinkled. "It won't turn."

"Don't force it. You must believe it will open—only then will it do so."

I felt helpless, wishing there was something I could do to make things easier for Danae. It was my fault she was even here.

Xanath continued, helping her work out the problem. Sweat began pouring from both their foreheads as they fought to open the barrier. The sorcerer didn't waver once and continued to speak in an encouraging tone that would make anyone want to follow his directions. Soon, Danae's expression took on a razor-sharp focus. She muttered something about Verena being a bitch and that this would never happen again. She would get that barrier down.

"Got it!"

Xanath took a shuddering breath. "Now you must pass through the door. I will be directly behind you."

They stopped talking after that. Whatever they were doing now, they didn't need to voice it aloud.

Time seemed to pass slowly as we waited. So slowly, in fact, that the ache in my stomach started to ease and the healing process began in earnest. I glanced at Aidan through lowered lashes, studying him. His head turned ever so slightly, and I caught a heated look enter his eyes. It warmed me to see it even as I told myself nothing more could happen between us no matter how much we wanted it. The bond between us might be incredibly strong—the kind that would make us risk our lives for each other—but it was also dangerous. The stab wound in my stomach emphasized that point. Neither of us had wanted it to happen, and yet we'd both willingly participated in the act to protect each other. What other lengths would we go to? Just being near him made me want to do things no rational person would consider. I wished the others weren't around so we could talk and work this out. No matter how we felt about each other, we had other factors to consider.

Danae cried out. My gaze shot to her, and I found her convulsing in her seat.

"What's wrong with her?" I cried, leaping forward.

Aidan grabbed my arm. "Xanath has found something. Do not interfere."

"But she's in pain!"

"You will only make it worse," Nanoq said, taking my other arm.

Between the two men, I couldn't move. They each held me with an iron grip I couldn't hope to break away from in my current condition. "If she dies, I swear I'll..."

"Patience," Aidan whispered in my ear. "You must trust me that Xanath would not be hurting her unless he found something dangerous to us."

"I can't stand to see her like this," I said, my voice nearly breaking.

Sympathy entered his gaze. "I know."

Danae continued to convulse in her chair. I waited helplessly, watching my friend shake and cry out as the sorcerer worked on her. What could possibly be causing the problem? As far as I could tell, she'd been cooperating.

"I've almost got it," Xanath said through gritted teeth. He looked about ready to fall over. His fingers dug hard into Danae's head as if he was trying to reach her mind physically and mystically.

Then all of a sudden, she slumped into her seat, completely still.

"There." Xanath breathed a sigh of relief.

He took a moment to collect himself before resuming the mind probe. Another fifteen minutes passed by with no more outbursts or convulsing. I wanted to ask what had caused the earlier problem but knew I had to wait to find out. Did Verena tamper with Danae's mind that much? Was it my fault for letting them work together? Maybe I should have stopped Danae from training with the sorceress, but there'd been no one else to teach her. And her powers had helped a lot of people, even saved a few lives, so it had to have been worth it, right?

"It is done," Xanath said, pulling away. "But she will need to rest for a while. The process was very difficult for her."

"Is she still...whole?" I almost choked on the question.

"I do not believe there will be any lasting damage." The sorcerer rubbed his face. "She eased my way as much as she could, but her mind was filled with barriers and traps. There was also something else."

"What?" Nanoq asked, his expression darkening.

"This young woman had a command buried deep inside her mind." Xanath looked at me. "After you acquired the orb, your friend was to take it from you if you did not bring it directly to the sorceress. She would not have had a choice."

And I would have had to fight her for it—even if it meant one of us dying. Verena had to have known about the orb for a while now if she'd planted the command before Danae stopped going to see her, though who knew if my friend remembered that last meeting correctly. For all we knew, they'd met yesterday. Verena could have even snuck into the house while Danae was asleep to place the compulsion.

Nanoq grunted. "Was there anything else?"

"Nothing else significant."

The pendragon put a hand on Xanath's shoulder. "You may rest for a while. Come to see me later when you've recovered, and we will speak further."

Something told me they were going to have a lengthier conversation about Danae when I couldn't be around to hear it. The sorcerer was in her mind for a long time and must have discovered more than what he'd revealed so far. I watched the older man go with a foreboding feeling. Was she really out of danger yet? Or was it that she'd seen things while with Verena that could be of use to them? It was hard to be sure.

"What about my friend and me?" I crossed my arms.

"You will both be taken to a cell. I will inform you soon about what will happen next," Nanoq replied, then turned toward the door.

"Which cell do you want them in?" Aidan asked.

Nanoq paused and turned his head. "Put them in the one across from your brother. Zoran could use a little company."

Aidan's features twisted. "With all due respect, milord..."

The pendragon shook his head. "They will be fine there. I suspect their presence will make your brother more miserable than them."

8

BAILEY

We'd been stuck in a dungeon cell that barely had enough room for us to stretch out for two days. I estimated our accommodations to be about five feet by eight feet. Danae and I took turns sleeping on the stone floor since neither of us wanted to lie near the chamber pot we'd been given to do our personal business. I'd thought outhouses were bad, but I'd since revised my thinking. At least the guards gave us a clean cell that didn't smell too bad, and they took the chamber pot away twice a day to be emptied, bringing it back freshly rinsed. Each morning, we were also given water to wash ourselves. It was more than the prisoner across from us was getting and most of the stench I caught came from that direction.

While sitting, I couldn't see Zoran, but if I stood up and looked through the barred window on the cell door, I could usually spot him. He paced the tiny space he'd been given for hours at a time. If he caught me looking, he'd stop and glare at me. It had been a while since I'd had trouble controlling my slayer instincts, but his feral expression, even in human form, made me itch to fight him. He just looked like he needed killing.

Danae made a noise, drawing my attention to where she slept on the floor. She'd barely said a word since they put us in our cell and spent most of her time resting. I'd only talked to her enough to ascertain the sorcerer's mind probe didn't do any serious damage. When I'd tried bringing up the things Xanath found in her head—the commands that might have made her attack me—she'd looked away ashamed. I'd told her it wasn't her fault, but that didn't seem to make a difference.

Standing, I stretched my legs and walked the three steps that took me to the back of the cell. If they left us down here for much longer, I was going to get bored out of my mind and do something really stupid. Though I couldn't hear anything from the fortress above, I could smell the scent of dragons everywhere. Being that close to so many of them and not able to fight or kill was pushing my slayer instincts to the edge. I hoped they realized they couldn't keep me in here long, or I'd end up as wild as the guy in the cell across from us.

I peered out the twelve-inch by twelve-inch window and caught Zoran pacing again. He made a weird grunting noise as he did it.

"Are you able to formulate any words or is grunting all you've got?" I asked.

He paused, snarled at me, and began moving again.

"Oh, good, you're expanding your vocabulary. There may be hope for you yet." This was about as far as our conversations had gone. He wasn't much of a talker. "Can you say 'hello, dragon slayer' for me? Come on, be a good boy and try."

He growled and rammed his door. It was made of out zaphiriam, a fire-proof metal the shifters used for all sorts of things, including weaponry. The coloring was mostly black, but there were hints of red veins running through it. Neither Zoran with all his brute strength, nor me with my slayer strength, could break our doors. The metal was thick and built to withstand even the most powerful creatures.

"He probably can't understand you," Kayla said, coming down the corridor. "I don't think he's bothered to learn English."

Well, that was disappointing. You could only have so much fun taunting someone if they didn't understand a word you said to them.

The sixteen-year-old human girl came into view, holding a couple of steaming bowls in her hands. She was on the skinny side with long, straight red hair and ivory skin. There seemed to always be a hint of mischief in her sparkling green eyes. Kayla had been living at the fortress for a couple of years, since accidentally crossing over to Kederrawien—the dragon realm—and when the dimensions collided, she'd returned to Earth. She didn't have a home to return to here since her parents had passed away when she was younger, so she chose to stay with the shifters. They protected her and provided for all her needs. Aidan used her as a spy sometimes, but mostly she just worked in the castle kitchen.

"Is that dinner?" I asked.

She looked down at the bowls of stew. "They call it midday meal here, but to us, it would be dinner. The sun just set an hour ago."

I appreciated the way she helped me keep track of time while locked down here. We'd become friends a couple of months ago, and while she couldn't do anything about me being locked in the cell, she did do all she could to make it more comfortable. Anyone who thought a sixteen-year-old wouldn't make a good ally had never been in this kind of situation before.

Kayla knelt down and passed the bowls through a small hatch in the door that could only be opened from her side. I grabbed the dishes and handed one to Danae, who had just woken up. She might be in a bad mood, but she didn't miss a meal.

"Thanks. It smells good," I said to Kayla. It really did smell amazing, especially when you considered I'd been living off of canned food and plain pasta for months.

She beamed. "I made it just for you and Danae with some leftover beef from last night. You don't want to know what the shifters are eating right now."

"That bad?" I lifted a spoonful of the stew and blew on it.

"Well, they prefer their meat cooked and flavored, so it's not horrible, but they're less picky than humans about what kind of animals they'll eat."

I took a moment to savor my food before looking at her again. "At this point, I'm half tempted to make them lock me up more often if I get this kind of food while I'm here."

She giggled. "Why do you think I haven't left?"

Shouts came from down the corridor.

"What's going on?" I asked.

She glanced in the direction of the sounds, her brows drawing together. "I don't know. Someone in the kitchen said some intruders were caught trying to sneak into the fortress. They must be bringing them down here."

"You should probably go. I don't want anyone knowing you're giving us special treatment."

Kayla gave me a weak smile. "Aidan told me he'd cover for me if they said anything."

That was good to know. I wanted to ask more, but the loud noises were getting closer. "Still, it's better if you're not here right now. I'll talk to you later when you bring the next meal."

"Alright." Kayla nodded.

She moved out of my line of vision, disappearing down the corridor. The interrogation room wasn't very far away—around the corner and about a hundred feet down the passageway—but she was going in the opposite direction, so whoever was coming wouldn't see her.

"Bailey," Danae called from behind me.

I turned. "Yeah?"

She looked up at me in consternation. Her pride had been stung by having her mind manipulated, and she was still processing that she'd allowed it to happen, even if she couldn't have stopped it. Of course, it was partly my fault it happened in the first place. I felt almost as guilty as she did.

"Thank you," she said, lifting her chin.

"For what? Getting you locked up in a dungeon cell?"

The corner of her lip turned up in a half-smile. "No, for talking me into letting Xanath clear my head. I was kind of angry with you about it at first, but I'm beginning to realize I'm thinking more clearly than I have in months. It was like I was moving through fog before."

"Really?" It hadn't felt that bad to me, but Verena hadn't messed with my mind as much.

"Yeah." She set her empty bowl on the stone floor. "While Xanath was in my head, he showed me all the places where Verena had invaded. It was...hard to take at first. The idea that someone could manipulate you like that and not even know it."

Sitting in this cell, I'd had a lot of time to ponder about that. If Danae didn't know she was being tampered with by a sorcerer, and she was one herself, how would I be able to recognize it in the future? This could happen again, and we wouldn't know it.

"It sucks," I said, sitting down next to her.

"There's got to be a way to protect ourselves from that happening again."

I met her gaze. "Let me know if you figure it out."

She nodded. "I will."

The loud noises and shouting had grown even closer. One voice, in particular, drew my attention. I jumped to my feet. "Is that Conrad?"

Danae joined me, both of us trying to peer out the barred window despite the fact we wouldn't be able to see anything.

"It sure sounded like him," she replied.

"What has that crazy idiot done now?"

9

AIDAN

Aidan soared through the skies on the western border of their toriq's territory, checking to ensure none of the Thamaran dragons had crossed. The dividing line between the pure and shifter's land was at what the humans called Interstate 35. He might have been relieved of his duties in the other part of the state, but Nanoq wanted to keep him busy. The pendragon still didn't fully trust Aidan and intended to keep him away from the fortress as much as possible until he left on the journey to recover the orb.

He hated being kept from Bailey, especially while she remained confined in the dungeon, but arguing wouldn't help his cause. It would only make Nanoq more suspicious of their relationship, and he'd already questioned Aidan heavily after seeing them together. The pendragon might not know everything, but he suspected a lot. At least Kayla would keep an eye on the slayer and ensure she received proper care. Aidan would have to find a way to thank the human for that.

Donar flew next to him. His cousin wasn't required to patrol, but he liked getting out once in a while and taking a break from his masonry duties. They also hadn't had many opportunities to spend time together in the last couple of months. In all the years they'd known each other, this was the longest they'd gone without seeing each other that Aidan could recall.

We should return to the fortress, he said to Donar. *The Thamaran are quiet this evening, and I see no sign of them attempting to cross.*

His cousin grunted his agreement. *They never do. Their territory is more than enough for them, and they know it.*

In fact, it had always been the Shadowan—who'd been pushed to the north—that gave the Taugud the most trouble. His toriq only continued their patrols along the western border to keep the pure dragons from getting any ideas. Bailey might battle the Thamaran often, but only because she entered their side of Norman to track them down. A slayer could roam wherever they wished. They might choose a safe place to rest, but they fought wherever they could find dragons near them. Bailey had to travel farther out now that she didn't have the Shadowan to attack anymore.

Aidan was surprised she didn't relocate to make things easier. He had visited his secret lair earlier in the day and found evidence she still inhabited it during his absence. At least, she must have been spending part of her time there. Many of her things were still in the house, and her scent lingered. He had asked her to stay there, but after his being gone so long, he hadn't been sure if she continued to do so.

Donar moved to fly on Aidan's right. *It must bother you that the slayer is in the dungeon across from your brother.*

Nanoq has reassured me he will not keep her down there for much longer.

*H*is cousin glanced over at him and narrowed his yellow eyes. *Still, I cannot imagine you like that he put her down there.*

Aidan snarled. *You are not helping matters by reminding me. I assure you she would not be there if I thought for a moment it would do her any real harm.*

You always were the patient one. If I cared for a female, I am not certain I could allow her to be subjected to such treatment.

Why are you baiting me, cousin? Aidan asked, annoyed. *You've never even liked the slayer and must enjoy her being locked up.*

Perhaps, but not as much as you think. She's grown on me—a little. I'm half-tempted to get her out of there myself.

Aidan jerked his gaze to Donar. *You can't be serious?*

His cousin let out a snort. *Perhaps my time down south with the Faegud has made me daft, but I've come to realize Bailey is not so bad.*

What made you come to that conclusion?

Donar was quiet for a moment. *We had trouble with a slayer in Texas. He attacked a group of warriors in training and killed three of them. A week later, he snuck into the jakhal during the early morning while we slept and murdered a mother and two of her hatchlings. It was after that I realized how much it must have taken for your female to discipline herself. This slayer had no regard for who he killed.*

Is he still alive? Aidan asked.

Yes. I have half a mind to send Bailey down there to take care of him. Do you think she would?

Aidan had no idea. *It hardly matters, considering we have an even greater mission ahead of us.*

True. Donar looked away.

They neared the fortress, and some sort of disturbance at the gates caught their attention. There were more than a dozen shifters gathered together and a great deal of shouting going on, though Aidan couldn't make out any clear words at this distance.

That is strange, Donar said.

Yes, it is. The fortress always appeared peaceful unless they were under attack by dragons or, in one case, human missiles.

There were no green dragons or missiles to explain this problem.

They soared down to the field near the fortress walls, landing on a patch of dried grass. Aidan and Donar shifted as quickly as possible in their rush to get to the gates. It was only once they got close and could hear distinct voices that the problem became apparent—Bailey's sidekick had come for her. Aidan cursed and ran up the hill toward the crowd, pushing through the spectators. One of the guards, who'd put on gloves to keep from burning human skin, reached to grab Conrad's arm.

"Back the fuck off, man!" Conrad yelled, pushing at the shifter's chest.

Donar grumbled, "This is not good."

Aidan agreed.

The guard shoved Conrad into a wall. The young man's head bounced against the stone, and his eyes turned glazed.

"Let him go," Aidan ordered.

The guard shot an annoyed glance over his shoulder. "This human and his friend were attempting to enter the fortress uninvited."

It was then that Aidan noticed Miles. He was the male interested in Danae, though he refused to acknowledge it, and he had no doubt come because of his concern for her. Miles was a stout man with short, blond hair. Unlike Conrad, he stood still and expressionless while two guards held his arms. He might not be struggling, but there was an expression in his eyes that said he could fight back if he wished. Like Danae, he'd once been a warrior for the human military, and it showed in his bearing.

"What is going on here?" Nanoq shouted from the other side of the gates.

The crowd parted to allow the pendragon to move past them. His gaze caught on Miles and Conrad, recognition lighting in his eyes. Both humans had been in the neighborhood when they came to collect Danae and Bailey. After seeing she had so many allies—most slayers lived solitary existences or only kept one or two people close—the pendragon had demanded Aidan tell him all he knew about Bailey's friends, including these two.

"What do you humans think you're doing coming here?" Nanoq asked, expression livid.

"It's been two days. We want to know what you've done to Danae and Bailey," Miles said, straightening to his full height. It didn't seem to matter to him that he was facing a powerful shifter who could kill him in a second if he wished.

Nanoq turned to Aidan and Donar. "You two, escort these men to the interrogation room." He pointed at the nearest guards. "Bind and blindfold them first. I do not want these humans seeing the inside of my keep or trying to run free."

He spun on his heels and marched away before Aidan could ask any further questions.

"This is bullshit!" Conrad came back to life, punching and kicking anyone near him. "What the fuck is this? Gitmo?"

"What's Gitmo?" Donar asked, glancing over at Aidan.

"I have no idea."

It took a couple of minutes, but the guards managed to lock manacles around Conrad's wrists and put a hood over his head.

Miles held his chin high and allowed himself to be restrained. Aidan might have thought he'd easily accepted defeat, but there was a look in his eyes that said he'd expected this and prepared for it. They needed to question these two quickly. Bailey's friends hadn't survived these past six months by doing something as stupid as trying to infiltrate a dragon fortress unarmed without a plan.

Aidan and Donar followed behind the guards. Conrad had settled down after they threatened to carry him and walked of his own volition. He and Miles couldn't see, but the shifters took care to guide them through the main thoroughfare. People stared and gawked from the edges of the stone path. This was exactly why they'd brought Bailey and Danae through the tunnel entrance. It was far enough from the fortress and concealed in a thick patch of woods so that no one in the toriq even knew they'd brought a slayer and sorceress inside—except those involved and sworn to secrecy. There would be mayhem if his clansmen found out. Thankfully, Conrad and Miles were human and smelled like it. Shifters would not find them as threatening.

They reached the interrogation room and sat both men in the chairs. The pendragon was already waiting inside with his arms crossed and an annoyed expression on his face. Just as Aidan was about to close the door, Kade slipped into the room. He moved over to Nanoq and whispered something in his ear. Aidan couldn't catch what he said since Conrad had started cursing loudly again.

"If somebody don't take this shit off my head, I'm gonna make ya'll regret it," he swore.

Donar let out a snarl and jerked the hood off Conrad. "I'm most interested to know what you could possibly do to threaten us."

The young man's dark skin reddened a fraction with anger. "You picked the wrong women to put in your black ops prison."

"Why don't you tell us what you really mean?" Aidan asked, getting impatient.

Nanoq and Kade stopped talking to listen.

"Ask him." Conrad jutted his chin toward Miles.

Aidan pulled the hood from his head, tousling his normally well-kept hair in the process. "What do you have planned?"

Miles looked up with a cold expression. "If we do not return home within the next twenty-four hours, my guys are going to spread the word around town that you've imprisoned the dragon slayer who has saved many of their lives. They're also going to tell everyone how you took the woman who has been healing them. There's been a flu going around, and Danae has helped a lot of people. As individuals, we might not be as strong as you, but I promise you don't want all of Norman coming here with every weapon we have."

Nanoq took a menacing step toward Miles. "You would risk human lives by bringing them here?"

"Bailey told me how you guys want to live in peace with us." Miles met his hard gaze. "Do you really want to make an enemy out of the people who live closest to your fortress?"

Kade cleared his throat. "Where do you hail from, young man?"

Aidan gave his uncle a confused look. "What does that have to do with anything?"

"I assure you that I ask for a good reason."

"That is none of your business," Miles answered.

Kade cocked his head. "The town—Norman— is not the place you grew up. You are originally from somewhere east of here."

Surprise lit in Miles' face, but he didn't respond.

"I had a dream about you early this morning. It came to me clearly that you were the answer I'd been looking for," Kade continued, undaunted. "Is there a cave near your childhood home where thieves might take refuge?"

Miles jaw dropped. "How would you know that?"

"Come on, man. Ain't you learned not to be surprised by anything anymore?" Conrad rolled his eyes. "This guy's got crazy written all over him—which probably means he's a seer or some shit."

Bailey's friend might be loud-mouthed, but he was also surprisingly perceptive.

"So you know of the place I seek?" Kade asked Miles.

The man's jaw hardened. "Even if I did, I'm not telling you anything."

Nanoq gestured at Aidan. "Retrieve the slayer. Let her know that her friend is in here, and he can give us the location of the first fragment but won't cooperate with us."

"Of course, milord." He bowed and headed out of the room.

As soon as he reached the cell where the women were being held, Aidan found both of them had their faces pressed close to the door, peering out the barred window. They must have heard enough to figure out who was in the dungeons with them.

"What is going on?" Bailey asked. "Why is Conrad here?"

Aidan stopped in front of the door and pulled the keys to the lock from shiggara. "He and Miles thought they would come rescue you."

"Oh, good grief." Bailey shook her head.

"It appears Miles may know the location of the first orb fragment, but he refuses to cooperate." Aidan unlocked the door and opened it. "We need you to explain to him why he must tell us."

Her brows drew together as she stepped into the corridor. "Why would he know?"

"My uncle is a seer. He had a vision this morning of Miles and that the fragment is located near his place of birth."

"Okay, well, that's not weird or anything."

Aidan held up a hand to Danae when she moved to come out as well. "The pendragon only wishes for Bailey to come. You will have to wait here."

She put her hands on her hips. "Will I get to see them soon?"

"I am certain you will."

If the timetable Miles gave them was any indication, they couldn't hold the women for much longer, and their group would be able to leave together. Even if it were only long enough to tell their friends in town they'd be gone again for a while. The pendragon had already decided Bailey and Danae would be going on the journey. The only reason he held them here was to prevent them from telling anyone else about it.

Aidan shut and locked the door before escorting Bailey toward the interrogation room. As soon as they reached the corner, he grabbed her arm and pressed her against the wall. If only for a moment, Aidan needed to touch her and take in her scent. He leaned close to her neck and inhaled deeply. She smelled like sugar and spice. It soothed him and his inner beast like nothing else could. With shaking fingers, he touched her soft, silky black hair. Despite being confined for two days, it still had a hint of the special soap she'd used to wash it.

"Aidan, we shouldn't be doing this," she whispered.

"I've missed you," he breathed the words into her ear.

She lifted her head, indecision in her eyes. "I've missed you too, but…"

"Just give me a moment."

Aidan pulled the bottom of her shirt up a few inches, checking the skin there. Only a faint line remained where he'd thrust his blade into her stomach. Had Bailey's time in the dungeons made the healing process slower? He did not like to think of her suffering these past two days and him not being able to reach her.

"How do you feel?" he asked, glancing up.

"I'm alright. It doesn't hurt anymore."

Aidan frowned. "I did not enjoy harming you."

"I know," she said softly.

Loud voices rose from the interrogation room, and he forced himself to pull away. Aidan shouldn't have gotten close to her at all, but it had been his first opportunity to see her since she'd been confined in the dungeon. Both he and the beast needed to see that she was okay. He was trying very hard—for both their sakes—to keep his distance, but it wasn't easy.

They walked side by side to the interrogation room and entered. Conrad and Miles both swung their gazes toward Bailey. She moved over to the wall opposite them, leaned against it, and smiled. Her entire bearing said she wasn't scared, hurt, or angry. It did a lot to relieve the tension in the room.

Conrad canted his head. "You don't look half as bad as I thought you would."

"The food is better here than what we have at Earl's." She studied her nails. "You'd be amazed what freshly cooked meat can do for your mood—no matter the accommodations." She waved an arm at her surroundings, making her point.

"They got chicken?" he asked, hope lighting in his eyes.

"Of course. It's good, too."

Aidan could see what she was doing. The more unconcerned she behaved, the less upset the men appeared. He turned to the pendragon. "Perhaps if we feed these humans, they might be more amenable."

"Is that true?" Nanoq asked the men.

Conrad's eyes lit up. "If the food is good enough, I'll beat the intel out of Miles for you."

Miles shot Conrad a scathing look. "Traitor."

"A guy has to have his priorities." Conrad shrugged. Aidan was willing to bet, though, if Bailey told him not to cooperate, he'd do exactly as she asked.

Miles addressed the pendragon. "I would be willing to consider telling you what you want to know if you take these chains off, and Bailey convinces me that talking is in our best interest."

Nanoq waved his hand at Aidan. "Tell the guards to get these men a meal. We will release their bindings and give them their food after we get the cave location."

"How do I know you'll keep up your end of the deal?" Miles asked.

"He will," Bailey said, lifting her unshackled arms for emphasis.

"Fine." Miles didn't look happy, but he didn't argue further.

Aidan left the room to speak to the guards, choosing the one he trusted most to give the orders. "Instruct the human, Kayla, in the kitchen that she is to prepare a meal with chicken for two of Bailey's friends. Tell her I told you to do so and do not return until she gives you the food."

The guard nodded and hurried away. He was one of the few shifters that hadn't looked at Aidan with distrust because of his dealings with the slayer. It was during times like these that one learned who they could truly rely upon. It would be a while before the others let go of their prejudice and accepted him again.

Aidan headed back inside and discovered Bailey had begun to explain the situation to Miles and Conrad. Nanoq must have given her the freedom to tell them everything because she wasn't holding back any details about the orb or its importance. How had Kade convinced the pendragon to let his guard down around these humans? Most of their toriq didn't even know about the orb. Aidan had been ordered not to speak about it to anyone outside the circle of those who already knew.

He moved next to the pendragon and whispered, "I'm surprised you are trusting them."

"Kade assures me they are no threat to us, but Xanath will be visiting them later," Nanoq replied.

Aidan should have guessed as much. "You know the sorcerer hates doing mind probes."

"He will hate it even more if someone other than us gets the orb first."

It was hard to argue that point, though Aidan hated to see the process performed again so soon and on more of Bailey's friends. Nanoq was relying on magic much more heavily than Throm ever had. Whether that was a good thing about the new pendragon or not remained to be seen.

"So, you see, we have to get the orb first, or else it could mean another sorcerer out there—possibly Verena—is going to use dragons to kill or conquer us all," Bailey finished, focusing on Miles. "You have to tell them where this cave is at."

Miles pressed his lips together. "How do we know anything these guys are telling us is true?"

Conrad spoke up, "I was there when Verena showed up, demanding Bailey get the orb for her, but the thing is..." he gave a worried look at the slayer, "...what happens when we don't give it to her?"

"We'll just have to burn that bridge when we get there." Bailey shrugged. "No matter the price—I can't let her have it."

"And we will do all we can to protect the slayer and her friends from the sorceress' vengeance," Nanoq added.

Aidan had insisted on that point once he realized the threat Bailey faced, discussing it at length with the pendragon the previous night. They couldn't let her cross a sorceress and be left vulnerable. Their toriq had more than enough resources available to help on that matter, so there was no reason they couldn't prevent any retaliation that might come.

Miles shifted in his seat. "If I tell you the location, then I'm going on this trip as well. It's close to my home turf, and I can navigate it better than anyone else here."

"I had hoped you would say that," Kade said, bowing his head. He must have seen more in his dream than he'd told them.

Conrad leaned forward in his seat. "I'm going, too. I've always got the slayer's back."

"I do not believe that is necessary..." Nanoq began.

"He goes," Bailey said, a fierce look in her eyes. "I know he doesn't look like much to you guys, but he's braver than ten men put together, and he's never failed me."

Aidan felt a surge of jealousy rise. Bailey had promised him that she felt nothing except friendship for Conrad, and he chose to believe she spoke truly, but he hated that the human man could be there for her in ways that he couldn't.

"If the clues in the prophecy are correct, the other orb fragments will be in pure dragon territory," Kade said, rubbing his chin. "It could not hurt to have another experienced fighter go along as well."

Bailey pushed off the wall and directed her attention to the pendragon. "Especially since we'll also be dealing with human threats, and the safest time to travel will be when Aidan and any other shifters who go are at their sleepiest."

Aidan couldn't argue with that point. If they moved during the morning hours, it would be difficult to stay awake to fly. They'd need some sort of transportation where Aidan and any other shifters who went on the trip could rest until their energy returned. There were a lot of things to consider and prepare for before they departed.

"Very well," Nanoq acquiesced. "Both human men may go. Now, I want to know where this thief's nest is located."

Miles hesitated for a moment, but finally his shoulders slumped. "It's called Robber's Cave, and it's in a state park just a few hours' drive east of here. I know that area like the back of my hand. If that's where we have to go, I can get us there."

"Are there any large human towns near there?" Aidan asked. He'd been patrolling that area enough that he might have seen something, and he knew which of the cities had not been destroyed by the pure dragons before shifters took over.

Miles shrugged. "The largest is McAlester. If we go the route, I'm thinking, we'll have to pass through it. The only thing I'm worried about is there was a state penitentiary there, and I don't know what happened with all those prisoners. It could be dangerous."

"The town still stands," Aidan said, remembering flying over the place and comparing it to his map. There had been some damage, but not too much. "The humans were not very friendly the one time I attempted to visit, though."

"Then maybe we should take a different route," Conrad suggested.

"No." Aidan shook his head. "I remember the highways north of there have several destroyed bridges. The only way I can think of by road that is manageable will lead us through that town unless we want to go farther south."

"Maybe there's…" Bailey began.

The door banged open, and a guard came through with two hot plates of food, interrupting her.

Conrad leaped to his feet. "Get these chains off. I'm ready to eat."

Aidan glanced at the pendragon for confirmation before pulling out his set of keys. The moment he freed Conrad, the young man was already grabbing his food and pulling his seat up to the table. Aidan unbound Miles next, who rubbed his wrists first before taking his meal.

"Now this is some good shit!" Conrad said between mouthfuls. Had the humans truly been suffering that badly? Could they not hunt and find their own fresh meat?

"For tonight, you will remain down here. We can discuss matters further after you've eaten and had time to rest," the pendragon announced.

Miles showed the first sign of a smile Aidan had ever seen on him. He'd just taken a bite of the baked chicken the guard had brought for him.

"Sounds good to me," Conrad said before shoveling a piece of bread in his mouth.

Bailey shook her head, amusement glinting in her eyes.

"You might never get him to leave now," she said.

Aidan grunted. "He will leave. I will make certain of it."

10

AIDAN

Aidan and Donar barely had time to finish their first meal for the day before he and his cousin were called into the pendragon's office. They'd expected as much, but they weren't the only ones there. Nanoq had summoned Kade, Xanath, and Phoebe to attend the meeting as well. What was his sister doing here? She hadn't been involved in anything related to the orb so far. He gave her an inquiring look, but she merely shrugged her shoulders.

The pendragon stood behind his desk, expression serious. "There are two important tasks that must be carried out in the near future. As you all know, the mating festival begins in a few weeks. I must send a group down to the neutral zone to scout for a potential site and begin setting up tomorrow. I must also decide who will travel on the quest to recover the orb. After much consideration, I've chosen Aidan, Phoebe, and Kade to go on the journey to recover the artifact."

Donar stepped forward. "I request to go as well."

"No." Nanoq shook his head. "The treaty we have with the Faegud requires at least one of the former pendragon's offspring mate with one from their toriq. I have chosen Ruari to be the one, but I will need you to go with him and ensure he makes a good match. You will both take part in the planning as well."

Aidan let out a breath of relief. He'd been worried for months that the new pendragon would force him to mate with a Faegud female, especially since he was the one who'd negotiated the treaty. With Zoran confined in the dungeon below, there were only three options. He hadn't guessed his other brother would be Nanoq's choice.

"Why Ruari?" Aidan asked. Not that he wanted to complain.

"If I am to be perfectly honest, it is because I want that troublemaker away from here," Nanoq said brusquely. "In fact, I want you and your sister to make an appearance at the festival as well, though you need not be there for the full week since I have other duties for you, and Ruari is the only one who must select a mate."

Aidan nodded. It was common practice for a new pendragon to keep threats to his position away from the toriq seat of power—the fortress in this case. Throm, Aidan's father, had done that by killing off most of his competition, but Nanoq had a stronger sense of honor than that. He also understood their people could not afford to lose more warriors. The new pendragon's behavior was in line with his sense of doing what was best for his people, rather than himself. Sending Aidan on border guard patrols had not only been about keeping him away from Bailey, but also because Nanoq had needed to strengthen his recently assumed position among their people.

Phoebe and Ruari had not been reassigned elsewhere yet. Aidan's sister trained the future female warriors of their toriq, which required her to stay at the fortress most of the time. Everyone knew she was quite good at her job, and it would be foolish to replace her. On the other hand, Ruari didn't have any particular skills of use. He was not reliable enough for regular patrol duty, and he was too conniving to be trusted with anything sensitive. This was the first opportunity Nanoq had to get rid of him beyond minor errands of little importance.

"You have no argument from me," Aidan said.

"You do realize Ruari hates me," Donar argued. "I nearly died because his paramour poisoned me."

Nanoq gave him a stern look. "All the more reason for you to keep a close watch of him during the festival. He must not do anything that would embarrass our people. I've already spoken to Hildegard on the matter, and she believes she has the perfect mate for him. Someone who can keep him under control—but you must ensure he gives this female a chance."

Donar gave a curt bow. "Of course, milord."

"Good. Then you can go inform Ruari that I wish to see him an hour from now. We will tell him the good news then, and I can introduce you to the others who will be helping plan the festival." The pendragon waved a dismissive hand at Donar.

Aidan's cousin reluctantly left the room.

"Now," Nanoq addressed the rest of them. "We don't have much time left before we need to release the slayer and her friends. Kade, have you found any more details from the prophecy that might be helpful?"

"Only that the other fragments are some distance apart from each other. I suspect we will have to travel through Shadowan territory at the very least to get the second piece, but according to the translation, we won't know the precise location until we acquire the first orb piece."

Nanoq frowned. "This could be an even more dangerous journey than we first believed. I am already concerned the sorceress, Verena, may try to follow you."

"I can do a spell on the travelers before they depart. It will shield them from any attempts she may make to find them," Xanath offered, stepping forward. "It will not last more than a week, though, so they'd need to return before that to be safe."

"Do you think it will take that long?" The pendragon looked to Kade for an answer.

"I am not certain. There will be trials we must undergo before we can acquire each fragment. There is no way of knowing how long those will take. We will also be traveling through dangerous territories with humans who cannot fly and must be protected from whatever difficulties we may face." He sighed. "It is too difficult to predict."

"We will have three shifters and a slayer who can fight. The humans we are bringing are experienced in battle as well," Aidan pointed out. "There are worse groups that could be assembled."

Nanoq lifted his brows. "Your uncle has been confined to the library for centuries. I am not certain you can count on his being useful in battle."

"That is not entirely true." Kade bristled. "Since you let me out of my confinement, I've been exercising every day and renewing my fighting abilities. I will not be as much of a liability as you think."

"Then continue your practice until you leave," the pendragon ordered.

"How soon before we depart?" Aidan asked.

"I will allow the humans two days to acquire transportation and supplies." Nanoq looked between Aidan and Phoebe, a warning in his gaze. "Both of you will escort them from here and stay with them at all times while they are in town. Make certain they do not tell anyone the sensitive details of this journey."

Phoebe had been quiet until then, but now she spoke up, "They will have to tell their friends something before they go. What should they say?"

"They can say they are going on a trip to assess the state of our territory. That they are acting as human ambassadors for us." Nanoq paused for a moment. "It is as good an excuse as any, and while you are traveling, you could gather information from the ground that we might not otherwise be able to acquire."

Aidan agreed with that plan. He'd had a very difficult time learning much of anything from the humans while out on patrol. They were either scared of him or preferred to try killing him. With Bailey and the others traveling with them, they could potentially learn a lot more.

"Okay," Phoebe said, apparently satisfied with that answer as well.

"Is there anything else?" Nanoq gazed between them, but no one spoke up. "Good. Release them and escort them back to town. The last thing I need is a human revolt on my hands along with everything else I must handle."

Aidan and Phoebe bowed and began to leave the room.

"One last thing," the pendragon called out. "Cover their eyes and do not let them see anything until they are well away from the tunnel exit."

"Of course, milord," Aidan replied.

11

BAILEY

"Lemme get this straight," Earl said, scratching at his beard. "You're gonna go with these dragons, shifters...whatever in the hell they are, and travel around the state doin' some kinda survey of their territory?"

We'd been sitting in his living room for an hour explaining our plans—the edited version, anyway. To say he was skeptical was an understatement. I glanced at Danae, who gave me a helpless shrug, before returning my attention to Earl. "Uh, yeah. Pretty much."

"And how long is this supposed to take?" He gave me a scrutinizing look.

Earl and my stepfather were good friends. Since Grady and my mom were stuck in Texas, cut off by a massive chasm running parallel to the Oklahoma state border, they'd asked Earl to watch over me. He took his job rather seriously.

Aidan's deep voice filled the room, "We do not expect to be gone more than a week."

"And I'm supposed to trust you with takin' Bailey and three more of my people on this trip?" Earl asked. For being an older man whose body had worn down over the years, he could still appear rather intimidating. Maybe it was the shrapnel scar on his left cheek he'd gotten while fighting in Vietnam or maybe it was his penetrating gray gaze. With his oily, silver hair framing his face and the thick beard covering his jaw, it made his eyes stand out that much more.

Aidan didn't flinch. "I will protect them with my life."

"I will, too," Phoebe said. She stood next to her brother, and it only took one look at her to believe she could hold her own. With her strong body frame, toned arms and shoulders, and the severe braid holding her hair back, she fit the warrior image. I'd fought with her and knew what she could do.

Earl crossed his arms. "Where are ya'll plannin' to sleep durin' this trip?"

"Seriously?" I threw my hands up. "I'll be twenty-three in a couple of months and everyone else going except Conrad is older than me. This isn't some teenage slumber party. We can take care of ourselves, and you don't need to worry about us."

"It's my job to worry and look out for ya'll," he said, expression stern.

Miles stepped forward. "You know I wouldn't be going on this trip if I didn't think it was important. Not so much for the shifters, but because it's time we find out how things look in other parts of the state. We don't get much news except..." I suspected he was going to mention the radio guy, Hank, and stopped himself. "... whatever turns up. It'll help to see how things are going out there by seeing it all for ourselves."

We didn't know if the shifters knew about Hank, but we'd decided not to inform them. There was no telling how they'd react. I might trust Aidan and maybe Phoebe, but their pendragon was a wild card. He might see Hank as a threat and try to shut him down. It was to our advantage that dragons and shifters knew nothing about the radio station.

Earl settled back in his chair, relaxing a little. Miles wouldn't endorse this trip if he hadn't asked all the right questions and considered it carefully. We'd spent hours in the fortress dungeon discussing it while waiting to be released. As much as he could be a stick in the mud, I was glad he was going. We needed someone from the area where we were going who could help navigate in case we ran into trouble, and he could think well on his feet.

"Alright," Earl said, gazing around at us. "Go on your trip, but you better make sure you take enough supplies to last you."

I glanced at Conrad. "We've collected enough dragon scales recently that I should be able to trade them to Javier for everything we'll need."

"And I've got some ideas for transportation," Miles added.

"Okay." I paused to mull things over for a minute. "There are still a couple of hours of daylight left. I'm going to go visit Javier before it gets dark to find out what kind of trade we can work out."

The sorcerer closed his shop at dusk, and the only things open in downtown after that were a restaurant and bar. I wouldn't take the supplies today, but I wanted to see how much the dragon scales could get me and figure out how we were going to transport everything. With a group our size, we were going to need more than one vehicle to fit everyone. Even the shifters would have to ride with us in the early morning hours since they'd be too tired to fly, and they might not travel by air much if we headed into pure dragon territory at some point in our journey.

"I am going with you as well," Aidan added.

Conrad nodded. "Me, too."

I'd figured they would—especially since neither of them liked me visiting the sorcerer alone.

"I'll check with my guys on getting some sturdy trucks with big gas tanks for the trip," Miles said and glanced at Danae, considering her. "She can go with me."

She frowned at him. "Do I have to?"

"You and I will both go with him," Phoebe said.

Danae sighed, recognizing she'd been backed into a corner. We were trying not to let on to Earl that the shifters had to watch over us, and that we couldn't go anywhere without them. He'd get offended if he found out—not that I could blame him. I was annoyed they didn't trust us, but in their shoes, I wouldn't, either. With what the orb could do, knowing anything about it and its location was powerful information to have.

Aidan gestured toward the door. "Are you ready?"

He wasn't wasting any time. Then again, we had to be prepared to go in less than two days. It wasn't much time to get organized.

I parked my truck in front of Javier's downtown store. Until about a month ago, I'd had to stop half a mile away and walk the rest of the distance. It was too hard to drive through the protection barrier the sorcerer maintained around his domain. Then Javier had worked out some kind of treaty with the Taugud clan which allowed him to continue his business downtown as long as he didn't impede shifters or humans from visiting. He still maintained a spell against pure dragons in case they snuck across the border, and he was required to fight on the side of the Taugud should a battle break out in their territory. I imagined there was even more to that deal, but that's all the sorcerer would reveal to me.

"With your pendragon's dislike of sorcerers, I'm surprised he let Javier stay," I said to Aidan after shutting off the truck engine.

His lips twisted into a grin. "Let us just say that your friend Danae went through a much easier process than Javier to earn Nanoq's trust. If he so much as moves wrong, Xanath will know right away and inform Nanoq."

"He agreed to that?" I asked, surprised.

Aidan shrugged. "He has too much to lose, and he is able to live in peace this way. It didn't take very much convincing for him to agree to our requirements."

"So does Nanoq have a tracking spell on him or something?"

"You could say that," Aidan said cryptically.

We got out of the truck.

The day was bright, if a little cool outside. Conrad had worn a light gray jacket over his favorite khaki pants and blue button-up shirt, but I'd stayed in my usual fighting outfit. Since becoming a slayer, the cold didn't seem to bother me as much anymore. Aidan had put on a thick, long sleeve shirt made of the same black camrium material as the rest of his wardrobe. It was tight and form fitting, but stretched enough around his muscles that he could still move easily. I couldn't help admiring him as I came around the truck. The look in his eyes when I met his gaze said he'd noticed my appraisal.

"Stop ogling each other. I want to get this over with," Conrad said with a roll of his eyes.

Guiltily, I looked away and forced myself to concentrate on the glass windows lining the front of the store. Like most of the other buildings nearby, it stood two stories tall and had a brick facade. It was well-maintained, and no one could have guessed an apocalypse had happened recently—which included all the earthquakes and storms that had struck the region as the dragon dimension collided with ours. Javier must have done something to protect downtown. Even Earl's neighborhood, which had held up surprisingly well, showed some signs of wear and tear. Many of the houses there had cracks in the walls, blown out windows covered with plywood, and there was a huge buckle in the pavement a block over.

Conrad held the shop door open, shooting me a warning look as I passed him. He might have finally accepted Aidan in our lives, but he didn't think anything good could come from me having a relationship with a shifter. The logical part of my brain agreed. I had a job to do protecting humans and helping the Taugud clan solidify their territory. Once that was over, Aidan had to take me to my family in Texas. They needed me there. I couldn't risk getting attached to someone when there was no chance we could be together on a long-term basis. The problem with that? It was a little too late. I honestly didn't know how to handle my feelings for Aidan or what to do about how we'd taken our relationship to another level. We'd yet to have a chance to discuss it without prying ears overhearing us.

I pushed those thoughts aside and waited for my eyes to adjust to the dark interior of the store. Even Javier didn't have electricity, which was partly why he closed shop after the sun set. If he was going to use up candles and lamp oil, he'd do it in the restaurant and bar where most of the humans preferred to congregate at night anyway. I hadn't visited those places when they were open, but I'd heard about them from other people. Even Hank, the radio guy, touted the good food and drinks the sorcerer offered.

All you had to do was trade something Javier needed for some of the silver credit coins he'd manufactured. Then you could purchase whatever you wanted from his establishments. It figured the arrogant sorcerer would make his own form of currency that people had to use with him.

"Bailey, it's been too long. What brings you here?" Javier asked, his voice coming from somewhere in the back of the store.

He appeared a moment later, walking up the aisle with a suave grace and confident smile. His skin had a medium tone, reflecting his Hispanic heritage, and he'd slicked his dark hair back. From what I'd learned about him, I estimated that he had to be in his early thirties. Javier was at that perfect age where his looks and body could leave most girls swooning, young or old. Except me, because I was already attracted to someone else.

The sorcerer had grown up in Oklahoma, but when he was halfway through college in Norman, he'd inadvertently crossed over into Kederrawien. That was when he'd learned he was a sorcerer—there'd been no magic on Earth for him to discover his abilities before. He met some sorceress over there who trained and guided him until he became powerful in his own right. Though Javier wasn't exactly resistant to telling me his story, he tended to change subjects often, so it had taken some time to piece together everything. There was still a lot I didn't know about him.

"How much credit can I get for all these scales?" I asked, holding up the two laundry bags' worth I'd carried from the truck.

He made a tsking sound. "You know I will need to inspect those first before I give you a price."

"I promise they're good," I said, though I knew it wouldn't make a difference.

"Yeah, yeah. That's what they all say, but seeing is believing."

I handed the bags over, and he peered into each of them. "You got a lot, chiquita. How many dragons did you kill this time?"

"A few."

He let out a chuckle. "Come to the back—just you."

"I think not," Aidan said, stepping around me.

Javier lifted a brow. "Surely a slayer doesn't need protection from a shifter."

"Where she goes, I go." Aidan stood his ground.

"Really?" The sorcerer looked at me.

"Aidan and Conrad are kind of a package deal for this visit." I shrugged.

"Alright, alright." He sighed. "Follow me to the back, and I'll see what I can do for you."

He led us past the aisles stocked with food, toiletries, and other essentials. There were people starving around town, yet he had everything they could need right in his store. The second floor held even more, and I'd heard he used some of the other downtown buildings for storage.

One day, he would run out of a lot of it as the town was depleted of its resources, but not for a while, and even then some things could be grown in gardens, hunted, or hand-made. Javier had made himself too useful for the shifters to kick out as long as he behaved.

We stopped by an empty table in the back. The sorcerer took one of the bags and dumped the green dragon scales on it. Conrad and I had taken extra care when removing them from the beasts I killed, making sure Javier couldn't complain about their quality. Why they had to be in such perfect condition I didn't know. He used them for protection spells against dragons, but he wouldn't let me see how he did it.

"Not bad," he said after sifting through the first batch. "You're getting better at collecting these."

"You mean I am." Conrad crossed his arms. "Bailey sucks at pulling them off so I have to do most of the work."

I cleared my throat and looked away. My knife skills were limited to sticking blades into dragons, not prying scales off. I was getting better, but it took me three times as long as Conrad to get them off without damaging them.

After Javier had finished going through the second bag, he looked at me. "I can give you two-hundred credit coins for these."

It was a fair price, based on past deals I'd made with him. One credit coin bought you a drink—of the alcoholic variety—or a small meal.

I considered my options. "I'm going to need to use over half of that right away for food and a few supplies. The rest you can put as credit on my account."

Javier was first and foremost a businessman. If you built credit with him, he honored it. Not to mention I was the only one who could get him dragon scales since he lost his previous connections in Kederrawien. He wouldn't dream of screwing me over.

A sly smile came over the sorcerer's face. "Going on a trip?"

"That is none of your business," Aidan said with a growl.

Javier held his hands up. "Hey, man, you don't have to worry about me. I've got a good thing going here, and I'm not trying to mess it up. It's just that I hear things and my sources tell me Verena is wanting some mysterious artifact she thinks only the slayer can get. Since you're staying at Bailey's side, I'm guessing you're making sure no one gets near her."

Aidan's eyes narrowed. "I suggest you keep that information to yourself."

"Yeah, man, no problem."

"Did you hear anything else?" I asked.

"Only that I'd rather you get that artifact before anyone else does." Javier's expression turned grave. "Even hearing about it freaks me out."

"Seriously? Why?" I had no idea how his magic worked, but the sorcerer always seemed to know a little about everything.

"The magic surrounding it is dark—real dark. Mess with that kind of power, and you'll lose your soul. I'm not saying I'm perfect, but I stay away from the things that will get me a ticket down to you know where."

That was debatable, but we all had our own ideas of good and bad.

"You better," Aidan warned.

It was time to change the subject. "Do you have a pen and paper? I'm going to write down the things I need from you. If you can get your people to pack it up, we'll be by tomorrow afternoon to get it."

Javier nodded and turned toward the shelf behind him, grabbing a notepad. "Whatever you need, I'm sure I got it."

"Thanks." I started writing down the food, fuel, and other things that would be important for a long trip.

The sorcerer watched. "If you tell the pendragon I helped, I'll even knock twenty-percent off the price."

"I will tell him," Aidan promised, yellow eyes gleaming. He didn't sound as positive about it as he should.

I finished the list and handed it over. "I'm pretty sure that's everything."

"Come by around 2 p.m. and I'll have it for you."

12

BAILEY

I gripped the satellite phone. "Mom, I'm going to be fine. I promise I'll call you when I get back."

"Bailey, it's too dangerous to be traveling. If something happens to you, we'll never know, and there's no way—"

"Nothing is going to happen. I'm not that easy to kill anymore," I said in a placating tone.

"Are you still fighting dragons?" she asked. I could almost see her give me an accusing look despite the fact she was all the way at our ranch southwest of Dallas.

"Yes."

"I told you to stop that." She made an exasperated noise. "It's bad enough your stepfather and older brothers are out doing God knows what. Between all of you, I'm going to have a heart attack."

She wasn't exactly exaggerating, considering she had a heart condition. I squeezed my eyes shut. The last thing I wanted was to be the reason my mother died, especially before I could get home. We hadn't seen each other for a long time, and it would be months before I could finally leave Oklahoma for good. I needed to be certain she stayed safe until then.

"So what are Grady and my brothers doing that has you worried?" I asked.

"Oh, you know…" An awkward moment of silence passed. "Trying to be men who protect the family, I suppose."

My mother could be rather old-fashioned at times. It was much easier for her to accept the men doing dangerous things than her daughter. "They aren't trying to fight dragons, are they?"

"Grady refuses to tell me much," she said, sounding frustrated. "But we aren't discussing them, we are talking about you. Your stepfather and brothers aren't going far from home like you are."

Of course she brought the conversation right back around to me. "I promise I'll be careful, okay?"

"I just miss you, honey," she said, voice turning softer. "You're still my little girl no matter how much you've grown up."

My chest tightened. We'd always been close, and she hadn't taken it well when I went away for college. Sure, I'd wanted to strike out on my own and become independent, but that didn't mean I couldn't still have a good relationship with my mother.

I turned and caught Aidan staring at me. He was supposed to be helping the guys load the trucks outside, but at some point he'd come to stand in the bedroom doorway, looking at me with a strange expression on his face. I might not have told him about radios, but I'd had to mention phones because there was no other way to explain how I stayed in contact with my parents. The satellite phones were still working, despite all that had happened. I had no idea if it was because there was no one to shut them down, or if the interim government on the East Coast had found a way to maintain them.

"I love you, Mom, but I have to go," I said.

Aidan continued to stare.

"Be sure to take your vitamins, Bailey. You'll need them." Her voice hitched. "And dress warmly—it's getting cold."

We'd already depleted our vitamin stock except what Trish needed for her pregnancy. "Of course. I'll take them every day, and I'll bring a jacket."

"Good girl. I love you and be careful," she sniffled. "I need you to come back to me."

My heart broke a little inside. Outside of my phone calls with her, I tried not to think about my family too much. That train of thought always depressed me.

"Tell Grady and the boys hello for me," I said.

"You know I will. They miss you, too."

It took another minute, but I finally hung up with her. Phone calls with my mom always left me feeling drained and like I'd been reduced to the state of a twelve-year-old again. All I wanted to do was go home to see her so she'd stop worrying.

Aidan came up and wrapped his arms around me, pulling my head into his chest. "She sounds like a lovely woman."

"She is," I mumbled. This was the first time he and I had been alone together since coming to Earl's. The old man had made us sleep in different rooms and watched us like a hawk when we weren't out with Conrad getting supplies for the trip. Earl was almost as strict as my mother.

Aidan sucked in a breath. "If all goes according to plan, you should be reunited with your family again in the spring."

"Really?" I looked up. "Why then?"

"The Faegud have requested my brethren assist them with taking over the territory around Dallas. The battle is to take place in the spring, and if it goes well, it will allow us to reach your family's ranch." Aidan brushed a lock of hair from my face. "No matter what happens, though, I will get you back to them."

"Even if it means never seeing me again?" That weighed heavily on my mind, and sometimes I worried he might try to talk me out of going.

Aidan gave me a weak smile. "What makes you think I would not come to visit?"

I rested my head on his chest again, enjoying the feel of him even though I needed to put distance between us. Aidan had always resisted getting too close unless absolutely necessary, but somehow, in the last couple of months that had changed. Wasn't it supposed to be the woman who got clingy after sex?

He reluctantly let me go. "It is almost time. They have finished loading the trucks."

We headed outside Earl's house and found most of the neighborhood standing around, saying their goodbyes to those of us leaving on the trip. Just beyond them were the two trucks we would take. Miles had come through with his promise to find just the right vehicles for our trip, including a Volvo RV hauler with a sleep area in the back and a utility truck with plenty of storage bins at the rear, as well as a spare fuel tank. They could each travel for more than a thousand miles without stopping for more diesel. Both also had steel plates welded to their bodies for protection against bullets, and wire mesh on the windows to catch any flying debris. Seeing them was like looking at something out of a Mad Max movie. Between the two, we had plenty of room to store everything we needed and carry all our passengers.

Earl caught my eye as he walked up. He pulled me into a hug that crushed my ribs and made me wonder if he'd ever let me go. "You be careful now, you hear me?"

"I will," I promised.

The older man squeezed one more time before pulling away. "And if you see anyplace with smokes, you get me some."

"I thought you were going to quit cigarettes," I said, teasing him. He'd cut back a lot, but he still had some stashed away that he lit up at least a couple of times a day.

"Not until I have to."

Trish, who'd just joined us, hugged me next. "You better be back before the baby is born."

I glanced down at the small rise of her stomach. At four and a half months along, she still had some time left. "You're joking, right?"

"No." She scowled. "I'll hold this sucker inside if I have to."

"It shouldn't take more than a week."

Trish blinked back the moisture building in her eyes. "Yeah, okay."

We finished telling everyone goodbye and loaded up in the vehicles. I was driving the utility truck for the first leg of the journey. The interior wasn't as fancy as the RV hauler, but it was better than most of the ranch vehicles my stepfather owned. I set my bag in the backseat and did a radio check with Miles. Both trucks had CB radios installed so we could stay in contact during the trip. His voice came over loud and clear, so I put the handset back in its holder.

Aidan appeared next to my window. "I will meet you at the location I mentioned before."

"We should be there in about twenty minutes or so," I said, turning the key in the ignition. The engine came to life, surprisingly smooth and quiet. Whoever the truck belonged to had kept it in good working order.

Aidan's gaze lingered on me a moment. "I will see you then."

Phoebe climbed into the passenger seat next to me. The interior upholstery for both vehicles had already been covered with camrium cloth to protect it when the shifters rode with us. Aidan's sister would stay with our group while he met with the pendragon, his uncle, and the sorcerer to let them know we were on our way. Xanath was going to do some kind of spell over us so Verena couldn't find us during our trip. He'd wanted to wait until the last possible moment since it had an expiration date on it.

"This is going to be fun," Phoebe said, grinning widely.

"Yeah, maybe." I only hoped I got a few dragon kills along the way because it had been too long since my last battle. With each additional day that went by without slaying, my nerves wound tighter and that could lead to trouble with the shifters if too much time passed. My control had its limits, even with Aidan. Other than that, though, I wanted the trip to be as uneventful as possible.

Miles pulled the RV hauler away from the curb, leading the way as we drove out of the neighborhood. I'd tried talking him into letting me drive it instead, but he hadn't budged. It had a lot more amenities than the utility truck, including a mini fridge and bed in the back. Conrad and Danae were riding with him, of course. With no shifters in their vehicle, they could listen to Hank on the radio without them overhearing.

We slowly made our way through the streets. The group who usually set up ambush points didn't have anything along our route, making things a little easier. The only thing to get in our way was the usual cracks and buckles in the roads and debris that had never gotten cleaned up. Conrad and I occasionally moved stuff out of the way when we were out hunting, such as tree limbs and trash bags, but we didn't have time to deal with all of it.

Heading in a southeasterly direction, we made it to highway 9. Then we followed it for a handful of miles until reaching a closed gas station. Aidan, the pendragon, Kade, and Xanath stood waiting for us in the parking lot. They had a crate of supplies next to them for the shifters that I assumed had food in it. We'd been warned ahead of time and left enough room in the back of my truck for it to fit.

Everyone climbed out of the vehicles.

Xanath gestured at us. "Please come forward."

Danae, Miles, Conrad, and I lined up as the sorcerer worked some kind of magic over us, chanting in a language I couldn't understand. Tingles went across my skin and I shivered. It didn't feel like anything I'd experienced before, but it reminded me of the sensation I got from being near fireworks going off. Behind us, Aidan and Kade loaded their crate onto the truck.

"It is done," Xanath announced. He gestured at the shifters so he could do them next.

"So we're good for a week?" I asked.

He nodded. "As long as you don't run into anything that interferes with the magic, it should last that long."

Danae frowned. "What would interfere with the magic?"

"You will know it when you feel it."

"That's not cryptic or anything." She snorted.

"It is up to you to recognize it. The others do not have the power to sense such things."

"You do realize I'm still a little a new at this," she said.

"I have seen your talents. You are strong and capable enough," he replied, sounding like a teacher with his student.

"Thanks for the words of encouragement."

The pendragon waited for Xanath to finish his spell on Aidan and the others before addressing all of us, "Humans and shifters alike are depending on you to recover the orb. Do not fail us."

The weight of our responsibility hit me. Until then, I'd been more focused on preparing for the trip than thinking about the gravity of it. Our success could mean the difference between a somewhat difficult post-apocalyptic world and one that would become unlivable. We had to do everything possible to ensure we got that orb back and tucked safely inside the shifter fortress.

Aidan did some kind of strange handshake with Nanoq where they gripped each other's forearms. "You can count on us, milord."

The pendragon stared hard at him. "Complete this task, and I will know I can trust you."

A few minutes later, we were back on the road again heading east. Kade had joined Phoebe and me in the truck, taking up the backseat. Aidan flew overhead, providing over watch for the first leg of the journey.

Through the windshield, I could spot him flying in the sky ahead. It was his job to look for any obstacles before we reached them. We'd gone over the route several times in the last couple of days, and he knew exactly which way to go.

To the south of us, I caught glimpses of the mountains when trees close to the road didn't block the view. Thin, hazy clouds covered the tops of them, adding to their mystique. Aidan had told me the range was from the dragon dimension just like the fortress, and the shifters were lucky both had crossed over. His clan depended on the mountains to get the stone they used for constructing their homes, and they mined the ore deep within to make their weapons.

Our drive was mostly through countryside for a while. The trees had lost their leaves so only random clusters of evergreens broke the monotony of beige coloring the landscape. Occasionally, we passed through a town. Tecumseh was the first but showed no signs of life. A few of the buildings along the highway had been burned almost to the ground with only parts of their walls remaining. I thought I caught a car driving down one of the side streets where a neighborhood still stood, but it disappeared before I could be sure. According to Hank, there were still people living in the town who he met when he visited for his news updates. They just preferred to keep to themselves.

We didn't have any problems until we got close to Seminole. Aidan flew back toward us and landed a short distance ahead on the road, shifting into his human form. Miles and I stopped our trucks. Before I could even turn off the vehicle, Phoebe was already getting out on the passenger side. We raced up to meet Aidan.

"There is a barrier ahead. It is made up of debris and blocking the road," he announced.

Miles pulled out a map he had tucked in his pocket. "Can you point to where exactly?"

"On the other side of this intersection." He put his finger down where Highway 9 and Highway 270 met.

"Will we be able to drive on 270?" Miles asked.

Aidan nodded. "Yes. I believe the humans living there just wish to prevent travelers from getting near their homes."

I stared at the map. That highway would keep us to the outskirts of town, though not entirely out of it. There was a chance there could be more road blocks once we made it farther along. "Did you follow the route very far? Are you sure it's clear?"

"Yes. You will not have any trouble passing by the town."

"Let's go that way then," Miles said, folding his map. "If you could check to make sure there's no one looking to ambush us while we're driving through, that would be great."

"Of course." Aidan glanced between Miles and me, caution in his eyes. "Do not travel too fast. The highway appears to have some damage, though nothing you cannot pass over."

"That's good to know." Miles made a circling motion with his arms. "Let's go!"

Phoebe grabbed my wrist. "I will stay with my brother this time. If you see us coming toward you, stop right away."

"Okay."

I hurried back to the truck. Kade joined me, taking the front passenger seat this time. Miles took off a minute later, and I followed him, keeping watch for any signs of danger. Maybe the people in Seminole were just trying to protect their town, but maybe they also caught travelers by surprise to rob them. There was no way of knowing.

We reached the intersection, and I saw what Aidan meant as I turned onto Highway 270. A handful of old junker cars were positioned across the four-lane road, the median, and the neighboring lawns on either side. There were also couches, old building materials, and construction barriers piled over ten feet high and went at least that far back. There was no way to drive through or around the haphazard barrier.

We turned and started going in a southeasterly direction. This had been one of our planned alternate routes anyway, so it wasn't a hardship to change direction. I glanced down the side roads that led farther into town. More old cars and debris blocked them. There were some houses and buildings on the west side of the highway, but I was guessing no one inhabited or used those anymore.

The road curved, taking us due east. There were a lot more businesses and homes in this stretch, but once again they didn't appear in use. Of course, appearances could be deceiving. I gripped the steering wheel tightly, expecting people to pop out any moment and attack. If it could happen in Norman, it could definitely happen in this town, too.

Up ahead on the north side of the road, an older man with a shotgun came out of an old, gray building that looked like it had seen better days. Aidan and Phoebe dove from the sky toward him. The guy's eyes widened, and he raced into some trees, disappearing into thick underbrush. It was wrong of me, but I snickered. That poor man didn't know the shifters wouldn't kill him. They just wanted to remove him as a threat. If there was anyone else lurking around, they'd think twice about showing themselves now.

We finally left Seminole behind, and I breathed a sigh of relief. Only a dozen more small towns to go before we reached our destination.

13

AIDAN

Aidan flew next to his sister as they scanned the area below, searching for signs of danger. It was a new experience for him to be escorting humans this way. The others might help, but he'd made it his mission to ensure everyone in their party reached their destination without coming to serious harm. The new pendragon had put a lot of faith in Aidan by allowing him to go on this quest. He would not let Nanoq down, and he would return with the orb no matter what it took.

He caught sight of a herd of cows blocking the highway. *Look there!*

I've got it, Phoebe said, swooping down and roaring at them.

The frightened herd stampeded their way through a fallen fence on the south side of the road, damaging it further, and into a nearby pasture. Their hooves left dirt and dried grass upturned in their wake. After his sister chased down a few of the remaining strays, she flew ahead to make certain no more had wandered off.

Aidan searched the area for any sign of the person who might own them. No human scents lingered, and the nearest houses didn't appear to have been occupied recently. His toriq occasionally hunted for cows and other animals near the fortress, taking those that would not be missed, but never more than they needed. The last thing they wanted was to deplete the resources of their territory. In fact, they wanted the land to flourish. He would have to inform the pendragon once he returned of this particular herd so they could keep an eye on it.

He caught up with his sister, and they continued on their way. The route they followed appeared to be in relatively good shape other than a few pot holes, as Bailey called them, and cracks in the asphalt. All of the bridges were passable as well. Small towns were dotted along the way—all of them quiet with no outward activity. If not for the fresh scents of humans and exhaust from their vehicles Aidan caught when he flew low enough, he might have thought the places abandoned.

It wasn't until he reached a larger town— McAlester—that he became uneasy. A light breeze blew in his direction, bringing the strong odor of people and their weapons with it. The gun powder especially irritated his nose. Whoever lived here was active even at this time of day and prepared for unexpected visitors. Miles had mentioned this town could be their biggest problem because the state penitentiary was located here. Aidan caught flickers of movement at the edge of the city and noted a road block had been set up.

He glanced at his sister. *Go back and tell the others to stop and wait.*

What are you going to do?

We do not have time to go around this place. Aidan eyed a couple of humans looking up at him with rifles in their hands. Didn't they know their puny weapons could do little to harm him? *I am going to convince these people that it is in their best interest to let our group pass through here.*

Phoebe hesitated only a moment. *I will return as quickly as I can.*

She turned and flew back in the direction they'd come. Bailey, his uncle, and the others were at least five miles behind them, which was good. They needed to stay out of sight until Aidan took care of this.

He swooped down, heading for a spot in the road approximately fifty feet from the barrier the humans had erected. As he got closer, they began firing at him. One of the bullets hit a soft spot in his wings, making him wince, but he ignored it. Their soft pieces of metal felt like little more than bee stings. They'd have to fire many of them in the same spot to do any real damage.

Aidan landed and allowed his inner fire to consume him. The gunshots came faster. As he shifted into human form, dozens of bullets disintegrated within the flames, going out in tiny sparks. Silly humans—they did not understand who they faced now. He could smell the desperation and fear leaking off of them in waves as they watched him change. Bailey had once told Aidan that he looked like a demon while transitioning between forms. No doubt these men had grown used to dealing with vulnerable travelers since the pure dragons left. After months of peace, these humans had grown too confident. If Miles was right, most of them were criminals—perhaps murderers and rapists. Who knew what they'd done to the innocents living in this town. Perhaps it was time they were reminded they were not at the top of the food chain.

He emerged from the flames and shouted, "Who is in charge here?"

No answer. The humans hid behind damaged cars, whispering to each other. They did not know he could hear them chattering on their radios and asking for assistance from others nearby. Aidan walked closer until no more than ten feet separated him from their hiding spot.

"I will ask one more time. Who is in charge here?"

A man with a bald head and thick beard slowly stood up. He reeked of terror, but he hid it well. "And who might you be?"

"Aidan of the Taugud. My toriq..." He paused, remembering most humans did not know what that meant. "My clan claimed this territory months ago and forced the pure dragons out. You have had the luxury of living in safety since then because of us."

The man edged around the car, gripping his rifle. "We make ourselves safe. You ain't got nothin' to do with it."

Aidan gazed beyond the road block toward the town. The pure dragons hadn't destroyed it, but the charred remains in their wake told its own tale. They'd destroyed at least a quarter of the structures that had once stood. Even from this distance, Aidan could spot the pieces of walls where houses had once been and buildings missing their roofs. Even closer, there was a large black spot on the ground where something must have stood, but it had been completely destroyed. Dragon flames only burned what they touched. They did not spread the way human-built fires could.

"Are you saying you fought the green dragons off yourself?" Aidan asked, cocking his head.

The burly man spit on the ground. "Didn't need to. They left."

"Because of my people," Aidan growled.

"Don't make no difference to me."

This was going nowhere, and he'd had enough. Aidan sprinted toward the man, took his rifle out of his hand, and threw it so far neither of them could see where it landed. Then he grabbed the human by his filthy, flannel shirt. "I have people coming this way in two trucks. You and your friends are going to let them pass safely through this town without incident."

The male's eyes rounded. "What the fuck are you?"

"Only now do you wish to know?" The human and his friend, who still hid behind the car, had seen Aidan shift.

"Shit ain't been the same since that day dragons showed up. This is the first time I've seen one turn human and your eyes..." He swallowed.

For some reason, that was the thing that always bothered people the most. Aidan could never figure it out. "The green dragons you've seen before are pure with strong animal instincts. Those of us who are red are able to shift to human form, and we can be more civilized." Aidan shoved the guy onto the car's hood. "But you are not making that easy."

A skinny human male stood up. Aidan caught the scent of urine coming from the direction of the man's pants. "We g-g-got orders from our b-boss," he stuttered, "not to let anyone p-p-pass."

Aidan glared at him. "Tell whoever gave you those orders that unless you let my people go through this town, I will take you and your friend here and dump you in the nearest lake. If one more person shoots a gun in my presence, the consequences will be far worse. Is that understood?"

The skinny man bobbed his head, but he just stood there doing nothing. Fear held him in place. The other male managed a verbal reply, "We got it."

"Good, now get on your radio and tell your boss what I told you," Aidan said, glaring at them both.

The bald man sat up, slid off the car, and went around the vehicle. He picked a hand-held radio off the ground and began speaking into it. Aidan listened as the guy relayed the message, noting that he was staring into the distance at a tall, brick building about a mile or so down the road. It had to be at least ten or eleven levels high. Was that where his boss was located? Could he be hiding there, watching his "territory" from a high vantage point? That was what Aidan would do.

"You two idiots get back here. I'll take care of this," said the voice over the radio.

"Leave now?" the bald man questioned.

"Yes!"

Both men darted a glance at Aidan, and then they took off running down the street. The boss wouldn't have told them to leave unless he had a plan. Taking a deep breath, Aidan searched for any evidence of explosives. Something like what the humans had tried using against dragons before. He didn't smell anything. Movement on the rooftop of the building where the boss was located caught his attention. A man was up there holding something over his shoulder in a way that sent Aidan's hackles rising. Not waiting a moment longer to find out, he began to shift. As the flames rose over him, an object soared through the air straight for him. Aidan didn't bother to move, staying directly in the rocket's path. A split-second later, it reached the flames covering his body and disintegrated with a flash of sparks.

He finished shifting and turned to find Phoebe landing next to him.

I take it they are not being cooperative? she asked.

No.

What do you need me to do?

Aidan gestured toward the road block. *Destroy this while I take care of the leader of this town.*

With pleasure. She gave him a sharp-toothed grin.

While his sister proceeded to burn the cars and other large objects blocking the road, Aidan took off into the air. His body protested, weakened from changing forms too many times in a short period, but he still had some energy in his reserves. He headed for the building where he'd seen the rocket come from, though the man who'd fired it had disappeared. All Aidan could see up there was the remnants of a sign that he thought was meant to say "Hotel Ald-*something*." Half the letters were missing.

As he got closer, gunfire erupted from one of the top-floor windows. Aidan jerked as several bullets hit him in his soft underbelly, puncturing the thinner scales there. Pain gripped his stomach, but he couldn't let it deter him. He flew straight for the window, letting out a roar of flames.

Someone inside screamed. As the fire died down, Aidan caught sight of a man scrambling away. He had made a point of blowing only enough for it to destroy the window and surrounding wall, creating a hole large enough for him to get inside. He touched down on the edge of the floor and tucked his wings into his back. In his dragon form, he stood taller. The top of his head almost grazed the ceiling. Aidan ran his gaze around the room, homing in on an injured man crawling toward a door. His right side had suffered deep burn wounds, especially on his arm and leg. Half the muscle tissue had been eaten away in the flames.

The struggling man gripped a hand-held radio in his good hand, holding it like a lifeline as he shouted into it for help. He managed to keep crawling at the same time. Aidan could not speak all that intelligibly in dragon form, and he couldn't afford to shift again. It had taken too much of his energy already and the bullet wounds in his stomach made matters worse. He pointed at the radio, and hoped he could make his point.

"Call them off," he said in a thick, growly voice.

The man's eyes widened on him, and he began to shake. Cursing inwardly, Aidan pulled a camrium blanket from shiggara and picked up the wounded male as carefully as he could. Then he took off out of the building, carrying his passenger away from town toward the waiting vehicles a few miles away. The whole time he put up with the man wiggling and crying in pain. It was all he could do to keep his passenger away from his wounded stomach. Why couldn't the damn human have just cooperated? Aidan didn't know if this was the boss, but even if he wasn't he might still be useful.

He landed and laid the human on the ground in front of where Bailey and her friends stood. After pulling the camrium blanket from the man's face, he backed away. His last flight had taken a lot out of him, and he had to stay on all four limbs to remain upright. At least with him in this position they wouldn't notice his wounds.

"What happened?" Bailey asked, giving the man on the ground a horrified look.

Aidan turned to his uncle. *Get the burn medicine and tell the sorceress to help this man.*

"Why did you bring him?" Kade gave him a puzzled look.

If we heal him, he may tell his people to let us pass.

"We could try killing every one of them that gets in our way instead."

Aidan had thought of that, especially considering how much his stomach hurt from where they shot him. He was angry, and the beast within him wanted nothing more than to lay waste to every stinking human he could find in that town. That wasn't the right way to do things, though.

There are too many people there—some of them possibly innocent—and it would take too long to get them all. He glanced back at the city. *And we must show them that if they cooperate, they will not be harmed. This is our chance to begin building relations with humans in our territory.*

"What is he saying?" Bailey asked.

Kade explained the situation to her, finishing with, "...and Aidan doesn't want to kill them all."

Miles grunted. "I'm willing to bet the ones shooting are criminals, anyway. It wouldn't be that big of a loss."

"No." Bailey shook her head. "Aidan is right. We need to use this as an opportunity to help them learn to cooperate."

Kade sighed. "I'll get the ointment."

Danae kneeled next to the man and looked him over. "I've never treated burn injuries like this before. I'm not sure how much I can do for him."

"Do what you can. The ointment Aidan's uncle is bringing will help."

The sorceress tore away the remnants of cloth near the man's wounds and made a sound of distress. "This is bad."

Kade returned with the ointment and handed it to her. "This won't fully heal burns that deep, but it will ease his pain and assist the skin in knitting back together."

She frowned at the glass bottle. "What is it?"

"Don't ask," Bailey said, grimacing. "It helped Conrad once so I know it works."

The young man in question shot a dirty look at Aidan. "Yeah, it definitely helps if you get too close to a shifter for too long."

Aidan wasn't about to apologize for a minor incident that happened over six months ago. Conrad had put his nose where it didn't belong and got in Aidan's way. The young man should have been grateful he didn't have to suffer through his little skin burn for long.

Danae took a moment to examine the ointment and sniff it. Once satisfied, she poured a dollop of it onto her fingertips and started rubbing it on the injured male's wounds. He struggled against her touch. Conrad and Miles dropped to the ground and held the guy's shoulders while Danae continued to work. She chanted healing words as she rubbed the gel-like substance onto his arm and then on his leg. Within a few minutes, the man's ragged breaths eased, and his body relaxed. Aidan hadn't expected much, but her powers were even stronger than he'd presumed.

They all watched as the skin and muscles began regenerating.

"Holy shit, girl," Conrad said, easing back on his heels. "This guy is going to be almost good as new."

Danae's brows were furrowed in concentration. The energy crackled around her as she worked. "Not quite yet," she muttered.

"I've never seen anything like it." Kade stared at her in awe. "She doesn't only have the healing touch—she is the very essence of a true healer."

And this is only after training for a few months, Aidan replied.

"One such as her is beyond priceless."

Miles glared at Kade. "Don't get any ideas. She is not up for grabs."

Phoebe arrived during the healing, shifting into human form, and shared her own surprise before giving them an update. "The road block is clear and the humans have withdrawn from the edge of town. I don't think they're ready to give up yet, though."

"What makes you say that?" Bailey asked.

"When I tried to get closer they shot at me."

Danae let out a sigh of exhaustion. "That's it. That's all I can do."

Everyone glanced down at the man on the ground. His skin was still somewhat mottled and pink, but she'd restored most of his missing tissue. He'd likely have some mobility problems for the rest of his life and would never regain full strength, but he'd live and survive to fight another day.

"That's amazing," Bailey said, giving Danae's tense shoulders a rub. "You did great."

The man's eyes had been glazed with pain, but now they were beginning to clear. Aidan directed his attention to his uncle. *Tell him to use his radio to call his people off. He should mention we saved him, but this is the only mercy we shall give. If they cross us again, we will not hold back next time.*

Kade dipped his chin. Then he leaned down and gave the human his hardest look. "Tell your people to let us pass safely through town. That is all we want, but if they attack us again, there will be no mercy the next time."

The man looked around at all of them, pausing for a moment on Aidan. Then he lifted the radio he'd been gripping since they left the building and spoke into it. "This is Granger. I'm ordering all of you to stand down. There are two trucks that are going to pass through going...?"

"We're taking Highway 270 all the way through town," Miles answered.

Granger repeated the information. After he'd made his instructions clear, he looked up. "There won't be any more trouble."

"There better not be," Kade warned.

I will return him to town, Aidan said to his uncle. Then he looked at Phoebe. *Stay with them and escort them all the way. After I have returned the human to where I found him, I will fly ahead to ensure his people followed his instructions.*

She narrowed her eyes. "Brother, you are wounded. I can smell the blood."

It is nothing. The half hour it had taken for Danae to heal Granger had bought Aidan's body time to start healing itself. He was still weak, but not as much as before.

"Wait." Bailey moved toward him, running her gaze over him. "You're hurt?"

Aidan pressed his nose into her stomach and let out a breath of steam. *Sister, tell her I am fine.*

Phoebe let out a sigh. "He's fine. I think it's just a flesh wound."

"Are you sure?" Bailey asked, knitting her brows. She still hadn't figured out Aidan's injuries were on his stomach, and her sense of smell wasn't as acute as the shifters. "You said there was blood."

"It's not much, and you know he's not going to let a small wound slow him down. Just let him go, and we'll check him over later if he's not better yet," Phoebe said.

"You better be okay." Bailey tapped on Aidan's nose before stepping away.

He glanced at his sister. *Thank you.*

She nodded. "I'll keep them safe, but you need to be careful."

He gave her a short bow of his head.

After Phoebe relayed his plans, Danae wrapped the blanket tightly around Granger to prepare him for the return trip. Aidan didn't waste any time grabbing the man—who glared at him with pure hatred—and flew him back to the building. He didn't take him through the window, though. Instead, he headed for the roof where he found several weapons lying around, including the launching device for the rocket. Aidan set the man down near the corner. Then he burned every weapon he could find, uncaring that he left a few holes in the roof. Those devices would not be hurting anyone again.

After shooting a threatening look at Granger, who'd managed to rise unsteadily to his feet, Aidan took off into the air. He flew slowly over the route Bailey and the others were taking through town. A few faces gazed out from windows, but no one fired a weapon. It only took him a few minutes to reach the other end of town where humans were finishing their road block removal on that side. He touched down a short distance from them and watched. They picked up the pace, five of them shoving a large truck aside while someone else steered it from the driver's seat. By the time Miles arrived in his RV hauler with Bailey following behind him, the path was clear.

The humans hurried away from the road and disappeared into nearby buildings. Aidan didn't move from his spot until his group was safely out of town.

14

BAILEY

I breathed a sigh of relief when I couldn't see the town of McAlester in my rearview mirrors anymore. Late afternoon had turned into early evening with the sun barely peeking over the trees in the distance. We didn't have much time left before nightfall, and I didn't want to be on the road when that came. Even though we could use our headlights without fear of drawing pure dragons in this area, there was still the human threat. I didn't want to face any more trouble today.

We were in a place I didn't know, and it was making me uncomfortable. Life had become primitive in ways I'd never imagined over the last six months. All those primal instincts passed down through our DNA from the cave man era were rising up now, bringing out a different side in people. Everyone's nerves were frayed. Traveling through places you didn't know was dangerous, and you sure as heck didn't do it at night.

"We will be fine," Kade said, almost as if he could hear my thoughts.

"What makes you so confident?" I asked.

He shrugged a shoulder. "All the potential dangers have passed. I trust we will arrive at our first destination safely."

"And after that?"

Aidan's uncle frowned. "I cannot say for certain yet."

"Well, that's a real comfort…" I started to say but stopped when I noticed Miles turning off the highway. "Where in the hell is he going?"

"To find closure, I suspect."

I glanced over at him. "What do you mean?"

"This is something he needs to do, but it will not take long," Kade said, staring straight ahead.

"How do you know these things?"

He didn't answer until I'd made the same turn as Miles and started following him down an empty country road. "I get small premonitions and feelings about things that may happen in the near future." Kade paused and furrowed his brows. "Not everything is clear, and events in the far future are much more difficult to discern."

"That figures." I tightened my hands on the wheel.

Up ahead on the left side, I spotted a lone house. It was small with white siding and a sagging porch roof. Other than a storage shed in the backyard, only trees and pastureland surrounded it. Miles turned onto the driveway leading to the place, tires kicking up dust from leaving paved road.

I stopped the truck behind the RV hauler. Miles had already gotten out of his vehicle and began walking toward the house. With the stiff set of his shoulders, one would think he headed toward an execution.

Danae raced up behind him. "Let me go with you!"

"No." Miles stopped and swung around. "I told you this is something I need to do alone."

She put her hands on her hips. "But if your father is in there…"

"Get back in the truck," he commanded and pointed toward the RV hauler.

Danae crossed her arms. "I'll wait right here. That's as good as you're going to get."

Miles glowered at her for a moment and then stomped away. He slowed his steps when he reached the porch, taking them carefully. The wooden slabs didn't look all that stable and desperately needed to be replaced. The rest of the house didn't look much better. One of the front windows was broken with half the glass lying shattered on the ground, and loose tree branches littered the roof. It didn't look like anyone had been living there for a long time.

"There can't be anyone in that house," I said, frowning.

"Not alive, no."

From what I understood, Miles' mother had died when he was a kid, and he didn't have any siblings. That left only his father.

I looked over at Kade. "Does that mean his dad…?"

"As I said before, he needs this closure."

Danae once told me that Miles hadn't spoken to his father in years. They'd had some sort of falling out, which was why he'd never tried to go home and check on his dad after D-day. I supposed now that the place was on his way, he'd decided to find answers.

Loud noises suddenly came from inside—like someone was tearing things apart. Miles screamed obscenities loud enough that even those without sensitive hearing could catch his words. "You sorry, bastard. If you'd just listened to me you might still be alive!"

It went on for several minutes. I left the truck and came to stand next to Danae. Miles would probably get all his aggression out before he left the house, but just in case he didn't, I wouldn't let her stand there alone. Aidan must have noticed we were no longer following him and turned back around.

He landed nearby, changing into his human form. Pure exhaustion lined his eyes as he began moving toward us. Whatever wounds he'd had before didn't show anywhere, but with the way he moved something was bothering him. If only Aidan would let himself rest. I didn't think he could take another shift today after having done it several times in the past few hours. It was all I could do to stand still and not help as he stumbled the last few feet toward us.

"What is going on?" Aidan addressed Danae.

"This is where Miles' father lived." She glanced at the shifter. "They weren't on the best of terms the last time they saw each other."

Aidan inhaled deeply and his gaze turned sorrowful. "I smell death in there."

"Any idea how long since it happened?" I asked. His nose could determine a lot of things mine couldn't—even with my enhanced senses.

"The scent has faded a lot. I would estimate at least a couple of months."

The shouting and other noises stopped, and we returned our attention to the house. Miles stumbled onto the porch, falling to his knees. Danae ran to him. She leaped over the steps, avoiding them altogether, and kneeled down to wrap her arms around him. Miles ducked his head so all I could see was his mussed blond hair and shaking shoulders.

"Come on," I said, taking Aidan by the arm. "Let's give them some space. You need to sit down and relax anyway."

"I'm fine."

I rolled my eyes. "No, you're not. What happened?"

His expression hardened. "It was nothing."

"Aidan," I dragged out his name in a warning tone.

He worked his jaw. "A few bullets struck me in the stomach. It is healing."

"What?" I grabbed his shirt and lifted it up. He tried to stop me, but I knocked his hands out of the way without much effort. I sucked in a breath when I saw the blue and black bruises covering his abdomen. Who knew how bad it had been when he'd initially gotten hurt. It was hard to see his muscular abs discolored like that, and his breaths were ragged. Add that to the fact he'd shifted too often today, and it spelled trouble. No wonder the man could hardly move.

"You see?" He jerked his tunic back down. "The damage is almost gone."

"Hardly—and if it was me hurt like that?"

He hesitated, and his expression transformed into a defeated one. "Very well. I will sit."

"Thank you." I led him to the truck, opening the back door to help him climb inside. The seat already had a huge camrium cloth covering it, so he didn't have to worry about burning the upholstery. He sagged into the cushions and tilted his head back, concentrating on breathing.

"Just sit here, okay?" I gave him a stern look. "You've done enough for one day."

He ran his hand through his shiny, black hair, letting a hint of vulnerability show in his gaze. "Is that an order?"

"Yes."

Kade barked a laugh from the front seat. "My nephew taking orders from a dragon slayer. Until recently, I never would have believed it."

"Don't make me show you my sword," I said, narrowing my eyes at him.

"The one Aidan made you? That would be ironic." Kade shook his head. "We both know you wouldn't hurt me."

I put a hand on the door frame and leaned into the vehicle. "And why is that?"

"Because it would hurt Aidan, and you wouldn't do anything to harm him."

I glanced at the man in question, who'd closed his eyes. "Don't push your luck."

With a parting glare at Kade, I shut the truck door. Something in his tone had disturbed me, and I needed to end that conversation fast. It was like he knew Aidan and I had grown a lot closer to each other than we let on in front of people. He'd talked in that same knowing voice that Conrad used when speaking about the topic. I hurried away before Kade could say anything else that might bother me.

On the porch, Miles and Danae had stood up and began talking in hushed voices. They probably didn't realize I could hear them if I concentrated.

"I can't leave without burying him," Miles whispered, shooting an anxious glance at the open doorway to the house.

She put a hand on his arm. "Then we'll bury him."

"It's going to get dark soon." He gestured at the sky. "I don't want to hold our group up over something like this."

Danae shook her head. "Don't be silly. If we work together, we could do it fast."

His expression wavered, and I recognized that look. It was the soldier in him not wanting to be the weak link. He needed to bury his father, but not at the cost of the mission.

"We've got a couple of shovels in the trucks," I said, walking up to the porch and stopping at the steps.

There wasn't much point in acting like I hadn't over-heard them. "You aren't slowing us down, so don't wor-ry about it."

Conrad and Phoebe joined us from where they'd been standing by the RV hauler.

"We'll help, too," Aidan's sister said, determination in her gaze. "It's important to mourn the ones we love."

"Is there someplace in particular you'd like to bury him?" Conrad asked. "We can do this—no problem."

Relief and gratitude filled Miles' gaze. He point-ed at a tree. "Right there would be good. We used to have a swing there where my parents would sit together when the weather was nice."

I looked at the spot, trying to picture what it would have been like in the summer. Right now, the tree was bare of leaves and looked forlorn standing in the yard by itself. It had plenty of branches, though, so maybe it provided plenty of shade when it was full.

"Okay," I said, returning my attention to Miles. "How about you guys grab the shovels from the truck and us girls will get your father ready?"

He drew in a deep breath. "Yeah, alright."

I hadn't been certain if he'd let us handle his fa-ther's body, but he hurried off like he was happy to leave that duty to us. Conrad followed him, talking to Miles the whole way to the truck. He preferred to fill awkward silences rather than let them stand.

Danae, Phoebe, and I entered the house. It took a moment for my eyes to adjust, but my nose picked up the smells in the still air quicker. The scent of death came from down the hall. I followed it with the other women behind me, Phoebe pinching her nose since it had to be even worse for her. Danae showed no signs of the odor affecting her at all, but I didn't know how strong it would be for someone with normal senses.

We found Miles' father in the back bedroom lying on his bed. His body had long since started the decomposition process, and I had to grip my stomach when I caught my first glimpse of him. I couldn't determine the cause of death, but there was an empty bottle of whiskey on the nightstand that spoke volumes about the man's state when he'd passed. The rest of the room was trashed. Miles had punched holes in the walls, thrown pictures and clothes around, and knocked a dresser on its side. We stepped over the debris and gathered around the bed.

"Let's get the blanket wrapped tight around him," I suggested.

Danae nodded. "Good idea."

Phoebe stood at the foot of the bed. "I'll wait until you're ready to carry him. If I handle this cloth for too long, I'll burn it."

Danae and I worked quietly, getting the stained sheets wrapped around the body first. Then we pulled a thick, blue comforter from the floor and started to roll the body onto it. My nose burned from the stench, but I did my best to ignore it. This was once a person, and no matter how gross it seemed, he deserved some respect.

"Do you have any idea what caused the rift between Miles and his dad?" I asked Danae.

She shook her head. "No. He refuses to talk about it."

"Maybe with time he'll open up."

She sighed. "Yeah, maybe."

We finished wrapping up the body. It was completely covered from head to toe so Miles wouldn't have to look at his father again if he didn't want to. Phoebe took the feet while Danae and I each took a side. Stepping carefully, we made our way out of the room and through the house. We didn't stop until we'd made it off the porch. Then we set the body down on the ground about twenty feet from where the hole was being dug.

Miles and Conrad had already started, but I caught Aidan leaning against the tree saying he'd help once one of them got tired. They'd only dug about a foot deep so far. I decided to humor them for a few minutes longer before taking over. With my slayer strength and speed, I could get it done a lot quicker. Kade came from the truck and brought canteens of water. While Miles and Conrad drank, I grabbed one of the shovels and dug into the ground. It was hard, packed earth and there were some roots to fight through, but I muscled my way deeper.

Aidan took one of the other shovels, and I paused to glower at him. "You're not helping."

"Yes, I am." He gave me a stubborn look.

Before I could argue, he started digging on the other end of the grave. I thought about tossing him back in the truck, but he would only get out again. It was better to just keep going. We both pushed ourselves to the max so that we made it to six feet within fifteen minutes. Everyone stood back and eyed the wide hole for a moment.

"Are you ready?" Danae asked Miles.

"Yeah, let's get him in there," he said in a gruff voice.

He and Conrad took hold of the body and moved it over, lowering it as much as they could before dropping it into the hole. Everyone looked around expectantly. Should we say or do something special at this point?

Without a word, Miles grabbed a shovel and started tossing the dirt back inside. A tear slipped down his cheek as he worked. I wasn't very close to him, but in that moment I wished I could do something to ease his pain. We'd lost too many people since D-day already, and it didn't seem like it would ever end. Most likely, his father would still be alive if not for the dragons invading. Maybe Miles would have even come home for the summer and visited. There were so many "what ifs" but it was futile to entertain them. We just had to quietly bury our dead one after the other while wondering if we'd be next.

Aidan picked up a shovel and started helping Miles. He was looking more worn out by the second, but he didn't let it stop him from helping a human in need. I had to admire that. There was very little about Aidan that I didn't like, which made it that much harder to keep my distance from him. Having a reminder that either of us could die at any moment didn't help.

They finished filling the grave. Miles sucked in a deep breath and ran his gaze over all of us. "Thank you for your help. If you could give me a moment alone, I'd appreciate it."

We all mumbled our sympathies, gave him hugs or pats on the back, and walked away. Danae took over the driver's seat of Miles' truck. I was glad she thought of it because he wasn't in any shape to be behind the wheel for the last leg of today's journey. After packing away the shovels, I climbed into my vehicle. Kade and Aidan had already settled inside. I noticed my filthy hands right before I put them on the steering wheel. Taking some moist tissues from the glove box, I cleaned my fingers and nails of dirt as best I could. Removing the grime also gave me a moment to concentrate on a simple task. Burying a friend's father really bothered me, and I wanted to get my mind off of it. Once finished, I handed the packet of tissues to Aidan so he could wash up as well. He took it gratefully. Shifters liked to be clean almost more than humans from what I'd seen.

"He will survive this," Kade said, breaking the silence inside the vehicle.

I looked at Miles where he stood over his father's grave. There was a wealth of pain, sadness, and regret in his eyes. This wasn't something he'd get over in a day or two. In fact, he might have to live with the pain for the rest of his life.

"How can you be sure?" I asked, turning to Aidan's uncle.

"Because he has no choice."

Sadly, he was probably right.

15

BAILEY

It was almost full dark by the time we reached Robbers Cave State Park. My truck's headlights were throwing off my night vision, but I could just make out the rugged countryside with its rolling hills and thick forests of trees. We'd left the remnants of civilization behind. I had to trust Miles and Danae to find us somewhere to stop for the evening. All I could think about was eating something, washing the rest of the dirt off my body, and getting some sleep.

Aidan let out a low growl from the backseat. "I can feel it."

"As can I," Kade said, his lips thinning.

"Feel what?" I asked.

Aidan leaned forward, poking his head between the front seats. "The orb. It is not far from here."

"What does it feel like?"

Kade grunted. "It is dark. The magic raises the hairs on the back of my neck."

I'd been getting that sensation for the past few miles, but I'd chalked it up to night falling and being in unfamiliar territory. I glanced at Aidan's uncle. "Then I'm feeling it, too. Think it does that to everyone or just those susceptible to it?"

"Most likely, anyone who can be controlled by it."

Up ahead, Danae pulled the RV hauler off the highway and turned into a visitor parking lot for Lake Carlton—a part of the state park. There were no other vehicles around, which was good. I'd been afraid some people might have decided this was a nice place to hide in the post-apocalyptic aftermath. We parked the vehicles and everyone got out, stretching their legs.

"Something happened here," Miles said, frowning as he looked around the area, lit up by the bright moonlight.

He would know better than anyone else what the place was supposed to look like. At first glance, I didn't see anything out of the ordinary. There were a few park structures of varying size, a playground, picnic tables, and a lake farther out. It was the kind of place families visited to enjoy the outdoors.

"What do you mean?" Danae asked.

Miles pointed to the area just past the parking lot. "There used to be a big building there, some picnic tables beside it, and a lot of trees. I know they were there when I came here a couple of summers ago."

Had that been the last time he saw his father? A touch of sadness lurked in his eyes, but he seemed to have buried most of his feelings during the drive.

We walked onto the bare stretch of land, and I ran the edge of my boot across the ground. The dirt was mixed with a tiny bit of black dust. Dragon flames didn't leave ashes, and it couldn't burn dirt, but it could scorch the top layer of it. Anytime they destroyed a place, they left a layer of black particles behind. After a few rainstorms, the dark dust mixed with whatever was underneath or washed away almost completely. Whatever happened here, it had mixed well enough that the attack must have happened a while ago.

"The building here was made of stone," Miles continued, pacing around. It was almost like he was latching onto this problem to distract himself from his grief over his father. "I don't see any sign of it now."

"There were likely some people hiding up here when the Bogaran ruled this area," Aidan said.

I lifted my brows. "The Bogaran? You haven't mentioned them before."

"We pushed them into Arkansas months ago. They held this territory before the Taugud took over."

"I'm surprised they didn't destroy that place, too." Danae pointed at a dark brown building across the parking lot. I'd noticed a sign that said it was a community center when I'd drove by it.

Aidan studied the structure. "Perhaps they weren't using it for shelter so the Bogaran left it alone."

Conrad came dashing out of the place—I hadn't even noticed he was missing. "Hey, guys," he yelled, stopping at the edge of the parking lot. "There's a bunch of food and bottled water up in here. You gotta check it out!"

Miles rubbed his face. "Well, that explains it. They were living in one building and using the other for storage. Most likely they tried to keep the dragons away from their supplies when they were attacked."

Except that meant if all the food was still here and the people weren't, they hadn't survived. No one pointed that out, though. It was enough that we were all thinking it. You could send yourself into a deep, dark pit of despair pondering over something like that for long. We'd already faced enough death and loss for one day.

Without a word, we grabbed flashlights from the trucks and followed Conrad inside. I gaped in amazement at the crates of food and other things packed into the building. He was right that there were plenty of supplies. In fact, we could take some of the goods with us if we divided it between the trucks. The rest we'd have to leave for other travelers who might come through later.

Everyone spent the next half hour digging through the food, checking that it was safe, and eating what they wanted. We hadn't stopped for a meal since leaving Norman, and we were starving. Afterward, we grabbed the sleeping bags and supplies we'd need for the night from the trucks and made space for everyone to lay out.

"We will wait until late in the morning to see about the orb," Kade announced once we finally took a moment to make plans. "There will be tests and everyone must be rested."

"Do we all have to take these tests?" Conrad asked, grimacing like Aidan's uncle had just asked him to walk the plank and jump into shark-infested waters.

"Everyone who is selected."

He shuddered. "Then I don't want to be chosen."

"Everyone on this journey must be prepared." Kade ran his gaze over us. "The only thing I can guarantee is at least one of each race will be selected. Perhaps more, but that was not clear."

"Well, that means Danae and I are already on the chosen squad," I said brightly. It didn't come as news to me, so I decided to accept my fate gracefully. I could always complain later if the tests didn't go well.

"Is there any way to study for this?" Conrad asked. "Exams and me don't get along too good."

Kade gave him a patient smile. "No, there isn't. The tests are meant to prove you are worthy of this quest. Either you are...or you aren't."

"I'm going to go check out the lake and see if it's clean enough to wash up," I announced. There was no point in hearing any more of what Kade had to say since it didn't seem to be very helpful.

Taking my pack that I'd grabbed from the truck, I headed outside. The sky was hazy with a few clouds, but there weren't so many that the moonlight couldn't bathe the land in its soft glow. I flipped off my flashlight and let my eyes adjust. It still amazed me how well I could see since becoming a slayer. While I could recognize it was dark, things still appeared crystal clear.

I walked around the building and passed by a playground with swings and a slide. Beyond that, there was a building with paddle boats. I headed toward it, figuring I could dip into the water there and use the place as cover in case anyone else came outside. It had been a long time since I'd stepped foot in a lake—or immersed myself in water for that matter. Since the apocalypse, we were all about using as little as possible. Sponge baths were about as good as it got unless you made a trip to a pond or lake. This place looked clean and inviting enough I wasn't worried about taking the plunge.

After one last look around to be sure I was alone, I stripped my clothes off and set them on the dock. Then I grabbed a bar of soap from my pack and jumped into the water. It wasn't very deep this close to the shore, making it perfect for washing my uniform before the rest of me. I pulled one garment at a time into the water, scrubbing the dirt and grime from each. It was a good thing camrium cloth wasn't a dry clean only sort of material. I scrubbed my boots too before leaving everything on the dock to air out. Due to the magical properties infused into my uniform, it wouldn't take long for all the pieces to dry.

After a glance around to be sure I was still alone, I walked deeper into the lake until I was able to immerse myself up to my chest. Most people would have found it too cold, but I found it invigorating. I ducked my head under water and scrubbed at my scalp. It felt ridiculously good. Over the next few minutes, I scrubbed every inch of my body with soap and reveled in the feeling of being clean. I'd had no idea how much I'd taken that luxury for granted until showers and baths became a thing of the past.

As I was rinsing the last of the soap away, a loud splash sent me spinning around. Other than ripples in the water, I couldn't spot what had done it, but the noise had been too loud for it to be a frog or something. "Who's there?"

A dark shape rose up, and I almost screamed. My heart started racing a mile a minute as I remembered Miles telling us that black bears inhabited this side of the state. Did they come this far into water, though? Why didn't I bring my sword with me just in case? Being a slayer didn't mean I wanted to fight a bear while naked in neck-deep water. I could drown just as easy as a normal person.

Then the shape took on a more distinct form, and I relaxed—Aidan. As he rose a little higher, being over half a foot taller than me, the water ran down his head and across his bare chest. His toned body called to me, and it was all I could do to maintain the ten feet separating us. My eyes were glued to all that naked, wet skin.

"I knew you weren't that immune to me," he said.

"You shouldn't be here," I replied, inching backward.

He waded closer. "Tell me to leave."

I swallowed. "Go."

"That wasn't very convincing."

There was something about seeing him in the moonlight, out in the middle of a lake, that made him that much more irresistible. Though we'd each fought our attraction at different times, both of us were drawn to each other like something out of the movies.

"Aidan," I gasped as he closed the distance between us. "We can't do this."

His face hovered inches from mine. "Did you not tell me just a couple of months ago that we should take whatever chances we can get, for however long we have together?"

"It's not as easy as I thought."

He ran his thumb over my bottom lip. "The best things never are."

"I don't think I can do this."

"Why?"

I closed my eyes, wanting nothing more than to wrap my arms around him. "Because I don't think I can survive it when I finally go home to my family and I have to leave you."

"I've told you before that it doesn't have to be one or the other," he whispered into my ear.

"Visiting once every few months won't be enough," I argued.

The water stirred as he swam around me. Like a mare caught in the lustful gaze of a stallion, I couldn't move. He came up from behind and wrapped his arms around my waist. The feeling of his hot skin against mine, contrasting with the cool water, was almost more than I could take. When the hard length of him brushed against my back, I jerked. It was all too easy to remember how he felt inside me.

"Don't end this before it's had a chance to begin, Bailey."

His deep voice ran over me like the water surrounding us. There was nothing more in this world I wanted than to give into him—to give us a chance. "This can never work, and you know it."

"Then perhaps one more night." He nibbled at my neck.

My thighs clenched. He was going to take over my body, and I'd never be able to find myself again afterward. "If we do that, it won't end there."

He was like a drug that I could easily get addicted to. I knew it, and he knew it. Peeling his arms from around my waist, I swam away. It was one of the hardest things I ever did.

16

BAILEY

The next morning I woke up sore and stiff. My sleeping bag had some cushioning, but it could only do so much with a hard floor underneath, and I'd tossed and turned a lot. It hadn't been easy walking away from Aidan the previous night—or rather, swimming away from him. There was a part of me that wanted nothing more than to give in to my feelings. Sure, I'd been the one to push for us to take a chance on each other a couple of months ago, but that was before I realized the full power of our attraction. Aidan could break the Richter scale when it came to the devastating impact he had on me.

Searching around the area we'd set aside for sleeping, I found the sleeping bags for Miles and Danae empty. All three shifters were fast asleep, though, and so was Conrad. A glance at my watch told me it was nine in the morning. Kade had said he wouldn't be able to wake up before ten, and he'd need an hour after that before his aging body would be ready to do anything useful. I needed to ask Aidan exactly how old his uncle was since he appeared to be not much more than fifty. With shifters, appearances could be rather deceiving, though. Aidan looked like he was mid-twenties rather than two-hundred and fifteen. That was enough to make a girl feel young.

Being as quiet as possible, I slipped out of the room, carrying my boots to put them on at the main door. There was no point in disturbing the others when we wouldn't be leaving for a while yet. I headed outside and found Danae and Miles sitting on a picnic bench. They had an array of snacks spread out on the table. I took a seat across from them, grabbed a granola bar, and started crunching on it.

"Hungry?" Danae asked, lifting a brow.

"Ever since I became a slayer, I have to eat something right away in the mornings, or I get cranky." I shrugged.

Her expression turned thoughtful. "Probably your metabolism. Gotta feed all the strength and energy somehow."

Miles pushed a thermos across the table toward me. "Coffee?"

"Where did you get this?" I asked, grabbing it like it was gold.

"Found some in the supplies and decided to make a pot." He gestured toward the grill about five feet away. Now that I was paying attention, I noticed there was still a bit of smoke wafting from the wood he'd burned inside, and the pot he'd used to heat the coffee remained on top. My hunger must have gotten the better of me that I didn't notice before.

I poured some coffee into the thermos cup and took a moment to revel in the taste. Earl made it about once a week, but I didn't always make it over to his place to drink some. The damn man wouldn't give me any to take back to Aidan's lair, and whenever people offered gifts in exchange for me saving them from dragons, I never got coffee. Not even a near-death experience could make them give up the goods. I needed to see if I could work out a deal with Javier to get some because if anyone had a supply, it would be him.

"We are taking *all* of the coffee with us, even if we can't squeeze anything else into the trucks," I said, setting my empty cup down. "And I get half. You two can split the other half."

"I don't think so." Danae whipped her arm across the table, taking the thermos away. I'd never seen her move that fast. Who knew she could be greedier about coffee than me?

I glowered at her. "Since I'm the one who has to fight any dragons we run into on this trip, I think that's more than fair."

"Two points." She ticked off her fingers. "One, I'm the person who heals you guys when you get injured or sick, which can be just as rough on me to do. Two, you've got the shifters to help you. Who do I have?"

Damn, she did have a point, and I could hardly cut Miles out of the deal since he'd just given me some of his freshly-brewed coffee. "Fine, we can split it three ways."

"Agreed." She nodded.

I drank one more cup before heading off to brush my teeth and wash my face. Conrad got up soon after that, and the shifters a short while after him. We packed all our things—and the coffee—into the trucks, barely fitting everything inside the storage boxes. We weren't going far so all three shifters rode with me. I was glad Aidan didn't appear to be mad about last night, but another part of me wished he would get angry because then he'd keep his distance. Instead, he gave me a look that said the war wasn't over yet. This was going to be a long day, and it had just started.

The humans in our group couldn't sense the orb fragment, but the rest of us worked out that it had to be around Robbers Cave down the road. Miles led the way with the RV hauler since he knew the best way to get there, but Danae stayed with him to make sure we were on the right track. The road we took led us through campgrounds along the way, then narrowed toward the end of our journey. After about ten minutes, we arrived. The dark sensation from the orb felt stronger than ever, beating against my skull.

We left the trucks in a nearby visitor parking lot. I wanted to station someone with the vehicles, but Kade said not to worry about them for now, which was the same thing he'd told us last night when Miles suggested rotating guard shifts outside. I hoped he was right because we couldn't afford to lose our stuff or the vehicles. It wasn't easy trusting the shifter's random predictions, but he had gotten us this far.

We hiked up the hill toward the cave. Since it had been a tourist spot, sidewalks and ramps had been built to reach it, but we bypassed those in favor of the direct route. Nearer the cave, there was a high wall of rocky outcroppings that went up at least a hundred feet by my estimates. A set of crude steps had been carved to get up there, but Miles waved me off from those. I couldn't figure out why, considering I felt the orb was somewhere deep inside all the rock and much farther back.

He pointed at a small opening at the bottom of the rocky outcropping. "This is the cave."

After the others peered inside, I took my turn and frowned. "That's tiny. It can't fit all of us even if we crouch down and scoot close together."

"I thought it was kind of strange, too." Miles shrugged. "This isn't a big cave."

Kade moved to the mouth of the opening. "This is the place. We must trust that the answers we are searching for will be inside."

He ducked down and made his way into the interior. Unsure what else to do, I followed with Aidan close behind me. It only took the three of us to fill up most of the space, and I had to straddle a tiny stream running through the middle.

"What now?" I asked.

"Check the walls," Kade ordered.

I began feeling along them, though nothing screamed "touch this to open a secret passageway."

"What about us?" Danae poked her head inside.

Kade held a hand up. "Wait there."

I was glad he told her not to join us because the air was becoming too thick inside the cave, and it was becoming difficult to breathe. Another person would suck what was left of the oxygen out. I began to get light-headed as I scooted along, checking the walls. Stars appeared in front of my eyes and my body grew tingly.

"Is anyone else feeling strange?" My voice came out slurred.

"Yes," Aidan hissed.

The next thing I knew everything went black.

My skull felt like someone had smashed something hard into it. For a moment, all I could do was lie on the cool stone and take deep breaths. It took a minute for the pain to subside to a dull ache. I opened my eyes and realized I wasn't in the tiny cave I'd been in before. I shot up into a sitting position, wincing when a sharp jolt ran through my head. After it faded, I scanned the cavern and found everyone in our group except Miles and Kade. We'd somehow been transported into a large cave that was about forty-feet by fifty-feet and twenty feet high.

Aidan rose to his feet and looked at me. "Are you okay?"

"Yeah. What happened?" I asked.

"I do not know." He walked over and gave me a hand getting up. I ignored the way the touch of his palm felt against mine, letting go of him as soon as I could stand on my own.

"It's like something knocked us out and moved us here," I said, studying the gray stone that emitted a strange glow. At least the illumination allowed us to see without using flashlights.

"It was magic from the spell on this place." He narrowed his gaze as he continued to look around. "I can feel we are even closer to the fragment now, but it's still not quite…here."

"That's the same impression I'm getting," I admitted. The longer I stood in the cavern, the less the orb fragment's presence bothered me, and yet I still knew it was close—as in almost right there.

"Whoa," Conrad said, sitting up. "What the hell just happened?"

Danae and Phoebe rose to their feet, looking around with bewildered expressions.

"You have each been chosen to be tested," a voice said from across the room.

An older man, wearing a light beige robe and sandals appeared. He had short, gray hair, haggard skin, and tired eyes. I was ninety-nine percent certain he had not been standing there a minute ago.

"Who are you?" I demanded.

His dark eyes narrowed on me. "Perhaps, the better question is who are you, and do you have the right to be here?"

"I was asked to come," I said. This situation was getting more confusing by the moment.

"That does not make you welcome," the imperious man said. He would have fit right in during the ancient Roman Empire as a senator. There was so much power lurking in his gaze, and he held himself regally. Of course, the robe added to the effect.

"Then why bring me and my friends into this cave?" I gestured at the others.

"As I said before—to test you."

"This guy is a real fountain of knowledge," Conrad muttered.

"You!" The old man pointed at him. "Have the least reason of all to be here. I can sense your displeasure at being given this task."

"What the fuck is that supposed to mean?" Conrad took a few steps closer toward the man, clenching his fists. "And you still didn't say who you are."

"I am Savion, and all will be revealed in time."

"What sort of test would you have us take?" Aidan asked, coming to stand in front of our group. We'd steadily been inching closer together, though I hadn't realized it until now.

"Your worthiness," Savion answered.

He held out a hand, and a spark of energy shot from it. I followed the burst of light to the far side of the room where a pedestal appeared. On it, there were five red stones about the size of marbles. Savion didn't have to instruct us. Instinctively, we all went over and took a stone into our hands before turning around to face him.

"And now, the test will begin," he announced.

17

Savion lifted his hands and the air thickened. With a twitch of his fingers, an invisible force swept through the room, dragging the five of them across the stone floor. Aidan dug in his heals, but it was no use. They stopped in a circle facing each other. A second later a weight came down, pushing them to the floor. Each of them sat with pained expressions on their faces.

The beast within Aidan growled. He did not like the way the old man controlled them so easily, but they had no choice. This was part of the journey. Kade had said their patience and willingness to complete the quest would be tested. Aidan needed to remember that—no matter how uncomfortable these trials made him. He only regretted that Bailey must suffer through this as well. Glancing over at her, he could see the strain on her face. Was it not enough that he'd caused her to stay in a dungeon cell for several days? It was no wonder she rejected his advances. Aidan had only made her life more difficult since the moment she met him, but he could also make it easier if she allowed it. He knew that he could.

"The five of you have been chosen to recover the orb and make it whole again, assuming you pass the trials," Savion said, meeting each of their gazes. "It must be all of you. If even one individual fails, you all fail."

Aidan found his voice. "We heard there is a chance someone else could get to it first."

"That is true." Savion nodded. "There are dark forces out there scheming to circumvent the orb's safeguards, but they are not strong enough yet. This is why you must do so quickly before it is too late—if you can."

"Alright, man, we get it. Quit beating around the bush and just tell us what to do with these stones," Conrad said, holding his up. "And do we get to keep them afterward? My girl likes red ones."

Savion gave Conrad an annoyed look. "They are not for decorative purposes. You must speak your truth into them, for that is the only thing that will free you from this place."

Aidan tensed. "Do you mean to say if we do not pass the test then we cannot leave?"

The old man nodded. "Precisely."

Everyone tensed, glancing worriedly at each other. Kade had not mentioned anything about these trials having permanent consequences if they failed—other than the obvious problem of the orb getting into the wrong hands. Had he intentionally left that part out?

And had he known all along he wouldn't be selected? If Aidan survived this, he and his uncle would be having a long talk.

Phoebe spoke up, "What truth do we need to tell?"

"The one you do not wish the others to know." Savion's figure faded a degree, becoming ghostly. "Only when your stone has turned clear have you said all you need to say. After they are all clear, the next phase will begin."

"The next phase?" Phoebe asked, but it was too late. The old man had disappeared.

"Man, this is like a drinking game without the drinking," Conrad said, giving his stone a disgusted look.

"Perhaps you should go first and get it over with," Aidan suggested.

Conrad drew his brows together. "I ain't got nothin' secret to tell. What you see is what you get."

"I know I would like to hear why you stay by Bailey's side the way you do." Aidan leaned forward. "No man stays that close to a woman he doesn't have some feelings for."

Bailey made a noise of frustration. "I told you there's nothing between us."

"She's got that right." Conrad nodded. "I got me a nice girl already. I ain't sayin' I'm an angel in disguise, but I'm not no player, either."

"Player?" Phoebe asked.

"A guy who goes around sleeping with a lot of different women," Bailey explained.

"Oh." She shrugged. "Shifters play around a lot when they are young and only commit when they find the one they truly love. What is the harm in that?"

"Um." Bailey frowned, glancing at Aidan with a question in her eyes. "That's...interesting."

"Tell us why," Aidan demanded of Conrad. The last thing they needed was to get into a conversation about shifter mating habits. That could be discussed another time.

Conrad opened his mouth and closed it. "It's kinda hard to explain. I guess it started when she offered to take me home to my grandma. Here was this girl I hardly knew at all willin' to ride with me across the state border, no questions asked. All my life, I've been moving back and forth from my parents—wherever they were stationed—to my grandma's house, but never really found any..." He paused and swallowed. "...good friends. She's had my back from day one, and I try to do the same for her. That's all there is to it."

His stone was still red.

Phoebe gestured at it. "There has to be more you aren't saying. Savion told us that we have to reveal something we don't want anyone else to know."

"Well, there's something else, but it ain't what Aidan asked." Conrad rubbed at a smudge on his boot.

Bailey frowned. "What is it?"

A full minute passed before he looked up. "It's about Christine."

"Okay, and..." she prompted.

"Well, we've been gettin' serious these past couple of months, and she doesn't like me being around you. I think she's either worried I'll get hurt, or she's jealous like Aidan."

"I'm not jealous," he said, even though he knew it was a lie.

Phoebe let out a snort. "Even I can see how you get around the slayer, brother. Don't try to deny it."

Bailey held a hand up, still staring at Conrad. "You mean Christine wants you to stop going out hunting with me?"

"Yeah." He hesitated, not quite meeting her eyes. "She wants me to move in with her and do the whole committed relationship thing."

"What did you tell her?"

"I said I'd think about it." Conrad's expression turned miserable. "I'm supposed to give her an answer when I get back."

Bailey drew in a breath. "Do you have any idea what you're going to say?"

Aidan hated to see the pain in her eyes. He might be jealous of Conrad's relationship with Bailey, but he was beginning to see they'd formed a strong bond that had nothing to do with romance or intimacy. They had become good friends, and she didn't want to lose him.

"I don't know what to do. She said she doesn't want to have anything more to do with me if I don't choose her," Conrad said, shoulders slumping. "And...I sort of love her."

Bailey was quiet a moment. "If you choose her, it's okay. I wouldn't hold anyone back from being with the person they love."

If only she would do the same favor for me, Aidan thought.

"I promise I'll let you know after I decide," Conrad said, rubbing his head. "I just can't make that decision until this is over."

Bailey nodded. "That's fine."

Conrad looked down at his stone. It had turned clear. He lifted it up and gave them all a half-hearted smile. "Guess that's one down."

"Why don't you go next, brother?" Phoebe gave him a sly look. "I know I would love to find out exactly what is going on with you and Bailey. Maybe we could take care of both your stones if you talk it out."

Danae nodded. "I know I've been trying to get Bailey to tell me what's going on for a while now. Maybe this test isn't so bad after all."

"She hasn't told you, either?" Phoebe asked, surprised.

"Nope. Changes the subject every time." Danae shot a disgruntled look at Bailey, who ducked her head.

"Someone is putting off their own revelation." Aidan glared at his sister.

Phoebe's lips thinned. "Don't act like you don't already have a question picked out for me."

In fact, he did. Aidan wanted to find out who Phoebe's lover had been in the Faegud toriq. She'd always been evasive about it, and this was his chance to make her confess. If only he didn't have to make his own revelation in the process.

"Very well." Aidan ground his jaw. "If I must..."

"We slept together once," Bailey interrupted, a blush creeping across her cheek.

Conrad snapped his fingers. "I knew it."

"Damn." Danae's eyes widened. "I hadn't guessed it went that far."

Phoebe's jaw hung open as she looked at Aidan. "Are you out of your mind? It's one thing to feel attraction for somebody who is forbidden—I understand that, really—but do you have any idea what will happen if members of our toriq find out?"

"Which is why I did not wish to speak of it." Aidan narrowed his eyes. "It is between me and the slayer, no one else."

"And it's not going to happen again," Bailey said, lifting her chin.

"That's what they all say." Conrad shook his head. "But the tension between you two tells me it ain't over yet."

"Yes, it is," she insisted.

"Why?" Aidan asked.

"You can't be serious, brother." Phoebe gestured at the slayer. "Even Bailey is smart enough to see it's wrong."

Aidan locked his gaze on Bailey. "Why? That is what I wish to know."

"I'm going to return to my family. It doesn't make sense to start something with you," she said, unflinching.

He didn't believe her. "I'm tired of that excuse and we've already discussed it. Try again."

She clenched her fists in her lap. "Why do you keep pushing this? You were the one who fought against it before."

The moment of truth had come. If he expected her to explain herself, he had to do the same—no matter the cost or the audience. Aidan drew deep from his well of courage, praying he did not come to regret telling her his feelings. For shifters, saying certain words aloud to another person meant a lifetime commitment. He would not be able to take them back later.

Aidan reached over and took her hand. "Because I love you, Bailey. You are a strong and incredible woman who has continued to amaze me every day since we met. I can't let you go without fighting for you and all we could become."

She stared at him, speechless. Aidan didn't look away or show any sign of shame or discomfort. He'd said it and meant it. She needed to know that.

"Dear Zorya, brother," Phoebe gasped. "What have you done?"

Danae knitted her brows. "It's shocking but not that shocking. What's the big deal?"

"By saying he loves her, he's forsaken ever being with another woman."

"Holy shit," Conrad said, then narrowed his eyes. "But I gotta ask. If you love her so much, why did you let her get locked up in that dungeon and let her get her mind probed?"

Aidan was still watching Bailey and the mixed emotions running across her face. She kept opening her mouth, only to close it again. He supposed he had just dropped a rather heavy load on her. It hadn't been his intention to do so, but the rules of the test had required it. There weren't many big secrets he hid from this group that could count for much. Bailey needed another moment by the looks of things. He'd give that much to her and hope she worked her feelings out in her head.

"The alternative would have been worse." Aidan turned his attention to Conrad. "No pendragon in recent memory has ever agreed to speak with a slayer, much less allowed one into their fortress. The only way Bailey could possibly earn his trust was to submit to every demand he made."

Conrad's lips thinned. "What if he'd decided to kill her?"

"I never would have allowed that to happen."

Phoebe leaned forward. "What is that supposed to mean?"

It appeared Aidan must give up another secret. "That I would protect Bailey with my life—if need be."

"Even if it meant you had to kill one or more of our people—maybe even Nanoq?" she asked, expression turning livid.

"I would have tried to avoid it, but if necessary…"

"No." Phoebe shook her head. "Your relationship with the slayer can't have gone that far. I refuse to believe you would kill one of your own people to protect her."

"Yes, he would," Bailey said, speaking up for Aidan. If those were to be her first words after his big confession, they could have been worse. He only wished she'd tell him how she truly felt.

Phoebe threw her hands up. "I can't believe I'm hearing this!"

Aidan turned his gaze to her. "If you ever truly fall in love with someone and they become your world, you will understand."

"What makes you think I haven't ever loved anyone?" his sister retorted.

He lifted a brow. "Have you?"

Sparks practically flew out of her eyes. "Yes—and I still love that person even if I haven't said it aloud to them yet."

"And who might that be?"

"It's not my turn yet. Bailey still needs to answer your question." She nodded toward the slayer.

"I don't...I can't..." Bailey stuttered, looking around as if searching for an escape.

Aidan had never seen her so flummoxed before. Up to this point, he hadn't tried to fully move from his position where Savion put him, but he did now. Aidan crouched in front of her and met her gaze. "No matter what your answer is, you can tell me."

"Aidan, I..." She paused and licked her lips. "This isn't easy."

He grazed a finger across her jaw, ignoring his sister's cursing behind him. "Be brave, little slayer. The sooner you tell me, the sooner we can work this issue of yours out."

She closed her eyes. "You don't understand how…"

"No, open them and look at me," he commanded.

Her lids flew open. "I hate you."

"No, you don't." He smiled.

Bailey drew in a deep breath. "This is exactly what's bothering me. It's like whatever is between us is so powerful that I get lost whenever we're close. I forget to breathe, and I don't care about anything else—my family, friends…nothing. It's too dangerous. We both have responsibilities to other people, and if we're not careful we're going to forget that."

"At least she has some common sense," Phoebe muttered.

"You got that right," Conrad agreed.

"Bailey, you and I can work this out. If we are patient and we take this one step at a time, I am certain we will find a way so that no one gets hurt," Aidan said, pretending he hadn't heard the others. "Did you not learn to control your instincts against dragons?"

"Well, yeah, but that's different."

"No." He shook his head. "That was the most difficult thing you could have possibly done."

"It's never going to work." Bailey tucked a strand of hair behind her ear. "You can't tell me anyone is going to accept us as a couple. Even Phoebe and Conrad are over there agreeing with what I'm saying, and if anyone should support us, it should be them."

Aidan shot a look at the two people in question. They didn't appear the slightest bit repentant. "If they wanted us to be happy, they would stand by our sides."

"It's impossible, Aidan," she said, shoulders drooping. "You never should have made your confession if it means what Phoebe says it does."

Her expression was so forlorn he wanted to kiss the unhappiness from her features. "Then let us take it one day at a time."

"That's like saying you're only going to eat one cookie out of the box even though you know it's a lie." Bailey's lips twisted into a sad smile.

Aidan sat back on his heels. He would do anything for this woman, even if it meant sacrificing his own happiness. "Tell me honestly that you do not want me to pursue you anymore, and I will not mention my feelings again."

"Despite the fact you can't have another woman now?" She lifted a brow.

It was all he could do not to pull her into his arms, kiss her senseless, and tell her that he would never let her go. This had to be her choice. No matter how painful to him, he couldn't force the issue.

"If that is what you wish," he said.

Bailey pursed her lips. "Will I still see you?"

"When it is necessary." He didn't think he could stand being near her beyond that.

She directed her attention to Conrad, studying him. What was she thinking? Was she considering how his own female had put him in a similar situation?

"I don't know," she finally said, returning her gaze to him.

Aidan took that hesitation as a good sign and cupped his hands over her cheeks, leaning close so that their noses almost touched. "One day at a time. That is all I ask. If it becomes too much, we will reconsider our relationship then."

She blinked. "By that point, it could be too late."

"Better to try than not."

"And what about everyone else? What do we tell them?" She gestured at Phoebe. "Your sister is already upset about it."

"This is between you and me. For now, there is no need to make a spectacle about it." Aidan wasn't ready to go that far. He could handle his people hating him, but he could not risk his toriq retaliating against Bailey. Even between the two of them, they couldn't fight that many shifters.

"Can you keep it quiet?" Bailey asked Phoebe.

She shrugged. "I might not like it, but I wouldn't do anything that could get my brother hurt."

"Okay, then we'll take it one day at a time—slowly," Bailey said, lifting her chin and meeting Aidan's gaze.

He felt as if a weight had lifted off his chest. He'd begun to believe he might not get through to her and that he would be doomed to loneliness forever.

Conrad sighed. "Why does love always have to get in the way?"

Bailey glared at him. "Don't make me come over there."

"Like you're really going to do anything."

Before Bailey could respond to Conrad, Aidan pulled her toward him and pressed his lips against hers. He kissed her gently until she relaxed in his grip, then he made it deeper. As their tongues glided against each other, he tried to impress every feeling and thought he had for her. He believed they belonged together, whether she'd fully accepted it yet or not. There were a lot of choices in life, but loving her wasn't one of them. She was the first thought he had upon waking and the last before he slept. Never before had he imagined one female could fill his mind the way she did, but now he knew it was possible to find a woman who completed him. And with every brush of his lips, he tried to convey all of that.

Eventually, loud coughing broke his concentration, and he reluctantly let Bailey go. A glaze covered her eyes that pleased him. She'd been every bit as caught up in that kiss as him.

"I guess the only question that remains is whether you love Aidan as much as he loves you," Conrad said, throat raw from his false coughing. "Because he's got me convinced he's revealed all he's got to say and his stone is clear."

Aidan glanced down at his palm and realized Conrad was right. The stone wasn't red anymore, but Bailey's hadn't changed yet.

She peered up through the fall of her hair, tangled from him gripping it during their kiss. "Of course, I love you. That's what makes this scary, and why I've been fighting it so hard."

He wanted to kiss her again, but he'd have to save that for another time. They'd already given the others enough of a show. Instead, Aidan caressed her cheek. "Perhaps I need to teach you how to slay your fears next."

She rolled her eyes.

Conrad started to laugh. "That's the cheesiest shit I ever heard."

Bailey started to lunge at him, but Aidan grabbed her before she got far. "Let him have his fun. He is only jealous because we've made our decision."

Conrad's mouth shut, and his expression hardened. Aidan ignored his penetrating stare to check Bailey's stone. It was clear. She'd said all she needed to say.

Deciding to save his sister for last, Aidan gestured at Danae. "What confession do you have to make?"

"Me?" Her eyes widened with false innocence. "I'm an open book."

Bailey snorted. "I think we'd all love to know what the deal is with you and Miles."

Danae averted her gaze. "I don't think it's fair to talk about that without him here to tell his side."

"You gonna let us sit in this cave for eternity instead?" Conrad asked.

She tossed some of her blond hair over her shoulder. "Okay, fine, but let's make a deal that whatever we say in this place does not get repeated without permission first."

"Agreed." Aidan could go along with that plan wholeheartedly.

The others mumbled their assent.

Danae fiddled with her nails. "The thing you guys don't know is that…Miles and I dated before. Um, a few years ago."

"What?" Bailey stiffened in Aidan's arms. "Why would you keep that a secret?"

Danae looked like she'd rather swallow a frog than answer. "Because it's my fault things ended. He proposed and…I took an assignment at another duty station that was as far from him as possible. It was ugly. I totally broke his heart, and he hates me for it."

"What the hell would you do that for?" Conrad asked, incredulous.

"I wasn't ready and he was just too intense." She threw her hands up. "It's hard to explain."

"Have you tried working things out?" Bailey asked.

"Yeah, sort of, but Miles isn't the forgiving type. I think short of crawling on my hands and knees, ripping my heart out and handing it to him, and giving the apology speech of the century, he's never going to get past what I did. That's something I have to live with," Danae said, shrugging. There was a look of despair in her eyes that Aidan had never seen before. Up until now, she'd hid her feelings very well, but her story did explain quite a few things.

He lifted a brow. "Do you still love him?"

She licked her lips. "Yeah, but it doesn't matter. He gave up on me a long time ago."

"If that was the case," Bailey said, leaning forward. "Miles wouldn't always act so irrational when he's around you. The only reason he'd do that is if he still has feelings."

"You think so?" Hope lit in Danae's eyes.

"Absolutely."

Conrad spoke up, "I gotta agree with Bailey on this one. That guy is hopelessly in love with you even if he don't know it right now."

"Your stone is clear," Aidan said, pointing to her open palm.

Danae smiled. "Yeah, I guess it is."

He turned to Phoebe. "It is your turn."

His sister gave him a nervous look. "I don't know where to start."

"Tell us about your lover in the Faegud toriq."

Her expression went blank. "That's over. It's been over for a long time."

"Who was it?" Aidan asked.

"No one you know."

He gave her a skeptical look. "We do have to tell the truth here."

"I'm telling you the truth. It was no one you know, and I doubt you ever met them," she insisted.

"Then what are you hiding?"

She worked her jaw. "Someone else—Ozara. I've been seeing her secretly for a while now."

"The…" Aidan started to say "spy" and barely caught himself. Ozara was the best female operative they'd ever had, especially since she could change the color of her scales and shift into any body type to match the dragons she came near. Few knew about her abilities or that she worked as a spy. He amended his response. "The one who is away often?"

"Yes." Phoebe nodded.

He'd had no idea his sister preferred females. She'd never said anything to him about it or given any clue. "When did this start? Did father know?"

"A few months before we crossed over from Kederrawien." She paused and worked her jaw. "Father did find out. He said we could see each other in private, but we must still produce at least one child each with a male before we could make our relationship open. Until then, I wasn't supposed to tell anyone."

On rare occasions, a shifter was born with a preference for their own gender. While some members of their toriq abhorred it, many others didn't care. The real problem was the shifters needed to increase their population. They could not afford to allow anyone to forego producing offspring if they were physically capable. The only way Phoebe would be truly free to see her lover, without bringing shame upon her, was to mate with a male first.

"This is why you have never settled on a male suitor," he surmised. She'd had more than a few offers over the decades.

Phoebe nodded. "I swear I've tried to give them a chance, but I can't find anyone who feels right. And Ozara is still young and too busy with her work to mate with a male. It could be a long time before we are free to be together openly."

"Does Nanoq know?"

"Yes. He told me the same thing as father." She paused. "But he let it be my choice if I go to the mating festival since he understands how difficult this is. I told him I'd go as long as I didn't have to choose anyone."

That was at least something. Nanoq's brother favored males, so the pendragon understood the problem Phoebe faced. He knew she had to find the right male in her own time.

"Wait." Bailey held a hand up. "Isn't it kind of cruel to make you mate with someone you're not attracted to?"

Phoebe drew her brows together. "They don't force us to do it. Eventually, everyone in my position finds someone they can mate with and not feel uncomfortable. It is a matter of waiting until the right one comes along."

"So maybe you and...Ozara could even hook up with the same guy?" Conrad asked, a wicked grin on his face. "Kind of knock out two birds with one stone?"

Phoebe looked at Aidan. "Does the slayer's friend always speak in such strange terms?"

"I find ignoring him works best."

Bailey folded her hands in her lap. "What Conrad is trying to say is could it be possible you and Ozara could share the same guy if you find one you both like?"

"Oh." Phoebe blushed. "Yes, that's happened before with other couples. I just don't know if we'll be lucky enough to find one who would agree to such an arrangement."

Conrad shook his head. "Too bad humans are off limits because I know a lot of guys who'd be happy to help."

Phoebe's eyes rounded. "Really?"

"Hell, yeah. If I didn't have my girl, I'd be down for it."

Aidan's sister let out a loud laugh. She had to have known all along where Conrad was heading with the conversation. "Not in your lifetime or the next, little man."

Outrage filled Conrad's expression. "Who you callin' little?"

In fact, he and Phoebe were about the same size. But Aidan's sister was a warrior with the large bone structure and muscles to go along with it. She saw any male who was not bigger than her as small.

"You know you could have told me about Ozara and everything else? Why didn't you?" Aidan asked. He was hurt his sister hadn't confided in him.

She gave him a weak smile. "It was nothing against you. I just promised father I wouldn't tell anyone and it sort of became a habit to keep it to myself. I've known I preferred women since before you were born."

Conrad shifted his gaze between them. "You don't look that far apart in age."

Bailey must not have told her friend about the difference in longevity between humans and shifters. "I am nearly two-hundred and sixteen years old. My sister is two-hundred and seventy-five. For us, we age very slowly, and shifter births are few and far between."

"You're like..." Conrad paused to do the math. "Sixty years apart. Holy shit. She could be your grandma or something."

"Don't be ridiculous," Aidan said. He'd gone through all of this with Bailey when he had first started teaching her about dragons. She'd had a difficult time understanding the differences between their races as well. "The gap between my sister and I is normal for our kind."

"Yeah, okay, man." Conrad let it go.

Aidan gave his sister a smile. "You know I suspected Lorcan for all this time?"

"Oh." She gave a nervous laugh. "We did have sex a few times—about a year before you two became friends—but I was going through an experimental phase. He was fine being my test subject."

Aidan spluttered. "Then he knew about your preferences, and you both hid this secret from me?"

"Don't blame him." Phoebe wagged a finger. "I made him promise not to tell."

The next time Aidan saw Lorcan, he would be having a long talk with him. Not only had he slept with his sister, but he had also aided her in seeing a female lover and hiding her secrets.

Phoebe lifted her hand, palm open. "The stone is clear."

Relief swept through Aidan. When Savion first said they would have to reveal private truths about themselves, he'd been nervous. There had been no way to know what to expect. Now that it was over, Aidan felt surprisingly closer to the others than before. Had that been the purpose?

Savion appeared before them, his expression stern but his eyes approving. "You have each done well. It is time for the final phase of your quest here."

"Another test?" Bailey inquired.

"I would call this more of a lesson."

18

"A lesson?" Aidan asked.

"Before the orb can be made whole, you must first learn the origins of how it came to be. Pay close attention, for every step of your journey will bring you to greater enlightenment. There are important moments in history that are long forgotten, but it is time they are remembered once more," Savion said.

With a bow, he disappeared, and the room plunged into darkness.

"What the...?" Conrad began.

Then an image appeared before them of a young man and woman—perhaps in their early twenties—wearing animal skins of a primitive design. Both had brown skin and long, dark hair. The female wasn't much larger than Bailey, and the male was lean. They faced each other near a grass hut. It was clear they were arguing, but it took a moment before Aidan could understand their words. They spoke in a language he'd never heard before.

"I want to be with you," the man pleaded, grabbing at the female's hands.

She pushed him away. "No, I have a duty to protect our people, and I cannot allow anything to distract me."

"You will die if you keep fighting them!"

She turned slightly, and Aidan caught sight of a blade strapped across her back. "Then I will die with honor."

"You choose dragons over me." He gave her a disgusted look.

The woman lifted her chin. "I do what I must."

"You are making a mistake," the sorcerer warned, standing over her with his greater height.

"Will you make me ugly like the last woman who rejected you?" she asked and lifted her chin. Despite her bravado, a fleck of fear entered her eyes.

The energy around the male almost made him glow. He was a sorcerer.

"No." He gave her an evil smile. "I will do something much worse."

She took a step back. "I won't protect you from our people anymore. If they choose to kill you, I will turn away and let them."

"My powers have grown. They cannot harm me." The man's eyes took on maniacal gleam . "You just wait and see!"

As the woman backed away from him, the scene faded and the room turned dark.

"What was that, and why could I understand what they were saying?" Bailey asked, gripping Aidan's hand.

"I suspect the magic that allowed us to see this story play out also gave us the power to understand," Aidan said, leaning close to her ear.

They couldn't see each other, but no one had moved from their positions. With the lack of other noises to distract him, he could hear everyone's heartbeats.

Conrad scraped his shoe across the stone floor, likely stretching his legs. "I don't get what that has to do with the orb."

A new scene appeared before them and everyone quieted. The same girl was now in a mountain pass, fighting a green dragon five times her size. Blood covered her left arm, and she limped heavily, though she did not let that deter her from striking the beast again and again. It was likely they'd been fighting for some time. Her chest heaved as she took heavy breaths, and the dragon moved sluggishly. The beast swiped his claws at her. She dove out of the way, barely escaping having her stomach torn open. The slayer landed hard on the ground. As the dragon lumbered toward her, she flipped over onto her back and lifted her sword.

A moment before she could impale the blade into the beast, the sorcerer appeared. He spread his hands wide and called out, "Stop!"

Both the young woman and dragon froze. In an impressive feat, he used his powers to lift them off the ground and levitate them. Slowly, he moved them toward a nearby cave almost completely hidden by bushes.

It had a wide enough opening beyond the brush that with the dragon's wings tucked close, it could pass inside. The sorcerer put them both in there, setting them on the ground, and then stood over the beast. Sparks flew from his hands, flying into the vulnerable dragon.

The sorcerer chanted a series of words, finishing with, "You will become a man now."

Aidan watched in amazement as the pure dragon slowly shifted into that of a human male. Once the transition was over, the man lay there naked with his wounds still bleeding onto the ground. He was large and muscular with short, black hair. Not unlike the shifters of Aidan's toriq. In his yellow eyes, there was fear. The young woman remained frozen as well, but there was anger and abhorrence in her gaze.

The sorcerer looked at her, giving her a pleased smile. "You chose dragons over me, so now you shall have your very own that you will live with for the next ten years. Neither of you will be able to leave this mountain until that time is over and once you do, you will become enemies once more."

With a final burst of magic, he finished his wicked spell and cursed them both to a life together. Then he left, laughing his way out of the cave. Several minutes passed before either of the still figures began to move. The woman was first, climbing up to her knees.

She looked around her. "My sword."

Aidan didn't see it anywhere. It must have fallen from her hands while the sorcerer moved her to the cave. She raced out to get it and came back. By this time, the former dragon had found his footing, but he had to grip the cave walls for support. He had no understanding of how to walk with human legs and feet yet.

"I'm not waiting ten years," the woman swore.

She lunged toward the vulnerable man with her sword pointed directly at his chest. He put an arm up, attempting to deflect it. A breath away from striking him, she came to a stumbling halt. Her hands shook. The expression on her face said she was struggling against some unseen force that would not let her go farther.

"I can't...I can't kill you." After another moment, she tossed the sword away. "That bastard!"

The man lowered his arm a fraction. Curiosity began to enter his gaze now that he knew she could not harm him, but he did not speak. He simply watched her as she began to pace the cave, cursing the sorcerer. Every so often, she would stop to glare at the former dragon and then begin her ranting again. Aidan could see what was happening. She still sensed the beast buried deep inside the man, and it brought out her instincts to kill him, but the magic had done something to prevent her from attacking him. For a slayer, that would be next to torture if she didn't learn how to get her instincts under control.

More scenes flashed before them after that. In the beginning, the woman kept her distance from the dragon man. She made it clear he was to stay away from her, but the food resources on the mountain were limited.

More often than not, he was the one to bring back an animal he'd captured. He'd offer her a portion of meat each time, and she'd refuse. It was only after three days of eating nothing except a few onions she found growing nearby that she gave in. He blew fire to cook the meat for her, and with reluctance she accepted it. Not long after that, she began teaching him how to speak.

"This is how shifters came to be," Phoebe said, awed. "I thought we'd been around as long as the pure dragons."

Aidan had believed the same thing. It was what they were taught growing up.

"How did the slayer line start?" Bailey asked.

"There were always foolish humans around attempting to kill dragons," Aidan answered, pulling Bailey closer into his chest. "One particular family made it their business to kill them. Eventually, they discovered consuming dragon hearts gave them greater strength and protection from fire. After a few generations of such practices, the children of the family began to be born as slayers, only needing to pass the ritual to gain their full gifts. You would be descended from them, and now we know where my race began."

The timeline moved forward, and they were shocked to discover the slayer and shifter became intimate. They'd developed feelings for each other over the long months that passed and began to work together to survive on the mountain. A few scenes later, the woman's belly appeared rounded. They had conceived! Aidan did not think such a thing was possible, but perhaps the sorcerer's magic had something to do with it. A little girl was born. The man and woman doted on the baby and took it everywhere with them.

Dragons came to the mountain occasionally, and the two fought them off, protecting the female child. Aidan glanced over at Bailey and caught a tear running down her cheek. He reached over and wiped it away. Two more boys were born after that, and then another girl. They were a family with no clan or other people to share their life with, but they were happy. The oldest girl eventually made her first shift into a dragon to the amazement of her parents. Later, the oldest boy did the same. They were the first true shifters, and though the father could not join them in the air, he still gave them instructions from the ground on how to fly.

"We were born from slayers," Phoebe muttered between scenes. "I can't believe it. What will our toriq think when we bring news of this?"

Aidan sighed, certain it would make little difference. "They will be in denial."

A new scene began, showing the dragon man collapsing while out hunting. The woman ran to him, frantic and screaming. He went into convulsions as she watched helplessly, and the children joined them, holding hands. Fire began to consume the man. A pit formed in Aidan's stomach as he realized what was happening. From that fire emerged the pure dragon the male had once been. His family backed away from him in horror. He roared with a wild look in his eyes that had not been there during the ten years he'd been human. The woman put herself in front of the children in a protective posture, shock and sadness in her eyes.

"You have to go," she said, her voice shaking a little.

The dragon stared at the family that was no longer his. For a moment, his gaze cleared and there was regret there. He extended his neck toward them, snuffling loudly.

"I promise I will take care of them," she vowed, then took a step forward to touch his nose. "And I will always love you, but please don't make me ever fight you."

A mournful sound came from the dragon's throat. He swung his head back and forth in a sign of grief, then he took off into the air, glancing back only once. The room went dark, and then the stone began to glow around them again like it had when they first arrived. Their lesson had ended.

"That was the most depressing movie I've ever seen." Conrad wiped some suspicious moisture from his eyes.

Bailey's face was pale.

"I had no idea," Phoebe said, shaking her head.

Aidan turned the slayer in his arms and pressed her head against his chest, needing to feel her close. "That wasn't us. You must remember that."

She shook a little. "I know, but it was still sad."

"Yes, it was."

Savion appeared and they broke apart. The older man gave them a knowing look.

"Now you know the first part of the story, but there is more to come." He gestured at Conrad to come forward and gave him a dark fragment of glass. "This is the first piece you are seeking. No one other than him may carry it until it is time to make the orb whole."

Conrad took the jagged piece into his hand and stared at it. "Why me?"

"You have been chosen to be its protector, and as long as you hold it, no other will be able to sense it on your person."

That explained why I suddenly couldn't detect its dark presence anymore.

"Where is the next fragment?" Aidan asked.

A piece of parchment appeared on the pedestal where the stones had been. "There is your map. It will guide you to your next location."

Bailey grabbed it before anyone else and looked it over. "There are no state borders or highways on here."

"No, but there will always be enough to help you find your way." He moved in front of her and put his finger over a spot near the top. "This hill cluster to the north is where you must go next."

Aidan leaned over Bailey's shoulder. He did not recognize anything around the section where Savion pointed, but he did find some of the other landmarks toward the bottom to be familiar. The old man was right that it should be enough if they compared it to the terrain maps they'd brought.

"Is there anything else we should know?" Phoebe asked.

"Your journey will only become more dangerous from this point forward. Take care and protect the man holding the orb piece. It cannot be allowed to fall into the wrong hands," he said, voice ominous.

Then he waved his arms, and a flash of light blinded them. When Aidan's vision returned, he found they were now standing outside the cave. Kade and Miles were a short distance away, staring at them in surprise.

Bailey tapped her watch. "We were in there for four hours."

That sounded about right, judging by the position of the sun in the sky. Aidan gestured at the map still in her hand. "By the looks of it, we must head north next, into Shadowan territory."

"How far into it?" she asked, staring at the parchment and worrying her lip.

He came to her side and studied it again. "We will need to compare this to your modern map before I can be sure."

Kade hurried toward them. "I cannot believe the cave did not take me."

"Are you truly surprised, uncle?" Aidan growled.

"Of course, I am!" Kade furrowed his brows. "I had thought I would surely be selected since I was the one to receive the visions."

He almost sounded convincing enough, but Aidan pressed further. "Did you know if we did not pass the test that we would be trapped inside there forever?"

His uncle shook his head vehemently. "No. Nothing in the prophecy mentioned that, though it did say those who were not pure of heart would suffer consequences for attempting the trials."

He gave him a hard look. "Then it is a good thing we were apparently pure of heart."

Kade gripped Aidan's shoulders, desperation in his gaze. "You must tell me what happened while you were in there. I swear to you I would have rather experienced it for myself if I could have."

His disappointment did appear genuine. Aidan kept his uncle in suspense for a minute longer—it served him right for not warning them—before giving a brief explanation of what occurred inside the cave. Kade didn't need to know all of it, but he did give his uncle the highlights about their test, and how the first shifters came to be. Many questions followed.

"I cannot believe I missed it," Kade said, still outraged.

Conrad crossed his arms. "I would have gladly traded places with you."

Kade narrowed his eyes. "I thought for certain Miles would be the human selected instead."

"Hey, I'm not complaining," the man in question replied.

Aidan looked up at the sky, noting they were losing daylight quickly. "It is too late for us to leave now. The Shadowan will already be roaming up north."

"We will leave as soon as possible in the morning," Kade said, glancing around them. "For now, we will shelter in the same place as last night."

Bailey nodded. "That will give us time to compare maps and figure out which route to take."

"Though it will mean losing another day of the protection spell Xanath placed on us," Aidan reminded them.

His uncle frowned. "Yes, we will have to make up time as best we can tomorrow."

And hope they didn't run into too much trouble.

19

BAILEY

We were on the road by shortly before eleven in the morning. Since the shifters could barely keep their eyes open, they rode in the vehicles with us for the moment. Phoebe took the bed in the back of the RV Hauler while the men rode with me. Kade sprawled in the backseat of the truck, and Aidan sat in his seat with his head resting against the window. I hadn't had many opportunities to watch him sleep before and couldn't help glancing over periodically while I drove. He'd stayed up later than me the last couple of nights, and every time I got up in the morning, he was burrowed in his camrium blanket with his arm over his face. Who knew a man that could turn into a fire-breathing dragon could look so peaceful?

Unfinished road construction ahead forced me to start paying attention to the highway. Most of the cones had been blown into the nearby ditches and fences, but the barriers still stood. No one had bothered to move them since D-day. I idly wondered if I came through here a year from now, would it all still be the same?

The construction crews had left the other half of the highway as dirt, having not repaved that section yet. It was probable that it would never be finished. I couldn't help but think that the world had more or less came to a halt and many things had been left undone. It was rather depressing, but also freeing. If we could get the dragon situation under control and begin to rebuild society, we could do so many things differently. What would it be like five or ten years from now? Would we be better off than we were currently? All those questions and more crossed my mind as I followed Miles' RV hauler and the miles passed us by in an endless sea of hilly terrain. Eastern Oklahoma wasn't nearly as flat as the central part.

We came up on the Robert S. Kerr Reservoir and crossed over it, driving along a divided highway. Not another soul was around aside from us and there were no boats on the water. That was the hardest part about traveling—not seeing many signs of life. Were people still living around here, but hiding? After getting past the reservoir, I spotted a general store ahead. Some silly part of me hoped it was open because it would have been nice to see something still up and running, but my hopes were dashed when I saw all the windows had been boarded up. I should have known better. Regardless, I needed to make a stop soon.

I grabbed the CB microphone and spoke into it, "Hey, Miles. Think we can make a pit stop before we cross the interstate?"

No way did I want to be caught with my pants down once we entered Shadowan territory. At least, not until it couldn't be helped. Taking a break now would give us that much longer until we needed to stop again.

"Yeah, give me a few minutes, and I'll find a place," he said, his voice crackling over the radio.

When he finally pulled over, we were next to a long stretch of woods. It wasn't worth trying to find an actual bathroom since the water didn't run anywhere and nearly every toilet was clogged and overflowing these days. Also, we needed to avoid places where people might be lurking and take offense to our using their place to do our business—hence why it was just as well we didn't drop by the closed general store. The less trouble we got into this trip the better.

Aidan stirred from his sleep and looked around. "Where are we?"

"Last stop before we leave your territory. If you need to, uh, use the woods, this is the time to do it." It occurred to me then that I'd never asked what sort of facilities the shifters used in their fortress. Did they all use chamber pots like they gave Danae and me in the dungeon or did they have something a bit more modern?

He noticed me giving him a funny look. "What?"

"Do you...do you use chamber pots everywhere in the fortress?"

"No." He shook his head. "We have something like your toilets."

My jaw dropped. "How? There's no running water."

Aidan's eyes lit with amusement. "Perhaps not in your human cities, but we've had a long time to figure out how to force water through pipes without…electric pumps, as you do."

"How do you know about that?" I asked.

"We have humans living with us, remember? The topic comes up every once in a while."

It was too bad they'd never let me stay at the fortress. I wouldn't care how many shifters I had to live with if it meant having running water. "You don't have washers and dryers, though, I bet."

He frowned. "I do not recall mention of those."

"They are machines that wash and dry clothes. Before you all arrived, we used them, but now we're stuck cleaning everything by hand without electricity."

"We wash by hand as well," he said, nodding. It was good to know they weren't a perfect little utopia in that fortress.

Kade rose from the backseat. "We have our human servants clean our clothes for us."

I scowled at them both. When they started laughing, I left the vehicle and headed for the woods. Since the season had changed, there wasn't as much vegetation to hide behind, but I managed to find a semi-secluded spot to relieve myself. I made sure there was no poison ivy lurking around first, though. The damn stuff might not have leaves in the winter, but it could still give you a rash if you came too close to it. A lesson I'd learned the hard way, of course. As I was leaving, I caught most of the rest of our group looking for spots to go, including Aidan. His uncle waited by my truck with his arms crossed. There was something in his gaze that told me he had something to say.

"You've grown close to my nephew."

I stopped in my tracks and looked up at him. "We've become friends."

He shook his head. "It is far more than that. Do not try to fool me."

"Are you saying you have a problem with it?"

Kade was quiet for a moment. "Seeing the future is a great burden, especially when it means you learn things that you dare not repeat for fear of changing what will come."

His tone was regretful. I could tell something was really bothering him, and he was having difficulty keeping it to himself. "You saw something about me, didn't you?"

"Yes."

I took a step closer. "What was it?"

"As I said, telling you would change things. I cannot risk that." He gave me a pitying look. "All I can say is that you have dark times ahead, but you must not lose faith—no matter how difficult life becomes or how long your struggles last."

My body turned cold, and it had nothing to do with the chilly weather. "Is this about Verena? About the promise I'll be breaking?"

His gaze bored into me. "Give Aidan a chance. It is through him that you will find the strength to get past the dark times."

"But I don't..."

Kade moved away from the truck. "I must go mark my territory."

As I watched him go, I caught Aidan coming out of the woods. He strode up to me. "What is it?"

"Your uncle." I gestured in the direction Kade went. "He said some things."

"What things?" Aidan asked, glaring at his uncle's back.

"He said I'm going to have dark times ahead."

Aidan moved closer to me. "I don't suppose he told you anything specific?"

"No. He said this was a case where it was important not to tell me the details so I wouldn't change what will happen." I sighed. "What does that even mean?"

Aidan pulled me into his arms, and I allowed myself to revel in his heat. "Whatever it is, he would only keep it to himself if there is something good that will come from the bad. I have learned this about my uncle before."

"So I've got to suffer through the terrible stuff first." I wished his uncle hadn't said anything to me at all. It was a lot easier to assume a bright future if you didn't know any better.

"I will be with you." Aidan leaned down and kissed my forehead. He didn't even care that most of our group was back and watching us. "We will face those troubles together."

"Kade told me you would be the one to get me through it somehow."

He nodded. "I promise I will always do my best to be there when you need me."

We broke apart when Miles walked up. "If you two can spare a moment from your cuddling, I want to go over the maps before we cross into Shadowan territory."

"What route are you thinking?" I asked, moving closer to Miles. Aidan hovered over my shoulder to look at the map as well.

"I figure we keep going north on Highway 59 until we link up with 62. We'll cross over into Arkansas there." He pointed at the border between states.

"From what our clan has been able to gather, the Shadowan hold the land all the way up to this part of…" Aidan paused as he traced his finger up the map and read the words, "Missouri."

Unlike the shifters, pure dragons didn't form their borders according to state lines. They did sometimes use landmarks like rivers, highways, and mountains, but they weren't exactly map readers. I didn't think they could read at all, actually. With the Shadowan, their territory crossed four states once you included a thin sliver of south Kansas. It seemed rather stupid that they'd fought so hard for the small part of Norman we'd taken from them—they had plenty of land.

I dug through a pouch on my leg harness, pulling out the other map the guide had given us at Robbers Cave and compared it to the one Miles held. "The next fragment is going to be somewhere in the southwest Missouri."

"We've still got at least a few hours of driving to do, and that's assuming we don't run into any trouble," Miles said, frowning.

"Then we need to go faster whenever we can because I doubt we'll get that lucky, and I want to get there before dark." I folded my map up and put it away.

"We will continue to ride in your vehicles for now." Aidan looked up at the sky. "If we fly, it will make it easier for the patrols to see us."

That was a good point. "And if they attack?"

Phoebe, Kade, Conrad, and Danae gathered around to join the discussion.

Aidan glanced at each of them. "The first thing you need to do is get the vehicles off the road and cover them with the camrium blankets. This is why we brought such large ones in anticipation of this."

"Yeah, we got that," Conrad replied. "But is there anything we can do to help?"

Phoebe narrowed her eyes at him. "Stay in your vehicles. The last thing we need is to be distracted by humans who can't survive dragon fire."

"You can keep your crossbow ready," I told Conrad. He didn't like feeling useless, and he'd get himself in trouble if he didn't have some sort of role to play. "If any pure dragons get to you and pull the blankets off, you need to be ready to defend the trucks. We're screwed without them."

He nodded. "I can do that, no problem."

Aidan looked at Kade. "You will stay with the vehicles as well and protect the humans."

"Is this your way of keeping your old uncle out of danger?" he accused.

I patted Kade's arm. "I'll be stuck on the ground too, but you know some of the dragons will try coming after the most vulnerable targets. We've actually got the rougher job."

"That's not..." Aidan began.

"Let's go!" Miles announced, cutting him off.

I tossed my truck keys to Conrad. "You're driving. I need to be able to hop out of the vehicle fast."

He grinned. "This is going to be fun."

We got the vehicles back on the road and continued our way north. Kade sat up front this time while Aidan and I took the backseat. Unable to sit still with Aidan and all his radiating heat next to me, I pulled my sword from my sheath and started sharpening it with a stone I had in my pack.

He watched me work. "You've gotten better at that."

I'd been horrible at sharpening blades when he first began training me. "The first time I tried stabbing a dragon with a dull sword, I learned."

"What happened?" he asked.

He knew it had to have occurred when he wasn't around because he never let me go out without the sword freshly sharpened. It pretty much had to be done after every couple of kills because dragon scales were tough to cut through even with zaphiriam blades. One of the first times I hunted without him, I forgot and paid the price.

"The dragon took a small chunk out of me." I held my left arm up. "It would have been worse if not for the bracers, so he only got a few of his teeth in my bicep."

Aidan ran his fingers over my smooth skin. "Take care. Getting bitten in the same place too many times will leave a scar."

I glanced at my shoulder where faint tooth marks remained. I'd nearly died in that battle. Not from the bite wound, but from being knocked off a three-story roof right after my shoulder was crushed in a dragon's mouth. "This one only took once."

"You allowed your opponent to bite too deeply." He sighed. "I wish I could have been there to help."

He'd been in Texas then. Neither of us bothered to mention that it had been my dad who came to my rescue. While I'd lain in a haze of pain and vulnerable to a dragon bent on killing me, my father had showed up and killed the beast. It was the closest I'd ever gotten to meeting my dad in my life. By the time I had recovered from my injuries, he'd left town to return to Tulsa where he did most of his hunting. He had only come down to see me once he heard there was a fellow slayer in Norman, but for some reason after the rescue, he'd decided not to stick around. Aidan suspected it was because I wore shifter clothing. To "The Shadow," as dragons referred to my father, it was an embarrassment that his daughter aligned herself with any type of dragon.

I had no way of knowing if that was why he left, but even if it was, he could hardly judge. He hadn't been around to help me. Sometime after he got my mother pregnant he'd accidentally crossed over into Kederrawien and stayed there until the dimensions collided back together. I didn't know how he'd survived that long in the other world, but he'd developed quite a reputation. Now, he hunted in the Tulsa area and left the Oklahoma City area for me to handle. That was what he told Earl just before he left, anyway.

"That's I-40 up ahead. You guys might wanna look sharp," Conrad said, pointing at the interstate about half a mile up the road.

It looked to be in good condition. The bridge didn't show any signs of damage, so people could travel on it if they didn't mind the risk of roaming dragons to the north. We were currently in the town of Sallisaw. There were no signs of life, but I noted that to my right was a very large cemetery with quite a few freshly dug graves. People must have been around somewhere if they were burying bodies recently. On my left, there was a gas station, but only the pumps remained. The building itself had been torched by pure dragons some time ago, along with several trucks that only had parts of their shells left. The farther we traveled on this trip, the more sights like that I saw. I might have grown used to it in Norman, but a part of me wanted to believe the rest of the world hadn't been as affected. This trip was taking away all my delusions.

Everyone was silent as we drove under the interstate bridge and continued our way north along Highway 59. On the other end, after we entered Shadowan territory,

I was relieved to find quite a few buildings still standing, including a motel and a casino. There were even some cars and trucks in the parking lots we passed, though I didn't see any people around.

"This town could be a lot worse," I said, noting only a few buildings had been burned in the area we currently traveled.

Kade twisted around to look at me. "That is because…"

"Uncle, don't," Aidan warned.

"What?" I looked between them.

"If the dragons don't destroy a place, they have their reasons." Aidan's face was like a mask. "Leave it at that."

Conrad gripped the wheel tightly. "What you're sayin' is they're savin' these folks for later."

Aidan expelled an annoyed breath. "Must you always make things worse?"

"She's a dragon slayer. You can't shield her from that shit."

"He's right," I said, going back to sharpening my sword. Inside, I was so angry I wished a dragon would show up right then so I could kill it. Naturally, none did.

We eventually reached the other end of town and went back to endless countryside. The land rolled and dipped, much like the area around Robbers Cave. It appeared most of eastern Oklahoma was full of hills and forests. In the central part of the state where we lived, you'd think almost every tree struggled with its last breath to grow and survive. It wasn't as apparent in the summer when leaves covered their limbs, but winter showed the deciduous trees for exactly what they looked like without their leafy decorations.

This was the result of the high winds that rolled through the plains in bad weather. They could easily reach seventy to eighty miles per hour, pushing cars around like toys. Strong thunderstorms, tornadoes, and even ice storms also worked to hit the land hard. That didn't show as much in the area we traveled now, though the trees did still appear rather barren. It just wasn't quite as bad since there were more hills and evergreens to give the terrain a fuller appearance.

I kept an eye on the sky, watching for any signs of green dragons. It was turning into midafternoon, and they would be coming out soon. We'd been lucky we missed the patrol when we crossed the border. Aidan had moved over to the far end of the backseat to look out the other window, and Kade had leaned forward to stare out the windshield. Conrad gripped the wheel like he could muscle his way through dragon territory. I hated feeling this vulnerable. It was different when I hunted in Norman where everything felt familiar, and I'd claimed it as part of my turf. Out here, we were the strangers invading someone else's land. The only good thing about it being dragon roaming time was that it reduced the chances of any humans bothering us. They lived in fear out here.

There was one big issue I was trying not to think about. The wild scent of the shifters was getting stronger the longer I sat in a closed vehicle with them. I hadn't killed a dragon in a week now, and the need to slay grew stronger every day.

Driving helped keep my mind off of the problem, but Conrad had taken over. If one of the Shadowan didn't show up soon, I didn't want to think about how difficult controlling my instincts might become. Aidan might be okay for a while since his scent was the most familiar to me, but Kade didn't stand a chance once I lost control. Even now, I was eyeing the back of his head and thinking deadly thoughts. I hated this part of myself. It seemed to have gotten worse while Aidan was away for two months.

It wasn't until we'd reached the town of Stilwell that Kade called out, "There!"

He must have had eagle-eye vision because I could barely make out the tiny shapes moving to the north-east of us. I grabbed the radio mic and informed Miles of the patrol. The brake lights on his truck immediately brightened as he slowed down. We were still far enough from the dragons that we kept going, but not nearly as fast. Only if the beasts turned in our direction would it be worth the trouble of stopping. Sometimes they had their eyes on other prizes, and it wasn't worth wasting time hiding when they had no interest in us. Still, I could feel my heart pumping harder with the increasing potential for a fight.

We finished passing through Stilwell and continued north. The dragons were still some distance away, but their figures had grown larger. I could now make out that there were three of them flying. The road started to curve northeast and we headed straight for them. Miles hit his brakes ahead.

Aidan reached through the seats and grabbed the microphone from the front. He'd watched me enough times to figure out how to speak into it. "We still aren't close enough to them yet. Keep going, but not too fast."

"Are you sure?" Miles asked, his skepticism coming through loud and clear over the radio.

"Until they notice us, we keep going."

We only had about three hours left of daylight thanks to sunset coming early at this time of year. If we hoped to make our destination by dark, we couldn't afford too many delays. Plus, we could easily take three dragons and be on our way soon enough. It was waiting for them to leave the area that could take a whole lot longer. We'd all had enough experience with them by now to know that.

The radio crackled twice before Phoebe's voice took over, "Brother, I'll let him know when to stop. He's just nervous about his borrowed trucks getting damaged."

Aidan pressed the talk button. "Your trucks will be fine, Miles."

There was no response after that. I could only guess he was arguing with Phoebe and Danae over what to do.

A few minutes later, the dragons turned in our direction. I could see them well enough now to tell they'd spotted us. They streamlined their bodies and started flying fast in our direction. Miles hit the brakes hard and pulled onto a narrow dirt road, waiting to park until he got us under some tree cover. The shifters and I didn't even wait for the trucks to stop before we leaped out of the vehicles and ran back toward the highway.

Aidan and Phoebe lit up in flames, shifting to dragon form. Kade and I pulled out our swords. The dragons were closing in on us fast, dropping altitude as they came closer. As the seconds ticked by, I prayed Aidan and his sister finished shifting quickly. A glance back revealed the others were pulling the large camrium blankets over the vehicles. The black cloth wasn't a perfect fit, but close enough that only the bottom of the wheels were left vulnerable. We'd brought extra tires in case they got damaged.

Turning back, I watched Aidan take flight with his sister a second behind him. They barely got into the air before clashing with two of the Shadowan. The third was farther behind, but it looked like it planned to bypass the ensuing melee and attack Kade and me. I met the beast's red gaze, letting it see its inevitable death in my brown eyes.

"I've got this one," I said.

Kade frowned at me. "Are you certain? This is a large dragon."

"I haven't killed one in nearly a week. If I don't get this out of my system, you're going to be one of my targets soon," I said through gritted teeth. "My control over my instincts still has its limits."

He stepped away, giving me space. "Then by all means, slay the beast."

The dragon rushed toward me with its jaws wide open. My blood pumped through my body and fueled me like gasoline poured on a fire. This beast was flying too low for me to use my favorite "crouch down at the last second and stab the belly" move. Twenty feet...ten feet...I dropped the sword, leaped up and grabbed it by its jaws, using the dragon's continuing momentum to swing to the top of its long neck. Wrapping my legs tightly around its throat, I let go of its head with one hand and pulled my dagger. There was a soft spot just behind the skull where a blade could push through.

As the dragon continued its flight, trying to get higher now that I was on it, I stabbed downward. The zaphiriam dagger went straight through the thin scales and into the soft spot, piercing the beast's brains. I twisted for good measure. The dragon floundered and crashed onto the road. I flew off, hitting the pavement hard and rolling over and over until eventually landing face down in a ditch. It took a moment for the stars to clear from my vision, but then I managed to get on my hands and knees.

A pair of legs appeared before me. "Are you insane?"

"No." I peered up through my fallen black hair.

Aidan's face was a mask of anger. He reached down and jerked me to my feet. "Did I not teach you to never jump onto a flying dragon? He could have taken you high in the sky and dropped you. Even a slayer cannot survive that."

"I knew what I was doing," I said, pulling away from him to brush off some loose gravel and dried grass from my body. Other than a few scrapes and small cuts, the damage was minimal. I'd be good as new in half an hour with wounds that minor.

"Bailey, that trick was not necessary, and you know it."

I glanced over at the dragon remains lying in the middle of the road. Its wings were crumpled and its tongue lolled out of its mouth. My dagger still stuck out from the top of its head. I'd have to remember to grab that on my way back, along with my sword.

Reluctantly, I dragged my gaze back to a very upset Aidan. "This is what happens now when I don't kill a dragon often enough. All I can think about is the fastest way to take it down and in this case…" I paused to point at the beast's body. "That was the quickest."

"Do you feel better now?"

I nodded. "Yes, I do."

He expelled a breath. "How often do you need to kill?"

"At least once every four or five days if I don't want the blood lust to start up. Each day after that, my control diminishes." I could see him doing the math and figuring out I'd gone a week.

He ran a hand through his thick, black hair. "And as long as you kill a dragon every few days, you will not take such high risks?"

I could see he was trying really hard to be patient with me because he knew this was a part of my nature. He might have helped me strengthen my discipline, but I could never be anything other than a slayer. It boggled my mind that he'd actually admitted he loved me the day before. How could he possibly care that much about a person genetically disposed to killing his kind? Every time I saw him, I couldn't decide whether to punch him or kiss him for making his confession to me. We still hadn't talked about it. I needed time to think through all the ramifications, so I'd told him to give me time. For now, we were close, but not too close.

"Right." I nodded. "It's easier to think and control myself if I've killed one recently."

Aidan pulled me into a tight hug. "Then, Zorya help me, I will make certain you kill a dragon every few days."

I looked up at him with a smile. "Every two days is even better."

He let out a martyred sigh. "Don't push it."

"You two need to help clean up this mess so another patrol doesn't find it," Phoebe called out from the road.

We broke apart reluctantly. The dead dragons would need to be dragged into the trees and covered with stinguise juice so their brethren wouldn't sniff them out before their corpses disintegrated in forty-eight hours. It was the only way to be sure the Shadowan didn't figure out we were in their territory and come looking for us. At least there were enough of us to get the job done fast.

20

BAILEY

For the next hour, we drove in watchful silence, waiting for another dragon patrol to show up. Crossing into Arkansas had been uneventful as we continued our way north. The land had become flatter and wider open with sparse trees dotting the landscape. There would be no way any pure dragons could sneak up on us in this area, but it also meant we wouldn't have anywhere to hide the trucks.

"You'd think there would be more of them flying around," I said, glancing at Aidan.

He shrugged. "We estimate the Shadowan have about five or six thousand members in their toriq. With their territory being vast, and their preference for nesting in larger towns, it is not entirely surprising we haven't seen more."

I supposed he had a point.

"Does that gas station look open to you, Bailey?" Conrad asked, leaning closer to the steering wheel.

We'd entered Siloam Springs and had been driving through it for a couple of minutes. I squinted at the large fueling station down the road with yellow trim and white-washed walls. It didn't show any signs of damage, and not only that—I could have sworn there were lights on inside. I frowned and checked both sides of the road. The whole town looked like it was in better shape than anywhere else we'd passed through on our trip. The traffic lights didn't work—no surprise there—but I could almost hear the faint hum from the electric lines with my enhanced senses. I'd never been able to do that before since I didn't become a slayer until after the power grid went down. There still weren't any cars on the roads, but when I peered down a side street, I saw a couple of people standing on their lawns. No fear of being caught out.

"We need a better map of this area anyway. How about we stop by there?" I suggested.

Conrad knitted his brows together. "You don't think that could be dangerous?"

It could, but we didn't have much farther to go before we reached our next destination, and it wasn't like we were easy targets. "We're never going to find out how life is anywhere else if we just pass every place by, and we've only got maybe an hour or so of driving left."

"The sun will set in a little over two," Aidan said, checking the sky though the window. "But I agree we should talk to the humans here. They could provide us with useful information."

I got on the radio and told Miles to pull off at the gas station. He argued but ended up doing as I asked. We parked the trucks in front with the shifters and I getting out first to check for any signs of danger. Around the side of the building, I noticed a man standing there smoking a cigarette. He appeared worn and haggard, maybe in his early forties, with thinning brown hair.

"Is this place open?" I asked.

He nodded. "Yep. They ain't got no gas left, though, if that's what you're lookin' for."

"Okay, thanks." I turned toward the others. "How about Aidan and I go inside? The rest of you can stay out here and keep an eye on things."

Phoebe gazed around with suspicion. "Don't stay too long."

"We won't." I gestured at Aidan, and we entered the building.

Going inside, I discovered I was right about the electricity. The overhead lights were on and even the coolers appeared to be running. My nose caught the scent of freshly brewed coffee. I wanted to go straight to the back where the pots were set up, but forced myself to search for the person running the place first. The last thing I needed was to die because of coffee, though there were worse things to get killed over.

No one stood behind the checkout counter. I noted the shelves weren't even half full with merchandise and nearly all the cigarette slots were empty, but a few packs remained. Earl would throttle me if I didn't get him some after he'd made a point of asking. They might be bad for his health, but these days smoking was probably one of the last ways you could go.

"Can I help you?" a woman asked, coming from the storage room in the back.

"Um, yeah." I took a few cautious steps toward her. "How do you have electricity?"

She narrowed her eyes at me. "You're not from around here."

"No, just passing through."

"We don't have any gas." She gestured toward the front window. "Stopped sellin' it months ago."

"But you have electricity?"

She nodded. "What's left of the fuel goes to keep our power plant runnin'. We're working on other ways to keep it goin' after that."

I noticed Aidan had left my side to inspect the store. The woman kept glancing between him and me like we might be shoplifters or something.

"Don't you have any problems with the dragons?" I asked.

She grinned. "Nope."

"How?"

"Magic," she said, not bothering to explain further.

I tensed. "There's a sorcerer here?"

"I suggest you tell me what you need and get goin'. As long as you don't cause any trouble and don't stay long, you should be alright."

Suddenly, I was all too happy to hurry up and get out of there. The last thing we needed was a run-in with an unknown sorcerer. "Do you have maps of this area?"

"Yeah, I do." She headed around the back of the counter and pulled one out. "You got somethin' to trade?"

I thought about the supplies in our trucks, particularly the spare stuff we'd picked up along the way. "We've got some hot chocolate packets and granola bars."

She lifted a brow. "That'll do, though I gotta see 'em first."

I glanced back at Aidan. "Can you get them?"

He hesitated, clearly not wanting to leave me alone with the woman.

"I'll be fine," I reassured him.

Aidan gave me a warning look to be careful before heading out of the store.

"That man has strange eyes," the woman said, a shudder passing through her.

"It's a genetic mutation." Which wasn't entirely a lie now that I'd learned how shifters came to be. "His whole family has the same problem."

"And what about you?" She looked me up and down.

"What do you mean?"

"As best as I can reckon, there ain't no more Comic Cons these days and sure as heck not around here." She gestured at my outfit. "Don't know what you're thinkin' wearin' that getup."

I wasn't about to explain. "It's more comfortable than you would think."

She shook her head. "I heard tell it's gonna get cold tonight—might even be some snow. You should consider a jacket."

"I'll do that," I said. There definitely had to be a sorcerer around here if she even knew about the weather, but it couldn't be her, or Aidan would have reacted differently.

He pushed through the door a moment later with two boxes of hot chocolate and a pack of granola bars. Moving aside, I directed him to put them on the counter. He backed up a couple of steps to stand behind me in a protective posture. I couldn't help but be amused that he thought I needed any kind of help against this woman.

"I want some of those, too." I pointed at the cigarettes. "Two packs."

She glanced down at the counter. "You got some rare items to trade, but they ain't that rare."

"There is more coming," Aidan said over my shoulder.

Conrad came in a moment later with a medium-sized box filled with canned soup. He brushed past us to put it on the counter with our other offerings. "You can have this stuff too, but..." He paused to search around the store. "I want a Snickers candy bar, a pack of gum, and two energy drinks."

The woman rifled through the box. There were about twenty cans of beef and chicken noodle soup inside. They had to be worth something, though I had no idea what kind of shortages this town had. It could easily vary from location to location in a post-apocalyptic world.

"Alright, ya'll got yourselves a deal." She handed me the cigarettes and map, then let Conrad grab his stuff. "Now I suggest you get goin'."

I eyed the coffee longingly, but decided it wasn't worth staying longer. "Thanks."

We headed back outside and found a strange man talking to Phoebe and Danae in the middle of the parking lot near the gas pumps. Conrad hurried toward the truck, fully aware of the orb fragment he carried on him. Miles appeared to be checking under the hood of his vehicle—though he hadn't mentioned anything was wrong with it—but he glanced up long enough to give me a brief shake of his head. Kade was nowhere to be found. His scent lingered in the air, though, which made me think he hadn't gone far.

Aidan made a growling sound as we approached the stranger, who had his attention on Phoebe. There was something about the tall man that bothered me. Maybe it was the black trench coat covering him from his neck to his ankles, or the spiked blue hair that stood straight up on top of his head. As we came around to face him, I decided his eyes stood out the most. They were the coldest ice blue I'd ever seen. I doubted he was much past his early thirties, but there was something ageless about him.

"Sorcerer," Aidan cursed under his breath.

"I am Bacchus." The stranger gave him an imperious look. "Who are you?"

Phoebe sidestepped in front of us. "He's my brother, Aidan, and next to him is..."

"Slayer," Bacchus interrupted, his gaze lighting on me. "I've never seen one who could tolerate the presence of dragons so well—even shifters."

The hairs on the back of my neck stood up. Normally, I wouldn't hide behind anyone in the face of danger, but Phoebe was the only one among us who had a way of deflecting magic. Not only could she shield herself against the worst of it—as I'd first thought—but she'd learned how to extend that protection a short distance. While the immunity might not be fool proof, it was close. As the sorcerer's gaze stayed on me, Aidan let out a snarl and started to go around his sister. I grabbed his wrist and held it tightly. If not for my slayer strength, I couldn't have pulled it off.

"She can be surprisingly disciplined when she wants to be," Phoebe answered, glancing back at Aidan and me with a warning in her eyes.

Bacchus flashed a set of even, white teeth. "And yet she's killed many in the short time since she began her career. I could use one such as her."

Aidan fought my hold. I had to wrap my arms around him to keep him from attacking the sorcerer. The magic emanating from Bacchus was so thick that it was a miracle we didn't all choke on it. Alarms rang in my head, telling me that touching him would mean death. Aidan probably knew that as well, but his jealousy had overtaken common sense. The sorcerer had baited him on purpose and maybe some of that magic had filtered past Phoebe's shield.

"Look, we apologize for encroaching on your territory," she said in a placating tone. "We promise to leave right now."

Bacchus dragged his gaze from me back to her. "You need not leave so quickly."

Says the spider to the fly attempting to leave its web.

"No, we really do." Phoebe waved at us to go.

Danae stepped next to Aidan's sister and spoke in a forceful tone, "You could put a lid on that, you know. No one likes a show off."

I grabbed Aidan and dragged him toward our truck. Conrad was already climbing into the driver's seat, and Kade was coming from around the back of the store, moving slowly enough you almost didn't notice him. As soon as we were all inside, Aidan's uncle twisted toward us with a grave expression on his face. "Say nothing until we leave this place. There are eyes and ears everywhere."

It took Phoebe and Danae a couple of more minutes, but they somehow talked the sorcerer into letting us leave. The women headed for the RV hauler where Miles had already started the engine. We didn't waste a moment before hightailing it out of there. I glanced back once to find Bacchus watching us from the gas station parking lot. Even at a block away, his cold eyes still felt like they pierced right through me.

SUSAN ILLENE

For the next few minutes, we rode in silence. Siloam Springs wasn't huge, but it was one of those towns that sprawled out as it grew and it had more than a few recognizable chain stores and restaurants to fill it. Eventually, we entered the rural countryside again. Kade turned in his seat to look at us and frowned at his nephew. Aidan was still breathing heavily from fighting the urge to hop out of the truck and go after the sorcerer. I was still keeping a tight hold on his arm. Bacchus had really gotten to him—even more than expected.

"I apologize for hiding while that…man was there. Just before he arrived I had a vision of him that told me I must avoid him at all costs," Kade said, lips thinning. "He is the most powerful sorcerer I have ever encountered."

"Why didn't you warn the rest of us?" I asked.

Kade ran a hand through his dark, wavy hair. "There was no time. You were already inside, and I had to act quickly. The vision revealed to me that Bacchus was capable of discerning an individual's abilities and weaknesses if he came close enough. Of all of us, it warned that I must not let him near me."

I supposed that made sense, considering his powers.

"He knew about me right away—even with Phoebe trying to block us." I expelled a breath. "And I could feel how strong his magic was."

Aidan's voice came out raw, "He knew exactly how to provoke me."

Kade nodded. "While his reactions to you two were problematic, Bacchus never would have let us leave if he had a chance to read me. My vision told me he would discover I was a seer, and he'd choose to keep me for his own uses."

"You don't think he could have overpowered us, do you?" I had wanted to avoid a fight with him, but mostly because it wasn't worth it if we could simply leave. Not for a moment had I thought our group could lose a battle to one man—even a very strong sorcerer.

Aidan's uncle gave me a pitying look. "He wouldn't have needed to overpower us. All it would have taken was him seeing that every one of us is willing to lay down our lives to protect the weak and innocent. He would have used that against us to get what he wanted."

I hadn't looked at my traveling companions as a whole like that before, but Kade was right. The need to protect people brought us together, but it could also become our downfall. If Bacchus had figured it out, he could have used the citizens of that town to bring us to our knees.

"As soon as we came out of the store and I saw that guy, I knew he was trouble," Conrad said, keeping his eyes on the road. "I thought about shootin' him, but then I remembered I had the orb piece in my pocket, so I stayed by the truck."

Kade gave him an approving look. "You did well. The guide in the cave must have chosen you to be protector for that reason."

271

Could Savion have known we'd run into trouble? How sentient, or even prophetic, could a mystical guy hiding in a cave for thousands of years be and still retain his sanity? Or maybe he had slept for all that time until we showed up. I supposed I could ask the next guide if one appeared there.

I grabbed the new area map I'd picked up at the gas station and checked it against the one Savion had given us, then stared closer. "That's strange."

"What is it?" Aidan leaned closer to me. It didn't take him long to notice the same problem. "Did the map change?"

"Yeah, it did. This was more of a regional map before, but it's like the whole thing zoomed in once we got close enough to the next fragment." There had only been major landmarks before, but now smaller ones appeared and even roads. The designers might not have programmed state borders—maybe because they didn't matter once dragons invaded—but they did somehow include stuff that didn't exist until recently.

"Was it like that before we stopped?" Kade asked.

"No." I shook my head. "It was all very generic with just a few terrain features and landmarks to guide us. If Savion hadn't pointed at the precise spot we needed to go, we wouldn't have even figured out the vicinity of the next fragment."

"It must have been a failsafe in case we lost the map," he concluded.

Aidan grunted. "And now that we are past the danger and near the next location, it is giving us more information."

I checked the magic map against the modern one. "Looks like we only have about twenty miles left to go."

A good thing too, since the sun was about to set.

21

BAILEY

We had to pass through the sleepy town of Noel, Missouri before reaching our destination. Most of the homes and buildings still stood, but I didn't catch any signs of life this time. Considering darkness was falling, I supposed that wasn't all that surprising. There could very well have been plenty of people still occupying the town who stayed hidden at the hour we went through. As the setting sun colored the sky orange and red, we caught sight of two dragons flying far in the distance. Everyone in the vehicle—except Conrad—could feel the next fragment getting close. Over the radio, we urged Miles to finish the journey.

It turned out the fragment was located inside a place called Bluff Dweller's Cavern. We had to follow a two-lane country highway to get to it and pull into a small tourist parking area across from a tiny pond. I got out of the truck, taking in our surroundings and noting the dragons had flown out of sight. From my vantage point, I spotted a couple of older stone houses and outbuildings—none appearing occupied—on my side of the highway spaced apart by vast, open fields. Another house sat on the other side of the road that looked like it had been built in the last decade or so. No lights were on in it either, but a white SUV was parked in front of the garage. On either side of the small valley where we were located, there were hills covered in dense forests of trees. They blocked my last glimpse of the sun as it set.

I took a moment to stretch my legs before joining the others who'd gathered around to study the row of rock steps on the side of the hill. We were tired, but we still had a mission to do and limited time to finish it. The sorcerer back in Arkansas might be able to track us if Xanath's spell wore off too soon.

"Do we make camp or go in now?" I asked.

Kade rubbed his chin. "We have no idea how long this may take, or how far our next destination may be. I would suggest going in now."

Danae sighed. "I agree. It's only 6 p.m. and even if we finish a little late, we can sleep after that."

"I guess I'm game," Conrad said.

Though I'd certainly had more strenuous days than this in the physical sense, I was already feeling exhausted. Spending the whole day in a hyper state of vigilance and fighting a dragon had worn me down. Still, I agreed with the others. We couldn't afford to waste another minute. I glanced at Aidan, who stared back at me. He was being generous enough to wait for my vote before giving his own preference. Little things like that made it even harder to resist him.

First, though, we needed to consider what we were getting into. "Anyone know anything about this place?"

"Nope." Danae shook her head. "But considering there's a sign for the cavern entrance, I'm guessing the cave is bigger than the last one we visited."

Miles nodded. "I agree. You all might want to take some supplies with you for this one."

We moved to the back of the trucks and stuffed two spare packs with food, water, and flashlights. As a precaution, I added a first-aid kit and a couple of emergency blankets in case we got stuck in there for a while. Small spaces didn't bother me much, but I sincerely hoped the cave was stable. It might have been a tourist spot before—meaning it couldn't have been too dangerous—but who knew what might have happened to it during D-day. This area may have been hit with earthquakes just like Oklahoma.

Once we were satisfied we had everything we might need, and we'd had an opportunity to answer nature's call, we made the trek up the stone steps. At the top, we reached a narrow stretch of flat area with a museum down to the left and a ticket office to the right. Spaced about a hundred or so feet apart were two separate entryways into the cave.

"Which one do we take?" I asked. Though I could sense the fragment somewhere inside, I couldn't get a precise lock on it to know where we should start.

Aidan pointed at the one by the ticket office closest to us. "Let's try that one."

We reached the doors and found them locked. It took Aidan and I pulling together to break them open. As soon as we did, a rush of warmer air hit us. Until then, I hadn't realized it was that cold outside despite the fact everyone else wore jackets. Only I had chosen to forgo putting one on because the chill didn't seem to bother me as much.

I frowned. "Are caves supposed to be this warm?"

"Yeah." Conrad nodded. "Most of them stay about fifty-five to sixty degrees all year."

"How do you know that?" Danae asked, surprised.

He shrugged. "My folks were in the military. Whenever I stayed with them, they tried to take me to do stuff and be a family and shit."

Conrad didn't talk about his past often, but he never ceased to amaze me at what he revealed. We flipped on our flashlights and headed inside. Kade and Miles watched us, staying by the doors. They'd go back and keep an eye on the vehicles once we left their sight. I shifted my light around to get a sense of the cavern, which was large enough that we didn't need to squeeze together tightly or worry about ducking our heads. As we went farther in, the ceiling opened even more and we found ourselves in a dome-like room. I spied hundreds of soda straws and stalactites coming down from the ceiling, formed by thousands of years worth of water dripping down—as Conrad informed us. They appeared like sharp icicles that could pierce a person if they dropped. We didn't have trouble with slipping on the floor despite the moisture in the cave. At some point, gravel had been added to the path.

In the dome room, I found there was more than one direction we could go. "Which way?"

"Uhh." Conrad moved his flashlight from one tunnel to the next.

"That way," Aidan said, pointing directly in front of us.

I'd considered the one with the stairs and railing, but my sense of direction was failing me inside the big, dark cavern. All I could think about was the tons of rock over and around me. Just because it appeared stable for the moment, didn't mean it was.

We moved forward. Our flashlights could only penetrate so much of the darkness and there were lots of nooks and crannies due to water carving the place, rather than man. It wasn't neat and tidy. Nature tended to make her creations like works of art that you could spend hours studying if you had the time.

Aidan led the way through the narrow tunnel. We couldn't all stand abreast anymore, so we moved in a single-file line. My shoulder brushed up against the limestone more than once. Conrad hissed at me, saying it could damage the stone. Since when had he become such a nature lover?

The cavern widened a little and Aidan stopped in his tracks, causing me to bump into him. He glanced over his shoulder. "There is a strange glow ahead."

I peered around him. He was right. A little ways down the path, a soft light broke the darkness.

Phoebe, who had taken the rear of our line, gestured at us. "Keep going. I feel like that is where we are supposed to be."

"Agreed," Aidan said, though like me, he didn't appear all that excited about it. Maybe the tight confines of the cave were getting to him, too.

We slowly inched forward and the light continued to glow brighter until we each turned our flashlights off. The shape of a person began to take form. I squinted and decided it was feminine. After a few more feet, my initial suspicion proved right. A woman with thick, black hair falling to her waist, tan skin, and square features watched us approach. I was guessing she might be Native American by her appearance. She didn't speak, but she lifted the palm of her hand toward us, and we stopped. Then she pointed toward the ceiling.

We turned our gazes upward, and the roof of the cave began to reshape itself. The stalactites disappeared, taken over by something that looked like a puddle of still water. It was silver and calm at first, but soon images began to form. The rest of the cave fell into darkness so that we couldn't see anything except the scene that began to play out before us.

A grungy-looking man with a spear in one hand and a bloody sack in the other walked through a thick patch of woods. I couldn't be certain, but I thought he might be in his late-twenties or early thirties. He had dark-blond curly hair, matted and stuck to his neck. His hands were caked with dirt and blood from hunting—maybe for his next meal? He walked with assured grace, hardly making a sound with his footsteps. This was an area he knew well, and he'd likely passed through it a hundred times.

He broke through the woods to a clearing where the sun shone brightly, and horror filled his gaze. Like a camera shifting position, the scene angle went from focusing on the man's face to coming behind him so we could see the same view. In the valley below, a village with thatched roofs sat nestled next to a small river. Several dark gray dragons were attacking it, burning and destroying everything in the place. My vision colored red, and I had a desperate urge to jump in there and fight every last one of them. This was what I was born for—protecting people from dying in such a terrifying manner.

People screamed and ran, some of them women with babies in their arms. Others were men attempting to fight the fire-breathing beasts with their simple spears, though it was no use. Anyone who fought died quickly. They only bought time for the others to try to get away to safety. I saw one family make it to the edge of the woods on the other side where they lifted some kind of trap door in the ground and jumped inside, disappearing below. Luckily for them, none of the dragons noticed. I could only hope for their sake that the beasts didn't sniff them out later.

"Gray dragons?" I overheard Danae ask. Her voice cracked when she spoke, and I glanced over to find tears filling her eyes.

Phoebe cleared her throat. "They are common in the far northern climates. Up close, you can see they even have a thin layer of fur growing from their scales. It helps them handle the cold better."

"Gray or green—they are some sons of bitches either way," Conrad said, rage filling his face. "I wanna jump in there and slam those motherfuckers with a few RPGs. See how they like that!"

I knew exactly how he felt, but I also recognized there was a point to us seeing this carnage. "This happened a long time ago. Nothing we can do about it now."

Conrad ground his jaw. "Yeah, I know, but a man can dream."

Aidan took my hand in his. There was an apology in his eyes as he looked down at me. "I am sorry you must see this."

"It's okay." I gave him a weak smile. "I'm sure we'll find out why soon enough."

Gazing back up at the ceiling, I found nothing of the village remained except black scorch marks in the dirt. The man who'd been out hunting when the attack began had fallen to his knees, sorrow written all over his face. A minute later, the family who had hidden underground appeared. There was a man, woman, and two girls around seven or eight years old. The father reached out to the grief-stricken hunter, hesitating before placing a hand on his shoulder. He was the older of the two and there was great wisdom in his eyes.

"Brother," I thought I heard him say. "I am sorry for your wife and children, I..."

The hunter lifted his gaze and his eyes began to glow. I gasped, realizing for the first time that he was a sorcerer.

"They have to pay," he said, rising to his feet.

The older brother shook his head. "I told you that is not the way, Finias."

"I don't care anymore!" the hunter shouted, startling the little girls and making them cry.

"Your magic is too dangerous—the price too high."

"I've lost everything." Finias took a step back, distancing himself from his older brother and the girls in both the physical and emotional sense. "It doesn't matter what I do now."

The scene faded away before opening to a new one. Some years must have passed because the hunter/sorcerer looked older and his curly hair had begun to gray. Finias sat at a table, hunched over something he worked on. The angle changed so that we could see his face and the fanatical gleam in his eyes. He lifted the object in his hands, and I caught my first glimpse of the orb fully intact. It was like glass—only a little murky in the middle so you couldn't see all the way through it. Despite the fact this had occurred long ago, the power and energy radiating from it reached through the scene to touch us. The shifters and I gasped.

"Oh my God," Danae said, dropping her jaw. "The magic coming from that thing reeks of death."

"What do you mean?" I asked.

"He sacrificed lives to make it."

"The fool." Phoebe's lips thinned. "He killed members of his own race just so he could get revenge on dragons."

Conrad snorted. "Bad guy logic has never added up for me."

"He does not care because his family is gone," Aidan said, drawing our attention to him. "Men such as him cannot handle a loss of that magnitude without their sanity going as well."

"That doesn't make it right, and he has to know that," I pointed out.

His hand squeezed mine where he still held it. "It is easy to judge someone when you have not faced their circumstances."

That was one more reason to love Aidan. He had a way of seeing through to the heart of the matter that most others could not. "Just do me a favor and don't ever go on a rampage if something bad happens." I lifted my chin. "I don't want to be the one who has to stop you."

He put a hand to my cheek, caressing it. "Then I suggest you don't ever die. I guarantee nothing if that ever happens."

"That's so sweet," Danae said, sighing. "I wish a man loved me like that."

Before anyone could comment further, the scene above us changed again. This time the sorcerer strode across a field with the orb raised high in his hand, fitting perfectly in his palm. Behind Finias, a hundred red dragons flew in perfect formation in the sky.

Aidan snarled. "He used shifters."

"That *fushka*," Phoebe cursed in her native tongue.

From beyond the next rise, nearly twice as many gray dragons appeared. They did not fly in perfect formation, but rather like a group who'd been called to battle at the last moment. The sorcerer called out, "Dijis!"

The red shifters zoomed toward the gray dragons with murderous intent. They collided together, blocking out the blue sky in a tangle of wings and talons. Roars and growls filled the air, as well as the harsh sounds of pain. Dragons had a way of yelping in a similar manner to dogs—if a little less high-pitched—when they were hurt. Over and over, we watched both red and gray beasts fall to the ground in crumpled heaps. The shifters were heavily outnumbered, but they fought as savagely as the pure dragons. Before long, though, no red remained. I thought I caught a sniffle come from Phoebe, but I couldn't tear my gaze away from the scene to check. It was enough that Aidan's hand gripped mine so tightly I thought he might break bones.

The sorcerer, surrounded by the mangled corpses of dragons, sent more power into the orb. It glowed bright. "Dijis!"

My jaw dropped when half of the remaining gray dragons moved to attack their brethren. They hesitated midway, the looks in their eyes revealing their helplessness as they were forced to battle their own kind. Finias' face was a mask of concentration. It was one thing to order one clan to fight another, but making them attack the ones they cared about took a lot more power. His hand was shaking by the time the battle finished, and only one horribly injured dragon remained. The sorcerer made his way over to it, sidestepping the corpses in his path.

"Galus," Finias said in a commanding tone.

The dragon struggled for a moment, but then it shut its eyes and expelled a final breath. *He must have commanded it to die. I might be a slayer, but at least I gave my opponents a chance to fight back. This man took all their free will away and made them do terrible things.*

A new scene appeared, and I discovered I'd only begun to see the lengths the sorcerer would go to in his crusade for revenge. Before our eyes, we watched as Finias led three humans through the snow. They were in a mountainous region where they had to take care with each step. They paused before a dark cave entrance, then the sorcerer gestured for his followers to go inside. Finias still had the orb in his hand, and the people with him walked almost like robots. No emotion reflected in their eyes.

The tunnel opened up into a huge cavern that must have been a couple of hundred feet high. There were nooks and crannies everywhere that dragons could use to build nests and most of them were filled with sleeping beasts. The three humans—two males and one female—gazed around. Finally, a hint of fear flickered in their gazes and their bodies shook. At least thirty dragons used the cave as a den. Even if these people were slayers, they couldn't hope to kill them all once the beasts woke up. This was a suicide mission.

"No." I covered my mouth with my free hand.

The sorcerer held the orb out and narrowed his gaze on his targets, whispering, "Dijis!"

The woman and two men struggled against the command, shutting their eyes and clenching their fists. The slayers would have felt an instinctive killing rage the moment they spotted all the dragons, a command to kill them only adding to that, but they still had some sense of self-preservation. Our kind would risk our lives even when there was just a small margin of success, but if it appeared death was an absolute and certain thing, we could fight our instincts. Otherwise, every slayer would die the moment they ran into a large nest. Something had been written into our genetic code to at least give us that much control.

"Dijis," Finias said a shade louder this time.

The slayers' eyes snapped open. They pulled their blades from their scabbards and each ran in a different direction. Their movements were silent and deadly at first, stabbing dragons in their kill spots so they never even had a chance to cry out a warning. Perhaps five died that way before the others awoke. Then the real battle began and the slayers were attacked on all sides. They hacked and slashed with a precision I hadn't quite mastered yet. These were experienced fighters who'd been hunting dragons for years so that they'd become the perfect warriors. I was both amazed at their abilities and terrified for them.

Then one of the male slayers failed to dodge a tail strike and went flying through the air, slamming into a cave wall. A dragon blew a billow of flames, blinding him, while another went in to chomp at his legs. A scream filled the air. When the flames subsided, the man lay with only stubs at his knees, bleeding profusely. A beast lunged forward and swiped at the slayer with its sharp talons. The man thrust his blade into its neck, twisting until the dragon choked on the metal. Then he withdrew the sword and plunged it into the creature's heart. It fell heavily to the ground, mixing its blood with the slayer's on the wet stone.

The man didn't get his sword free in time, opening him to another dragon. The beast finished him off by chomping his head and ripping it from his shoulders. I flinched and had to look away for a moment. Even after all the battles I'd fought, this was the most gruesome one I'd ever seen. Aidan pulled me close to him. Though I didn't want to appear weak, I couldn't resist the warmth and security he offered. Something told me he needed the reassurance just as much. We were watching slayers die after all, and he'd fallen in love with one.

When I forced my gaze back up to the scene, I found the remaining man and woman standing back to back. Both were bloody with their clothes ripped and gashes covering their exposed skin. Part of the woman's long, blond hair had been shorn off, revealing her high cheek bones and striking blue eyes. She was a beautiful warrior, and she had her back to a large, muscular man who could have given Brad Pitt a run for his money. They fought, calling commands to each other and facing off against the remaining twenty dragons. The battle seemed to last forever. One-by-one the beasts went down, barely able to get at the slayers now that they worked in concert. The sorcerer stood on the sidelines. He watched the man and woman fight with a satisfied expression on his face.

I wished I could jump in there and stab him to death.

Eventually, two of the beasts purposely thrust themselves on the slayers' blades. I thought Finias might have commanded them to do it, but then the other dragons climbed over their fallen brethren—the swords still stuck in them—and clawed at the man and woman.

The talons ripped into their heads and faces, pulling them apart. After that, it only took seconds for the beasts to finish them off. The man died quickly, but a sign of life remained in the woman as she lay bleeding out on the cold stone. She inched her hand toward the fallen man, not quite able to reach him, and whispered something I couldn't catch. Her breath shuddered once and her body went still.

Eight dragons remained. The sorcerer turned them on each other, and as the battle played out to its sad conclusion, the scene faded away. This time, the murky pattern in the ceiling didn't change to another scene. Instead, the natural cave roof returned with all the stalactites hanging down. A soft glow filled the walls, enabling us to see everything around us in detail.

"I'd kill for one of those cat videos on YouTube right about now," Conrad said, grimacing. "That shit was depressing."

He had no argument from me there.

A breeze brushed by us, and we turned to find the silent guide standing at the end of the tunnel again. The Native American woman stared at us with ancient eyes. Then she clapped her hands, and everything went dark.

22

PHOEBE

Phoebe found herself in a different part of the cave she didn't recognize. She spun around, searching for the others. It was quiet—too quiet. She inhaled deeply, but the only odors she took in were the subtle hints of limestone and a slight mustiness in the air. Phoebe suspected no one had been in the caverns for months before they arrived.

The tunnel was narrow enough that if she spread her arms wide, she could touch the walls on either side of her. A soft glow emanated from the limestone, enabling her to see her surroundings well enough. There was a small pool of water beside her feet, and a reddish-orange salamander sitting next to it. Was it looking at her? She narrowed her eyes on the creature but couldn't be certain.

This had to be another test. They might not have gotten the chattiest guide at their last stop, but this newest one made Savion appear sociable. After what they'd been forced to confess, she worried what they might have to do at this one. She'd already told her brother her deepest secret, and though Aidan took it well, it left her feeling vulnerable. Phoebe enjoyed having a few things she kept to herself, and with her lover being a spy, she didn't want to bring unnecessary attention to Ozara. They'd each agreed to keep their meetings private. On the other hand, it did give her some measure of relief to no longer hide such a big part of herself from her brother.

"Is anyone there?" Aidan asked, his voice drifting over to her.

Phoebe spun around, spotting his head poking out from around a curve in the tunnel. Where had he come from? She hurried in his direction, ducking under a large piece of flat stone that protruded from the wall at shoulder height. In the section where her brother stood, the tunnel opened wider and gave her a measure of breathing space. Though dragons enjoyed dark caves as nesting places, Phoebe wasn't certain she would want to live in one if the fortress was ever not an option.

She reached her brother, grateful to see a familiar face. "Did you just arrive?"

"Yes, a moment before I called out to you. When you disappeared, we did not know what to think." He leaned against a stone wall, defying Conrad's earlier warnings. "Maybe the others will join us soon."

"Maybe." Phoebe checked one end of the tunnel, finding only darkness where she'd stood a minute ago. She turned to check the other way and caught a glimpse of light coming from that direction. "Do you see that?"

Aidan moved next to her and squinted. "I think someone is down there."

She took off first, leaving him to follow behind. The tunnel narrowed again so that they could barely fit through the passage without brushing against stone. As they got closer, a distinct figure began to take shape in the light. Phoebe skidded to a halt, almost tripping as her boots caught in the gravel.

"Father?" she cried out.

Aidan grabbed her arm. "It can't be."

In the circle of light, only Throm's head and chest showed. Then the rest of his body formed, and he almost appeared whole, but there was a luminescent quality about him. Phoebe resisted the urge to reach out and touch him. If she found nothing except air, it would only make the pain of seeing him again that much worse. It was difficult enough having him standing right there and not know whether he was real or not. What sort of test forced them to face a lost loved one?

"Children." Throm nodded. "I have missed you."

Phoebe and Aidan exchanged glances. Their father almost never expressed his feelings.

The figure chuckled. "You do not believe it is me, but I assure you it is. Zoyra has allowed me to come here so that I might help you in your quest."

"You were angry with me the last time I saw you," Aidan said, a hint of pain in his voice. He'd suffered the worst of all because of his estrangement with their father. "I find it hard to believe you are happy to see me now."

Throm gave Aidan a pitying look. "I see much clearer now, son. Death has a way of removing everything except the simple truth, and I've discovered a lot about you."

Aidan stiffened. "Such as?"

"Your actions of late greatly disturb me." Their father shook his head. "It is my own fault for not watching you more closely and guiding you as I should have. The fact you have fallen in love with a slayer only proves my failure."

Aidan sucked in a breath, and his gaze filled with hurt. Phoebe might not agree with her brother's choice of a female, but she could see how happy he was with Bailey. Aidan had never shown such passion for life. Before he met the slayer, he seemed to do everything without any true drive or purpose. Now, he behaved like a man who cared and wanted to make a difference in the world. Phoebe might be having a difficult time accepting the slayer as something more than a passing interest for her brother, but if Bailey could make Aidan a better man, then perhaps she was meant for him. Who cared what their father thought?

"What do you want from us?" she asked.

"And the daughter who failed me when I only wanted one thing from her—to succeed me as pendragon." Throm's expression twisted. "But you could not even win a simple battle against another female, could you?"

"We do not have to listen to this," Aidan said, moving in front of Phoebe. "If you've only come back to judge us, we've heard enough."

Throm's eyes sparked. "I have but one simple task, and the orb—fully intact—can be yours. Your journey will be over and you can return home."

"What? How?" Phoebe asked, stepping around her brother.

"Kill the slayer."

"Absolutely not!" Aidan barked. Then he leaped through the air as if to tackle their father but fell through the image and landed hard on the ground. He climbed back onto his feet to glare at Throm. "This is just a trick—you're not even real."

"Am I not?" Their father looked down his nose at Aidan. "Then how is it I am able to upset you so easily? You may have shown a measure of discipline around your brothers, but I could always see through your act. More than two centuries have passed and you still behave like a child. I should not have been surprised when you disappointed me in the end."

Phoebe balled her fists, shaking with anger. "You had over a thousand years to learn and grow, father, yet your entire emotional capacity could fit into a single raindrop. The fact you cannot see what an amazing person Aidan has become astounds me. As far as I am concerned, you're just a cold and bitter old man who is best forgotten!"

"How I mourn Zoran's poor decisions near my death." Throm shook his head. "Because he was the only one smart enough to cast his emotions aside. He understood they would only cloud his judgment and weaken him."

"I'm done listening to this," Aidan said.

He spun on his heels and began walking the other way. He'd barely made it a few steps when the ominous sound of stone sliding against stone filled the tunnel passageway.

Aidan came to a sudden halt, pressing his hands against a wall of rock that had not been there before. Phoebe's heart skipped a beat. Had their father just trapped them inside this cave? She'd never been fond of small spaces, but as long as she could get out of them she could handle it. This was like her worst nightmare coming true.

"Let us out of here," she said through clenched teeth.

Throm's expression turned pleased. "Swear a blood oath that you will kill the slayer as soon as you leave here, and you will be free."

Aidan marched back toward their father. "I will never do that!"

"What about you, daughter?" Throm gazed at Phoebe. "Are you willing to spend an eternity here to protect your brother's lover?"

She swallowed. The walls were closing in on her, and she could hardly think beyond wanting to find a way to escape. Would she be willing to kill the slayer if it meant not having to stay in this place a moment longer? Not just that, but they could get the orb and go home. This entire journey would be finished.

Then she looked at her brother's face and saw the panic there. He truly loved Bailey. If Phoebe chose to kill her, she'd lose Aidan forever. They would fight, but she didn't think her brother had it in him to hurt his own sister even at the cost of the slayer's life. This decision fell completely on her whether she was willing to go that far to get what she wanted.

Closing her eyes, she uttered the words that would damn her forever. "No. I won't do it."

"Very well." Throm's form began to fade. "Enjoy your new home."

As soon as he disappeared, Phoebe fell to her knees. "Dear Zorya, what have I done?"

Aidan moved to crouch down next to her. "Thank you, sister. I know that was a difficult decision to make, but I am indebted to you for it."

Her throat was closing in and she couldn't breathe. "I need water."

"Here." Aidan handed her a canteen from the pack he carried.

They had enough supplies in there to last them for a few days, but after that, they would slowly starve to death. A shifter could go a month without eating. They might grow weaker by the day, but as long as they had water, they could survive for a while. Between the canteen that refilled itself every hour and the water filtering down the cave walls, they had plenty. But how would she survive being stuck in this cave for that long, waiting to starve to death?

23

CONRAD

Conrad paced back and forth along the tunnel, no longer impressed when the limestone lit up whenever he got close. They could keep their hocus-pocus crap, tryin' to keep him trapped inside this place like a caged animal. He just wanted out of here, and if it didn't happen soon, he was gonna start bustin' up some stones till he found a way out. Protecting a cave was only worth the trouble if you weren't trapped in it.

What kind of messed up shit was this, anyway? One minute he, Bailey, and the others were standing together, and in the next they started disappearing one by one. Only he got left behind, still stuck in the same spot where they'd watched that jacked up movie, or flashback, or whatever in the hell they wanted to call it. That was hours ago. At least, he was pretty sure, but his watch stopped working so he couldn't figure out the time anymore.

Movement at the top of the tunnel caught his eye. Was there something up there? The magical glow didn't light up the roof of the cave like it did the walls, and it was hard to see anything. He squinted, trying to make out what had captured his attention. Just as he focused on a dark shape, a bat came flying straight for him. Conrad squealed like a little girl and fell on his ass. Fuck, that gravel didn't feel too good.

He took a quick glance around to make sure no one had seen him. Ha! Who was he kidding? Wherever the others were, it wasn't here. He'd walked from one end of this cave to the other and hadn't found a dang thing. The way out no longer existed. Conrad couldn't even find the other tunnels they'd seen when they came in, so all he had was this one.

He climbed to his feet and dusted his pants off, cursing because he'd gotten them dirty. No way was he going to have a chance to wash and press them smooth during the rest of this trip. Conrad hated dirty, wrinkly clothes.

His mouth was getting dry. He'd passed on carrying one of the two packs they'd brought with them, and now he regretted it. How was he supposed to know their group would get split up? Then he remembered a small pool of water down the passage with a plastic duck sitting on a rock above it. What the hell a yellow ducky was doin' in this cave, he couldn't say, but it had an old design with its red mouth yawning open that wasn't common anymore. It may have been there a while.

Conrad returned to the pool, ignored the duck, and cupped his hands to scoop some water. He didn't worry about it being contaminated or anything. He'd been on enough cave tours growing up to know that ones like this—especially if they were made of limestone—had pure water. It all got filtered through the rocks as it came down. He drank several mouthfuls before his thirst finally went away, but then he was left to wander around again. Too bad that guide wasn't here so he could tell her exactly what he thought of the quest locations and their damn tests. She might not have anything to say, but he had plenty.

At the end of the tunnel where it had been dark, a soft light appeared.

Conrad tensed. What if the people who set this place up decided to test them by havin' strange creatures attack them when they least expected? Like those fools in the movies, he still couldn't resist moving closer. One careful step at a time, he walked toward the light all while planning his battle strategy. As he got closer, he slipped a folding knife from his pocket and glided it open. If they wanted to mess with him, they'd get a fight.

A dark figure moved within the glow, but he couldn't make out a distinct shape. Whatever it was, he hoped it had eyes cuz he was gonna sink this blade in one of them. Let the creature try attacking him if it couldn't see.

Then what had been a blobby shape took on form, and he stumbled to a halt. "Grams?"

"Hey, baby," she said, smiling at him like it was all good. "I'm so glad to see you."

Conrad wanted to believe it was her, but it just didn't seem possible. Still, he folded the knife closed behind his back in case it was her. She always took his blades away. "Is that really you?"

"They said you might not believe it." She sighed and moved a little closer to him. "But do you remember what I did for your eighth birthday?"

"Yeah," he said, still skeptical.

She looked just like he remembered, other than the weird glow all around her. Same curly, gray hair from her putting it in rollers every night, and curvy body that said she cooked real good and had no problem eating everything she made. Her skin was dark like coffee without the cream, and she had the kindest eyes he ever saw. If she wasn't his grams, they'd produced a perfect replica of her.

"I baked you a cake in the shape of your favorite toy car. What was it?" She tapped her chin, thinking. "Oh, yes. It was a Lamborghini, though I think you changed your mind about it the very next week when your dad sent you a Porsche."

Holy shit, this woman knew things that no one else could...but that didn't mean it was her. "They could have pulled those memories from my head or something. If you are my grandma, how did you get all the way up here? Last time we talked, you were still in Dallas."

She ducked her head and let out a shuddering breath. "I am sorry you have to find out this way."

"Find out what?" he asked, taking a step closer.

"I passed away two months ago," she said, giving him a sorrowful look.

All this time, Conrad had been keeping hope alive that she was okay. He'd needed to believe that, figurin' that when Bailey found a way home he'd go with her since they'd be going in the same direction. Her family's ranch wasn't too far from Dallas.

"It can't be." He backed up a step, shaking his head. "I would have felt it or somethin'."

"It's true, but I am in a better place now, baby. It's okay."

"They always say shit like that, but I ain't ever bought it," Conrad said, starting to get angry. He didn't want to believe his grandma was dead. He couldn't.

She shook a finger at him. "What have I told you about that language?"

It was her scolding tone that broke him. Conrad fell to his knees and trembled as tears ran down his face. He'd told himself so many times that he would get back to his grandma as soon as he could find a way, and now it was too late. Maybe he should have just tried jumping the damn chasm to get to her. Why had he thought he had more time?

She hovered close to him. "If it helps, your cousin Bryan was there. I wasn't alone."

"How—" Conrad swallowed. "How did it happen?"

"In my sleep," she said, her voice gentle. "My medication ran out, so we knew it was only a matter of time, but I didn't suffer."

"I'm sorry." He wiped his wet cheeks. "I shoulda been there."

She gave him a teasing smile. "And what could you have done?"

"I woulda found you some more medicine. No way would you have gone out like that with me around." Conrad stood, anger rising. "Bryan should have gotten it for you."

She sighed. "He tried and almost died twice. The streets weren't safe."

It was easy to forget that most people didn't have a dragon slayer with them when they went around town. Even with Bailey, Conrad had gotten shot by looters once and almost died. He had to remember Bryan wasn't much of a fighter and trying to grab anything from a pharmacy would have been dangerous. Conrad supposed the fact his cousin tried at all should have counted for something, though it was hard to acknowledge that. Letting Bryan off the hook wasn't easy when it meant they'd lost their grandma.

"So what are you doing here now?" he asked. As much as he appreciated getting to see her again, he didn't think the people who'd designed the test did this as a favor.

"They brought me back so that I could make you an offer," she said, clasping her hands in front of her.

"What offer?"

"Your parents are living in the new American government territory," she began.

Conrad's chest tightened. He hadn't even let himself think about what happened to his parents. Since they served in the army, he figured they would have been on the front lines fighting the dragons as soon as they arrived. He and Bailey had seen up close how hard it could be for the military to take them down. Conrad had figured he'd lost them, though he'd never voiced that fear out loud. Bailey had tried asking him about it, and he'd just told her he didn't know where they were.

"You mean that safe zone they set up on the East Coast?" he asked. The suggestion that his parents were still out there left him stunned. He wasn't as alone as he thought.

She nodded. "Yes, baby. The military has them working in Asheville, North Carolina. They've been there...well, since soon after the dragons came, and they're helping protect people. I know they're worried about you." Her gaze softened. "If you leave now, you could be with them in no time."

Conrad frowned. "I can't even get out of this cave, much less all the way to North Carolina."

"Don't worry about that." She took a step closer. "If you promise to go straight there and leave all this behind, you'll find your path open."

Conrad put his hand in his pocket and grabbed the orb fragment. "What about my friends? What about us stopping anyone from getting the orb?"

"Take the single piece you have with you. You'll be so far away no one will ever find it, and without your fragment, no one can ever put the orb back together," she said and smiled. "Everyone will be safe, and you'll be with your parents again."

He didn't know what to say. It all sounded so reasonable, and the thought of finding his family after all this time was like dangling a carrot on a stick. He'd hardly let himself dream he might see his mom and dad again, much less believed it. Could his grandma be telling the truth? Could Conrad leave, never look back, and make his way to the East Coast on his own?

"Grams." He worked his jaw, trying to figure out what to say. "I got a girlfriend and Bailey and other friends who count on me. Are you sayin' I gotta leave them all behind without even tellin' them goodbye?"

Her gaze turned sad. "Your friends here...some of them are already failing their tests. This is the only other way to keep the orb fragments from getting in the wrong hands. I know it sounds difficult, but you'll be protecting them. This is why you were chosen to hold the first piece because those who designed these trials suspected something like this might happen."

"I don't—" He rubbed his face. "I don't know what to say."

"Say 'yes' and everything will be fine." She gave him an encouraging smile.

Conrad turned his gaze in the direction he knew would be the way out if they opened it back up. If his friends really were failing, could he leave them behind?

24

DANAE

anae sat huddled in the cold and dark, shivering. She'd pulled the blanket from the supply pack and wrapped it around herself, but she still couldn't seem to get warm. Being trapped inside a dark cave for who knew how long and unable to see had taken a toll on her. She'd been afraid of the dark as a little girl, but she thought she'd gotten past that. Guess not.

When Danae first found herself separated from the others and sealed inside a cave room alone, she'd tried finding a way out. She'd ran her hands over the rocks, searching for a crevice or some sort of exit. There was nothing. Who knew how far into the caverns they'd taken her, and for that matter she could be stuck in an unexplored area. These bastards who'd designed the trials probably thought it was funny to make them miserable in their quest to get the orb. She wished she had some kind of magical powers that could force the rock open so she could leave, but that was definitely not a part of her skill set.

A soft light began to form about ten feet away. She squinted, trying to adjust to it after sitting in pitch-black darkness for too long. It brightened at a slow and steady pace, giving her eyes the time they needed. About five minutes passed before two shapes began to form inside the light. She stood, shrugging off her blanket.

"Who's there?" she asked.

No answer. The shapes began to coalesce into human forms. Though her heart pounded hard against her chest, she moved closer. Something about those shapes seemed familiar. Then the faces began to emerge and she cried out when she recognized them.

"Mom? Dad?" She leaped forward in an attempt to wrap her arms around them, but went right through their silhouettes to smack into the cave wall. The pain stunned her for a moment, but it wasn't that bad—just a scrape across the cheek.

She spun around and discovered they'd moved to the middle of the cave room. Both of them watched her with love and happiness in their eyes. She'd thought she would never see them again since they'd been vacationing in Scotland with her younger sister, Candace, when D-day came. There'd been no way to find out what happened to her family or contact them. She'd tried to imagine they were okay, and that things weren't as bad over there as in America. Maybe it was silly, but sometimes a person had to lie to themselves if they wanted to keep getting up in the morning.

"Hello, sweetheart," her father said, his brown eyes as comforting as ever.

Since the last time Danae had seen him during Christmas break almost a year ago, he'd grown his brown hair out so it was medium-length instead of super short like he'd kept it while she was growing up. Other than that, though, he hadn't changed much. Her father still looked strong as ever despite being in his mid-fifties now.

Maybe it was a stupid question, but she had to ask, "How are you guys here?"

Her parents exchanged glances, then her mother met her gaze with regret lingering in her eyes. "The mystical forces that run this place brought us."

"All the way from Scotland? That's impossible!" Even with being a sorceress, Danae found that hard to believe. Nothing was powerful enough to transport people across thousands of miles and do it in such a short span of time. This had to be some kind of trick. These people might look like her parents, but they couldn't actually be them.

Her father cleared his throat. "If we were still alive, that might be true—"

"You're...you're dead?" she said, a hitch in her voice. She didn't want to believe it, but she had learned enough from Verena to know some sorcerers could bring back the dead temporarily in forms like this. Her chest tightened. If that was the case, this could all be real.

"I am so sorry, honey," her mom said, taking a step closer to Danae.

Her mother looked ethereal standing there with her long blond hair hanging down, and her golden skin still amazingly smooth and blemish-free. Most people believed she and Danae really were mother and daughter with such similar features, but Danae had actually been adopted when she was two years old. Her real parents had died in an accident.

She backed up a step, shaking her head. "This has to be some kind of trick they're playing on me. You guys can't be here—or, uh, dead."

Danae just couldn't allow herself to believe it.

"This isn't a trick," her father said. "We survived as long as we could, but when the dragons attacked our hotel, we weren't able to escape in time. I hate to say this, sweetheart, but we passed away months ago."

Danae's gaze ran between her parents, and somehow she suspected it could be true. She couldn't explain it, but in her heart she knew she had truly lost them. "What about Candace?"

"Your sister is fine," her mother reassured her. "In fact, she has just boarded a ship with some other Americans to return home."

"Really?" Danae asked. "Isn't it dangerous to travel that far these days?"

Her father nodded. "There are water dragons, but we are in a place now where we know for certain she will make it back to America safely. She only needs you to find her and protect her after she arrives."

"How would I even know where to look? From what I've heard, most of the port cities on the East Coast have been destroyed, and that's assuming I can even make it that far on my own." There was no way anyone she knew here in Oklahoma would make that kind of journey with her.

"If you leave now," her mother said, glancing at her father. "Your paths will cross not long after she arrives. This is your best chance to find her."

Danae furrowed her brows. "You mean abandon my friends and the quest?"

Though she loved her sister, they weren't close. Candace had been a surprise for her parents who came three years after they'd adopted Danae. Five years separated them, and her sister had always liked to throw it in Danae's face that she wasn't *really* family. That point of contention had been so bad that it was partly what drove Danae to join the military. While their parents had always loved and accepted her, Candace had not. They said it was jealousy. Her sister looked less like their parents than she did, and she had an inferiority complex. Danae couldn't take it anymore and found the fastest way out.

Her mother gave her a pleading look. "We know you two have had your differences, but there is no one else who can protect Candace like you can. It's going to be dangerous when she returns. We know we can count on you to help."

They'd always relied on her. Danae was the dependable one while Candace broke every rule and did whatever she wanted. Still, could she tell her parents no? Could she live with herself if she abandoned her sister and left her to face this world alone?

"What about the quest? My friends are depending on me to help them, and if we fail, the orb could get into the wrong hands. Hundreds or even thousands of people could die." And one thing she'd learned in the military was when your choice was between saving one or many, you always picked many.

Her father's expression tightened. "Your friends are already failing their tests. You wouldn't be abandoning them because your quest is over, and now you have to think about your sister."

"In case you haven't noticed..." Danae gestured at the surrounding walls. "I'm trapped here."

Her mother gave her a reassuring smile. "Promise you will leave right away, and you will be able to get out."

Danae stilled. "So what you are saying is all I have to do is agree to go find my sister, and I can leave this place? And if I say no, I'm stuck here forever?"

"I'm afraid so, honey," her mother said. "This is the only way we can save you."

She looked between her parents, torn as to what to do. Danae wanted them to be real and to know she was at least getting this one chance to talk to them. But she didn't like the ultimatum they'd given her, which didn't seem right. The magical forces could be feeding them what to tell her and manipulating Danae's parents to force a certain conclusion.

"Mom, Dad," she began, looking between them and memorizing their faces. "I love you both more than life itself, but I'm calling bullshit."

25

BAILEY

I paced around a large, stone pillar, feeling like a caged animal. The guide had transferred me to a cavernous room that had a sign on the stone wall marking it as a bomb shelter. A couple of hundred people could fit inside the space, and with the tons of rock overhead, I could see how the cave could probably take a good beating if a nuclear war ever started—though that was unlikely to happen these days.

Why had the guide separated me from the others? And why leave me here with nothing to do? The way back to the tunnels was sealed with only a couple of the stairs leading that way remaining. There were a set of doors by the bomb shelter sign, but they wouldn't budge. I'd even tried banging on them in case Kade or Miles might overhear and come to my rescue—to no avail. I did find a wide pool of shallow water to drink from near the rear of the cavern. It required crouching close to the ground and squeezing past low-hanging stone to get to it, but at least I wouldn't die of thirst. No, worry and boredom would likely get to me long before that. At least the limestone emanated strong enough light that I could easily see every nook and cranny of my prison.

"You never could sit still for long," a man said from behind me.

I swung around, jaw dropping in disbelief. "Grady?"

My stepfather stood there, looking like the old cowboy I recognized with his flannel shirt, jeans, hat, and scuffed boots. His dark-blond hair was a tangled mess, and he'd grown his beard out some since the last time I saw him. Otherwise, nothing about him had changed beyond the soft glow emanating from his body. He even had that shit-eating grin on his face that he always got when I did something to amuse him. Boy, was he a sight for sore eyes.

"You never could keep yourself out of trouble, could you, Bailey?" he asked with a slight Texas drawl.

I put my hands on my hips. "Are you implying that me being trapped in a cave is business as usual?"

He laughed. "Let's just say it ain't a surprise."

"What are you doing here?" I frowned. "Shouldn't you be with Mom?"

Grady took the cowboy hat off his head and held it to his chest. "I'm sorry to be the one to break this to you, but…"

"Please don't tell me she's gone," I interrupted, moving toward him. The sorrow that now filled his gaze told me something very bad had happened.

"No." He shook his head. "Your mother is fine—it's me."

I froze. "What do you mean? What's wrong with you?"

His lips twisted in irony. "Your mother warned me more than once not to go out to the west pasture, but the dragons kept steelin' from my herd. I couldn't just let them keep doin' it with winter comin' and too many mouths to feed."

I'd heard they'd been gradually gaining a lot of guests on the ranch. People in the cities had been steadily leaving in favor of the quieter—and safer— countryside. My parents let friends come to stay and occasionally strangers if they had kids with them. At last count, over twenty people lived at the ranch now.

"So you tried to fight them?" I gaped at him. "You had to have known you couldn't possibly go up against dragons!" I was having a hard time grappling with the idea of Grady being dead while he stood right there. It was easier to just argue with him like old times.

"Well, I'd set up some explosives to get them." He paused to wag a finger at me. "Don't look at me like that—it's worked a few times before. Anyway, it means you have to lure them into the trap and this time...let's just say it didn't go too good."

I was quiet for a moment, trying to take it all in. "And my brothers?"

"They're fine. I took the heat so they could get away." He smiled. "You like how I managed that play on words?"

I balled my fists. Usually, I loved his quirky sense of humor, but not this time. "This isn't funny. You're... you're dead!"

He slicked his hair back and put his hat on again. "Yeah, ain't that the crux of it, but your brothers are strong. They'll take care of your mother and the ranch."

"But they won't have you. I won't have you," I argued, my voice breaking. I loved Grady and couldn't believe he was really dead. It wouldn't sink in no matter how hard I tried to comprehend it. "When did this happen?"

"Two nights ago."

I began pacing. "I knew I should have tried to find a way to you guys. This is my fault. If I'd been there, I could have taken on that dragon and..."

"Stop!" he commanded, his light-hearted side gone. "You can't take this on yourself, Bailey. Even if you had been around, I might have still gone out there. It was my job to protect our family, and that herd could feed us for years to come."

He could say what he liked, but I knew better. "So why are you here?"

"To make you a deal," he said, expression turning all business.

"What kind of deal?"

"I've been told your friends have failed their tests, and you're gonna be stuck in here forever unless you agree to this offer." He paused. "All you have to do is promise to come home straightaway, and they'll let you go."

I narrowed my eyes. "You mean leave my friends behind? Give up the quest?"

"They've all been offered their own deals." He shrugged. "It ain't so bad."

This man might look and talk like my stepfather, but I had no way of knowing for sure if it really was him. "This is part of the test, isn't it? You're trying to turn me against my friends."

"Now, Bailey—" He put a hand up. "I'm not tryin' to cause trouble. I'm just givin' you a chance to go home and be with your mother and brothers. They miss you. And as you said, you could protect them."

It was tempting, so tempting, but I didn't buy a word of it. "No. I'm not leaving, and I refuse to believe anyone from my group would take a deal. This mission is too important for that."

"They've all got family to worry about—you aren't the only one." He gave me a sad smile. "When it comes to protectin' the people we love, we'll do almost anything."

I crossed my arms. "Nope. I'll find my way home when the time is right—and not a minute before."

It wasn't only that I'd made an oath to Aidan, but also because it was the right thing to do. I hated the idea of the rest of my family being down in Texas, vulnerable to dragons, but if they could survive the winter, I could be there in the spring. Aidan had said he was certain he could get me home around then.

"Are you sure?" Grady asked, skeptical. "If you don't take the deal now, there's no turnin' back."

"I'm positive," I said, standing my ground.

A wide grin split his face. "That's my girl!"

Before I could ask what he meant, he faded away. I spun around searching for him, but the room was empty again. Long moments passed, and I began to second guess myself. Then Danae suddenly appeared in the room.

"Bailey!" she cried out and raced over to hug me. "I have never been happier to see you."

I patted her back. "Same here."

Danae pulled away to study me. "Did your test involve seeing people you care about who told you they're...dead?"

"Yeah," I said, surprised. "You, too?"

"They tried to trick me by saying I could only leave if I promised to go find my sister. It was...it was my parents." Danae ducked her head. "I don't know for sure if it's true, but they said they died months ago."

I pulled her into another hug. "Same thing happened to me with my stepfather, except he said he passed two days ago after we left on this trip."

For a few minutes, we commiserated with each other over what we'd experienced. I was about to think the others might have taken their deals, but then Conrad showed up. His face was pale, and it wasn't until he spotted Danae and me that he perked up.

"Man, I ain't never been more happy to see you two." Next thing Danae and I knew, we were being pulled into a group hug. He told us about his grandma, and how close he came to agreeing to the deal she offered. "But in the back of my head, I just knew you guys weren't really failing your tests, and they only wanted to test me."

"Surely you have more faith in us than that!" I teased.

He shrugged. "It was tough. I figured if they were workin' at your weak spots like they were mine, you might give in. They shouldn't be messin' with our dead relatives like that."

We continued to talk and work out the horrible experiences we'd been through, finding comfort in each other. One thing I could say for these tests, they were making our group closer. The strongest bonds of friendships come from standing by each other through the bad times when it seems like all hope is lost. I was worried, though, when Aidan and Phoebe still hadn't shown up. It had to have been an hour we'd been waiting with no sign of them.

"Think they failed?" Conrad asked.

We'd all been thinking it, but he was the first to say it aloud.

"I don't know." I worried my bottom lip. "They're both smart, so I hope not."

Another half hour passed before both the brother and sister appeared. Phoebe's face was haggard and worn, as if she'd been through hell. Aidan fared a little better, but his guarded gaze revealed he was holding most of his emotions in check.

I ran toward him, and he took me into his arms. "Slayer, I do not ever want to be put through a test like that again."

"Who did you see?" I asked, gazing up at him.

"Our father came to us." Aidan glanced at his sister. "And he was the worst version of himself."

I knitted my brows. "They kept the two of you together?"

"Were the rest of you alone?" The question came from Phoebe.

I nodded and gave them a brief explanation of how our tests went.

"It must have been difficult," Aidan said, caressing my cheek.

I put my hand over his. "I'm okay, though I have no idea if we were really seeing our dead relatives or not. That could have been a trick, too."

"Our father truly is dead, and he behaved real enough." Aidan glanced at his sister. "But his offer almost made us turn on each other."

"What? How?' At least my stepfather hadn't appeared cruel or mean.

Aidan's expression turned bitter. "He said we would be trapped in the cave forever unless one of us agreed to kill you."

"Seriously?" I was horrified. At least the rest of us had only been asked to abandon each other. It was bad, but not that bad. I turned to Phoebe. "I'm surprised you didn't take him up on that, considering how unhappy you are with the idea of Aidan and I being together."

She lifted her brows. "You're lucky you look good in your camrium uniform, or I might have considered it."

I laughed. At least we could make light of the matter now, and it was reassuring to know even a bribe couldn't make her turn on me.

A crackle of energy sparked in the room. We turned toward the exit doors where the guide appeared, stoic as ever. The Native American woman gestured at Conrad to come forward. He hesitated, but went to stand in front of her. She lifted her hand and held out the second orb fragment, waiting for him to take it.

"So we're done here?" he asked.

She nodded.

He took the orb fragment from her and put it in his pocket. "Where do we go from here?"

She turned her gaze toward the doors and they opened wide, letting in faint traces of daylight and blistering cold. How long had we been in this place? Judging by the sky out there, it was either dawn or sunset, but I couldn't be sure while still in the cave. And a light snow had fallen while we were gone. Most of it had melted in the sunlight, but a few small patches in shaded areas remained.

Pulling my map out, I glanced down at it. The scale had widened back out, and if I judged the landmarks correctly, a large part of Oklahoma was now showing. I assumed the tiny groups of building in two spots represented Tulsa and Oklahoma City, leaving the corner of Missouri where we were located at the top, right corner. It all lined up.

I walked toward the guide. "Where do we go?"

She pointed at the far left side of the map at a single tree. It was to the northwest of Oklahoma City—probably near the panhandle. I couldn't be certain without any state border lines to guide me.

"This is where we need to go? To the west?" I asked.

She dipped her chin. Before I could ask anything else, she disappeared.

I sighed and put the map away. After all the time we'd spent in the cave, I needed sleep before I could formulate any kind of coherent plan. We all took one look at each other, and then hurried toward the exit. No way did we want to stay in the caverns for a moment longer.

Kade was huddled on a bench just past the gem panning station wrapped in a camrium blanket. He rubbed at his reddened nose and came to his feet as soon as he saw us coming out. "It's about time!"

"How long have we been gone?" I asked. Aidan and Phoebe shivered next to me. I estimated the temperature to be around forty degrees, which was dangerously close to the temperature that would send them into hibernation.

"Almost twenty-four hours, and you missed the snow," he said, disgruntled. "I was about to give up on you when I got the sense you'd be coming soon. Miles is over at the house across the way, making you all something to eat since we figured you'd be hungry. He brought out some kind of cook stove that was in his truck since we didn't want an open fire attracting any attention."

Conrad's stomach let out a loud growl, agreeing with that assessment. He rubbed at it. "Please tell me it'll be ready soon."

Kade nodded. "He started on it a couple of hours ago with a couple of rabbits I caught when it warmed up a bit this afternoon, and he's using some fresh vegetables I brought with me from the fortress. Almost thought about eating without you since I could use something warm in my stomach. Try to make it quicker next time—we can't afford delays like this."

He received a lot of sour looks and glares, which he ignored. While we were having our hearts ripped out by possibly dead relatives and making the most difficult decisions of our lives, Aidan's uncle had been out hunting rabbits. Who cared if it was a little cold? But somehow he'd been the one to suffer while waiting. I was half tempted to throttle him, but I was too tired and hungry to bother at the moment.

"Is there enough room in the house for everyone to sleep?" Danae asked.

Kade nodded. "I'm all rested up, and if Miles takes the couch, the rest of you will each have your own bedrooms. There's plenty of space."

Aidan gave me a look that said we weren't sleeping in separate beds.

"We will rest together, but that's it," I whispered. My mind was on that scene we'd watched with the slayer and her dragon man. I wasn't ready to risk ending up in a situation like theirs until I could do something to control it.

Understanding filled his eyes, and he nodded.

26

BAILEY

The truck hummed along as we made our way across northeast Oklahoma, toasty warm despite the cool weather outside. I ran my fingers through Aidan's short, spikey hair where his head rested on my lap. It was almost noon, but I sort of hoped he didn't wake up for a little while longer. I enjoyed having a strong man, who despite me being a slayer, could sleep that securely with me close.

We'd gotten up just after ten in the morning, and managed to drag the shifters to the trucks where they passed out again. Before that, I'd enjoyed a night in Aidan's arms with no one watching us. We had only held each other and kissed, but it couldn't have been more intimate. He watched me as I lost my battle with fatigue and fell asleep. It had been nice having him there. Just as he trusted me now, I'd trusted him to keep me safe while I was unconscious and vulnerable. Taking our relationship slow seemed to be working for us. There was no point in rushing into anything, especially under the circumstances. If it was meant to be, it would be.

Conrad was driving the truck. Kade snoozed in the front passenger seat, snoring lightly. We'd just entered the Tulsa city limits, though our route would only take us partway through town and allow us to circumvent the rest. I kept a close eye out. The dragons might not be awake yet, but we'd entered my father's territory. Wayne was out there somewhere, and there was always the chance he might show up.

"I recognize that look on your face," Conrad said, meeting my gaze in the rearview mirror. "You're nervous."

"You know why."

His fingers tightened on the wheel. "Daddy issues?"

"Yeah, something like that." I turned my gaze toward the window, noting Tulsa had its fair share of damage from dragons.

With every mile we drove along the highway, I found plenty of half-destroyed buildings and bare spots with only scorch marks remaining. The city might have a dragon slayer, but he was outnumbered by a thousand to one, maybe more. He could only do so much against those odds.

"Think he'll turn up?" Conrad asked.

"I hope not." Though a part of me wouldn't have minded a chance to get answers from him, I didn't want him coming near the shifters.

Aidan stirred and lifted his head. "How far have we gone?"

"About a third of the way. We're in Tulsa now," I replied.

He sat up and rubbed the sleep from his eyes. "I assume there has been no trouble yet?"

Conrad snorted. "*Yet* is the keyword in that sentence."

Damage to one of the highway's bridges forced us to take a slight detour. Kade woke up when we moved onto a bumpy city street for a mile before finding a ramp to get back on US-412. We'd gotten used to having to work our way around obstacles for this trip. Aidan's uncle gazed around for a moment, clearly trying to make sense of where he was at.

He turned in his seat. "Water?"

Aidan handed him the canteen he'd just finished taking a drink from, and his uncle gratefully took it. Shifters were always very thirsty when they first woke up. Prepared for his next request, I dug through the pack sitting on the floorboard and handed him some trail mix. It made for a decent breakfast when you couldn't stop to cook something hot. He munched down on it like he hadn't eaten in a week, finishing the bag.

We finally reached the west end of the city, heading back into the countryside, and I breathed a sigh of relief. It was almost one in the afternoon. I hadn't thought we would actually make it through Tulsa without running into some kind of trouble.

I dug out a granola bar and chewed on it. The land around us was mostly flat or rolling plains. If anything came along, we'd probably see it long before it reached us. I wanted more than anything to hurry up and get to our final destination. When I pulled out the map to see if it had changed, though, I got nothing other than it had re-centered itself so everything east of Tulsa no longer showed. Interstate-35 had popped up to help make things clearer. We'd probably reach it in a little over an hour if nothing happened to slow us down.

"Dragons are headed toward us," Aidan said, gesturing to the north. "I count five of them."

Should have known the peace had lasted too long. They were still some distance away, but we were in their sights. Ahead of us, Miles sped up the RV hauler. Conrad gunned the truck's engine to stay close behind him as we made a mad dash for the exit ramp coming up. They veered onto it, barely slowing down. As soon as they reached a crossroads section, they slammed on their brakes and turned north. We had the choice of either a gas station or storage facility to give the trucks some cover. Not much else was in our direct path since we'd just passed the town of Sand Springs and entered remote territory again. At least for the moment, a cluster of trees blocked the dragons' view of us. Miles chose the gas station.

Aidan and I glanced at each other, and as the trucks careened toward the shelter of the canopy in front of the place, we leaped out. I hit the ground running. We needed to divert the dragons' attention away from the vehicles and force them to battle us on open ground. There was a large field across from the station to the west. Aidan and I headed toward it with Phoebe not far behind us. Kade stayed with the others but began shifting into his beast form.

A chain-link fence ran parallel to the road across from the service station. It was low enough that I managed to leap right over the top. Aidan and Phoebe overtook me as we raced up a hill. When they reached the crest, they began shifting into their beast forms. I pulled out my sword and searched the sky. All five dragons were coming over the trees northeast of us. As I watched them fly closer, I prayed they didn't pay any attention to the gas station and kept their attention on us.

"Try to wound the first ones you fight and send them to me," I told Aidan. He was about a heartbeat away from taking flight.

I will do as you ask, his beast replied in my head.

Then he took off into the air, following Phoebe as they met the dragons a short distance away. I was surprised Aidan had allowed Beast to take over for this battle, but perhaps I shouldn't have been. He'd said his inner dragon was a ferocious fighter and could finish his enemies off twice as fast. Considering we were outnumbered, we needed every advantage.

Aidan clashed in the air with a large, green dragon. With his beast in control, he moved at an incredible speed, ripping his talons across his opponent's face. They wrestled for a moment longer before he managed to toss the wounded creature down to the ground in my direction. I raced toward it, sticking my boot on the dragon's side as it struggled to get up from where it lay on a crumpled wing. Raising my sword high, I drove the blade into the creature's heart.

I barely had time to make sure it was dead before another green dragon landed with a thump twenty feet away. Good grief, Beast was a killing machine. I'd watched Aidan fight enough times to know he didn't finish his opponents off quite that quickly.

My newest target didn't land in as awkward a position. The dragon was already getting to its feet and staring at me with its beady, red eyes. Blood pumped hard through my body as I reached the dragon. It poised to make a leap, and I kicked my foot out, nailing it in the side of its face where Aidan had already carved a deep wound. My opponent made a grunting sound of pain. I began hacking and slashing at it wherever I could strike, weakening it as fast as I could. The dragon let out a roar of fire. For a moment, I was blinded by the flames, but I kept my sword pointed outward. The creature rammed straight into it with the sharp tip going into its chest. His tough ribs stopped the blade from going far, but the resulting wound had to hurt. His flames died down.

I jerked my blade out, dropped to one knee, and thrust lower this time. My sword sunk into the softer scales just below the ribs and straight toward the dragon's heart. It roared and tried to snap at me, but I managed to lean far enough to the right to avoid its razor-sharp teeth. With a twist of my blade, I finally cut into the beast's heart. Shock entered its eyes, and then it fell over on its side. I watched the dragon expel its final breath before withdrawing my sword.

Glancing up, I didn't spot Aidan or Phoebe in the air anymore. It wasn't uncommon in a battle with many opponents for them to eventually end up on the ground. I scanned the area around me and found them about two hundred feet away—with my father and another man attacking them.

"No," I said under my breath, panic rising.

Wasting no time, I sprinted toward the battle. I passed the three dead dragons along the way, whose corpses lay in crumpled heaps. It seemed to take forever to reach the fight. All I could do was watch as my father tore into Aidan with his blade while the shifter dodged the strikes and didn't fight back. He was trying not to hurt my father. At some point, though, he was going to get tired of that and strike back. It was animal nature to protect one's self. Phoebe did fight against her attacker, and they'd traded several wounds if the fresh blood running down their bodies was anything to go by.

"Stop!" I commanded.

The slayers barely spared a glance for me. They were in battle mode, and the shifter dragons posed the greater threat. I waited for a break in the fighting, leaped toward my father, and pressed my blade to his neck. "If you strike him one more time, I don't care who you are, I will kill you."

Though I meant every word, I hoped I didn't have to carry through with it.

"You are a slayer. Why would you choose a dragon over me?" he asked, holding still with his sword remaining high.

I glanced at Aidan, and by the look in his eyes, could tell he was in charge of his body. He must have forced Beast back in his mind as soon as he realized who he fought. That explained the control I'd seen. Still, I ached for all the cuts and tears in his scales that had to have mostly come from my father. He'd suffered for my sake.

"If you haven't noticed, he isn't trying to kill you," I pointed out.

Wayne jerked his brown eyes toward me. My father was half Cherokee, and it showed in his features. He looked to be middle-aged, wore his dark hair long, and had a sturdy build well suited for fighting dragons. His skin was medium brown and on the leathery side. With my mother being half Malaysian and half white, I had inherited a distinct appearance.

"I do not care whether they fight back. All that matters is they die," he replied.

"These shifters are my friends." I pointed at Aidan and then Phoebe. "Go after the green dragons all you want, but don't touch the red ones."

"Who does this woman think she is to order us around?" the other slayer asked, walking toward us. Beyond him, I caught Phoebe covered in flames as she shifted. It was almost impossible to hurt her right now, so he must have decided to join our conversation. He was maybe a few years older than me with medium-length blond hair and a muscular build.

"She is my daughter," Wayne answered. There wasn't a hint of emotion in his voice—he'd stated it like a fact.

The other slayer lifted his brow, and looked at me in surprise. "I didn't know you had a daughter."

"He wants nothing to do with me, so don't feel bad," I informed the guy.

"That is not true," Wayne said, drawing my attention back his way.

I leveled my gaze at him. "Could have fooled me. You decided after one brief meeting that you hated me so badly you left all of Oklahoma City for me to defend by myself. I didn't even become a slayer until August! Now I discover you've even got help up here—for a city that is not nearly as populated. Talk about picking and choosing your enemies."

That probably sounded a bit whinier than I had meant for it to come out, but it had been bad enough when I'd thought my long-lost father abandoned me to take care of his territory. Now I'd discovered there was another perfectly good slayer in Tulsa who could handle the job, and still he didn't come down to help me cover my larger territory. It was a small miracle steam didn't come out of my ears.

Wayne thrust his sword in the ground. "You wear dragon-made cloth and consort with our enemies. I could not stay."

"My mother—the woman you left behind when she was pregnant with me—is down in Texas where I can't get to her. She's running low on the medicine she needs for her heart, and I need to do whatever it takes to get to her. If that means allying with shifters who don't hurt humans, and even protect them, so be it. These two you're trying to kill..." I said, gesturing at Aidan and Phoebe, who'd both changed into their human forms now, "have chosen to put aside their differences and help me, which is more than I can say for you."

"Damn, Wayne. I had no idea you were training me while you had a daughter who needed you," the second slayer said, gazing between us. "I would have told you to help her."

It was good to know my speech worked on someone. It didn't fail to escape my notice that both slayers were able to control themselves. Over and over, I'd been told it was almost impossible. I'd considered that if I could do it, maybe my father could too, but he must have taught this guy as well.

"Quiet, David." Wayne gave him a disgruntled look. "This is between me and my daughter. You can get the truck ready for us to leave."

David hesitated, clearly not wanting to miss what was said next, but he left when my father's furious glare didn't let up. I watched him go, wondering how the two men started working together. Had they known each other long? I didn't want to feel jealous, maybe my father wasn't worth the trouble of getting to know, but after so much time spent wondering about Wayne, I wasn't quite ready to write him off yet.

I crossed my arms. "Does this mean the fight is over?"

"For now." He glanced at the shifters. "But I don't want to find them in my territory again. What are you doing up here anyway?"

"Passing through."

He lifted a brow. "From where?"

"What does it matter?" I asked. This was not a conversation I wanted to get into since I'd sworn not to reveal our mission and even our alternate story wouldn't sound good to my father. He wouldn't like the idea of us scouting his territory.

"I am aware the Shadowan and Taugud are enemies," he said, running his gaze around to all of us. "It surprises me that any shifters would dare cross this deep into pure dragon territory—even with a slayer on their side. You must have a good reason, or you would not be here."

As I stood there trying to come up with some sort of plausible excuse, Kade walked up and nodded at Wayne. "It is good to meet the man who sired such an amazing woman."

My father narrowed his eyes. "Who are you?"

"I am Kade of the Taugud, and I am the one who insisted on us going on this trip," he answered.

"What for?" Wayne asked, impatience in his eyes.

"Let's just say we are working to stop a sorcerer from doing something horrible and leave it at that," Kade answered.

"How bad?" my father addressed me.

"We will be saving a lot of lives by doing this," I said.

"That is all I need to know." He waved an arm. "You are free to leave."

"That's it?" I'd expected a little more conversation or at least uncomfortable questions.

Wayne nodded. "You have your sources, and I have mine. I knew a group would be passing this way on a very important mission, and they must not be impeded. The only thing I did not know was that my daughter and shifters would be involved."

For the first time, I saw a hint of pride in his gaze. How much did he know about our quest and how? "Assuming we pull this off..." I swallowed and decided to take a chance. "Will you come visit me sometime soon?"

He lifted a brow. "Would I be welcome?"

Aidan came to stand by my side. "As long as you do not attack members of my toriq, we will allow you into our territory to visit your daughter."

I held my breath.

Wayne was silent for a moment. "Christmas is coming in a few weeks. I will see you then."

A small thrill ran through me. We might have started off on the wrong foot, but maybe there was a chance we could work things out after all.

"That would be great," I said.

He stared at me. "Travel safely, daughter. Your journey is not over yet."

27

AIDAN

Aidan glanced at Bailey for the dozenth time. She'd been quiet since they left her father behind to continue their journey. He was thankful he'd managed to wrestle control from Beast in time, so that he did not hurt the older slayer. It had not been easy, especially knowing he was The Shadow and could very well kill Aidan. Though he'd been proud of his control, he'd sensed Bailey's father had held back from the start as well. Had he known how much it would upset his daughter if he killed her travel companions? Had that scene been played out on purpose?

To Aidan, it almost seemed like too much of a coincidence that the famous slayer waited to show himself until after they were well out of the city, and then he'd accepted an invitation to visit his daughter without needing much encouragement.

"Bailey," he began, turning his gaze toward her. "Do you want to talk about your…"

"No, not now," she said, and her face tightened. "I need some time to think."

"I would not have tried to kill him." Aidan took her hand. "As long as he didn't pose a threat to you."

She gave him a weak smile. "I know."

Conrad tapped his fingers on the steering wheel. He'd missed the reunion scene between Bailey and her father, but he'd heard about it from Phoebe while they cleaned their wounds after returning to the trucks. Knowing the slayer as well as Aidan, Conrad stopped discussing it as soon as it became clear Bailey was uncomfortable. It was written all over the young man's features that he wanted to ask questions, though.

Several minutes passed in silence. More than once, Bailey looked like she was about to speak. Aidan pretended not to notice, deciding she would open up when she was ready.

"Do you think…" she paused and cleared her throat. "Do you think Wayne really wants to get to know me? That he's actually coming to visit for that reason."

"Girl, I think he's curious what you're up to, and with the way he watched you the last time he was in Norman, it's probably harder than he's lettin' on to stay away," Conrad said, jumping at the chance to finally discuss the topic.

She threw up her hands. "Then why stay away at all?"

"Perhaps it is an issue of pride," Aidan suggested.

Kade turned in his seat. "Your father knows more about you and your activities than he revealed to us today. A slayer does not live as long as him without powerful resources at his disposal. He is cold and calculating, but I also sense he has a soft heart somewhere in there. You are a link to a past he thought long gone. Though he might not be pleased with your choice of allies, he still wants to get to know you."

Bailey narrowed her eyes at him. "Is this coming from another one of your visions?"

Kade smiled enigmatically. "Visions are only one of my many talents."

"Is he always this annoying to be around?" Conrad asked Aidan.

"Yes, but I've grown used to him the same way I have you," he replied.

"Hey, man." Conrad shot him an annoyed look. "Don't ever piss off the driver."

"Then don't ask silly questions," Aidan said.

The radio crackled, ending their conversation as Danae's voice came through the speaker. "Are you guys seeing this up ahead?"

They had been so caught up in their conversation that Aidan had hardly been paying attention to their surroundings. He knew better than that and wanted to kick himself. Moving closer to the side window, he looked ahead toward the west. A sheer wall of dust and dirt rose from the ground all the way up to high in the sky.

"Oh, my God," Bailey gasped. "What is that?"

As if he'd heard her, Miles came on the radio. "It looks like a dust storm. If it is, it will be too dangerous to drive through."

Bailey grabbed the microphone. "Didn't dust storms stop getting this bad decades ago?"

Aidan had no idea about such things in this place, but back in Kederrawien this type of weather phenomena occurred frequently. Dragons could not fly through the storms because it was impossible to see where they were going, and the swirling sand could tear at their scales and eyes. They always had to take shelter until the weather cleared.

"The worst of them did," Miles answered. "But sometimes a less severe dust storm comes along and darkens the sky. They just don't look anything like this."

Kade frowned. "There is something strange going on here. A normal storm moves, but I've been watching this one for a few minutes now, and I am almost certain it is staying in one place."

Aidan took one of the modern maps from Bailey's pack and studied it. He remembered hearing something a few months ago about a hazard forming in the northern part of Thamaran territory. They'd crossed into the toriq's land when they'd passed Interstate 35 a little over half an hour ago. He traced the highway they now drove until he reached their current position.

"It appears there are salt plains and a lake ahead. Perhaps that has something to do with this storm," he said, showing Bailey what he found.

She repeated Aidan and Kade's observations over the radio to the others.

"I don't know if that makes any difference," Miles replied. "There is a lot less vegetation in this area because of the high salt content, and the wide open spaces could be contributing to the storm, but it doesn't explain why it isn't moving."

"Are you going to turn around?" Bailey asked.

"Since it's not moving, I want to get a closer look. This may only be a problem here, but we can't be sure we'll never run into something like this again. Might as well study it, so we can warn others if they come this way," Miles replied.

Aidan had to admit to a certain amount of curiosity himself. He had never seen a stationary storm, and if this was the same problem he'd heard about with the Thamaran, it had been going for months—perhaps even since the dimensions began colliding. It wasn't easy getting reliable information on places this far north, and the details had been more than a little vague. The one thing he did know was that the pure dragons avoided coming anywhere near it, which explained why they'd had no sightings of them recently.

Miles stopped his truck a couple of hundred feet before the edge of the storm. Everyone climbed out, noting it was warmer in this area, and moved to the front of the vehicles to gape at it. The dust wasn't a solid wall—they could see bits of debris flying around in there—but it stopped at a precise line across the highway and fields on either side. There was a good deal of debris scattered just outside the storm, including vehicles stripped of their paint, animal bones, and tree branches bare of any bark. Anything that had been in there did not fare well.

Bailey furrowed her brows and glanced at Aidan. "Shouldn't we be hearing something? I mean, it's clear that the wind is blowing hard inside there and pushing sand and stuff around. Why is it so quiet?"

"I do not know, but it is strange," he replied. Even with straining his ears, he couldn't hear the storm. At night, if the moon wasn't full to light the surrounding area up, this could become an even bigger hazard. People would go right into it without seeing the danger.

Danae began walking closer to the storm, but halfway there she doubled over. Miles raced to grab her. He was able to guide her back without feeling the same effects. Once she was a safe distance, she moved to the side of the road and vomited. After finishing, she turned toward them.

"It's some kind of natural magic creating the effect. Not from a sorcerer, but something from nature or the Earth." She shook her head. "I could feel how wild and strong it was."

"It is peculiar that I did not see this coming," Kade said, rubbing his head. "Normally I get some kind of warning about magic-related troubles."

"Yes, but often not until the last moment and only if it is a threat to us. We could see this coming for ourselves," Aidan replied.

Danae drank deeply from a canteen of water Miles handed her. He was fussing over the woman quite a lot for a man who presumably hated her. No one in their group had brought up the topic of Miles and Danae's relationship since the cave, but Aidan had observed them. The human male had certainly showed signs that he was still in love with the sorceress. And with each day they traveled closely together, it became even more apparent.

"We were warned about it," Danae said, handing the canteen back to Miles. "Xanath told us to expect something that could remove the spell he put on us. This storm is it."

Aidan stilled. "Is it a problem at this distance?"

"No." She shook her head. "We'd have to enter the storm for it to remove our anti-tracking spell."

Movement from the storm caught their attention. Some dark shape flew through it and came soaring out from about a hundred feet high. Aidan grabbed Bailey's arm, pulling her with him. "Get back!"

Everyone ran toward the vehicles. The remains of a two-door truck slammed down on the pavement a mere dozen feet from where they'd just stood. It was stripped of its paint, the windows had been broken out, and all that was left of the interior seats were metal springs and wires.

"Holy shit!" Conrad said. "And here I thought I'd seen it all by now."

"Let's turn back," Miles said, always prepared to take charge. "It's going to take us longer, but we have to go around."

⚜

Their detour added hours to their drive. By the time they reached Alabaster Caverns State Park, the sun had long since set. They'd discussed stopping for the night to avoid Thamaran dragon patrols, but decided against it. There didn't seem to be many in the area, and they only had two full days of their protection spell left. They couldn't afford to waste any more time than necessary.

Miles continued to lead the way in the RV hauler, using a pair of what he called "night vision goggles" to see since they could not risk using the vehicle lights. Bailey took over driving the truck. Her enhanced night vision was more than enough to let her follow Miles, especially with the moon out.

They made their way through the park, following their sense of the orb fragment now that they were close. It amazed him how as long as Conrad held the other two pieces, Aidan could not feel them—even from a few feet away. Somehow, the guide had given the human the ability to block the uncomfortable sensation. It was only when they neared a new fragment that the dark feeling returned.

"Not another damn cave." Conrad moaned from the backseat where he rode with Kade.

"It makes sense if you think about it," Bailey said. "Where else could they hide the fragments and be sure the places remained intact thousands of years later?"

"Also accessible," Aidan added.

Conrad sighed. "Yeah, I guess lakes and oceans would be out of the question if we're actually supposed to get it."

Miles stopped his truck in front of the park office, and Bailey pulled up next to him. The clock on the dashboard said it was a little after 9 p.m. Today had been their longest drive yet, and everyone was hungry and exhausted. Their group got out of the vehicles to take a look around. Aidan was pleased to find the temperature warm enough that they almost didn't need their jackets. Except for Bailey, who only wore hers once so far on this trip, and that was the previous evening when the temperature dropped to freezing after the sun set.

Aidan gazed at the area around him. There were a few buildings nearby, including what appeared to be human homes, a restroom for visitors, and picnic areas. No people seemed to be around, though.

"I've been here before," Miles said, studying their surroundings. "My parents brought me when I was a kid, but I forgot about it until now."

Aidan found it interesting the young man offered such personal information, considering he rarely spoke of himself and especially not since they'd buried his father. Perhaps this journey was making the normally reserved man open up more.

"Do we go in the cave now?" Bailey asked, nodding in the direction of where the orb fragment called to them.

Danae shook her head. "If the final test is anywhere as bad as the last one, I think I'd rather wait until I've eaten and gotten some sleep."

"We have no idea how long you may be in there and time is of the essence," Kade pointed out.

"Then you go in there, man," Conrad replied, giving him a disgruntled look. "Because some of us aren't ready to face whatever else they got planned for us."

"I agree with Danae and Conrad," Aidan said. "We have no idea what the final test may involve, and the last one was difficult enough to pass after a long day of travel."

"Very well." Kade sighed. "Let us see if we cannot find sleeping quarters in any of these buildings and prepare a meal for ourselves."

Everyone mumbled their agreements and began unloading the trucks.

28

BAILEY

I woke up to bright sunlight filtering through the bedroom windows. Sitting up, I ignored the unfamiliar furnishings around me and focused on the man lying next to me in bed. Aidan was still fast asleep. I glanced at my watch, noting it was almost 11 a.m. He probably wouldn't wake up for another hour without a little help.

Leaning down, I pressed light kisses on his chest and up to his neck. His breathing changed, no longer light and soft. He sucked in a deep breath of air and his eyelids fluttered open. I met his yellow gaze and smiled.

"Good morning," Aidan said, pulling me on top of him. "I normally do not condone being woken up early, but you may use your kissing method on me anytime you wish."

"I thought you might appreciate that," I said, reveling in his heat.

Aidan's hands found their way under my t-shirt, and his fingertips traced their way up my back. I arched into his touch, enjoying the feeling of him being so close. He burrowed his head into my neck, breathing me in before placing tiny kisses there. I didn't want it to end.

His muscles bunched, and in the next moment, I found myself flipped onto my back. He burrowed between my thighs with only my underwear and his pants acting as a barrier between us. Last night, I'd insisted on some clothes or else who knew what might happen. No way were we doing anything until I got Trish's birth control supply from her. Still, I couldn't help letting Aidan practice for what we'd eventually be doing once the time was right. It felt too good playing the happy couple to give him up just yet.

"I don't suppose you've changed your mind about us becoming more intimate?" he asked, staring at me with a lust-filled gaze. Every muscle in his body was strained to keep control of himself. It was the sexiest thing I'd ever seen.

I shook my head. "Nope."

"This is torture," he said, lifting his head to stare at the wall.

I ran my hands down his back and squeezed his butt. "Then move."

He grunted. "I do not have that much willpower."

I laughed. My amusement fled when it was followed by loud pounding on the bedroom door. Whoever it was couldn't knock just once. They kept going like they were the police demanding entry.

"What?" I yelled.

"You two lovebirds need to get up. We've got work to do," Conrad answered.

I sighed. "Guess it's back to the real world."

Aidan gave me one last lingering look, then rolled off of me. "May I kill him?"

"I'd consider it," I said, yanking my t-shirt down where it had ridden up my stomach, "but he is the guardian of the orb fragments so we can't take him out just yet."

"I heard that," Conrad called through the door.

"On second thought, we could hurt him a little." I swung my legs over the side of the bed and reached for my camrium uniform on top of my pack. Aidan didn't move from where he lay, watching me get dressed. His gaze was so intense that I didn't bother to hide my body as I changed tops and pulled on my pants. It was one of those intimate moments that made me feel even more like we were really together.

Only after I sat down to pull my boots on did he start getting dressed. We finished getting our things together and headed out, stopping just outside the front door to brush our teeth. Could this actually become a routine if Nanoq allowed him stay closer to the fortress? I wanted that more than I dared hope.

We walked over to the picnic pavilion to join the others, who were already enjoying coffee and snacks for breakfast. Aidan's uncle was the only one left unaccounted for from our group. I gulped down a cup of hot coffee before bothering to talk to anyone.

"Where's Kade?" I asked.

"He's coming," Conrad answered. "But it's not like we need him to go in the cave, so there's no point in waiting for him."

"He's always in such a rush to keep going on this quest—until it involves being awake in the morning," Phoebe said with a scowl, tossing an apple core into some nearby bushes.

The shifters had special greenhouses and gardens where they could grow fresh fruits and vegetables year round. Their selection used to be limited, but since returning to Earth, they'd gathered seeds, plants, and trees from around the area and began to increase their variety. Aidan had explained everything to me after I got a peek inside the crate the shifters brought with them.

We cleaned up our mess and started heading for the cave. Kade came dashing out of a house up the road, hurrying to catch up. He might not get to go inside, but he wouldn't miss seeing us off.

"Whatever test they give you," he started, giving us all stern looks. "You must not fail. We are close to completing this journey, and we cannot afford to be unsuccessful now."

Conrad snorted. "Wow, man. I'm glad you reminded us, or we might have forgotten how important this is, and what we've already gone through to get this far."

"Do not be snide," Kade said, pointing a finger at him.

"Let's go." I gestured to our group, not wanting to wait any longer.

We headed down the hill to the wide mouth of the cave. I almost stopped in my tracks when I saw a young woman standing there, watching us come toward her. She had long, red hair, pale skin, and looked to be in her early twenties. And if I wasn't mistaken, she seemed to be wearing a park service uniform. What the heck?

"About time you guys showed up," she said, putting her hands on her hips. "I've been waiting for months!"

"Who are you?" Phoebe asked, narrowing her eyes.

She smiled brightly. "I'm Allison, and I will be your guide today."

Everyone looked at each other confused. I turned back to her. "There must be some mistake. The last two guides weren't…"

Allison lifted a brow. "Modern? Young? Friendly?"

"Yeah, actually," I agreed.

She nodded. "Your original tour guide sacrificed herself to get rid of the dragons in this area. She was a slayer like you, except a really old one who'd been around for ages. Since I happened to be in the area when she died, I was chosen to take her place."

"Oh." I frowned. "I always figured the other guides weren't actual people."

Allison shook her head. "Oh, they were people a long time ago, but their spirits have been stuck in their caves for thousands of years waiting on you, so they've gotten a little…antisocial."

"Right," I said, feeling like I'd just entered an episode of the Twilight Zone—which was saying something, considering the way my life was these days.

"Anyway, if you all will follow me, we will begin the tour." She gestured at us, then turned and led the way into the cave. It was dark at first, but as we started down a set of slippery steps, the glow we'd seen at the other fragment locations started emanating from the walls. "As you can see, magic runs this place now, but we did have electrical lighting effects before."

"Were you an actual tour guide here?" Danae asked.

"Yes." Allison glanced back at her. "That was one of the reasons I was chosen."

Aidan frowned. "Who selected you?"

"You'll get all the answers you need to know soon enough," Allison said, continuing to lead us through more series of steps, plus some twists and turns that seemed to go on forever.

The place was huge. The roof went up nearly fifty feet in some spots, and the paths were often much wider than the last cave we visited. I found deeper pools of water and many sunken areas below the path we followed. This was the kind of place dragons would love to nest inside. There was so much space and interesting rock formations.

Allison paused for a moment as we worked our way across a bridge of sorts. "As you may be wondering, this cavern is made of gypsum or more specifically—it is mostly alabaster. There are only a few places in the world where black alabaster can be found, and this is one of them. For you, Aidan, you should know that alabaster is tolerant to your second fire and can be used for building materials."

"My toriq does not own this land," he said, though I could see interest in his eyes.

Allison shrugged. "The Thamaran won't come within fifty miles of this place, so if you wanted to make your way back here someday, you'd be fine once you got close—or you could send others."

As much as I could understand Aidan wanting to try out a different material for building stuff, I hoped he didn't return. I addressed Allison, "What happens to you after we're finished with our quest?"

"That's not for me to say," she said in a clipped tone.

I must have hit a sore spot, or maybe she didn't know. She spun on her heels and continued the tour, pointing out various rock formations, most of which had been carved out when a fast-moving river had run through the underground area. We discovered that the path we followed through the cave was three-quarters of a mile long if we followed it to the end.

I began to wonder how much of that distance we would be traveling when Allison stopped in a wide, open area. She turned to face us. "When I used to give regular tours, this was the spot where I might turn out the lights so people could see how dark it gets. Now, this is where you'll see the final part of the story on what happened with the orb Finias created."

As she faded away, so did the glow on the rocks. Bright light started to shine from the back wall where a scene began to appear, featuring Finias riding a black horse. The sorcerer had aged since we last saw him so that he looked like he was in his sixties now. He carried the orb in the palm of his hand, holding it close to his chest. In the sky above him, at least a hundred drag- ons—green this time—flew in formation. The angle changed to show a fortified city ahead of him with high walls and guards posted at the gates. Half a dozen men sat on horses in the middle of the path leading there. Despite their overwhelming odds, they didn't back down as the sorcerer approached them.

Finias came to a stop a short distance away, two dragons landing on either side of him. "Surrender now, or else I will destroy your city."

A stately-looking man wearing leather armor shook his head. "We have seen what you've done to the other cities you have conquered. Your people suffer while you grow rich from their labor, and when you are not happy with them, you feed them to your dragons. Enough is enough, Finias. You cannot have every place you set your sights on."

"Even if it means you will all die?" the sorcerer asked.

The city leader lifted his chin. "We would rather cease to exist than live under your control, but if you had any sense, you would stop this madness. Using dragons to manipulate and kill people? You are no bet- ter than the beasts you lead."

"Very well," Finias said, his face turning red. "You will not be troubled by me any longer."

He raised the orb. "Dijis!"

The dragons swarmed toward the city, blowing flames of fire. The screams from men and women rose up. Some of the beasts grabbed people, chomping them into pieces. Others concentrated on burning everything in sight. Finias kept the two dragons at his side, prepared to have them burn the men across from him if they dared to move.

It took almost an hour for the beasts to eradicate any trace of the city from ever existing. All the while, the leaders sat frozen on their horses, watching it happen in horror. Every time one of the men would start to ride forward with the intent to kill the sorcerer, the dragons would snarl at him. The leaders could do nothing except watch their people die.

After it was over, a satisfied smile crossed Finias' face. "I will leave you men to spread this day's events to others so they might learn from it."

With that, he turned his horse around and rode off into the distance.

The next scene opened with a group of people gathered around a trestle table. One, I was surprised to see, was the slayer we'd seen during our first history lesson—the mother of the shifters. I'd known my kind could live forever if we weren't killed, but it was still incredible to see her alive after what must have been thousands of years. She hadn't aged at all. It was only in her eyes that you could view the toll it had taken on her to live so long. The joy I'd seen when she looked upon her children was gone, and I couldn't find a trace of happiness in her demeanor. She simply existed now. The man/dragon she'd once fallen in love with had likely died millennia ago.

The leader of the destroyed city spoke to her. "Finias must be stopped—no matter the cost!"

"Are you certain you are willing to sacrifice anything?" the female slayer asked, lifting a brow.

"Yes! He murdered my family and my people."

An older man who looked just like Savion spoke up. "There is a way."

Hearing his voice, I was certain it was him.

"How?" another man with yellow eyes like a shifter's asked. He stood next to a woman who also had yellow eyes.

"We must get the orb from the sorcerer," the slayer said.

"Everyone who has tried has failed," the city leader argued.

Savion clasped his hands together. "That is because there has never been a pact between all the races to be rid of him. If we stand together, we can do it."

The female shifter furrowed her brows. "Your magic is strong enough?"

Several of us gasped, having not realized he was a sorcerer when we met him before.

"With enough help and the right planning, my powers will be sufficient, but doing this will not come without sacrifice," Savion warned. "Most of us will die to accomplish this task."

The city leader laid his hands flat on the table. "How certain are you that this will work?"

"I am absolutely certain if we swear a blood oath now to do what we must," he answered.

The female slayer rose to her feet. "I will gladly do whatever it takes."

After a few more questions, everyone else agreed as well. The scene faded away.

A new image appeared before us of Savion and the female slayer walking through the corridors of what appeared to be a palace. It was night, judging by the dark windows. They passed several guards along the way who did not acknowledge them or look in their direction. Deeper and deeper into the palace they went, taking one turn after another and climbing several sets of stairs. Eventually, they stopped in front of an intricately carved door with ferocious dragons depicted on it.

Savion furrowed his brows and light glowed from his hands. He reached for the handle, but when it shocked him, he jerked back. Taking a deep breath, he tried once more. The light emanating from his fingertips increased until it lit up half the corridor. It was a good thing the nearest guard was around the corner because I wasn't sure he could have hidden that with whatever invisibility spell he was using.

A light pop sounded, and he sighed in relief, pushing the door open. He went in first with the slayer following behind him. They exchanged looks once, and there was a wealth of meaning in their expressions. They weren't a hundred percent certain their plan would work, but they would try anyway. Creeping across the room, the slayer moved somewhere out of sight. Savion continued forward until stopping a few feet from a large bed. Finias slept on it with two naked women sprawled on either side of him. His eyes were closed, and he snored loudly.

Savion drew out a knife and sliced it across his palm, then lifted his hand into the air. It stopped at some kind of invisible wall that briefly lit up. He began chanting words I could not understand, but he repeated a series of them over and over again.

Finias jerked up in bed, his gaze shooting to Savion. "What are you doing?"

The chanting continued without pause.

The evil sorcerer knocked one of the women to the floor in his haste to climb out of bed. She landed with a thud, crying out. He barely spared a glance for her as he jerked on a robe to cover his naked body. There were some things I could have definitely lived without ever seeing, and that was one of them.

"You will die for this," Finias said after strapping his robe tightly around him.

Savion continued his chant, sweat starting to form on his brows.

"You will not break my spell in time." Finias grabbed a knife from the bedside table. "It was foolish of you even to try."

Savion chanted louder, and the magic thickened so much that we could feel it even though we weren't there. As the evil sorcerer raised his knife upward, a bright series of sparks crackled between the men and the protection shield broke. He'd done it!

Finias drove his knife downward, and my stomach clenched. He plunged it straight into Savion's chest.

The sorcerer fell to his knees, but he managed a smile for Finias.

"You think you've won, but you haven't."

I caught sight of the female slayer leaping across the bed with her dagger raised. Finias didn't hear her until the last moment. He began to turn, but it was too late. She plunged the blade straight through his neck with such strength it came out the other side. The evil sorcerer fell to his knees. Shock flickered in his gaze in that brief moment before he went slack, slumping to the floor. The slayer rushed toward the bedside table and grabbed a wooden box from on top of it. She flipped it open, revealing the orb inside, and took it out to stuff into a pouch hanging from her belt.

The female slaves began to cry. The slayer rounded on them and spoke in a hushed tone, "Be quiet, and do not alert the guards for at least a few hours, do you understand?"

Both of them looked at her like she was their savior and nodded their heads. There was no telling what Savion had done to them. The girl who'd been knocked off the bed spoke in a whisper, "His sons will come after you."

"I know," the slayer answered. "But I will be long gone by then if you keep quiet for a few hours."

"We will," they both promised.

The slayer gave Savion a sorrowful glance, knowing she could do nothing for her partner, and moved toward the door. She paused there to clutch at a crystal hanging from her belt, squeezing it until it began to glow. I wasn't certain what it was for until I caught her passing the guards again unnoticed. Savion must have made it for her, anticipating that she might be the only one to survive. The slayer hurried through the palace, only slowing when she neared guards so as not to make a sound.

My heart stuck in my throat as I watched her make the long journey back through the palace, noting that the crystal was beginning to fade. The slayer noticed it as well. When the gates to the palace appeared up ahead, she raced toward them. They were already opening for a supply cart to pass through, but she was out of time. She jumped onto the back of the cart and pulled a woolen blanket over her. No alarms were raised, and she made it through the gate with no one the wiser.

The scene flashed forward to the slayer meeting with the city leader deep in the woods. He waited there with a spare horse, handing over the reins when she got close.

"Savion?" he asked.

She shook her head, mounting the horse. "Finias killed him right after he got the shield down."

"He was a good man—for a sorcerer," the leader said.

"Yes, he was." The slayer guided her horse around and into a trot.

We watched in brief glimpses as the two of them rode for what seemed like days until they reached a coastal area. I couldn't even begin to guess where since it was empty without any special landmarks. On the beach, they met with the two shifters we'd seen before. They asked about Savion, and the slayer gave them the same answer as she'd given the city leader. Exhaustion lined her face, and the human leader appeared half dead where he sat on his horse. Their pace had been grueling to make it to the coast.

The slayer handed the orb pouch over to the male shifter. "Guard it with your life."

"Of course," he said, taking it from her. It disappeared, and I could only assume it went into shiggara. That was probably the safest place for it.

The sound of thundering horse hooves in the distance drew their attention. The angle changed to show a group of soldiers riding for them. They were led by a man who looked like a younger version of Finias. It didn't take much to put two and two together. As the evil sorcerer's son continued toward them, the shifters began to change into their dragon forms.

"Hurry!" the slayer urged. "All he needs is to be close to the orb to call upon it."

The shifters finished their transformation and took flight over the water, picking up speed quickly. After the slayer was satisfied they'd gotten far enough away to be out of danger, she turned to the city leader. "Are you ready?"

"Yes," he said, straightening in his saddle. He might have had fancy armor for the time period, but he didn't look to be in good physical shape. Most likely, he'd led an easy life before his city had been destroyed. Still, he lifted a sword and appeared ready to face the over-whelming odds.

When Finias' son was about fifty feet away, the slayer pulled a slim knife from her belt. She muttered under her breath. "Can't let him close, or I'm dead."

She threw the blade, landing it in the man's eye. He cried out, then fell from his horse to land with a thud on the ground. The slayer drew her sword and attacked the men with the city leader following close behind. She fought with such viciousness that the first three went down under her blade alone. The city leader barely finished his first opponent, and was already wounded from that battle, but he went after another. His next fight didn't go as well, and he ended up with a blade in his belly. The slayer finished off her last opponent and the one who struck the city leader. She didn't even appear winded.

The city leader slid off his horse and fell to the ground, blood soaking the front of him. As he lay there gasping his final breaths, the slayer kneeled next to him. Sorrow filled her features.

"You completed your task, and you have done well," she said.

Blood leaked from the corner of his mouth. "Only one...of the six sons are dead."

"I know," she said, "but I will hunt them all down no matter how long it takes."

His gaze went to the ocean. "Let us hope...the shifters make it to that faraway land."

"If they are committed, they will," she promised.

The scene faded away, and a new one began with the red dragons flying over an endless sea of water. I glanced at Aidan. "Can you really fly across an ocean without stopping?"

"Not exactly," he said, still watching the scene. "But there is a way to float in the water for a while to rest so that one could keep going."

"What about storms?" I asked.

"If they are strong, we cannot fly through them."

We watched snapshots of the shifters flying for hours without breaks, then lying on the water with their wings spread wide while they rested. They shifted to human form occasionally to catch fish and eat, as well as drink from the water skins they pulled from shiggara. More than once, they were attacked by water dragons and had to fight for their lives. During one particularly difficult battle, the female shifter died. For a few hours, the male held her in his arms before he finally forced himself to continue on his journey.

Though we only watched glimpses of his trip the rest of the way, it was exhausting to see. The wear and tear it took on the male shifter's body was brutal, but at least he was lucky the worst weather was only light rain. Eventually, he reached land and rested for a day before continuing onward.

His journey through America was almost as tough to watch as the one through the ocean. Dragons lived there too, and the shifter fought battle after battle while searching for the best place to hide the orb. He must have spent months altogether to make the journey before coming across a Native American tribe. He met with a female shaman who looked just like our guide in Missouri. She appeared to have been expecting him— she wasn't much of a talker back then, either—and readily agreed to help.

Using her magic, she broke the orb into three pieces. They traveled together to the three locations we'd visited and used the shifter's blood to help fuel the protection spells she made. I almost didn't recognize the caves as they appeared nearly three thousand years ago. They'd hardly been touched by humans back then. In fact, the places where the shifter and shaman went didn't appear inhabited at all. It was about as remote and difficult to reach as you could hope to find—especially against sorcerers from Europe.

At their final stop, the shaman used the last of her strength to make the protection spell. She warned the male shifter there would be a period where there would be no magic, but no one who knew about the orb would be around to search for it, so the fragments would be safe. And once magic returned, the spells would come out of their dormancy to work again. Of course, she said it in such vague terms that unless you knew about the dragons being banished into another dimension, and the magic going with them, it wouldn't make sense. The shifter just nodded his head. Then she told him never to speak about the orb to anyone and to protect the caves until the day he died. He promised he would.

After she said all she needed to say, which was a lot for her, the shaman crumpled to the ground in front of the shifter. She'd died between one heartbeat and the next. For the sake of every race out there, she'd given every bit of herself to hide the orb. Her face was peaceful as the scene faded away.

29

AIDAN

Aidan stood in stunned amazement at the journey he had just witnessed. He'd tried more than once to imagine how the orb fragments had come to be in their recent locations and failed. Now he knew the difficulties a small group had faced to make it happen.

The tunnel walls resumed glowing, and the guide appeared before them. "As you saw, most of the people who sought to keep the orb out of the wrong hands died. They gave their lives so that others might live."

Aidan didn't say anything—none of them did. There were no words that could capture the sacrifices six individuals made, one of whom had not even been part of the original pact. He was humbled by the lengths they were willing to take. If not for them, would anyone currently in the cave be standing here now?

"This leads us to your final test," Allison said, clasping her hands in front of her. "To be responsible for the orb, you must be willing to make similar vows as that first group. It must be protected at all costs."

Bailey cleared her throat. "Why does it need to be re-assembled? Wouldn't it be better to take the pieces and dump each one into a different ocean or something?"

"For the same reason the others didn't do it," the guide answered.

"And that would be…" Conrad prompted.

Allison drew in a deep breath. "Because it was fore-seen that someday it will serve a higher purpose, and the only place you can reforge it is here. This is why there had to be trials before you could take it. Only those with hearts who are honorable and true may safe-ly possess the orb."

Aidan mulled that over. "How will we need it? It only targets dragons and slayers."

"Unfortunately, I don't have those answers." She gave them an apologetic look. "I could pretend like I know and speak riddles or allegories to confuse you, but I always thought that was lame. Plus, I'm too much of a modern woman for that. Whatever the original six wanted me to know is all I've got, and they didn't reveal those details to me."

He had to appreciate that she was at least being honest with them. "Do you believe it is something where we'll know what to do when the time is right?"

"That pretty much sums it up."

Danae shoved her hands into her jeans pockets. "How about we rewind back a bit and talk about this vow we have to take. What exactly are we promising to do?"

"It's a combination of things," Allison said, running her gaze across all of them. "You must swear to protect the orb with your lives until such a time as it can be destroyed—which will happen, someday. Also, there is going to come a time when your group is split up. By taking the vow, you will be linking yourself to the others, which means when you feel *the call*, you must answer it by returning to the place where you all met."

"Norman?" Conrad asked.

Allison nodded.

Aidan frowned. "What do you mean by *the call*?"

"There will be no missing it. You'll feel an urgent need to get back to Norman as soon as possible—no matter how far away you are from there," she said.

"Wait." Bailey put a hand up. "Are you saying some of us are going to be traveling really far away before this big emergency comes up? And will that be when we need to use the orb?"

Allison smiled. "I'm beginning to see why the other guides choose not to be very helpful. *Yes* to the first question—please don't ask which of you ends up where because I don't know. *Yes* and *no* to the next question. The call will be the beginning of the crisis, but it's not like you'll need to use the orb as soon as you meet up. That will come sometime later. I don't know when, how, or why. Anything else?"

"Just one," Bailey said. "Do you know if we're going to have any trouble with people trying to take the orb from us in the near future?"

Allison laughed. "I think you already know the answer to that question."

Bailey's lips thinned, but she didn't say anything else.

Conrad shifted his weight from foot to foot. "This is basically like a lifetime commitment, isn't it?"

"You could say that," Allison agreed. "If you don't think you can put your duty first above everything else, you shouldn't take the vow. The process for reforging the orb will not work if all five of you are not fully committed."

Bailey put a hand on Conrad's shoulder. "Your girlfriend, she…"

"…can't be first," he finished, ducking his head. "By coming on this trip, I pretty much committed myself to this already and sidelined her."

"I'm sorry. This is my fault," Bailey said, her gaze deeply apologetic.

Conrad shook his head. "No, it's not. If you remember, I'm the one who insisted on going on this trip. You didn't make me do shit."

"Perhaps you can talk to her more when you return," Aidan suggested. Even he didn't want to see Bailey's friend suffer.

"I've actually been thinkin' a lot these past few days." Conrad glanced between them. "Here you two are with every reason for your relationship not to work, and yet you're still tryin' to be together. Neither of you cares that you're supposed to be enemies. You totally accept each other exactly as you are. So if my girl loves me, why is she tryin' to change me from the man she met? And am I really gonna be happy if I give up things I care about for her?"

Some of those thoughts had crossed Aidan's mind, but considering he and Conrad were barely civil to each other most of the time, he had not thought it his place to say anything. It was good to see the young man showing a new level of maturity.

"Does that mean everyone is ready to take their vows?" Allison asked.

Phoebe cocked a hip. "As long as there are no vows of chastity involved."

"No." The guide laughed. "There aren't."

"Tell us what to say and do," Aidan said.

Allison waved her hand to the side, and a pedestal appeared. This one had a basin on top with the third orb fragment jutting from the middle, almost as if it had been glued or welded in place there. A silver dagger rested at the basin's edge.

"First," she said. "I will need Conrad to put his two orb pieces with the third. They won't attach themselves or anything, but they need to be together."

He pulled the fragments from his pocket and laid them in the middle of the pedestal. "Like that?"

"Yes," Allison answered. "Now you must take the dagger and slice a cut across your palm. Let the blood drip across the fragments while repeating after me."

Conrad glared at her. "Seriously? You kind of forgot to mention this part."

She lifted a brow. "Are you saying you're too much of a baby to make one cut?"

"No." He worked his jaw. "A man just likes a little warning first."

Conrad grabbed the dagger, sucked in a breath, and sliced his palm. Several curses were muttered under his breath directly after that, but he managed to move his hand over the stones in time for his blood to begin dripping on them.

"Repeat after me. I—*state your name*—swear to protect the orb with my life," she began.

He cleared his throat. "I, Conrad Alberts, swear to protect the orb with my life."

"And heed the call when it comes," Allison continued. "No matter the personal sacrifices I must make. For better or worse, the orb and my companions will always come first above all else."

Conrad repeated her words.

"And that's it. Who's next?" Allison asked, looking around.

Bailey stepped forward. "I'll do it."

Conrad handed the dagger over to her. Danae was already digging through one of the packs to get the first aid kit. She helped Conrad clean his wound and said a few chants over it to make certain he healed quickly. Meanwhile, Bailey cut her palm and hurried to squeeze blood over the fragments before the wound started healing.

"I, Bailey Monzac, swear to protect the orb with my life," she said, her voice carrying clearly through the cavern.

After she had finished, Aidan went next with Phoebe and Danae going after him. It almost seemed like the air in the room thickened with each person's vows—as if there was magic building and leading to something bigger.

"Now for the final phase," Allison said, flicking her hand at the bloody dagger, so it disappeared. "For those of you without fireproof clothing on, I suggest you remove whatever you would like to keep."

"Hold on." Conrad lifted a finger. "Are you saying any clothes we wear aren't going to survive what is coming next? Because if that's the case, then I don't see how our bodies will make it, either."

"You'll be fine as long as you meant your vows," Allison reassured him.

His jaw dropped. "What's that supposed to mean?"

"Yeah, I'm a little curious about that, too," Danae said, her brows furrowed.

Allison slapped her forehead. "I forgot to tell you that this last stage will make everyone fireproof who isn't already—as long as you meant your vows, of course."

Conrad opened and closed his mouth. "Damn, that's just...scary. I felt like I meant them, but now you're making me second-guess myself."

"You'll be fine," Allison said. "Probably."

"That's not helping!"

The guide looked at Aidan. "It's now time for you to reforge the fragments. I assume you know what to do."

He nodded and walked toward to the pedestal.

"Wait," Danae called out. "I happen to like these clothes, so just give me a moment."

She raced down the passageway and out of sight. After a moment of hesitation, Conrad went in the opposite direction. Danae returned a couple of minutes later wearing only a pink bra and underwear. Aidan averted his gaze, but he did catch enough to know the woman didn't behave the least bit shy about her lack of attire and walked confidently. Conrad ran back to them in nothing except blue boxer shorts and a deep scowl on his face.

Aidan waited until Allison nodded before taking hold of the two loose fragments and pressing them into the third. Drying blood coated his fingertips, but it would be cleansed away soon enough. Once he was certain he'd positioned everything just right, he inhaled deeply and let the second flame flow out.

To his shock, the blue and purple fire lit up the entire room. He could hardly see anything as the flames took on a life of their own. They pulled and pulled at him, sucking the energy from his body to keep them going. The temperature rose inside the cavern until even Aidan began sweating from it. He shook as the flames continued to flow from his mouth, taking every last bit of his breath and somehow finding more. Aidan felt as if they took everything he had.

It seemed as if five minutes had passed before the fire abated and the room returned to normal. He sucked in a lungful of oxygen, grateful to finally be able to breathe again. Once his light-headedness had passed, he glanced down and found the orb whole again with all of the blood gone.

"Damn, that was wild," Conrad said behind him. Aidan turned and discovered the young man cupping his private parts. He'd survived unscathed, but his shorts were gone. "Can I go get my clothes now?"

"Sure," Allison answered.

Aidan studied the walls while Danae hurried past him. The guide had said the stone there was like zaphiriam and could handle the second flames. She'd been right. The cavern room where they were located was now sealed with no cracks for water to run through. If they'd been in a cave without the right stone, it could have been disastrous. The rock in the next layer above might have crashed down on top of them. No wonder it took the shaman and shifters so long to select the right location for this part of the quest.

Danae and Conrad returned with their clothes and shoes on.

"So, uh," Conrad gestured between himself and Danae. "We don't have to worry about getting burned by dragon fire anymore?"

Allison nodded. "Fire of any type won't be a problem for you, but keep in mind you are still mortal and dragons can hurt you in any other way. You won't heal quickly like a slayer or shifter can."

"Excuse me." Conrad grabbed Aidan's arm and held on for a minute. When he didn't burn, he grinned. "Can't hurt me by touch, either!"

Bailey rubbed her face. "I just know this is going to cause problems."

Allison took the orb from the pedestal and handed it to Conrad. "This is still your responsibility until it can be placed in a safe location—such as the one being prepared at the shifter fortress. I don't have to remind you of your duty, do I?"

"Nope." He took hold of the orb. "I got it."

The guide waved at them. "You are free to go, and I wish each of you the best of luck. Please take care on your journey home."

Aidan took Bailey's hand, and they made their way back through the tunnels, going the same way they came in. He still felt weak and walked slower than usual to navigate the slippery steps. The others followed behind them. When they emerged from the tunnel, they found Kade and Miles waiting for them.

Miles zeroed in on Danae right away, frowning at her chest and the long-sleeve t-shirt she wore. "Weren't you wearing a bra when you went inside?"

Bailey snickered.

"Who has the orb?" Kade asked.

Conrad held it up long enough for Aidan's uncle to see it, then stuffed it back in his pocket where it left an odd bulge. He'd have to find an alternative way to carry the orb now that it was whole.

"Let's go!" Miles called out. "We've still got a few hours of daylight, and I don't want to waste them here."

Aidan found it rather amusing how much the man enjoyed being in charge.

30

AIDAN

Aidan grew restless, sitting in the backseat of the truck with Bailey. They'd acquired the orb, but they still had the journey home to complete. This was the time when they had the most to lose. And yet as he stared out the window, watching the countryside go by, all he could think about was leaving the confining truck and soaring in the open skies. His inner dragon had grown quiet—too quiet. Something had happened at the last cavern when he blew his second flames. It had drained him of almost all his energy, and now that he thought about it, Beast had been the one to send that final surge. They might not have survived it otherwise. Aidan wasn't used to the other part of him lying dormant. He kept thinking if he shifted and flew, it might help.

"There is trouble ahead," Kade said, leaning forward in the front seat. "Dragons are attacking that town."

Aidan caught Bailey's fingers curl around her sword hilt. She glanced at him. "That's Watonga up there. It's not a big city, but it is big enough there could be a lot of people still living there."

"Man." Conrad slapped the steering wheel. "We only got a couple of hours until we make it home. Can't we go around this shit?"

"The orb is our first priority," Kade agreed.

Fire spewed from the dragons' mouths as they ravaged the town in the distance. Aidan could only imagine the fear and terror they were spreading to innocent people. "Every death from this point forward is on us if we don't do something."

He might be feeling weaker than usual, but he had high hopes a battle might bring Beast back out. This was his chance to be sure, and if they saved a few humans while they were at it, all the better.

"I have to fight them," Bailey said, glancing at Aidan. "How about we leave the trucks here, and you can fly me the rest of the way?"

Kade turned in his seat. "I have counted at least six dragons so far. If you and Aidan go alone, it will be too risky."

"I'm sure Phoebe will go with us. You guys just park next to that farmhouse up ahead, and you should be fine," Bailey replied, determination in her gaze.

Aidan nodded. "It is a good plan."

His uncle pointed a finger at him. "Do not let any of the dragons get away or they will spread the word that we are here."

"I'll take care of it," Aidan promised. He believed he could do that much.

Bailey got on the radio and let Miles know of their plans. As soon as the trucks pulled off the road, they jumped out of the vehicles. Phoebe appeared ready for a good fight as well. Aidan and his sister quickly shifted into their beast forms and then he picked Bailey up in his arms. Had there ever been a time when one of his kind actually carried a slayer into battle to kill dragons? He rather doubted it.

He gripped her in his arms as she trembled with the need to kill the beasts attacking the human town. As she had mentioned, Watonga was small compared to Oklahoma City or Norman, but the rising cacophony told him a sizable population of people made their homes there. Perhaps there were even refugees from nearby places.

Two of the dragons were attacking businesses and homes on the edge of town. Aidan swooped low to drop Bailey in a field across from a cemetery. One of the green beasts saw them coming and headed straight for them. Aidan streamlined his body, colliding with the dragon midair. He grabbed hold of his opponent's lower jaw, shoved it upward and bit into its elongated neck, crunching down hard enough to make it difficult for the beast to breathe. It clawed at Aidan's chest deep enough to draw blood, but to no avail. Once he was certain the dragon had been sufficiently weakened, he dropped it to the ground for Bailey to finish. She'd already killed its partner.

Aidan flew higher in the air, searching for more opponents. Phoebe had gone farther ahead and currently fought a large beast a couple of blocks away. She didn't appear to need assistance if the way she castrated the male dragon was any indication. Aidan winced. His sister could be vicious when she wished.

Aidan searched for the other dragons and found three of them near a cluster of gray silos. They'd already burned one of them almost to the ground. He swooped down to grab Bailey again and then raced in that direction. Phoebe joined them along the way. As soon as he got close, Aidan dropped the slayer off on a road next to the silo complex and a warehouse. He went straight for the dragon doing the most fire damage, grabbing its wings from behind.

The beast roared as Aidan squeezed his fists tight, breaking the uppermost bones. His opponent could not maintain flight with its wings so badly damaged. Aidan tossed the dragon in Bailey's direction where she waited with her sword at the ready. He caught her running to the fallen body as soon as it struck the pavement, her sword raised high. There was nothing more alluring than watching the slayer take down her opponents with brutal force. One day he hoped to catch her right after a battle while still on the field. Aidan wanted to experience all of Bailey's passion and lust for himself . Some might find it too dangerous and a little depraved, but that was what made his and Bailey's relationship work. They loved the best and worst parts of each other.

The sound of flapping wings came from behind him. Aidan turned as quickly as he could, but not quite soon enough. A green dragon bit into his shoulder hard. Breaking a jaw lock was no easy task, and as pain surged through his body, it was all he could do to stay aloft. The small surge of energy he'd felt at the beginning of the battle was fading fast. Aidan called for his beast to rise up, but got no answer.

Phoebe was fighting her own opponent and could not help. Another dragon headed toward the silos, coming straight for Aidan. With his shoulder steadily being crushed, he could not handle a second assailant at the same time. He clawed at the first dragon's eyes but only caught the right one before it snapped the left shut. Aidan lifted his legs and dug his toes' talons into the beast's lower stomach. He ripped and tore into its body until the dragon finally let go of his shoulder. As blood poured from his wounds and ran down his chest, Aidan tried to force back the unbearable pain.

He rammed into the beast's wounded belly and drove it toward the ground. At less than ten feet from the pavement, the dragon's wings lost air. It fell the rest of the way on its own, finding Bailey ready and waiting to greet it.

Aidan surged back up higher as the other incoming dragon reached him. Gritting through the pain, he grabbed his opponent's jaws and jerked them wide. His strength was nearly depleted as he lost more blood, and he needed to kill this one quickly. Aidan reached for his second fire and blew it into the dragon's throat.

The beast's eyes widened in shock as its mouth and esophagus hardened, and it lost the ability to take deep breaths. This was a trick Aidan learned last summer. It would not work on a dragon's exterior body but proved quite effective on soft, inner tissue.

His opponent made a strange gurgling noise, then its wings went slack. It spiraled down, landing on a warehouse roof and crashing through it. Aidan followed the fallen beast and went through the hole it left in the building. The green dragon would lay there dying for a while if he did not finish it off. While Aidan might not like the Thamaran all that much, he did not believe in letting his opponents suffer for prolonged periods. There was no need for that. He used his talons to claw and tear a hole in the beast's belly just below the ribs. Once he'd made the opening large enough, he forced his fist inside the cavity, found the heart, and crushed it. The light from the dragon's eyes faded away.

Turning his gaze up to the roof, Aidan blew a stream of flames to enlarge the hole so he could fly back through it. Though he hadn't noticed it at the time, he'd sliced his right wing coming down. Gritting through the pain of his injuries, he made it back outside to land next to Bailey. It was all he could do not to collapse at her feet.

"I think we got them all," she said, then turned to look him up and down, eyes widening. "My God, Aidan, you're injured all over!"

As she fussed at his injuries, he searched the sky. He could not shift until he was certain no more dragons were around. Phoebe flew toward them, landing a short distance away. She'd suffered a few injuries herself to include a broken talon and several deep lacerations on her stomach.

There are no more dragons here, she said. *I checked the whole town.*

Relieved by her news, especially since Kade's count had been off, Aidan let the fire consume him and shifted to human form. While he did that, Bailey asked his sister to go back and check on their group. She flew away about the time Aidan emerged from the flames.

He checked Bailey over, seeing nothing except cuts and scrapes until he spotted her right ankle. She wasn't putting much weight on it, and her pants were shredded at the bottom. Blood poured down her boots and onto the ground. He kneeled to take a better look at her injury, finding her ankle swollen with deep gashes in her skin.

"I'll be okay, Aidan. It just hurts a little." She grabbed his good arm and pulled him up. "It's you I'm worried about."

"I will be fine," he said, though inside he could barely contain his pain. The dragon had crushed his collar bone and shoulder socket. Once he also considered his blood loss and nearly nonexistent energy, Aidan knew he must rest soon if he hoped to begin healing.

Taking hold of each other, they limped toward the main street that ran through town. Several humans jogged toward them. There was shock and weariness on their faces as they took in the sight of Bailey and

Aidan. Then their gazes shot to all the fallen dragons littering the pavement.

"You fought them off!" a middle-aged woman said. "We've been having trouble with those damn creatures for two days now, and you killed them all so fast!"

Bailey attempted a smile. "Hopefully this will be the last you see of them for a while."

An older man pointed at her. "What are you that you can survive dragon fire? I saw it try to burn you, but you just kept fightin'."

"I'm a slayer," she explained.

"And him." The man gulped. "I could have sworn I saw him change from some kind of red beast with wings into what he is now—and those eyes!"

Bailey went into a short explanation about shifters and the differences between them and the green dragons. Several more people gathered around to hear the story. They must have figured out the danger had passed, and wanted to know what happened. Aidan couldn't blame them. Out here, they didn't have slayers or shifters to help, and they were on their own.

"I'm Elen." The middle-aged woman smiled kindly at them. "How about we get you two set up someplace where we can tend to your wounds? There's a motel just down the street, and we've got some clean beds there. It's the least we can do."

"Oh, you don't have to…" Bailey began.

"Nonsense. It's the least we can do," Elen insisted.

"And I'll be happy to feed you supper at my restaurant. We've had to modify things a bit without electricity, but I promise we serve good, hot meals there." The first guy gestured toward a place across the street. The sign read "Hi De Ho Café."

Aidan could scent the faint trace of bacon and eggs that had been cooked there this morning. It did smell good, even a handful of hours later. Once his body began to heal, he would need sustenance to speed his recovery and the offer was tempting.

"We're waiting on our friends," Bailey said, glancing down the street. "That's them coming now."

The RV Hauler and service truck rumbled toward them, and Aidan caught sight of his sister riding inside the lead vehicle. After Miles and Conrad had pulled up next to them, Bailey's sidekick leaned out the window with a concerned expression on his face. "You all alright? Phoebe said that fight was rough, and you guys were injured."

Aidan tucked Bailey under his arm, knowing the two of them must look like a bloody mess. They were both in pain, but they would survive. "We are fine."

One of the townsmen looked them up and down. "You two look like you should be in a hospital—if we had one of those."

"All of you are welcome," Elen said, undaunted by the new arrivals. "We'd surely be dead if you hadn't shown up when you did. I don't care what you are, or how you did it."

"Help! Please help!" A woman screamed from down the street, hurrying toward them. Next to her, a man carried an unconscious little girl. The whole family appeared to have suffered from burns, but the child had it the worst. Her face, shoulders, and arms were mottled from dragon fire grazing her. If it had touched any closer, she would have been dead already.

Danae leaped out of Mile's truck. "I've got this."

"Is she a doctor?" Elen asked.

"She's a healer," Aidan answered.

Danae asked for blankets, and after they pulled the camrium one from the backseat, she had the couple lay their little girl on it. She gave them an urgent look. "There's no time to wait. I must treat her here."

Kade handed her the burn ointment, which she began rubbing on the girl without hesitation. It took the rest of the bottle they'd brought to cover all the girl's wounds. Then Danae began chanting, using sorcerer words.

"What's she doing?" the mother asked.

Aidan considered saying something, but he feared his appearance would only frighten the parents further. Not only was he covered in blood and wounds, but his yellow eyes stood out. The best thing he could do was keep quiet and not interfere.

Conrad joined them, speaking in a reassuring voice. "Trust me. Your little girl is going to be much better once Danae is finished with her."

Both the parents looked down at their child with worried expressions on their faces. It couldn't have been easy to let strangers near their daughter, especially after all that had happened to them. To permit an unknown woman who was chanting and placing a glowing hand over their little girl must have been difficult to allow.

Nearly thirty minutes passed before Danae stopped, slumping against Miles where he kneeled next to her. The young girl opened her eyes. "Mom?"

"Dear God," the father said, running his gaze up and down his daughter's body. "She's almost completely healed."

In fact, the only signs of her burns now were overly pink skin.

"The rest should fade by tomorrow." Danae dragged in several deep breaths. "She will need rest and plenty of fluids."

"Of course." The mother leaned down and kissed Danae's forehead. "You are a miracle worker!"

"Now how about we get the rest of you folks fixed up? Most of you look like you're about to fall over on your feet," Elen said, gesturing at them.

With a little more encouragement, Bailey, Aidan, and the others walked the short distance with Elen to a nearby motel where she set them up with rooms to rest. They wouldn't be going any farther today until they could recuperate.

31

BAILEY

Our group was split up between a handful of motel rooms. Elen must have been one of those people who enjoyed playing hostess because she went out of her way to take care of us. She even managed to get some of the town's sparse water supply so we could wash the blood off ourselves. My camrium pants were ruined after having my ankle half crushed, but I'd brought a spare set to wear. Aidan promised he'd make more for me once we were back at the fortress.

After taking a couple of hours to tend our wounds, rest a little, and clean up, we headed to the café where we were served steak and mashed potatoes. A local rancher supplied the beef to the restaurant in exchange for other things the owner traded with his customers. The town ran surprisingly well despite the post-apocalyptic circumstances. They said the dragons had mostly left them alone until recently, so they'd been trying to get by as best they could. I was definitely impressed with how well the meal was cooked and plotted ways to get back up to visit again someday. Risking life and limb was worth it if the food was good—only the fuel expenditure held me back.

I came out of the bathroom after changing into my t-shirt and underwear. Aidan was just coming in after going to talk to his uncle. His eyes were sunken with weariness, and his shoulder only looked marginally better. With his black camrium tunic on, I couldn't be sure how the gashes in his stomach looked.

"Don't you usually heal faster than this?" I asked, limping closer to examine his wounds.

He'd been bitten in the same spot where a dragon had gotten me a few months back. His bones had been crushed, and they would take a couple of days to mend, but even the punctures and gashes in his skin had barely begun to close. Those should have sealed shut by now. If Danae wasn't already worn out from healing the burn victim, I would have asked for her help.

"Yes, but something strange occurred in the last cave," he said, shaking his head.

I frowned. "What do you mean?"

"When I breathed my second flames, the magic drew a lot from me to reforge the orb and everything else in the room. It left me drained afterward." Aidan sunk onto the bed.

I sat down next to him. "Why didn't you say anything? If I'd known, maybe I wouldn't have suggested we jump right into battle when we found this place."

"Bailey." He took my hand. "You and I both know you couldn't have left the people here to die. In fact, I am certain you would have run in by yourself if I didn't offer to join you."

"So?" I shrugged, feeling guilty he'd fought because of me. "Out of all of us, I'm the one who is least injured. I probably could have fought the rest if I'd had to."

He lifted a brow. "You're being ridiculous. I just witnessed you limping a moment ago, and we both know it would have been much worse if you'd been on your own."

"Maybe," I mumbled, knowing he was probably right.

Aidan lay back on the bed and stared at me. "Come here, slayer."

I was on his good side, so I curled into him and rested my head on his undamaged shoulder. There was something comforting about listening to his strong heartbeat. "Tomorrow we'll be home. Do you think Nanoq is going to send you away again?"

"I do not know." He was quiet for a minute. "But I am hoping our success on this journey will be enough to convince him to let me stay in my lair."

The idea of Aidan and I living together sounded almost too good to dream about. "If I have to make more vows for that to happen, I'll do it."

He kissed my forehead. "I do not think I can survive putting a knife in you again. Please do not ask that of me."

"Even if it means a chance for us to be together?" I asked, lifting my head to meet his gaze.

Aidan sighed. "I do not know, but I promise I will try to work out something."

I drifted off to sleep, scheming ways to make our relationship work no matter what it took. We'd been through so much together during this trip and grown closer because of it. I didn't think I could give Aidan up if he was sent away again. What that meant for my future with my family, I didn't know. It wasn't a choice I had to make for now.

❧

I was pulled out of a nice dream I was having of Aidan and me in his lair, cooking dinner together and behaving like a normal couple. There were voices outside the motel room. I lifted my head and strained my ears, trying to make out what they were saying.

"You won't get past me, sorceress," Phoebe said. "I'll kill you first."

"How did you find us?" Kade asked.

Verena laughed. "Worried your sorcerer's spell didn't work? Oh, it did, but there is more than one way to locate those who do not wish to be found. I have spies everywhere."

My heart leaped into my throat. I glanced at Aidan, who was still fast asleep. His severe injuries had taken such a toll that I doubted much of anything would wake him. A quick glance at my watch told me it was only an hour before dawn. Phoebe and Kade would be getting tired by now too, and I couldn't leave them alone to handle this.

Dashing across the room to my pack, I dug out my spare pair of camrium pants and pulled them on quickly. The arguing outside continued. Good God, I couldn't let anyone get hurt for my sake. If Verena had found us, she must have a plan for how to subdue everyone so that she could get to the orb.

Not bothering with my boots, I grabbed my sword and ran outside. "Leave them alone, Verena. This is between you and me."

"Hand over the orb, slayer," she said, staring down her nose at me. "I must have it."

I shook my head. "No. It's not going to happen."

It was then that I realized she had her left hand upraised toward Kade. He was holding his own dagger against his neck. Phoebe was moving her head back and forth, watching all of us, which told me Verena couldn't control her. Instead, the sorceress was using Kade to keep Aidan's sister back.

"Would you let your lover's uncle die to protect the orb?" Verena asked.

I glared at her. "Threatening me will not work. It will only prove you are the absolute last person who should ever get a hold of it."

Anger flashed in the sorceress' hazel eyes. "You think I would use it to control you, but you are wrong. I am only trying to keep it from getting into the hands of another who would use the orb for ill purposes."

"That's what you say now, but you can't be sure the power of it won't lure you to use it," I said. For the moment, I had to keep her talking and keep her attention on me. I'd say whatever it took to make sure she didn't hurt Kade or anyone else.

Verena used her free hand to dig through a large purse hanging over her shoulder. She pulled out a wooden box. "You can put it in this. The wood is specially treated so that none can sense it inside, and I will not feel its call."

"What makes you think we have the orb?" I asked.

She clucked her tongue. "I may not be able to sense it, but I know it's here somewhere. Do not try to deny it."

I studied the box. It looked suspiciously like the one that the sorcerer Finias used to store the orb next to his bed—before the slayer took it out. After three thousand years, how could Verena have it? Sure, she'd been alive a thousand years ago, but that was still a long time gap. Was she somehow related to the man who originally designed it? She already had the magic to control a couple of us at a time, so it wasn't a big leap that if power like that was put into an object and magnified, it would become just like the orb. So many things began to make sense now.

I crossed my arms. "Finias is your ancestor, isn't he?"

Though if that was true, it meant the old slayer was not able to track down all six of the sorcerer's sons to kill them.

"Yes," Verena nodded, surprise flickering in her eyes that I had figured out that much. "He had a daughter no one ever knew about. One of the serving maids got pregnant by him and fled before he could find out. She kept the child a secret but returned the night after he was killed to take the box. It was her intention to track down the orb and protect it from ever being used again."

"But she failed," I surmised.

"And the duty to find it has been passed down every generation since."

I frowned. "Is that why you were so quick to meet me after D-day? Did you already know I'd be part of the group sent to find the orb?"

"Not right away," she said. "I just knew you would be important for something. It was only in the last few weeks that the details became clearer."

I was letting Verena think I was considering her request to take the orb—anything to buy just a bit more time before help arrived. And it was useful to get a little more history out of the sorceress while she was here, even if I couldn't trust anything she said. It helped to understand her motivations, so I could predict what she might do in the future.

"Why are you certain the shifters and I can't protect the orb?" I asked.

Verena's expression softened and pity lit in her eyes. "Because I know. If you let the shifters control it, you will come to regret that decision."

"How?" I took a step forward, unable to help my-self. "You have to be a little more specific if you want me to buy your story."

"I don't know yet!" Verena cried in frustration. "I only know you will regret it if you do not give it to me. The consequences will be greater than you can imagine."

She was giving me empty threats just to get the orb. I wasn't buying a word of anything she was saying. "You're not getting it. Not now—not ever."

Verena lifted her free hand and pointed it at me. She whispered ancient words and power sparked the air, surging into my body. Pain unlike anything I'd ever felt before lit up every nerve until I was left screaming and falling to my knees.

"I had not wanted to resort to this," Verena said.

I barely heard her over the blood rushing in my ears. The next thing I knew, I was curled on the ground, rolling from side to side. There was no escaping what she was doing to me. From the top of my head down to my toes, everything was on fire with invisible flames.

"Leave her alone," Phoebe screamed.

"Move a step closer," Verena warned, "and your un-cle will start cutting through his own neck. The only way this ends is by you giving me the orb."

"I can't do that," Phoebe said helplessly. She knew Kade and I would both sacrifice ourselves rather than let anyone else have the artifact. I was glad Conrad had stayed in his room, so we could work this out without worrying about protecting him.

"Now!" Verena demanded, then ramped up the pain in my body until I screamed even louder.

Through pain-glazed eyes, I watched as the dark figure I'd seen skulking around earlier snuck up behind Verena. That person had been biding their time and waiting for the right opportunity. It was why I'd kept the sorceress talking for so long.

Miles lifted the shotgun in his hands and fired it directly at the sorceress' back. Verena cried out, falling to her knees. All of the sudden, the agony I'd been experiencing went away. I gulped in several deep breaths and climbed to my knees. Kade was lowering the knife at his throat, relief in his eyes. A second later, Aidan pulled me up and into his arms. He'd been sleeping so soundly that I didn't think he got up until I started screaming.

I turned my head and saw Miles going to stand over Verena, still aiming the shotgun at her. She ignored him, her gaze on me instead. "You will come to regret this, slayer. Mark my words."

Energy crackled the air, and before Miles could pull the trigger, Verena disappeared. The only sign of her presence was the traces of blood she left on the parking lot pavement.

Danae came running outside in only a tank top and underwear with her blond hair a tangled mess. She looked like she'd just woken up. "Miles, what are you doing out here? And was that you I heard shooting?"

I turned my attention back to the man in question, noting for the first time that he didn't have a shirt on, and there were suspicious scratch marks on his chest and shoulders—the kind that came from a woman's nails.

"The better question would be," Conrad said, stepping out of his motel room, "where was Miles before he came out here?"

Phoebe's jaw dropped. "Dear Zorya. Did you two finally make up?"

Miles' cheeks turned red. "Maybe we can concentrate on where the sorceress went instead of what I do in my spare time?"

He had a point. I searched the parking lot, not seeing any sign of Verena.

"Do you smell her anywhere nearby?" I asked Aidan.

"No." He shook his head. "I suspect she is long gone—for now."

Kade nodded. "She will need to tend her wounds. That will buy us enough time to get the orb safely put away where she cannot reach it."

I certainly hoped he was right because her final threat left me with a sick feeling in my stomach. What kind of consequences would I be facing? Was that threat real or false?

32

BAILEY

It was just before noon when we reached Oklahoma City. Aidan still slept on my lap, where his head had fallen as soon as we'd climbed into the truck that morning. It was a good thing my ankle had mostly healed during the night, or I wouldn't have been able to half carry him out of the motel room. At least the remaining tenderness didn't bother me much. It was Aidan who I worried about since his wounds were still mending at an abnormally slow pace. He promised he'd see his clan healer once he returned to the fortress, but I couldn't be there for that.

The shifters missed our going away breakfast, but the rest of us enjoyed it. The town had given us a nice farewell meal, and we gave them some tips on how to hide from dragons in the future—such as digging underground tunnels. Since they'd only recently begun to have serious dragon problems, they hadn't known dirt was the trick to hiding from the flames.

I looked up as we neared downtown and gasped. Hearing about the destruction of the buildings was one thing, but seeing them was another. The top part of Devon Tower, which was once the tallest structure, had been obliterated by dragon flames so that the highest remaining floors opened up at a jagged angle. Many of the other high-rise buildings were just as bad off or completely obliterated.

"Damn," Conrad said, letting out a whistle. "They messed downtown up!"

"Yeah, they did."

I was really glad we still had a little time left before the dragons would be up and about. It allowed us to see the area without risking getting caught. There were guards sitting on rooftops, but they would stay near the buildings to protect the sleeping inhabitants. Aidan had told me there were hundreds of dragons nesting in the large openings the beasts had made on the sides of the structures. Keeping them safe was the guards' priority, and we wouldn't be getting close enough for them to find us a threat. Not as long as they didn't realize we had shifters with us, anyway. I'd insisted we roll up our windows just in case the wind picked up and blew in that direction.

Conrad followed Miles as he took the Interstate 35 ramp and headed south. In a few more minutes, we would cross out of pure dragon territory and enter the edge of shifter land. Driving down the interstate was a bit tricky, though, because it was technically neutral and either clan could travel over it. The Thamaran had mostly stopped using it after I made it one of my favorite hunting grounds. Hopefully, they hadn't figured out I'd left town for a while.

Kade began to stir in his seat. I grabbed a canteen of water and passed it to him as soon as he opened his eyes. He gratefully took it, gulping down the entire container. I handed him an apple next—the last one we had. He munched on it, his eyes becoming more alert with each moment that passed.

"That is our territory up there." He gestured toward the I-240 bridge that marked the boundary the shifters had set in their peace treaties with the pure dragon clans. Everything to the southeast of that intersection with I-35 belonged to the Taugud.

"Yes. We're almost home." And I'd never been more grateful to be nearing Norman.

It took driving another twenty minutes, passing through Moore first, before we turned off on our exit. I kept a watchful gaze to the west the whole time, daring any Thamaran to come out and play. Aidan continued to sleep until we hit our first buckle in the road on Main Street. That jolted the truck enough to stir him.

He picked up my canteen and began drinking from it. I examined the town, making certain nothing was out of the ordinary. The shifters might consider this land part of their territory, but I considered the whole of Norman mine. For as long as I lived there, it would be my responsibility to keep its citizens safe. Thankfully, it didn't appear anything had changed except someone had finally moved a fallen tree off the road. It had always been annoying to drive around the damn thing, but since it only blocked one lane, I'd just left it there.

We made our way down a side street and reached Earl's place a few minutes later. Justin was standing at the gate when we pulled up. He spoke to Miles for a moment before opening the way for us. By the time we parked the trucks in front of Earl's, half the neighborhood was outside and heading our way. I supposed our journey made for interesting news, but if Hank the radio guy showed up, I planned to disappear fast.

Earl walked up the sidewalk as we got out, his eyes on me. "Got my cigarettes?"

I'd been prepared for this. I tossed the two packs I'd gotten for him through the air. "Enjoy those. You have no idea what I risked to get them."

"I will," he said, opening one of the packs right away. It wasn't until he lit a cigarette up that his gaze met mine again. "Glad you made it back safely, Bailey."

Trish came running up and bowled me over with a hug. "I've been worried about you!"

"I'm back right on time," I said, pulling away.

She pouted her lips. "It still seemed like forever."

Justin joined us, checking out the trucks. "Doesn't look like you ran into too much trouble. Don't see any damage."

"That's because Miles insisted on protecting these things like they were precious jewels." I patted my service truck, thankful it had done such a great job. "They never even got near the action."

"Looks like you guys did, though." Justin nodded at Aidan, who'd finally climbed out of the truck. The poor guy was still trying to wake up, and his injuries were slowing him down.

"We had a few battles, but we all came back whole," I said, putting my arm around Aidan. No one needed to know I was half propping him up.

Several more people came to greet us and ask questions before Earl finished smoking. Then he gestured at me to come with him to the house. I frowned. There was a look in his eyes that told me I wasn't going to like whatever he had to say. My stomach churned.

"I'll be back in a few minutes," I told Aidan.

He nodded. "I'm going to send Phoebe and Kade ahead to the fortress to let the pendragon know we'll be there shortly."

Aidan left out the part about how we needed to hurry and get the orb there, but I could see the message in his eyes. I glanced over and caught people already beginning to offload the trucks. Miles had said he would return them to their owners as soon as we got back. We'd have to take my personal vehicle to ride to the fortress.

I gestured at Conrad. "Could you transfer mine and Aidan's stuff to my truck?"

"Yeah, sure." He frowned. "What's going on?"

"Earl wants to talk to me." I shrugged.

"Alright, I got ya, girl." He patted me on the back and hurried away.

I walked into Earl's house and found him sitting at his rickety kitchen table. There were two coffee mugs sitting in front of him. He slid one, steam flowing from the top, toward me. When I took a seat next to him, he didn't meet my eyes. Instead, he waited until I'd drunk a few sips and reveled in the taste of it. Earl didn't need to know I'd acquired my own supply while I was away.

He cleared his throat. "I got a call from your mother while you were gone."

The tone of his voice told me my suspicions might be correct. I took a deep breath. "Was it about Grady?"

He tensed, his gaze shooting to me. "How did you know?"

"He's dead, isn't he?" I asked, just needing the truth.

"I'm sorry, Bailey. He passed away shortly after you left." Earl drank deeply from his coffee mug. "Don't know how you knew that, though."

I couldn't exactly tell him the truth, but I could come close. "He came to me in a dream a few days ago. Told me he'd died, but not to worry because my brothers are taking care of mom."

"That about sums it up." Earl nodded.

He and Grady had been good friends as well, so this couldn't have been much easier on him. The weight of the death seemed to sit heavily on Earl's shoulders. He wasn't one to show emotion very often, and even when he was bothered by something, he usually covered it up with his gruffness.

"I know you lost him, too," I said, reaching over and giving him a hug. "But he seemed to be happy in my dream—like he's going to be alright."

That was my one consolation. I had a strong suspicion that the Grady I met in the cave had been the real one, and though he'd had to say a few things for the sake of the test, he'd also gotten a chance to say goodbye. Not many people were given an opportunity like that. I still needed time to sort out my feelings and mourn him, but I'd do that once I finished my mission. That came first, as I'd sworn in my vows back at Alabaster Caverns. There was some comfort in knowing I now had a higher calling that didn't just impact the town I lived in, but possibly the world.

"You should call your mom," Earl said, finishing the last of his coffee.

"I will—tomorrow. There's something else I have to do first." I stood. "Just do me a favor and don't tell anyone about Grady right now."

Earl scrunched his brows. "Why?"

"I have my reasons."

Heading outside, I caught Conrad talking to Christine across the street. She had tears running down her cheeks, and his shoulders were stiff as if it was killing him to see her so upset. I went to my truck in Earl's driveway to check it over. It was exactly as I'd left it a week ago, except better. Someone had fixed my broken windows and patched up the bullet holes. The black paint they used didn't quite match up, but I didn't care. My baby was looking better than she had since last summer.

Aidan made his way over to me, moving at a slow pace. I remembered what it was like to have my shoulder crushed. You might not walk on it, but every step jarred the bone and shot pain through your body. He settled in the front passenger seat of the truck, and a few minutes later Conrad hurried toward us.

"How did it go?" I asked.

He shook his head. "Not good. It's, um...over."

"I'm sorry," I said, wishing there was something I could do.

He opened the back passenger door and climbed inside. "How about you tell me what Earl wanted. I don't want to talk about my problems right now."

I sighed and got into the driver's seat. This was going to be a tense ride. I didn't dare tell Conrad the news about my stepfather because that would mean there was a very real possibility his grandma was dead, too. After what he'd just been through with his girlfriend, I couldn't add to his pain.

33

AIDAN

The silence in the truck was deafening. Aidan was as curious as Conrad about what Earl had discussed with Bailey in the house. She was tight-lipped, though, and didn't offer anything as she drove down the city streets. Bailey kept her eyes on the road, holding the wheel a little more tightly than Aidan thought necessary.

"Are you going to tell me?" Conrad asked.

"It was nothing." She shook her head. "He just wanted an account of how things went on the trip is all."

Conrad lifted his brows. "And he couldn't do that outside?"

She gave him a brief smile that didn't quite reach her eyes. "You know how he is around, uh, Aidan. He just thought I might be straighter with him in private."

While that was a plausible excuse, Aidan could sense a hint of sadness in her features. Bailey wasn't telling them everything. He wouldn't push her now with Conrad in the truck, but if he caught her alone later, he would ask for the truth. Something told him she was barely holding herself together.

No one spoke for the rest of the drive. They reached the gas station near the fortress and found Kade, Nanoq, and Xanath waiting for them. Bailey pulled the truck up next to them and parked. Aidan watched as she took a deep breath and blew it out before shutting the engine off. Was she nervous about meeting with the pendragon again or was it something else?

They got out of the truck, and Bailey stopped him by his door. She whispered in a low voice, "My stepfather passed away just like the vision of him in the cavern had said."

Aidan stilled. "I am sorry to hear that."

"Please don't tell Conrad or the others."

It took him a moment to grasp why, but then he understood. Before, only he and Phoebe knew for a fact that the relative they met with was dead. Most of the group chose to believe their meetings with loved ones were a trick. But if Bailey revealed the news about her stepfather, they'd begin to think what they'd heard was true as well, and yet there wasn't a lot they could do about it. Aidan could understand why she didn't want to tell them that this soon after their return. It was something that could wait. At least, for a little while.

"I won't say anything," he promised.

They walked side by side toward the pendragon. Aidan still felt weakened by yesterday's events, but he did his best to hide how much his injuries affected him.

Bailey was kind enough to keep pace with him so that his slow walk didn't appear as obvious. Conrad already held the orb out to let the pendragon and others see. He'd had it wrapped in a piece of black camrium cloth before to protect its smooth surface.

Nanoq studied it closely. "I don't feel anything from it."

"The human was designated guardian of the orb," Kade explained. "As long as he is holding it, no one can sense or find it."

The pendragon lifted his brows. "Truly?"

"I'll show you." Conrad pulled the black cloth from his pocket and set it on the pavement. Then he placed the orb on top of that.

Everyone except him flinched. The dark power coming from the artifact was so heavy now that it was fully intact that it gave Aidan a headache. Bailey grumbled and rubbed at her head. Xanath and Kade appeared as if they might lose their last meal.

"For Zorya's sake, pick it back up," Nanoq ordered, grimacing.

Conrad scooped the orb off the ground and carefully wrapped it in the cloth. Everyone sighed a breath of relief when the dark energy dissipated.

Xanath shook his head. "Only a very corrupt sorcerer could handle such an object. Anyone with a healthy amount of goodness inside them would know that they'd lose themselves with that kind of power at their disposal."

"That is interesting to know," Nanoq said, then ran his gaze across Aidan, Bailey, Conrad, and Kade. "I want to thank each of you for making this journey and recovering the orb. From what Phoebe has told me, it was not without its difficulties and sacrifices. The Taugud are indebted to you for this."

Each of them nodded their heads in acknowledgment.

"Is the chamber ready to hold the orb?" Aidan asked.

"We worked day and night for the past week, designing a specially built vault with every conceivable protection spell we knew," Xanath said. The lines of exhaustion on his face proved he'd outdone himself. "Once the human guardian has placed it inside, we will seal it shut with his blood and that of the pendragon's so that they will be the only ones who can access it or monitor the orb's presence."

Conrad's lips thinned. "Am I going to get blindfolded again?"

"No, you have earned my respect and gratitude. The guards will be instructed to allow you into the fortress anytime you wish to visit, though you may never remove the orb without my permission," the pendragon said.

"Really?" Conrad's brown eyes lit up. "I can come anytime?"

The pendragon nodded—reluctantly.

"So if I just want to stop by and eat with ya'll, that's okay?" Conrad pressed.

Nanoq's shoulders relaxed a degree once he realized what the human truly wanted. "You will be welcome at our table anytime. Though the toriq must not know the story of the orb, they will know you did a great favor for us that has earned our esteem."

"And I'm fireproof now, so I don't have to worry about one of you burnin' me." Conrad reached out his free hand and grabbed Nanoq's arm for a few seconds before releasing him. "See?"

"I heard," the pendragon said, looking like he just ate something that didn't sit well with him.

"And the slayer?" Aidan asked.

"While she has earned my gratitude and a measure of trust I never would have thought I'd afford a slayer, her situation is a little more complicated." Nanoq paused and studied Bailey. "Allowing you free access to the fortress is not something I can give at this time, but I do believe we can allow supervised visits upon occasion."

Bailey crossed her arms. "No chains or blindfolds?"

"No, none of that. As long as you continue to prove loyal and useful to the Taugud, I will not subject you to such treatment again." He cleared his throat. "In fact, your first appearance as a guest among our toriq may be soon."

Aidan tensed. "What do you mean?"

"Your brother," Nanoq began, eyes darkening. "He may have let it slip to the Faegud pendragon that we allow a slayer to run loose in our territory and that she has the discipline not to attack shifters."

Aidan's jaw dropped. "He did what?"

Nanoq held up a hand. "Believe me. I was no more pleased about this than you, especially because I only found out after checking on preparations for the upcoming mating event and meeting with Hildegard. She has requested that Bailey should come visit her during the third day of the mating festival."

"What is he talking about?" Bailey asked, turning to Aidan.

He had chosen not to tell her about the event since he would not be required to mate. It appeared he'd have to explain himself now. "Part of the peace treaty with the Faegud requires some of our toriq members to join with the Faegud."

"Who exactly must do that?" Annoyance burned in her gaze.

"Ruari and some of the others," he said.

"But not you?"

"No." He shook his head.

The pendragon watched this exchange, lips thinning until Aidan feared Nanoq might lose them altogether. Anyone within fire-breathing distance could sense the interplay going between him and Bailey. He'd hoped to keep this from anyone else for a while longer.

"I see that there is more to you two than you prefer to let on," the pendragon said.

Kade cleared his throat. "They have become very good friends, especially during our arduous journey— we all forged bonds together."

"I am not a fool," Nanoq growled.

"Then you should know better than to try keeping them apart anymore," Aidan's uncle answered to everyone's surprise. "I have seen for myself what they can do together, and it is to our people's benefit."

Nanoq shot him a dark look. "I did not ask for your opinion."

"Will you lock me away in the library like my brother for speaking my mind?" Kade lifted a brow.

"No." The pendragon rubbed his face. "I have sworn I would not go to the extreme lengths he did."

Xanath stirred from his silent observation. "I am afraid I must take the seer's side on this matter. Whatever you think of Aidan and Bailey's..." He cleared his throat. "relationship, keeping them together would be wise."

"Why?" Nanoq glanced at each of them.

Kade was silent for a moment, considering his words. "I have seen several possibilities for the future. Each of them is dark with distressing events tied to them, but the one that will work out best for our people is the one where Aidan and the slayer are allowed to be together."

"You will explain this in greater detail later," Nanoq said, a warning in his tone.

Aidan's uncle shrugged. "I could, but to reveal anything more would alter the future as well, and nothing good will come of that."

Nanoq looked up at the sky and mumbled something about needing Zorya to give him patience. "Very well. What would you have me do? It is bad enough you insisted Aidan not be required to mate at the festival."

That was news to Aidan. He had no idea his uncle had stepped in for him.

"This is the way I see it going best," Kade began, brightening. "You do not like keeping Aidan at the fortress because it threatens your position. Let him stay at his lair with the slayer instead, and he can assist in guarding the nearby borders or conduct any other missions as you see fit."

Nanoq's face turned red. "You are telling me I should allow a shifter under my command to live with a woman born to kill our people?"

"Yes." Kade nodded. "I believe that covers the gist of it. She has a great deal of control over herself, but part of that comes from regular exposure to us. When she doesn't see any of our people for protracted periods, it makes it harder for her once she does—trust me on this. Allowing Aidan to stay with her full time ensures our safety and her cooperation in working with us in the future."

Aidan could hardly believe he was hearing these things from his uncle. How long had Kade been thinking all this up? The man had insisted Aidan meet Bailey since before the dimensions collided. Could he have known even that far back how things might play out?

Nanoq turned to Xanath. "What is your opinion on this matter?"

"I have seen into the slayer's mind, and Kade's assessment is correct. It is Bailey's exposure to Aidan that proves to help her the most. If not for how close they've grown, I doubt their quest to recover the orb would have succeeded," Xanath replied.

Aidan glanced down at Bailey who watched the exchange with varying degrees of horror and amazement. Neither of them could add their own arguments. All they could do was wait for their fate to be decided for them.

Nanoq directed his attention to Bailey. "You would agree to live with a dragon shifter full time and believe you can refrain from harming him?"

"I'd hurt myself before I'd hurt him," Bailey said with no hesitation, then glanced at Aidan. "And I'd have no problem sharing a home with him."

"Would you accept orders from me if I have missions for you to carry out?" Nanoq asked.

Bailey knitted her brows. "As long as you don't ask me for something I find morally wrong."

Aidan was proud of her answer. The pendragon could hardly argue with that.

"And will you attend the festival in two weeks?"

"As long as you can guarantee I will not be attacked while I'm there," she said.

Nanoq took a deep breath. "Very well, then you and Aidan may live together, but I ask that everyone here refrain from spreading the news. It will get out, of course. I would just prefer we not make a bigger issue of it than absolutely necessary."

"Agreed." Aidan nodded. It felt as if a weight had lifted from his chest. He would never have thought the pendragon would agree to this sort of arrangement, and he would do anything necessary to keep from jeopardizing it.

"Congrats, Bailey." Conrad gave her a pat on the back. "If these stiff guys can accept your weird relationship, then I guess I gotta, too."

"Um, thanks," she replied.

Nanoq ground his jaw. "Let us get on with relocating the orb. Aidan, you will accompany us, and you can meet with the slayer later to discuss your...plans, after you return the human to his home."

"Of course, milord." He turned to Bailey and gave her a meaningful look. "I will see you tonight."

She lifted her chin. "You better."

The pendragon, Kade, Aidan, and Conrad began the walk to the fortress. He glanced back once to watch as Bailey headed for her truck and opened the driver's door. She paused before climbing inside to grin at him. Aidan memorized that moment, hoping there would be many more like it to come.

DRAGON LANGUAGE GLOSSARY

Alefire: Thick and potent ale with a spicy aftertaste that the dragons drink (more than two mugs will make them drunk).

Bitkal: Ritual which decides who will become the next pendragon.

Camrium: Leather or suede-like clothing worn by shifters and the humans living with them that is fireproof and spelled with magic for protection.

Cryas: Soul.

Dijis: Attack.

Fushka (pl.- fushkan): Fool, idiot.

Galus: Die/be dead

Jakhal: The clan seat of power—their capital.

Kederrawien: Dimension the dragons lived in for the past thousand years.

Petroes: Dragonflies (not the ones native to earth) who only come for a short period each summer. They can breathe tiny flames that will harm humans much like being sunburned.

Shifitt: Dragon curse word similar to damn or shit.

Shiggara: Stasis or limbo (an invisible place for dragons to store a small amount of supplies).

Stinguise: A foul smelling juice that can temporarily cover up other scents.

Sude camria: Black Camria, the plant used to manufacture the garments worn by dragon shifters while in human form. The end result can have a leather or suede-like appearance, depending on the process used to weave the cloth together.

Toriq (pl.- toriqan): Clan/Tribe.

Zaphiriam: A fire-proof metal with qualities similar to steel that dragons use to forge weaponry. It is black with red veins running through it.

Zishkat: Dragon dung.

Zorya: The dragon goddess.

DRAGON CLAN NAMES

SHAPE-SHIFTER CLANS:

Taugud- Clan in mid-western U.S. (southeast Oklahoma) that Aidan belongs to.

Straegud- Clan in eastern U.S.

Craegud- Clan in western U.S.

Faegud- Clan in north/northeast Texas with a mixture of pure and shape-shifter dragons.

PURE DRAGON CLANS:

Shadowan- Dragon clan in Oklahoma that holds the *northeast* part of the state, as well as parts of Arkansas and Kansas.

Thamaran- Dragon clan in Oklahoma that holds the *west* side of the state and the Texas panhandle.

Bogaran- Dragon clan that holds the southern half of Arkansas.

Ghastanan- Dragon clan in Texas that holds the central portion, including Dallas.

Don't want to miss Susan Illene's next novel?
To subscribe to Susan's newsletter visit http://eepurl.
com/-pk_f. If you prefer to only receive email alerts
when she releases new books, visit http://eepurl.
com/-pb-L.

You can also join her Facebook fan
group here: https://www.facebook.com/
groups/1657437984566674/.

Dragon's Breath Series
Stalked by Flames
Dancing with Flames
Forged by Flames
Christmas with Dragons (coming late December 2016)

Other Works by Susan
Darkness Haunts
Darkness Taunts
Chained by Darkness (novella)
Darkness Divides
Playing with Darkness (novella)
Darkness Clashes
Darkness Shatters
Darkness Wanes

ACKNOWLEDGMENTS

As always, I have a lot of people to thank. My family are my greatest support with my husband making sure I eat when I'm spending an especially large number of hours in the day working on a book. My father who is happy to help critique chapters and research topics for me. And all my extended relatives who are always happy to support me in any way they can (this includes you- Aunt Connie and Uncle Jerry for going with me on the research trip).

Special thanks to my editor, Angela, and to all my beta readers. This book would have all sorts of issues without the helpful feedback I've gotten from you all.

A huge thanks to my cover artist, Jeff Brown, for the beautiful cover. I appreciate photographer Josh McCullock for his great work getting the model shots, as well as Rahela Mahmood for posing! I honestly couldn't have asked for a better team. Also to my design brain storming group- Rachel, Kristy, Sarah, and Heather. They help give me great concept ideas and feedback for my covers and track down the best places to get the model's wardrobe. On top of that, Rachel and Sarah have taken over running my Facebook fan group page and they're doing an outstanding job with it.

For research on the novel, I have to thank my guides at Bluff Dweller's Cave in Missouri—Jay and Mary Jane. And a big shout out to Britany for doing such a fantastic job on the photo tour at Alabaster Caverns. All my guides were great about answering questions and going out of their way to help. There were so many other people I spoke to during my research trip for this novel and didn't get their names, but they deserve recognition as well for their assistance. Of course, any mistakes I made in the story are my own, or may have been on purpose for the sake of the fantasy world building elements.

The list goes on and I can't possibly thank (or remember) everyone who has contributed in some way. There are so many of you, but that doesn't mean I don't appreciate your help. And last but not least, thanks to all my readers. Your motivation and love for my books are what helps keep me going!

ABOUT SUSAN ILLENE

Instead of making the traditional post high school move and attending college, Susan joined the U.S. Army. She spent her eighteenth birthday in the gas chamber—an experience she is sure is best left for criminals. For eleven years she served first as a human resources specialist and later as an Arabic linguist (mostly in Airborne units). Though all her duty assignments were stateside, she did make two deployments to Iraq where her language skills were put to regular use.

After leaving the service in 2009, Susan returned to school to study history with a focus on the Middle East at the University of Oklahoma. She no longer finds many opportunities to test her fighting abilities in real life, unless her husband is demanding she cook him a real meal (macaroni and cheese apparently doesn't count), but she's found a new outlet in writing urban fantasy heroines who can.

For more information visit: www.susanillene.com

You may also find her at:
Twitter- @susan_illene
Facebook- www.facebook.com/SusanIllene1
Goodreads- www.goodreads.com/author/show/6889690.
Susan_Illene

Made in the USA
Middletown, DE
30 April 2017